Un-natural Selection

By

James Donnelly

Published by James Donnelly

First publication 2014

From an idea conceived in 2009

ISBN 978-0-9928229-0-3

Human interference - how much rope?

The growing demands of us, the dominant species currently on the planet with our needs for energy, food and living space, will inevitably impact on the world we inhabit and not least, upon the species that we live the closest to. On this planet for just a dog's watch and already we have deliberately interfered with life's natural rhythms. Plants genetically modified and animals domesticated or hybridised to suit our purposes, no matter how whimsical. But in everyday life there is cause and effect and as a species, we cause to operate on a grand scale and should expect the resultant effects, to be equally as considerable. Should we not be surprised at the notion and enormity of global warming, or that rubbing shoulders with black rats and their fleas, made humans die in their millions, or that scavenging bears, taking advantage of Man's encroachment of their remote forests, would lead to confrontation?

Whatever we do and wherever we do it, we influence and disturb and cannot be sure of the outcomes. Therefore, we should expect that, as with our deliberate meddling, the unintentional interferences, may cause us to create natural anomalies, on the one hand, unremarkable and low impact, but on the other, well… who knows what unacceptable aberrations might we conjure, ominous, threatening; horrifying even…the stuff perhaps, of genuine nightmares!

The Parish of Parley

approx 1 mile

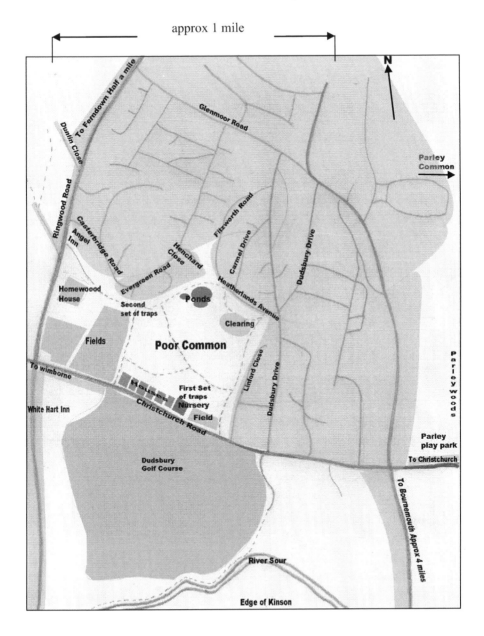

Chapter 1

August 5th 2009

"Our boy's dead then?"

The disgruntled doctor, who'd been called out, could pronounce him dead. "As could anyone with half a wit Inspector," he moaned. "Disconcertingly", he added, "not only is he dead, but he isn't all there."

"Oh great!" It was just getting better and better thought the experienced officer.

However, the doctor could not say with any certainty as to how or when he died. In fact the remains, indeed literally what remained, in that secluded spot would prove to be a mystery for some time to come. The carcass of flesh and bones, that was once a living thing had been found by local children out playing. It had been well hidden but not deliberately or maliciously. In reality, the only person you could probably blame for this choice of final resting place was the deceased himself; the torso draped over a substantial bough half a metre off the ground and in amongst a particularly large clump of rhododendrons. The sprawling mass of big leathery leaves covering most of this little-used part of Poor Common created a living barrier some three to four metres high in places and its darkened undergrowth had been ideal for the victim's purposes. However, the reassuring cover it had once afforded him would only serve to delay the find and allow the forces of nature, a very welcome slice of the action!

From behind, through the sparser undergrowth, where the victim had originally entered, the body looked like the casualty of a nasty fall that, had you not known it, might just that second have happened; the person perhaps stunned and momentarily winded. But that wasn't the case here; for the living version of this lifeless shell, had picked this isolated and unused spot well. And should anyone have fought their way through this jungle for a frontal approach, the sight befalling them would leave only the strongest stomachs with any content.

The police on attending a body would normally have been keeping an open mind as to what had happened. More often than not, foul play had little to do with it, but on this occasion and despite the lack of any obvious weapon, the Inspector had had few doubts. It was murder, surely? Coincidences were something he found difficult to ignore and there were already too many clinging to this body. Besides which, this untimely demise would now throw up even more questions; not least about the manner of his death, but also regarding the disastrous impact it would have on the harrowing abduction investigation in which the Inspector was already entrenched.

Kidnap and now murder, possibly two of the most emotive crimes the Inspector would ever have to deal with. The pressure would be racking up. And, as if that wasn't enough! The media and newspapers had their own theories on the abduction and this particular corpse's involvement, from the absurd to the very plausible. Like the police, they had little or nothing to base them on, but unlike the cops, this didn't appear to matter just so long as it gained them a wider audience. Whilst this death may have pulled the rug from under both parties, the ever optimistic press would be only momentarily stunned, for when one door closes there are usually plenty more to pry open! The local Ferndown constabulary, on the other hand, had a much narrower and less creative view: This now lifeless form was really the only solid lead they'd had. It would seem like they were on their way back to square one and, as ever, the press would already be there to welcome them!

"Everything all right Inspector?" the ranger called from the behind the tapes, craning to see.

"And he is?" asked the Inspector, without turning to look.

"Ranger from the country park that oversees this area," the Detective Sergeant advised his superior and scanning his notebook for a name, added. "He brought the key for the gates. Let our boys in, a Mr Nash."

The word ranger was all it took to remind the Inspector... his eyes flicking skywards with annoyance, "Him again." He'd had a brief telephone conversation with Tony Nash, just after the abduction; a warning, his take, apparently on the potential perpetrator. As if! But it was the recent chance meeting with Mr. Nash, and the incredible notion he was now suggesting, that had been enough to relegate the so-called Park Ranger...Warden, whatever! - Very swiftly, to near 'nutter' status. He'd seemed a straightforward enough chap, the Inspector reflected. Why though should anyone want to stir things up like that? Had he not even considered the impact on the family, let alone the rest of the public at large? The man was a bloody nuisance, he thought wearily; a constant worry like some pestilent wasp at a picnic.

On his way back to the station to update his superiors, the Inspector took his time. He was not relishing the thought. Consciously driving within the speed limits, slowing purposefully at junctions and traffic lights, his normally lively Peugeot sluggish as it pulled away under his reluctant instruction. In reality, the journey was but a few miles. Somehow though, he was going to stretch it out. He needed time to think. Deliberately taking a longer route, and glancing over to the right, his eyes were drawn over the open fields, to the copse that hid the solid perimeter wall of Homewood House a few hundred metres away. Distracted for a moment, he reflected on not so recent events at the property.

There had been a suspicious death back in, I suppose.... "April" he concluded to himself. He knew why his mind had so readily grabbed the information, not because of it being recent history but because she too had been found outside, in this instance in her secluded garden. As with the current corpse, the local wildlife had had time to have their fill. They reckoned she had been dead for a couple of weeks, probably longer than this new one, because more of her was missing. This, though, was where the similarity ended. Hers, it seemed, had been an unfortunate accident with no insidious implications. As he drove on, the Inspector's mind flipped reluctantly to the immediate challenge awaiting him back at base. What he could not have comprehended, as he manoeuvred his car, was that answers to the many questions that had been flung his way in recent weeks would all in some way stem from the property he'd just passed. But even if there had been a reason to search it, he would not have found any evidence - nothing tangible, no murder weapon, no incriminating documentation, no specific piece of forensics: it would be as if a barren wasteland. And yet, the clues had been there. He might even have seen them, their relevance at the time disjointed and unconnected to future events. But something had taken place within those walls: A simple act, which for the residents around Poor Common, would have long term consequences; natural, basic, commonplace and yet... not exactly normal.

Chapter 2

Earlier, that same year, January 10th 2009

Many would not hear the harsh and shrill sound, which cut through the chill January night heralding the start of another year and, more importantly, the beginnings of a new season.

The not too distant estates with their seemingly random but planned modern housing would be locked down tight against the winter's grip; windows bolted, condensation already glistening inside the frames, curtains drawn, children and adults alike snuggled into duvets.

The witching hour had come and gone some forty-five minutes earlier. A few night owls though, would still be watching, square-eyed, the flickering screens of TV dross. They would not hear it, either too wrapped up in their programme, or dozing heavy eyes, imploring them to bed and sleep; but just not quite able to drag themselves away from the relative warmth of their favourite chairs and sofas, as the outside temperature plummeted.

Consequently, most of the human inhabitants living on the fringes of Poor Common would be asleep and blissfully unaware of the dreadful sounds urgently assaulting this quiet patch of land; an area of common ground, insignificant in the great scheme of things, but so typical of virtually every village, town and city the length and breadth of the country.

It had brought Tony Nash to a halt though; ears and eyes scanning the blackness around him. *That wasn't far away*, he thought and, feeling the familiar thrill, walked on with a softer step.

On the other side of the common, just under half a mile away from where the noise emanated, Janet Coleman, a waitress at a local pub, had finished her busy shift and was just unlocking the front door to her mum's house in Fitzworth Road, where she lived. Although tired from her long hours at work, she was still wide-awake: on a high in fact. The shift had gone really well. She hadn't stopped and all her customers had gone home satisfied - as her tips reflected. The cold night air and the short walk home had revived her. Usually she would slip inside and settle down with a hot drink and unwind but the violent sound stopped her instantly. She knew it was distant and that she was safe, her key already turned and the door just needing to be pushed.

"What the fuck was that?" she half whispered half mouthed to herself. She froze, her pulse quickening, listening, waiting, her breath condensing as it hit the cold, sending wispy plumes of vapour into the night air. Nearly a minute passed and, just as she had made up her mind to go inside, it came again. Her skin crawled as the hairs unfurled to counter the growing icy fear, senses racking the deepest recesses of her brain's database for any clues. It sounded like a strange dog bark; no not a dog bark –

a high pitched shouting or perhaps a combination. Either way, she was sure it was like nothing she had heard before. A spasm of fear flushed through her body and, pushing the door more forcibly than it needed, she scurried inside. It slammed noisily against an adjacent wall, waking her sleeping parent. Cursing to herself under her breath, she quickly and carefully closed the door. Heading towards the kitchen she called softly up the stairs to her Mum, apologising for waking her. However, the warmth of the house comforted her and by the time she had turned the light on in the kitchen and flicked the switch on the kettle, she had begun to relax. She stared blankly out through the oblong void of the window, aware of the liquid becoming agitated in the pot and seeing nothing more than her own reflected world. Feeling safe and secure in her home she rationalised, "Probably just some bloody animal" and, taking her tea, crept into the lounge for a bit of late night viewing.

Betty Thomas was also one who was still awake. At 87 years young, sleep was not something that she seemed to need. Often waking before the dawn chorus in the summertime and usually up and doing by 7.00am in the winter, bedtime was whenever she fancied. Even when her husband had been alive, she would retire usually way past midnight, with him having been tucked up an hour or so before her.

She heard it! The staccato reports making her start and prick a finger on the needle she was using to mend a blouse.

"Shit," she cussed. "You noisy buggers". The noise hadn't frightened her; indeed it would take a lot to put the wind up Betty. The fact that it was almost outside the back door wasn't a problem either; it was just that the first blast set the dogs off around her feet. As they rocketed upwards, paws scrabbling wildly on the polished flagstones like cartoon characters, their bulk connecting heavily with the table legs, they sent a flood of sweet sherry onto its well-worn surface. As the harsh sounds fired off intermittently outside, the hounds inside bellowed, five or six barks each, to everyone they heard.

"Quiet!" Betty commanded, and the dogs dutifully stopped until the next time and the process repeated itself.

After five long minutes, Betty's fuse blew. Charging out of the back door, she put an end to the persistent sounds outside and the cacophony inside. Even though the sound was as familiar as the barking of her own dogs, it still sparked the exclamation as she walked back in, "What a bloody racket that is!"

After mopping up the spilt sherry, Betty poured herself a fresh schooner, talking to the dogs as she did so.

"I know you'd like to go out and play but it's too late. Besides, I don't think you'd be welcome out there just at the moment". The excited dogs, sitting expectantly, tails sweeping the floor behind them, gazed lovingly up at her. As she returned to her sewing, they soon settled down, both appreciating the continuous heat from the kitchen's oil fired Aga; unsurprisingly, their favourite spot at this time of the year.

A few hundred yards across the common from Betty's secluded grounds, Jim Bennett, the owner of a small nursery, was checking the doors to the shop. He'd already rattled the gates and walked the perimeter fence and was ready to turn in. Grudgingly, he had taken to doing this most nights now, ever since his struggling business had been broken into, just before Christmas.

He and his wife had bought the little nursery some thirty years ago but the last ten years had been a struggle. His wife had died of cancer, losing her long battle six years ago. Since then he had run it virtually on his own and, as the days drew further from her death, his resolve and drive seeped away. It had been a life-style change to buy the nursery, way before such ideas would become fashionable. Deemed their retirement plan - working together with plants was something they both delighted in. Their ideas had offered such hopes and now, at 69, he could barely find the will to keep it going. The negativity flowed through him like the cancer had in his wife. It appeared to touch everything around him, dwindling sales, the stocks of plants seemingly blighted by every disease or pest known to man, suppliers hiking up the prices, equipment breaking down, those little bastards breaking in, the rates, the Vat man, the Tax man.... who the hell was he working for anyway? His despair and loneliness were almost too much, save for his faithful companion Cockles.

Half-blind and with a somewhat stiff gait, Cockles was always ready at the door when he felt that his master, for whatever reason, was about to go out. The elderly cocker spaniel was by his side, even now, as he moved back towards the house. The first unearthly shout had barely burst through the still night air and the dog's hackles were up. A low warning grumble rose in crescendo to a deep menacing growl as the alert dog stared out hopelessly towards the trees and the darkness they trapped.

"Alright boy," Jim bent down and stroked the dog's feathery head, "Nothing to worry about, is there? You've heard it all before, haven't you?" Cockles evidently was not fully convinced, the low rumbling growl persisted off and on for a while, as they continued up the path to Jim's bungalow.

"Funny though," Jim mused continuing the one sided conversation, "I've heard that sound so many times in the past, but it still leaves me cold; makes the hairs on the back of my neck stand up. Bit like yours I suppose: no wonder you get so worked up. It always sounds so..." His voice trailed off as he struggled to find the right words to describe it. "Chilling, desperate... No, not desperate, urgent... Oh I don't know."He opened the back door and the light flooded out. He stepped inside. "Puts the willies up me that's for sure." Satisfied that he had probably found the right words, he closed the door and the path darkened for the night.

The eerie blackness of Poor Common was relative, thought Tony, treading lightly and not wishing to disturb the silence. Looking from the outside into the heart of the trees, it would be as if staring into a huge void: where all light and movement was consumed; a dense blank space silhouetted against the moonless backdrop of the night sky. The opposite view though, one he could see now, from near the centre of the common outward, proffered a completely different perspective. It was an area of land, he guessed, similar to that of the average eighteen hole golf course, so not huge. As if to reinforce this and looking northwest a few hundred yards through the slender pines, he spied the occasional lighted window on Fitzworth and Wollaton Roads. But turning one hundred and eighty degrees, the artificial aurora from the conurbation of Poole and Bournemouth polluted the whole southern aspect. Lighting up the east-to-west running Christchurch Road and its large houses set back from the busy highway, marking the southerly boundary of the common. Unseen from his current position, and over to the west some half a mile away, he knew Homewood House lay. Surrounded by paddocks and open woodland it ran adjacent to the well-lit Poole to Ringwood Road, the A348.

The wintry landscape of twiggy beech and birch, stark and bleak against the cold hues of the Carmel Scots and Corsican pines, reflected a barren quality. Many would think nothing lived in this outwardly lifeless and insignificant slice of countryside. It was just too small and hemmed in. Humanity had encroached at every turn: housing, horses, dogs, cats – people! Tony however, knew otherwise, reflecting that much of the wildlife in the UK had learnt to live with human activity; some even thrived on it. Poor Common was no different: still home to a wide representation of the country's indigenous inhabitants albeit at this time of the year many would be hibernating. Tony wondered if those that weren't, would still hear the strange shrieking perhaps setting them on edge. He suspected that even the lucky ones in 'seasonal sleep mode' would be aware of it, dulled senses measuring the threat level and subliminally wriggling deeper into their winter bedding in the hope of further concealment.

Either way, man or beast, awake or not; these unfamiliar calls, albeit quite normal as it happens, for the most part would go unnoticed. An excited Tony Nash had known exactly what it was and had lingered in the vein hope of catching a glimpse. Aware that this animal was almost certainly in season and that the unearthly call was in fact an urgent clarion to attract a male and time would be of the essence; the animal's body, only receptive for but a short few days. The necessity to mate being as base as it gets, an innate and supreme effort to preserve the bloodline and further the species. What Tony couldn't have known was that only one male will answer. Her good fortune will be that, at just a year old, he is a prime specimen, not least because he has survived to adulthood, but because he possesses subtle traits that will set him apart from others of his species.

Chapter 3

Friday 13th March

Staring out with more than a little angst and trepidation, twenty-seven-year old Tony Nash, Forest Ranger and self confessed outdoorsman, tanned and gently weathered, had not expected these waves of self-doubt and nerves. After all, he was used to talking with people. The crowds that descended daily and, in particular, at weekends to the popular Country Park where he worked, could number up to 5,000. Often, he would lead groups out for walks and expeditions around the 250-acre site, no problem. He could speak confidently, assertively if necessary, and of course knowledgeably to these groups, from the liveliest and demanding children all the way up to the not so lively and less demanding pensioners and grandparents. He could handle awkward and difficult situations in a calm assured manner but nothing; nothing had prepared him for the gut-wrenching nerves he was now experiencing. Butterflies didn't even come close!

Gazing back at him were 24 pairs of eyes, most wide with expectation, some feigning boredom, others accusing, some defiant, two or three just downright flirty; their bright orbs sizing him up and evidently liking what they saw. The unsubtle probing emanated from class 11B of Ferndown Upper School. These were the young men and women of the lower sixth form: sixteen to seventeen year olds, feisty, belligerent and "full of it". In this formal alien environment, over-warm and clammy, Tony felt like the proverbial fish out of water.

It had slowly dawned on him what his co-ranger and immediate boss, John, had dropped him into. 'Go and give a talk about what we do, to some kids at the local school'.

"Ok," Tony had said. "No problem".

His mind already conjuring up bright-eyed and eager eight or nine-year olds, all jostling to impart their own innocent and sometimes humorously distorted view of the wild and dangerous forests of Dorset. Take a few animal bones and skulls and a few other interesting items. Throw in a young, unattached female form teacher and yes, it could be fun. And so this idyll remained in his mind, the teacher's part swelling with every visitation of the thought.

It wasn't until three days ago that John had mentioned which School he was going to. The 'Ferndown' part was all right; it was the 'Upper School' bit that had set alarm bells jangling in his mind.

"They're not kids," had been his reply to the Senior Ranger, half joking but with rising concern. As he learnt they were going to be lower sixth, he protested: "All they're interested in is where to score, where the next shag's coming from and what they could do with one of our chain saws! Not how many types of deer do we have or the fact that we look after endangered reptiles."

"Ooooh, hark at Mr Cynical," John, feigning shock, fired back in typical good-humour.

Tony's protestations deflated. "Well you know what I mean: half of them probably won't want to be there."

"And half of them will," countered John. "Go on," he urged. "It will be good for you and I think you might be surprised. Don't forget these kids have made the choice to stay on at school, so I think you're over-reacting, just a tad".

"I know," Tony agreed without much enthusiasm. "Still…" Tony's optimism rallied, "So who's the teacher?"

As Mr Lynes, the somewhat battle-weary and rotund form teacher, began to introduce him, Tony only half took in what he was saying.

What the fuck am I doing here? Was the question he kept asking himself, *I'll bloody murder that John volunteering me for this.*

"Tony Nash," concluded Mr Lynes.

Shit, the smile belied what Tony was thinking right at that moment; then somehow he turned and thanked Mr Lynes. Mouth dry and a barely perceptible wobble in his voice; he began to address the class. Using the notes that thankfully he had taken the time to prepare, he started by telling them the role of a Forest Ranger at Moors Valley Country Park.

"As Mr Lynes mentioned, I am a Ranger at the Moors Valley Country Park… um, although my employers are actually the East Dorset District Council: part of their Countryside Management Service. The Park is er, actually a joint venture between the Council and the Forestry Commission. The park and visitor centre are run by us and the forests by the Commission".

Once Tony had begun to speak and the audience seemed to be listening, he began to relax: errs and ums disappearing very quickly. Using some maps that he had put up on the board, he was able to indicate where the park was in relation to the surrounding area. Most of the students would know it was about eight miles north east of Ferndown and it was likely that many had been there at some time in their short lives. The Park boasted play trails, cycle tracks, high rope courses, golf, fishing and a miniature railway. With abundant car parking, set amongst an open woodland of tall pines, it was a very popular place to walk the dog, walk the kids and just generally… spend time in, 'getting back to nature.'

Tony's job varied with the seasons. As a junior ranger he would be involved with conservation and countryside management tasks during the winter months. Invasive scrub clearance, fence and path repairs, and his particular favourites, pond and stream regeneration. With the huge influx of more visitors in the summer months and longer days, the shift pattern changed, as did the role of the rangers. They would still effect minor repairs where needed, but mostly, they kept a watchful eye on the visitors; "We're on hand for questions, directions and first aid." He smiled, adding, "I'm one of 12 full time rangers at Moors Valley and we have also twenty other smaller sites which we manage. So, there is always plenty to keep us busy."

He explained the main Park and the twenty other sites also in the East Dorset area covered a range of habitats. These included woodlands, heaths, grass and wetlands supporting a number of rare species. A couple of these sites, Tony mentioned to the rapt audience, were of particular interest to him, as they were virtually on his doorstep from his home in West Parley. Suggesting that, because of their proximity and not least because one of them, Poor Common, was en route to his favourite Pub, he often visited them.

He'd chosen the ranger job as part of his loose plan to do something ultimately in conservation or countryside management. Right from his earliest years the fascination he had for animals had swept him inevitably towards the outdoors type of life. From helping with the livestock on his parents farm in West Dorset, to grubbing around in the local woodlands searching for bugs and all manner of creepy crawlies. As an adult, he hadn't changed much. So, although now his flat was in a fairly leafy suburb, and his job got him out into his favoured environment, he still couldn't get enough. Besides, at work, he was often too busy to notice what was under his nose. Consequently walking sites close to home in his time off, gave him the opportunity to actually see things: plants and animals and the landscape changing with the seasons.

For twenty-five minutes Tony had held his audience. He had been asked to give a general talk to the group as part of their Personal, Social, and Health Education curriculum. Mr Lynes had set it up, in an attempt to 'broaden their minds and get them thinking'. Apart from explaining about his role in the ranger service, he had expanded it, giving mention to the management of the unique Dorset heaths and their rare reptiles. He was passionate about how his job made a difference in this respect albeit, he knew, in a limited way. Winding up his talk he advised that anybody could be involved, from joining Wildlife groups to volunteer days, where groups of people from all walks of life, under the supervision of the rangers, help to coppice woodlands, dig ditches or clear ponds.

"Thanks for listening;" he said with obvious relief, "I have some leaflets here about the park and volunteer days if anyone wants one".

Turning to Mr Lynes, "Do we have time for any questions?" He was actually enjoying himself now and he felt connected with most of the kids. They'd seemed a really nice bunch, chipping in with helpful remarks or seeking clarification when he hadn't explained something particularly well. Casting his eyes back to the lively crowd, he noticed a number of waving hands indicating where questions were ready and waiting. After a couple of questions, one about snakes and how you could tell the difference between the three species found locally and another about how important were gardens for wildlife, a voice at the middle of the classroom called out, before another waving hand could be picked, "What about the big cats of Dorset?"

"What about them?" Tony cheerfully challenged back, although somewhat guardedly.

"Well aren't you like, the bloke who was in the paper, talking about them?"

A flutter of anxiety resurfaced in his guts, "Yes, that's right," Tony replied, still more than a little wary as to where this was going.

"Sorry what was your name?"

"Stephen... Stephen Bishop, sir," The 'sir' bit surprised Tony. None of the others had chosen to use this - they had all used his Christian name, not that it bothered him either way.

"Sorry, Stephen, what specifically is your question?" It wasn't a challenge but Tony was not going to be drawn on this particular subject, at least, not without some idea of what the boy's motives were. Tony eyed him suspiciously. The skinny lad was more smartly dressed than his classmates, not overly so but enough to notice. His open, bespectacled face suggested an intelligence, and the forward-leaning body, arms resting on the desk, hands clasped but relaxed, implied an earnest and attentive listener.

"I was just wondering whether you really believe that there are big cats, you know yeah, like, Pumas or Panthers in Dorset or anywhere in Great Britain? Only the papers, they like, said you were... an expert"

And not for the first time in recent history, Tony cringed!

Chapter 4

Saturday 14th March

Tony was still on a bit of a high as he walked along the path through Poor Common on his way to the pub. He had woken at the usual time seven-fifteen am, although no alarm had roused him. A quick accusing glance at the clock was followed by a pleasing sensation relaxing his whole body, luxuriating in the warmth of his four tog duvet, as he remembered: a weekend off. As he lay there, wondering how to spend the day, the early morning sun was desperately trying to break through the curtains and beams of light took advantage of every fold and chink: it was going to be a lovely day.

He had some shopping to do in the morning: groceries, plus he needed some new jeans, needed to get some money out from the hole in the wall before playing badminton at 11.00am and then (he had decided this reward fairly early on in his planning) a pint at the Angel and perhaps lunch.

He had driven home after his badminton session so that lunch need not be restricted to one pint! It was now twelve-thirty. Being a single man had its advantages, he thought, as he strode purposefully along the gravel track that the council had recently laid around Poor Common. He had been long enough out of a relationship for the usual guilt to subside but not so long that he was missing the company. The modern one-bedroomed flat in Glenmoor Road was, once again, his.

"If I want to go to the pub for lunch… Then why not?" It was a simple statement to himself, but he found the need to justify it as a bonus, a pat on the back even, for the trauma he'd gone through at the school the previous day. It wasn't something he did often; his ranger salary only went so far. And growing up on a farm, with its own fresh produce and a mother who cooked had its advantages, making him self-reliant and economical in his own way.

But not to cook once in a while is a pleasure that most people these days value. That wasn't to say Tony didn't take advantage of modern living either; often grabbing a sandwich, a pasty and a can of coke or similar for lunch at convenience stores if he was in a hurry. The combination of his 'on the go' working life and active leisure time plus a reasonable diet meant he was fit and healthy. At quarter of an inch under six feet and his square shoulders tapering to a half decent six-pack, he readily turned female heads. Most of Tony's male colleagues and friends would give their eye teeth to look that good but to cap it all, even at twenty-seven; Tony had been blessed with a face that didn't seem to age. Schoolboy good looks would be how most people would describe him as reflected in a bashful grin, neat sandy coloured hair parted on one side and a fringe casually swept across the forehead.

"You, you lucky bastard, are going to be pulling the birds even as they nail the bloody coffin shut," a regular had quipped across the bar, during one of the normal good-natured sparring bouts that made the pub such an attraction.

He had entered the common from the North East corner, through a narrow tarmac path off Heatherlands Avenue between the houses. The partially cracked and weed-dotted surface led on to the gravel path, which immediately split, left and right, to form part of the circular route close to the perimeter of this small public area. Taking the right hand fork, as he had done on many occasions, the path gently wove its way out of the tree line and on towards his goal.

Although the Angel was about a mile and a half away from his flat, the relatively short walk, a good deal of it over the common, was what he enjoyed. Even in this non-descript area of woodland with the odd clearing and semi seasonal ponds and horse's fields on the western edge, he was able to see deer, foxes, badgers and occasionally some of the tinier creatures: mice, rats, rabbits and, if really lucky, the odd stoat or weasel. Not exactly big game but he relished the expectation of seeing something new or unusual.

Passing the now flooded ponds - roughly the half-way marker to the pub - the question posed by Stephen Bishop yesterday, edged its way back into his consciousness. It had reminded him of what he really hoped to chance upon, somewhere, someday as he went about his life amongst the Dorset countryside. Frequently he had imagined an encounter, often in various rural settings and scenarios. He was, though, sure that one day he would come face to face again with one of the most secretive (if you actually believed they existed) and exciting creatures to roam the modern British countryside: a big cat.

Widely reported for many years, it is believed that possibly Puma, Panther, Lynx and other similar felines, not indigenous to Great Britain, do survive in our rich countryside. There have been way too many sightings for it not to be true, Tony had argued with some of his more sceptical friends. However, these days he had not been quite so outspoken, at least not since the newspaper article that Stephen had referred to had caused Tony a lot of grief from all quarters.

The incident had occurred a couple of years back, not long after he joined the ranger team at Moors Valley Country Park. On one of his patrols around the almost empty play trail on a Tuesday afternoon in late September, he had been approached by a mother of two young children, clearly panicky and out of breath. If she had not had a child under each arm, she would almost certainly have grabbed him, such was her agitation.

"Over there," she blurted out, "by the spider". The spider, in question, was nearly 30 feet long from mandibles to hind leg and was just one of the huge wooden structures laying in wait around the trail for the swarms of children to climb over.

"A Black Cat," she'd yelled. The frightened look and tremulous voice told Tony this was not some diminutive moggy gone awol from one of the local residences. The hairs on the back of his neck shot up, excitement took hold and, without a word, he was off. Running like a gazelle on steroids, jumping over logs, leaping ditches, cutting corners through the trees towards the spider: no way was he going to miss this.

Twenty minutes later, red-faced and seriously out of breath, Tony had caught up with the woman on her way back to the visitor centre. He wanted to question her. Inviting her in for a cup of tea in the café, he sat her down. Now much calmer, it was the noisy children that needed to be quelled, thought Tony. As if sensing his thoughts, she reassured him that this was normal behaviour for 'over caffeinated' kids; coke at lunch time, she explained apologetically.

So why am I buying more? Tony had wanted to ask. Instead, he'd asked her name and then to clarify what she thought she had seen. Clearly, having had time to cool down on the walk back and begin perhaps to rationalise it, she was still adamant that it was a large black cat. It had been about 75 yards away and moving in the open woodland. The ground cover was negligible and so she had had a very clear view. The beast, as she had referred to it, was probably a bit bigger than a large Labrador. It was completely black from its cat's head to its long tail and was definitely cat like in its movement. There was no question in her mind as to what it was.

Tony had got into a bit of trouble because of the way he had handled the incident.

"You should have radioed it in. We could have got some more people over there. No," the senior ranger said as patiently as he could, "not necessarily to look for it, but to be on hand to protect any of the visitors if it showed its face again."

As senior ranger, John had heard similar stories, but not from his own back yard! He had asked Tony to call the Police just to inform them - out of courtesy as much as anything: he was not expecting them to do anything about it. He was right on that count, however somebody must have blabbed to the press and the "Beast of Dorset" was born. The country Park had come out of it really well: the publicity was great and visitor numbers took the park to capacity for the next week or so. Tony's ego on the other hand had taken a bit of a hammering.

The press had dubbed him a wildlife expert. Flattering - but embarrassingly way off the mark. He loved wildlife and the outdoor existence he was privileged to have and, yes, he probably had a wider grasp of flora and fauna than most people, but expert was definitely not where he felt comfortable at all. His work colleagues had ribbed him unmercifully. It had been good-hearted enough. Maybe, it was just him, reading more into it than was meant. He couldn't help taking some of it to heart though and, being the new boy and now seemingly the font of all knowledge, he couldn't help wondering what his fellow rangers really thought. However, if he had felt a little hard done by from his work mates, the onslaught he received from the lads at the pub the day it hit the papers was stomach churning. To begin with, it was remorseless, high-spirited and a good laugh and he'd have expected nothing less. Underneath though, he was quite a shy person. Normally chipping in with odd comments here and there at the bar and laughing along with everyone, he felt like one of the lads, but he wasn't brash or over the top, nor one of the life-and-soul types that held court, with quips and jokes for all occasions.

Perversely, the initial attention he received elevated him within the drinking circle and it was gratifying. The trouble was - it still haunted him even now. Conversations, whether drink-enhanced or not, that delved anywhere near the natural world would inevitably require comment from the "expert". It wouldn't matter where he was in the pub or that he was not even part of a particular discussion, being sat with other friends or a girlfriend. Over the hubbub of the busy pub the call would go out, "Let's ask the expert", followed by huge guffaws and laughter all round and Tony wincing inwardly, hoping his company would see the funny side of it. Yeah hilarious… but now, it was beyond a joke!

Turning off the circular gravel path to a cut-through track that, after a quarter of a mile, led down to the main Poole to Ringwood Road, Tony remembered the talk he'd been to recently about the area of Poor Common and its immediate surroundings.

He had learnt that, back in the eighteenth century, Poor Common had been part of a much larger and unenclosed heath land stretching from the New Forest in the east, to Bere Regis and beyond: a vast tract covering hundreds of square miles. West Parley, as a settlement, featured in the Doomsday book and was much older than its overshadowing neighbours, Ferndown and Bournemouth. In fact, to the west of the village and immediately south of Poor Common, at Dudsbury, was a hill fort dating back to the Iron Age. The name Poor Common indicated that, at the time of enclosure sometime in the nineteenth century, part or all of the site was left open as an area where the poor of the Parish would have kept the right to collect fuel but not to graze livestock. As Tony understood it, that right still existed today. Not that he'd seen anyone dragging off the odd Scots Pine. Unfortunately, little of the vast heath actually remained today. There were merely small pockets dotted around Dorset, fragmented by the various requirements and activities of man. The great irony of the heaths was that they were not a natural habitat but an ancient "made" landscape. Originally woodland, cleared by farmers at least four to five thousand years ago for arable and grazing purposes, prevented the re-growth of trees. But left alone in more recent years and, if it hadn't been built on, the now nutrient poor sandy soils were soon colonised by a variety of specific plants and animals suited to those conditions and creating a unique landscape. Ferndown, with its population of around 20,000, lay pretty much in the centre of the old heaths mass. History? Yes, perhaps not in the same league as the Roman Empire, Napoleon or the Second World War, but interesting all the same: it helped him understand and connect a little more with the place he lived in and was happy to call home.

It was now one-twenty-five pm. Better get a shift on, he thought; his stomach growling in agreement. The ponds he'd passed just back around the corner had diverted him in a search for frog spawn. It was typical of him, unable to resist any body of water or wetland, he could happily lose an hour without batting an eyelid.

After walking a few hundred yards along Evergreen Road, he turned left into Casterbridge Road and the pub came into sight. It was still sunny: the sky remarkably blue and a slight chill freshened the air; always a good time of the year, he reflected.

The sighting of frogspawn in the pond - a first indicator that temperatures were warming up and that spring was on the way - had further lifted his mood. Small as it was to Tony, the green swathe that was Poor Common still proffered the same feelings of expectation as any other wild area; maybe round the next corner? Little did he know it but, as the year would progress, its bends and boundaries would not disappoint.

Chapter 5

March is the month of expectation. Beneath its lingering hard exterior, dormant life is patient. Waiting; waiting for warmth; waiting for the sun. It is also a month where the weather is changeable, harsh and wretched, icy frost-covered days, bleak and depressing, with biting winds and stinging precipitation, all reminders of the winter's grip. Some years, it could seem as if spring would never come and April almost done before any noticeable change. But, usually by late March, the countryside is winter-weary and as the days slowly lengthen, glimmers of sun become longer and more frequent; the hint of warmth stabbing life into the chilled mornings to become fresher, cleaner, brighter. It's as if Mother Nature herself has had enough of the dark days of winter and is throwing open the shutters, spring-cleaning the landscape with bright yellow duster and sweeping winds. Many creatures anticipate the future months of plenty and stir themselves at differing times, their biological clocks honed to the earth's seasonal waking. The red fox is one of these. Unlike many, they do not need to be awakened from hibernation. Timing, though, is still important and Tony on one of his many forays to the common was endeavouring to do the maths.

He reckoned the vixen he had spotted was young, perhaps a year old, maybe two. By rights, she would have been in season a few months earlier, had probably mated and could even now have young. She looked healthy and strong and in prime condition, for the rigours of motherhood. What he could not have guessed was the story behind this particular vixen's upbringing.

When she had been fourteen weeks old, she had followed her parents, ranging further on each excursion from their secure den, under one of the sheds at the Guide Camp - situated within the ancient rings of Dudsbury Hill Fort. The territory they covered was wide, occasionally crossing over on to Poor Common. By eighteen weeks, like any other fox, she had begun foraging on her own. In the months that followed she strayed further from the natal range, exploring and probing, staying out and away for longer periods of time like some belligerent teenager in the human world. As luck would have it, she found a ready source of food. The 6-foot high walls of Homewood House might keep less agile and more intelligent beings than her out, but she had found her way in and life would prove good there.

But now in her den beneath a huge rhododendron, in an abandoned badger set, the vixen warm and secure, is now a mother. Born on the fifteenth of March just after two am, four healthy cubs weighing in at around 100 grams each and just 10 centimetres long, suckle greedily: two male and two female. Like all foxes at birth, they are blind and deaf. With short, black fur they are totally reliant on their parents: the mother for milk and warmth and their father to keep the vixen fed and healthy. For the next four weeks she will hardly leave the den, enabling the cubs to feed only on her milk. Her mate, an unusually large dog fox will hunt on behalf of both of them, bringing the food back to the den for sharing.

Lucky here too: he is a very healthy creature, bearing all the usual hallmarks of the red fox. Erect ears and cat-like eyes, kindly but piercing, suggesting a heightened intelligence and razor sharp alertness. Moving with the same jaunty gait, he differed from the archetypal smart red coat and white bib, by being a dirty mottled brown virtually all over. His throat and belly were of a lighter hue but nowhere near as distinctive as the sartorial elegance of the classic Reynard.

Despite a number of attempts, Tony had not been fortunate enough to see this elusive animal. If he had, the chances were it would be no more than a fleeting glimpse. A waving brush disappearing through a gap in a hedge, or perhaps caught in headlights away in the distance: momentarily stopping, turning to look - just two shining points of light; then unruffled, nonchalantly moving on. A fox like any other, Tony would probably have surmised.

Chapter 6

Thursday March 19th

One of the great advantages of a patch of land like Poor Common, situated right on the doorstep of a number of housing estates, is free and easy access for the local residents. The compacted hardcore of its circular route, ideal for all sorts of activities, ensured that the user need not venture anywhere near vegetation, get wet or muddy feet, and could therefore adorn themselves in any form of impractical footwear from open toed sandals to stilettos, and yet still feel healthily virtuous. Brilliant as well for wheeled access to buggies, prams and wheelchairs, not to mention bicycles and the occasional prohibited motorbike. A little slice of, 'walking on the wild side', without actually having to go too wild or indeed too close to nature. So at any time of the day a wide range of humanity could be found ambling and perambulating safely; without risk of tripping on an uneven tree root or a wayward blade of grass. A place therefore to slip out for a breath of 'fresh air' or a burst of activity then be home in seconds to veg out in front of the box.

For some like Tony Nash, still naive about modern family life, this slightly cynical view was how he often saw the common being used. For the most though it was a useful facility – lives lived at such a pace that, in amongst all the day to day drudgery, kids to school, washing, hoovering, cleaning etc, etc, the dog had to be walked. On the plus side though, children could walk to the common unaccompanied and find themselves in a living Play Park; climbing trees, building dens or pond-dipping, all within the relative safety of the community umbrella.

For Bridget Morley it was a good place to grab some much needed exercise and fill her lungs with unfettered air. Grandma Graves could not kick the habit. She was good around the baby, Declan, and since moving in with her, smoked only in the kitchen. Bridget wished she would try to give up; not wanting to see her mum in an early namesake. She would need her for the foreseeable future, childcare whilst at work; inexpensive but above all safe.

Not long out of a messy divorce, Bridget and baby Declan had been warmly welcomed back into her mum's house. Dorothy Graves, a widower of some 5 years would relish the company; it was more than she could possibly have hoped for. Dorothy had lived at number 12 Linford Close for 25 years. The garden backed on to the east side of Poor Common but it had no direct access, unlike some of the others in the road.

It was just after two pm when Bridget, with a day off work, had decided to take Declan out in his pushchair for a walk around the common. She had given him his lunch and was hoping that the gentle movement might get him off to sleep. To access the common with the pushchair meant a short walk around to the pathway off Heatherlands Avenue. The weather had turned again, the sunnier days at the weekend had held such promise, but now it was cooler, and the sky was dark and threatening. She pressed on quickly in an effort to use some energy up and keep warm. By the time she reached the gravel path Declan was asleep. Debating with herself about going back and finishing some forms she had to fill in or take advantage of the peace; she opted to carry on; the walk would do her good.

Glancing around, she noted the common was very still and hushed. Not eerily so but that peaceful sort of calm that occasionally preceded snow. There was no breeze and the muffled air, moisture laden and heavy, had only a slight chill to it. A dog barked not too far away, breaking the magic.

A further 200 yards along the path, recently cleared from the encroaching wilderness, Bridget drew level with a particularly large Corsican Pine. Hearing a boisterous rustling sound coming from the remaining mature rhododendrons some 20 metres away, she shot round to where the noise had emanated, just in time to see two heavy-set-looking dogs tumbling out of the huge shrub. Wild and excited they bobbed and weaved about each other, momentarily stopping to face off, deep-throaty growls giving way to short bouts of seemingly ferocious barking. Eying each other they waited for their opponent to display some vulnerability or weakness: a subtle movement, a feathering of the tail, a twitch in the eye, a slight dip in posture, all potentially signalling a change in attitude or readiness. Within a matter of seconds a gesture made resulted in both dogs tearing off as one. A sudden lurch whilst in full motion would send one somersaulting over the other. Back on their feet in a trice and taking in the lone woman they hurtled towards her. Bridget momentarily froze, her mind racing through thoughts of futile flight on to maternal defiance. As she reached down for her umbrella, stashed in the basket beneath the buggy (the only potential weapon in her armoury) Bridget saw out of the corner of her eye the familiar figure of Betty Thomas striding up the slight incline towards her. On seeing Betty, the initial anxiety over the dogs left her. Re-holstering her weapon, she realised whom they belonged to and knew of their steady, if a little exuberant, temperament.

Like a gunshot, "Halt!" exploded into the air, once again making Bridget jump. As if the dogs hadn't been loud enough Bridget smiled to herself, at the same time checking Declan for any signs of stirring. On the command, the dogs slewed to a stop some three metres from Bridget; sitting bolt upright, side by side, faces expectant, tongues lolling out of their mouths, panting heavily and steam rising from their backs.

"Hey ho Bridget, looks like snow." The voice was strong and confident. "How's that young chap of yours?" Acknowledging the pram with an incline of her scarved head and seemingly oblivious to Bridget's attempts at signing that he was asleep, finger raised to pursed lips.

Betty continued "I expect your mother's happy to have you both around. How is she, by the way?"

"She's fine thanks," Bridget replied. "And yes, a different woman by all accounts. I think having Declan around gives her something to focus on, you know, since dad died".

They chatted on for about 5 minutes, Bridget updating her about work, her lack of social life, men! Betty was good at asking the right questions, drawing out the problems, listening and chipping in with helpful tips and ideas. All the while the dogs remained sitting, heads occasionally turning to distant noises.

After making some comments about moving on, Bridget said, "Look at those two," casually nodding in the direction of the dogs. "They're so good. They're a real credit to you. What breed did you say they were?"

"Bull terriers," Betty swiftly replied and with a backwards wave, she continued on her way. Bridget watched them for a while. She'd got the vibes that the question had jarred with Betty momentarily and that the reply had been too quick in coming, defensive in some way. Her instincts had been right and if she'd had any inkling of future events, Bridget without hesitation, would have had no trouble in condemning them.

Chapter 7

Monday 23rd March

Gary Brown had finished the tuna roll his mother had made for the obligatory lunch box that he preferred. He didn't want to have to go out and buy a sandwich. He wasn't being tight, but he could often use his lunchtime more profitably! A half-eaten packet of custard creams lay open beside him. They had been attacked at morning tea break and he was now dipping into them once again. It was not long after midday and it was looking very doubtful that they would last for the afternoon cuppa. Grabbing his bottled chocolate milk drink and standing up, his heart quickening slightly, excited at the thought of what he was about to do, he pondered where to start. He'd probably got about twenty minutes, half an hour top whack, he assessed. The bedrooms first - that way he reckoned, by the time anybody was due back he would be downstairs nearer to where he was supposed to be working. Good plan, he thought, tactics that's what it was all about.

He had arrived in the house only that morning. His boss Michael Jones had met him on the doorstep at about quarter past eight.

"Bloody dogs!" had been Gary's greeting as he parked his bike against the fence in the drive. He was a bit flustered and annoyed with himself. Being late was not something he was known for.

"Sorry I'm a bit late boss," he gasped, trying to catch his breath.

"Oh I knew you would be here," Michael replied, trying to placate him. "One thing you're good at is being on time." This was a true statement of fact; Gary was a good timekeeper. What the statement might also have implied was that he wasn't good at much else. Fortunately for Michael he knew Gary well enough to know that he could be bloody infuriating at times. Painting a small wall could stretch to a whole day job, if needed. Conversely, if he had to be somewhere after work or finish before time, he could be a minor whirlwind. Nor was he self-motivated, always needing to be shown what to do, never looking for the next job or indeed what might need doing (unless it suited him, that is). He also seemed to lack any common sense; an unfortunate failing, for it was a useful trait in such a manual job. However, Michael was sure this was a deliberate tactic to ensure he was given little or no responsibility, no one really knew. Nonetheless he was very reliable, always prompt for work, rarely missed a day off sick, and, if working with someone who would keep him 'motivated', was a useful and relatively skilled member of his small family painting and decorating firm.

The job they had started that morning was to paint the hall, stairs and landing at number 23 Dunlin Close.

It was actually only about a mile and a half from Gary's house and he had decided to make his own way there.

"What happened then?" Michael asked Gary.

"Well I cut through Poor Common to get here, and I was happily scooting down the path to get on to Evergreen, when this bloody dog shot out in front of me. Weird it was, a dirty brown colour, thought it was a fox at first. Too big though. Anyway, I slammed me brakes on and skidded off the path into a bush. Of course when I got back on again and tried to cycle off, my fucking chain had come off." Michael winced at the expletive, so close to a customer's house. Hopefully they hadn't heard it. Not a good start, otherwise, he reflected.

In fact, Mr Smith had already left, as had the eldest daughter. David the twelve-year-old was about to leave for school and the baby was, thankfully, still incarcerated in its high chair at the kitchen table. Mrs. Smith had let them in as she shooed David out the door, calling after him absently, "have a good day." Her mind dragged in different directions, was silently ranting, "Yes I'll get breakfast, I'll make the sodding packed lunches, again, I'll see to the baby, I'll sort the Painters out. You go off and have a nice day at work." If Gary and Michael only knew!

"Cup of tea before you start?" she enquired cheerily, hiding her annoyance well. After all, the painters had been at her instigation.

Her husband, despite months of nagging, had been reluctant to get on with it, so she'd brought it to a head. His capitulation had been surprising. He'd suggested that the high aspects of balancing on ladders whilst hanging paper might be tricky… perhaps needing the professional touch. So **she** had found them, quickly sorting out a quote and leaving little room for him to manoeuvre.

Jessica brought her back from the brink of rage, with a tantrum of her own. Decidedly pissed-off at still being strapped in the high chair, she had resorted to the age-old attention getter. With the whole kitchen in which to throw her porridge, the innate accuracy never ceased to amaze. Cleaning the cupboard fronts would be one thing, Linda grimaced, but that open drawer with all those bits in, was going to be a bloody nightmare!

"It's all in the preparation," Michael had said to Gary after they had drunk the proffered bonus cup of tea. Gary had heard it all before. It was often said to him within earshot of the customer as if to give further reassurance, that they had made the right choice of decorator. Today's speech had been no exception and Linda had seemed grateful for it. The preparation that he had been alluding too, and Gary had been at all morning, was sanding down the woodwork, all the skirting boards and doors downstairs. The upstairs had yet to be done and thankfully, to Gary's relief, there were no stairway spindles, just solid panels.

Soon after his arrival, Michael had opened all the doors in the hallway to check what needed to be done. As he did so his eyes eagerly took in the scene that was revealed behind. "Nice sunny room," he commented, on the rear-facing lounge. "Kitchen, ok" …and, "toilet, useful", he joked. He hadn't really needed to open them like any home owner, he was just being nosey. Gary on the other hand, had not been particularly bothered. It wasn't until the mid-morning tea break that his ears had pricked up.

Linda had been explaining that they had done most of the decorating themselves, as of course, Michael being a professional could probably tell. She had run through the trials and tribulations of decorating the bathroom, their bedroom of course, each of the three children's bedrooms, the older ones now twice, and the difficulty of them wanting themes. Gary was only half-listening when the relevant information registered. He sipped his brew as furtive thoughts rushed in. Ideas and images congealed quickly. *Just need to check a few things out,* he mused excitedly; heart skipping in expectation.

He now climbed the stairs treading cautiously. Michael had nipped off to get some paint and Mrs Smith, Linda as she had asked to be called, had gone up to Sainsburys to get some shopping in and had taken the baby with her. Brilliant, thought Gary in heightened anticipation, time for a recce.

Not far away, and also on his lunch break, Tony Nash was doing his own furtive investigations. As part of a three-person team they had been tasked for scrub bashing on an area of Poor Common. They would be up against a familiar foe; namely the dreaded rhododendrons that would need hacking down to ground level and some weedy Scots Pine, designated for removal. Tony had been helping with the tree-felling all morning.

Now though, having sat and consumed his sandwich, fruit and packet of crisps, he was itching to explore. He knew the common pretty well, but the large stand of rhodies that his other mate had started to clear with the aid of a JCB, was worth a quick look. The large front bucket had been used to break through the upper foliage and bash down the aged plant's twisted superstructure. Whilst the long mechanical arm at the back with a narrow bucket at its extremity, was favourite to dig up most of the trunk and roots. Although, it was unlikely that all of the resilient vegetation would be removed, five to ten years would, as like as not, see the floor virtually covered once more, but as Tony understood it, what it did achieve, was to allow other indigenous flora to take root and get a hold of an area; a sort of beachhead against the onslaught of established invaders. So where some of the clearing had taken place, saplings of beech and birch would be planted. These would eventually grow up between the sparse pines to change the dynamics of the woodland, encouraging different species of both plants and animals to inhabit it.

With the light-blotting foliage removed and the area exposed, slow-moving reptiles and amphibians were often disturbed; but reluctant to move, lest they draw unwarranted attention from beady eyes perched on high. Tony moved through the area, eyes fixed to the ground and watching his footfall. The common was home to grass snakes, frogs, palmate and smooth newts and the odd toad. Most of these, apart from the grass snake, would more likely at this time of year be found in and around the large ponds a short distance away. The frog spawn Tony had already seen in there would suggest that many of these adult creatures would be leaving their watery mating ground in the next month or so, to scour the surrounding countryside for food. It was perhaps a little early to see them out of the water, but as Tony reflected, there could also be some, running late for the party and still making their way there. So he kept his eyes open looking for enforced movement as he drew near and disturbed logs or parted any lower foliage.

His mind wandered, as his body did and he remembered, this week held the last Thursday of the month. The relevance would only be obvious to those looking to attend the regular meetings of the local Dorset Wildlife group. The interest in all things to do with wildlife had been the initial draw, and he had been attending the regular 'get togethers' for just over the year now; enjoying the walks and talks that they had put on. His thoughts though on this occasion had drifted, and not as one might have expected; from his current activities, chasing mini beasts, or the evident and normal focus of the meetings, (the flora and fauna of Dorset) but to a different incentive for his attendance. Stronger motivational reasons were luring him, and it had now become a necessity to go to every occasion. It had nothing to do with a rare species, or discussions about Natterjacks or Great Crested Newts (his particular fascination). It was baser than that, and certainly from a looks point of view far more attractive. It was a girl called Jenny, and he was hoping she would be there at the next gathering.

It was not a large house, Gary had assessed earlier. It was detached, just, and set in its own grounds albeit long and narrow; the width in fact of the house with a side path. All the houses in the row were the same. With no garages to widen the plots, they had looked somehow squashed, as if the architect had been under pressure to get five into the available slot, instead of four, which would have looked less mean.

Moving into the first room off the landing, the door already open, and with his heart still thudding in his chest, Gary assessed very quickly that this must be the boy's room; the football paraphernalia, a bit of a give-away. He noted the computer on the small desk; an older model, probably a hand-me-down from dad he thought. Across the room, which was only about eight feet wide, was a portable television fighting for space amongst endless clutter all perched atop a pine chest of drawers. Clothing, books, comics and toys lay strewn across the floor, the bed unmade, its duvet pushed untidily against the wall where it had been thrown that morning. On the small window ledge he spied a piggy bank (which felt quite heavy), an mp3 player, and a cheap digital camera and, amongst the clutter on the chest of drawers, a PSP poked through. Very nice, he thought. Those portable play stations are worth a bob or two. Right, let's have a look in the next room.

Slightly calmer now, he realised he was at the back of the house and, as he pushed open the door that had a cute bunny sign on it saying Jessica, it became obvious that it was the baby's room. The traditional wooden cot was the main feature of the tiny room, hemmed in by bland, flat-packed furniture; a single-fronted wardrobe and next to it a lower chest of drawers. On top of this, a changing mat and an array, Gary noted, of wipes, creams, talcum powders and cotton buds. Something he guessed, for every orifice the little creature possessed. The white furniture had been doctored with a variety of homemade stickers, featuring the regular nursery crowd, Peter Rabbit, Winnie the Pooh, the Hungry Caterpillar and many more. Standing by the cot, he looked out through the small window only a few feet away and in to the garden below. The narrow pane would offer only a limited view, Gary judged. *Besides*, he thought, *the room was so small, I doubt Linda spent much time in here*. What he did notice, though, was the ramshackle fence at the end of the garden, about twenty metres away. It was covered in places by a dense coating of ivy, probably the reason the fence was still standing, he joked to himself. Behind this ideal screen, a small field led down to, what looked like, a lane. The high hedgerows snaking away behind the other plots suggested it went down to the main road. *Excellent!*

Wasting no more time, he moved quickly, checking his watch as he slipped into the adjacent bedroom; also at the back of the house. The sixteen-year-old's, he deducted - a reasonable-sized room with windows on the two outer walls; the larger, at the back. Moving to this window, he eyed the garden and beyond. "Not bad," he said to himself quietly reassessing, "Not bad at all; in fact... almost perfect!" Once again the pounding in his chest grew. Glancing around the room he took in the laptop, a new one, and an I-Pod Touch complete with docking station.

"Typical girls' bedroom," he said with more than a hint of derision. "Clothes everywhere." A large double wardrobe, a bit imposing in such a confined space, was stuffed to the gunnels with dresses, skirts, jeans, trousers and blouses all hanging on and off the rail, its floor a jumble of shoes. "Why do they always have loads of them?" he asked himself.

He had only been upstairs for a few minutes but it had been enough. It was all looking very promising, he thought. Just need one more bit of vital information and checking his watch again, felt he ought to get a move on. He was actually in plenty of time but was nervous and excited and it made him jumpy. He needed to get this done and do a bit more work. He wanted whoever got back first, to get the impression that he had been working through most of his lunch break. As a consequence, he didn't bother with the parent's room but instead went back downstairs into the hallway. Looking around the walls, he was confounded again.

"Fer goodness sake" he said out loud, frustrated that what he was searching for wasn't obvious. He thought about his own house, Mum had them everywhere; you couldn't turn round without a recurrent feeling of over-familiarity. It was almost embarrassing, so many, and at every age, and with every available relative. What he was now looking for, disturbingly, he hadn't seen much evidence of in any of the rooms so far. Weird? Moving quickly and urgently with rising panic, lest he run out of time, to where he knew the lounge was, he opened the door. And there, on the mantelpiece, and on almost every available horizontal surface, they were clustered; what Gary desperately, and quickly, needed to see, in order to confirm suspicions and fulfil his hopes...

He needed to see the family photographs.

Chapter 8

Thursday 2nd April

Betty Thomas was having trouble remembering. Her brain kept starting the journey of a particular thought only to find at a later moment, it had diverted on to another topic; something completely random. Her consciousness was fuzzy and emotions chaotic; with feelings of euphoria, panic and then of imminent doom. Rational thoughts kept sliding in and out; *what's happened to me? Where am I?* They were interspersed with dream-like sequences; the dogs barking, the butcher's smiling face merged into a Hoover being pushed by Julie her cleaner. Round and round they went. When at last there was a period of 'lucidity', she was so cold and trying to move was impossible; her body leaden, as if welded to the floor. Trying to shout, her mind screamed, but not a sound issued from her immobile lips. Panic came again, her usually robust demeanour crumbling at the horror and appreciation of her plight. Knowing, now, that she was in the garden, her eyes flicked around the darkening scene. Not a useful muscle moved. Waves of panic submerged her frustration. Uninhibited tears welled, and silently, Betty wept.

After a time, Betty had no idea how long, and with the cold seemingly banished, she tried to remember what had happened and the disjointed journey of earlier. She remembered, going to the butcher, *that's right,* she said to herself, *meat for the animals.* She also remembered driving back home ... catching Julie on her way out ... saying goodbye to her... the hall clock chiming five o' clock ... and hastily calling out to the disappearing woman. Betty couldn't remember what she had yelled, but for some reason, felt it was something important; relevant. Then, in a moment of revelation, *the animals, I came to feed the animals!* Realising she had come to put out food for the foxes helped orientate her within the garden. *I must have fallen on the path?*

The path lead from the back door towards the outhouses, where she kept all the garden equipment. It was pitch-black now and just a huge dark shape indicated the low building. *That means behind me is the herb garden,* she reasoned. Anger and frustration got the better again as she tried to turn her head. *Why can't I bloody move?* But it put her on the east-facing side of the house, where the ground sloped gently down to the southern wall, some 200 feet away, meaning that she was hidden from the main gates and the front of the house. *So anyone calling won't see me!* Not that that was going to happen, she considered, hardly anyone came to the house apart from the postie. Then her spirits soared remembering Julie the cleaner and Neil her husband. *Neil will be in to do the garden tomorrow- Friday. God knows what time it is now; I wonder how long I've been here?*

The darkness told her it was night but stubbornly gave no other clues. It was a clear night sky, no cloud cover, just stars. The moon was not in her narrow field of vision and whatever light she was trying to shine gave only cold comfort. Movement in the inky blackness drew her waning attention. There was no way she could tell what it was, but from over by the sheds something stirred. Ordinarily the dark never frightened her, but now, now that she couldn't move her *damn body*, her wits allowed fear and terror to stalk the neural networks. The dark shapes, flickering and fleeting, conjured demons from the furthest recesses of Betty's failing cerebral architecture. A huge creature loomed out of the blackness towering over Betty's prostrate head. *Oh my lord* she cried out silently and in utter dread. Betty shut her eyes in a desperate attempt to banish the apparition. *It's not real,* she inwardly shouted at herself.

Warm, vile breath assailed her nostrils. *Sweet Jesus*, she begged in dire realisation. Eyelids flinched as it buffeted her lashes. Upwards it swept, caressing perversely the hairs on her forehead, tickling like a wayward insect desperately manoeuvring for escape. Her skin crawled. "*Getaway, getaway,*" she sobbed, pleading in absolute terror.

She had had enough; involuntary spasms now shook her whole body. Her eyes shot open and in an instant of final recognition, took in the familiar beast, one that had so often visited her this past year. In near delirium she suddenly remembered what she'd yelled to Julie, and it hit her hard… "Have a good holiday." Nausea took a vice like grip and cold cruelly 'put the boot in'. Slipping out of consciousness, it would be the last thing she would ever think of.

Chapter 9

Wednesday April 15th

Eight minutes after Sandra had put the call in to the Police, she heard the distant wailing of sirens. The disturbed post-woman sat on the cold front steps staring at the gravel, trying to come to terms with what she had just seen. All the while the incessant two-tone sound grew louder. Two minutes later and one of the officers was opening the gates to gain access to Homewood House, pulling up outside the front door with an unnecessary stab on the brakes, the tyres digging into the gravel as the car slewed to a halt. The two officers jumped out and walked over to Sandra. One of them knelt down to eye-level.

"Hi there, I'm PC James Ryan." Sandra looked up absently. "I believe you've just called in about... a body," he said as calmly as he could. She seemed to have trouble taking in what he was saying and guessing that she was probably in shock, tried again.

"Sandra. It is Sandra isn't it?" The other officer was beginning to wander around taking in the lay of the land.

"I'll have a look round the back," he called to his colleague and disappeared through the gate past the garage. By now, Sandra was beginning to speak, albeit a little shakily.

"Sh... she's round the back by the vegetable garden."

"Who is?" asked PC Ryan.

"Betty, Betty Thomas. This is her house." At the mention of her name Sandra let go another flood of tears. "Who could have done such a thing? Why would they want to?" she implored.

Stepping over a splash of vomit (Sandra's) the roaming PC drew level with the back door. Concentrating on avoiding, it he grabbed the door handle and opened the back door. Calling out as he did so, "Hello, any..." there was no time to finish the sentence. As it opened, and without warning, vice-like jaws grabbed his leg.

At the front of the house Sandra was giving PC Ryan her details. A scream of sheer pain and terror reverberated off the hushed building and cut her short. A couple of pigeons took flight from the nearby vegetable plot, the sharp clap of wing beats adding to the mayhem.

"Oh my god," she cried out in horror. "The dogs!" With that, more cries and profanities issued through the narrow gated portal. Within seconds, PC Ryan was up and running towards the noise, grappling to release his baton.

"Steve?" he bellowed, letting his colleague know he was on his way, but fearing what he might encounter. Turning the corner of the house he could see the top half of his fellow officer lying on the floor hanging out of the back door, wildly thrashing with his baton at something inside the door. The deep blood-curdling snarls and growling filled James Ryan with dread.

"Steve" he yelled again and, reaching the door, was momentarily stunned by what he saw. Two large dogs were just hanging on to his colleague's leg. Sharp teeth had already shredded his trousers and were ripping through the flesh beneath. Steve had somehow released his baton and was lashing out at the frenzied animals. The dogs' movements were frantic. They pulled and shook at him in an effort to tear flesh. Panicked, his violent blows were often glancing and having little effect. Each time he'd managed to dislodge one dog with a well-connected blow, the other would be back to take its place. The pain was almost unbearable but adrenaline was in control; anger, hate and aggression were now driving him to survive. James's blood was up too and he waded in with his own baton. From a standing position his blows were more accurate and forceful, the metal baton thwacking heavily against their heads and bodies. Eventually with stinging metal raining down on them, the dogs began to back off. Seizing the moment, James charged at them, yelling at the top of his voice and wildly hitting out at them. They retreated, scampering away into the Day room at the back of the kitchen. Swiftly he closed the door behind them, just as the dogs seemed to rally and, turning on their heels, charged once again. They slammed into the door just as he pulled it home, their weight forcing it shut the final inch. Without stopping James ran over to his mate and surveyed the damage. The leg was badly mauled, blood was leaking everywhere, the gashes looked deep, and there was no way he could deal effectively with so many wounds.

"Hang on mate, I'll get some help" Grabbing his radio he got through to the control room.

"Ambulance requested urgently at Homewood House. Officer wounded". Turning casually, he glanced out of the back door, and another horror scene transfixed him. Like an automaton he requested, "CID to attend. We have the remains of a body."

James collected some cushions from the drawing room and tried to make his colleague comfortable. Steve was in great pain and deathly white, the shock kicking in. James tried to talk with him, struggling to find a topic that didn't seem too contrived.

"What sort of dogs were they, do you think?" James asked, knowing as soon as he had said it, that it was a stupid fucking question. Steve looked at him, and in the moments when his face wasn't contorted with pain, the expression said it all, and he lashed out viciously.

"Like I give a fuck what they are." Crestfallen, James looked on helplessly. Steve knew he'd cruelly over-reacted but the pain, *Christ! The fucking pain,* he screamed at himself.

In near delirium he managed, "You don't think they were Chihuahuas then?" He flashed a forced smile.

36

"Dickhead," was James's reply, grateful that his friend was still capable of the sort of humour that generally got them through a day. After what seemed like an hour to James but, in reality was 13 minutes the response ambulance and paramedics swept through the open gates and down to park next to the Police car. While the medics were stabilising Steve and getting him stretchered, James called back to control. "I have two dangerous dogs on site which will need removing. Any chance you can get a dog warden here pronto? Better tell them to bring some serious fire power. These dogs are fucking wild." A glint of sun flashing off a windshield up at the main gates told James that the cavalry had arrived and he strolled round to meet them.

The drive was beginning to get congested as the CID's car rolled gently to a stop on the other side of the wide turning circle. From the driver's door Inspector Patrick Stimpson struggled free from the seat belt and swung his legs out on to the gravel.

"Hello Ryan, heard you might have something for us?" He said, as he lifted his substantial frame out of the car.

"Yes sir, we have a dead body, well what's left of it".

"Bit messy then?" Patrick concurred.

"Fraid so sir."

"Well, where is it then constable? Let the dog see the rabbit, as they say."

"Speaking of dogs Sir, there are a couple of vicious bastards in the house, at the back. Whatever you do, **do not** go into the room at the back of the house, the one off the kitchen. The dogs are in there."

"Thanks for the tip-off Ryan," Patrick acknowledged.

"Oh yeah, and I've put a call out for the dog warden. Hopefully they'll be with us soon." Ryan led the way around to where the body lay gently warming under the sun's spring glare.

"Christ what happened to you?" Patrick asked the dazed policeman as he was being taken to the ambulance on a stretcher.

"Fucking dogs," was all he managed to say. The dogs in question had quietened, just occasionally though they fired off a few salvos of violent barks from their refuge, to make sure that whoever was out there, kept a distance.

Patrick turned to take in the carnage that lay a few yards before him. "Do we know who she is yet? I presume it is a she?" he asked uncertainly.

"Yes Betty Thomas. This is her house, I haven't had a chance to find out anything else sir."

"The woman on the front steps?" Patrick queried.

"Her name's Sandra – Postie; the one who found her," informed Ryan.

"Right, you go and have a quiet word with her, find out what you can about the Thomas's, I'll be along in a minute." With eyes still assessing the grizzly scene, he added soberly, "And you'd better call control, get some more help. Tell them also to give SOCO a heads up. We've no idea what we're dealing with."

37

Chapter 10

Staring blankly at the ghoulish sight in front of him and desperately trying not to focus on any one particular thing, Patrick's mind started to grasp at ideas and possible scenarios. His eyes moved purposefully around the body, widening their arc on each sweep. He noted an empty and overturned plastic tub laying about 6 feet up the path, and the fact that the outside light was still on over the back door, although it was daylight now. *Did she come out to get something, with the tub as a receptacle, some vegetables from the garden?* He looked over at the relatively bare plot. *Maybe, maybe not*, he thought, glancing over to the shed, and the obviously fenced pen. *Or did you have something in the tub? Maybe you came out to feed something, chickens perhaps?* Not that he could see any. S*till, whatever was in the tub has been eaten now. Looks like it was dark when you came out, hence the lights' still on,* he reasoned. Noticing the path was a little uneven he wondered if she had just taken a tumble. At that thought, his eyes went back to the body and in particular the head. He was rewarded with what he thought was a huge gash around her left temple and eye. The wound he felt was not consistent with just someone bashing their head on something, it was too wide and spread out. He was aware though that the body must have been out overnight, *by the look of it probably longer, much longer,* he mused, assuming that the massive damage to the stomach was probably made worse, like the head wound, due to animals and insects. *But that injury could be originally from falling and hitting something, I suppose, or perhaps being hit over the head with something.*

As if drawn by unknown forces, experience, instinct perhaps, Patrick focused on the low retaining wall around the raised bed that followed this section of the path. It was made up of what looked like the local Purbeck stone. Irregular shaped boulders had been expertly arranged and cemented on top of each other to form a metre high barrier. Patrick noted that whilst the overall effect created a neat uniformity, the individual stones still jutted out rustically in places. *Hitting your head on one of those wouldn't be too clever,* he thought.

Having seen more than enough outside, he reasoned that somebody else would be able to discern much better than he how she might have died. Gingerly, he stepped in through the back door. He had noticed an unpleasant smell hanging around, but had assumed that it was the remains of Betty Thomas. As his eyes took in the devastation in the kitchen, his nose took the full force of the stench.

"Oh great! Dog shit," he said through gritted teeth and wrinkled nose.

"How long have you been stuck in here I wonder?" he said under his breath. The rhetorical question was naturally lost on the dogs but a couple of barks answered anyway. *Quite some time by the look of the floor,* he pondered and surveying the virtual bog of faeces and urine. Shitty footprints told their own story. The trails led all over the house. It was clear that they had managed to find food in the walk-in larder. *The old wooden door must have given way to a sustained attack,* thought Patrick, surveying the weakened with decay and now splintered quarter panel, just above floor level. Food packets had been shaken open, odd bits crumbed the floor, flour, sugar, lentils, the discarded bags and cartons scattered.

"You've not starved then," he said in admiration of the dog's tenacity. "But what have you had to drink, I wonder?" Picking his way carefully through the minefield of excrement, he wandered into the corridor, which he guessed, was a sort of back hall. Wellington boots and heavy shoes, paired off and neat, lined the floor. Coats hung off pegs and leads dangled lifelessly. A single entry door led out onto the patio and another went back, Patrick guessed, into the day room, judging by the scrabbling noises made by the incarcerated animals. Along one wall was an array of 'built-in' cupboards and shelves, a utility storage it looked like, all made of a rich dark wood. His eye though was drawn to a glass-fronted cabinet containing two shotguns and a sort of sporting rifle. Boxes of ammunition stood regimented on the shelf. It was academic now as to whether the old girl had had a licence for them.

Climbing the uncarpeted stairs, in the presumption they would lead on to the rest of the house, he wasn't looking for anything in particular but wondering if he might find something - information, photographs, letters, documents anything really, that could be of use. The dogs obviously hadn't had the full run of the place. Some of the doors still remained closed. They had been able to get into the back hall and stairs leading to the small rooms above including an old bathroom. The door to the room stood against a wall, the rotten architraves unable to support it. Patrick took in the dust and cobwebs and the dilapidated nature of the decoration. *Obviously not the main bathroom,* he thought. The constant trickling of running water into the toilet bowl through a worn ballcock, alerted Patrick to the dog's fresh supply of running water. *You lucky bastards,* he smiled.

Finding nothing of significance as he carefully moved around the upper rooms, he decided to go downstairs. From the wide landing adorned with some fabulous local landscapes, *bet they're not prints,* he descended the rather grand stairway that would take him to the main hall at the front of the house. Halfway down, he stopped to admire the view out of the window above the front door. Looking up the drive to the front gates he took in the formal rose garden off to the left and the orchard on the right. "Very nice," he said to himself in an appreciative manner, reflecting it was a far cry from his own attempts.

The sight of a small white van turning tentatively into the drive through the gates distracted him. *The dog warden*, he assumed. And remembering the look of agony etched on the young coppers face as he was being carried out, thought; *rather you than me mate!*

Chapter 11

"This is Jenny sir, Jenny Spader, the dog warden." Ryan evidently knew Jenny from previous occasions, there was an obvious familiarity.

"Hello, pleased to meet you," Patrick quickly replied, giving her only enough time to smile in response. "I don't suppose you've been told much, but the situation is going to be difficult, and I'm afraid, a little upsetting".

A brief shake of the head and "No," was all that Jenny had time to offer.

"Let me explain," Patrick continued, eager to get on. He was, though, taking in the somewhat diminutive, slim and shapely figure, of the warden. At five foot seven and a half inches, Jenny was actually above average height. He noted the fashionable and heavy rimmed square spectacles perched above high and healthily-coloured cheek bones, dark brown eyes, hair severely swept up into a high pony tail. *She was very pretty* he thought, *if it wasn't for the beige cargo pants and green fleece with East Dorset District Council emblazoned on it, she could have been the archetypal haughty P.A., or glamour model even.*

"Just around the corner here," he continued, pointing to the gate by the garage, "we have a body. We think it is the old lady who lived here, but I warn you, she is in a bit of a mess. The local wild life, or maybe these dogs we've got locked up, have had a go at her, if you understand my meaning." Jenny's grimace told him she had understood.

"My problem is that we don't know, as yet, how she died and so, I have to treat this as a suspicious death, which means…" He paused and ran his fingers over his forehead as if still trying to extract the thoughts physically. "We might have a potential crime scene or scenes if you include the house. Now, without knowing how long these dogs have been trapped in here, and just how dangerous they might be, bearing in mind one of my officers has just been taken to hospital with his legs ripped to shreds, we both need to tread carefully".

As Patrick drew breath, Jenny acknowledged his concerns with a sympathetic, "Ooh sounds nasty."

"Yes, and by that I mean - the dogs need removing, somehow, to allow access to the whole house but at the same time, without disturbing said potential crime scenes."

"You wouldn't want them running amok then?" Jenny added with a trace of sarcasm. The black humour deliberately deployed to give an air of confidence. She'd seen the way his eyes had scanned and knew he was questioning her ability.

"Well quite," was Patrick's acknowledging and amused reply.

"Tricky one then," said Jenny, continuing in the same light-hearted vein. "Right," she said more seriously, "I had better make my own assessment of the dogs and the situation before deciding how to handle it. Is it ok if James shows me were to go?"

"Yes surely," Patrick smiled wickedly at them and swept his hand towards the gate. "Off you go JAMES," he said, emphasising the name. James duly led on; his neck and face colouring with a fiery glow. Patrick watched them go still wondering how this slip of a thing was going to subdue two vicious canines. She looked so young, probably not much older than his own daughter who was fifteen. *Mind you, the high ponytail flouncing around didn't help,* he thought as she disappeared around the side of the house.

To get his own version of events, and determining he wasn't going to be able to speak to James for a while, the Inspector went over to Sandra who was now looking lost, her uniformed inquisitor having deserted her. Sandra told him why she had come up to the house. Quite apart from delivering the mail, her concerns were that Betty had been missed by the butcher in town. He'd mentioned it in passing and she had offered to check on Betty when next delivering her mail. And that was how she had come to find her lying there. Sandra also explained that Betty was a widower and that it wasn't unusual for her to call in and have a cup of tea whilst on her morning round. She also advised that Betty had a cleaner, whose husband came in and helped out in the garden. She gave the detective their address, but seemed to recall that they were away on holiday. Betty had told her this about three weeks ago now.

"They were going to see their daughter in the States," she said her brow furrowed as she tried to reclaim the information buried deep amongst other snippets of information similarly gathered.

"I would think they are due back any day now," she concluded.

"So potentially," Patrick began, assimilating the information, "you haven't seen her, the butcher hasn't seen her and the home help hasn't been here for a week or so. Just how long has she been lying there?" He was really talking to himself but Sandra had been following his train of thought,

"She could have been there for a couple of weeks then! That's dreadful."

"Well yes, anything up to two weeks but probably not that long." Patrick said, almost defensively, as if it had been the Police's fault she hadn't been found. "No wonder those dogs are pissed-off," he added.

Meanwhile, around the back of the house Jenny and James were cupping their hands around their faces as they tried to see in through the French windows. The dogs had immediately taken offence to this intrusion of their privacy and had charged the expanse of safety glass. With seemingly no thought to the pain, their thick heads repeatedly slammed up against the glass, barking and snarling sending gobbets of spittle and slime to smear the clarity. Both Jenny and James had recoiled at the first thrust, the panes shaking violently and threatening to leave their wooden frames.

"Jesus," James had exclaimed.

"I don't think he's going to be much help," Jenny pointed out grimly.

"Why?" James asked, noting Jenny's look of concern, "What are they?"

"Well," she said choosing her words carefully, "if I'm not very much mistaken, I think these are a type of Pit-Bull, probably an American Pit-Bull."

"Nasty then?" James enquired.

"Not normally," She hesitated. "If handled correctly. But potentially, and particularly under these circumstances, then yes, very nasty, very nasty indeed. But what is intriguing, is how an old lady ends up with two dogs that are banned in this country under the Dangerous Dogs Act. Assuming they are hers, of course?"

"No doubt there," said James, "Sandra the Postie has verified them as hers."

"Okay," she said slowly and deliberately as her thoughts now followed a different tack. "How long has the old lady been dead?" Jenny enquired.

"We don't know yet for sure," answered James, "Sandra hasn't seen her for about two weeks, not that that is anything to go by, from all accounts. Why what are you thinking?"

"One way to a dog's heart is through its stomach, not always of course, but in this case these dogs are probably starving and thirsty. I think I'll try and soften them up with some food and water. If I can get it to them that is, before I make any attempt at catching them."

James looked aghast, "Catch them? Are you mad? Haven't you got an Ouzie dart gun or something?"

"No, we don't dart them," she laughed at the obvious nonsense. "I've got a long pole with a noose on the end of it that slips over their heads. It's called a grasper."

The young PC grinned, "Sounds a bit kinky."

They walked companionably around to the back door; Jenny's eyes were immediately drawn back to the forlorn body of Betty Thomas. Revolted and saddened she averted her gaze over towards the outhouses. Casting her eyes over the wooden sheds abutted against the high wall, she began to turn as if to go into the house. Something had registered in that momentary glimpse and she swung back round to credit it.

"Look at that," she exclaimed incredulously. On the wall above the sty, stock still, staring at them intently was a fox. She stared back at it for a moment and felt uncomfortable, ill-at-ease at being scrutinised in such an obvious way. Uncharacteristically unnerved, she made to go indoors again, but something still bugged her and, turning back again, she was just in time to see its tail disappear behind the wall. *That was odd,* she thought beginning to break it down in her mind's eye, *you don't often see foxes quite so bold and particularly not during the day.* But there was something else, something she couldn't quite get to straight away, her mind triggering some sort of querulous alert. Because much of her thoughts were still taken up with how to deal with the dogs, it didn't click for some moments, but as James and Jenny picked their way carefully into the kitchen, avoiding the foul-smelling deposits, the incident flashed back into her consciousness. She suddenly recognised the disturbing and unmistakable glare for what it really was; calculating, unrestrained and definitely predatory. "Blimey, he was a big beast," she said loudly, aiming it towards an equally perturbed James whose hand covered nose and mouth, indicated where his immediate concerns really lay, the sickening stench, rather than some animal.

"Yeah and you don't often see them out at this time of day," James replied, his voice muffled and distorted by his hand.

"Sorry?" Jenny queried automatically, but at the same time guessing what he had actually said. "No you're right, very strange."

******

Later that evening, as Tony strode out along his usual route to the Angel Pub across Poor Common, he once again marvelled at how quick the evenings lengthened. It seemed like only yesterday that it was still dark at five in the afternoon and now, here they were mid-April, and it was only just getting dark at seven-thirty. As a result the activity around the common had picked up, notwithstanding the extra dogs and humans, thought Tony scathingly, the wild life too had seemed to perk up. Birds were trilling away, their evening choruses soon to be swelled by summer migrants while, in the fields, horses were noisily playing, and amongst them rabbits grazed oblivious to the heavy hoof-fall, although he didn't think they were anywhere near as abundant, as in previous years.

And away in the distance Tony could see, a probable reason for that anomaly crossing a field. Close to the copse that hid Homewood house; a fox was trotting. He was right out in the open and moving with intent. It wasn't particularly unusual. He'd often seen them traversing these open spaces, although, where this one was going with such obvious determination he had no idea; *some well stocked bin I shouldn't wonder,* Tony thought. He loved the foxes though, they were, he'd always felt about the closest animal that Great Britain got to being dangerous; that and a badger. Not that, in reality, they were any kind of a threat to humans. Contact between them and man was negligible, the fox probably seen more often than a badger, well alive anyway, Tony smiled coldly. He'd seen too many mangled forms at the side of the road.

The fox had disappeared from sight a few moments earlier whilst Tony had been 'away with the animals', but just as the view would disappear behind a dense holly bush he caught sight of another two foxes following the first. He stopped walking and immediately went a few steps back up the path, to broaden his field of vision. There had always, it seemed to Tony, been quite a high percentage of foxes in this limited area but it was very unusual to see three almost at the same time. Even at this distance, he knew they must be adults. Besides, it was far too early in the year for cubs to be out and about. He watched them to see where they went. From the edge of the paddocks they left the open ground and disappeared into the large shrubs just inside the common.

Tony made a mental note to check around that area. It was quite likely there would be cubs and it wouldn't be long before the vixen would allow them to play above ground. That, Tony thought would be a treat to watch, providing he could find them.

Chapter 12

Thursday April 30th

Tony finished clapping and quickly averted his eyes from the bobbing ponytail of Jenny Spader. *Why hadn't he gone and sat next to her when the chair was free?* He chided himself.

He knew why. He had walked into the cosy hall, with the twenty or so chairs all lined up in the centre, ready for the talk, and there she was sitting one row from the front. There were about five other people already seated. A couple, Mr and Mrs Johnson, were sat together while others were dotted around in various seats and, as usual, nobody was in the front row. A few people were standing at the edge of the hall chatting. They acknowledged Tony as he walked in.

"All right Tony," one called out. Other heads turned, and a cursory wave and a swift, "Fine thanks," was Tony's self-conscious reply. He often felt that people were watching him. He knew they weren't, but just couldn't help himself. It was a minor flaw in his character. He had been dogged with a shyness through his school days and it had carried on through, to a lesser extent, in his teen years. But life after, and particularly the agricultural college, had helped to boost his confidence and his reticence was pretty much a thing of the past. However, there were times, like now, when he had a wobble, a throw-back and he was annoyed with himself. He had wanted to talk to Jenny. He'd thought about this meeting for the last few days, hoping that she might be there. This branch of the Dorset Wildlife Trust had seemed a little staid when he had first joined six months ago. Many of the regular attending members were quite a bit older than he, not that he'd joined for any nefarious social reasons. Despite there being a couple of young women his age, it was the third one that had done it for him. Jenny. Smitten from the moment he had laid eyes on her. Disappointingly, she was not one of the regulars, and had not been at the previous meeting but he had overheard she was coming to this one.

Slim, athletic and shapely, Tony had noticed, and a little shorter than himself, but boy was she a looker! Was it the eyes, or the glasses? Perhaps the combination, but whatever it was, it had sent a familiar jolt and stronger, it seemed, than he'd experienced before; his heart had sprinted, lungs had dragged in air, in fact his whole insides had been in turmoil, as he had recoiled from the first instance of her smile.

And there she'd been. She too, looked round and flashed him that same wide smile. It was at that point, he felt, all eyes seemed to be watching with interest. They hadn't been. But Tony's returning smile was perfunctory and not at all what he wanted. *They're all expecting me to go and sit next to her,* he thought. *The two youngsters, it's only natural,* he imagined them thinking, the old boys in their corduroys and tweed jackets exchanging glances; '*Know what he's after?*' insinuated, across their grinning faces. And so he had sat halfway down the hall, some two rows behind, and as far down the row of chairs as he could get. Six chairs? *Bloody miles away, I might as well be next door!* He'd thought irritably.

Throughout the talk, billed as 'Meet the Moths', Tony had been distracted. Moths were not really his thing; under normal circumstances, though, he would have listened with genuine interest, all grist to the naturalist's mill. But the high pony swishing gently side-to-side and occasionally dipping as Jenny looked down in an attempt to re-position herself, on the hard plastic chairs, drew his gaze. He had been running it through in his mind, *I'll speak to her at the coffee break after the talk,* he had decided. But much of the speaker's rhetoric and accompanying photographs had washed over him as he grappled with possible opening gambits and topics of conversation. By the time the presentation had finished, about an hour later he was a bag of excitable nerves, *they all sounded so naff and besides everyone will be listening,* he thought, irrational though it was. He was only half listening when the chairman, thanked the guest lecturer and then followed it with a brief announcement.

"We have had a couple of requests in, one from the local constabulary, their wildlife officer, and, the other from the vets, down the road. They have come in independently, I might add, but the topics are somewhat similar. The police appear to have had a flurry of missing pets, more than usual it seems, rabbits, guinea pigs chickens etc. No doubt foxes or badgers, it's that time of year – extra mouths to feed, I should think." He looked over his glasses knowingly and smiled. "The vets have echoed this natural crime wave with domestic animals being mauled, from scratches to torn flesh." He looked down at his notes, "I think they thought this was nearer our domaine and wanted us to keep our eyes open for anything unusual. "No doubt," glancing pointedly at Jenny, "your offices will be contacted too, if they haven't already."

Jenny's head bobbed in acknowledgment. "Yes, the police have mentioned it to us, but as you say it's probably just that time of year."

With coffee perched precariously on a mismatched saucer, and cornered now by one of the local landowners keen to hear what was happening at Moors Valley these days, Tony felt more comfortable. Talking with somebody actually seemed to settle him down and help take his mind off Jenny.

"Plenty of frog's spawn in your ponds I expect," Tony asked Piers.

"Oh crumbs! Tons of it," he replied. "I love this time of year, don't you? How's your father these days, by the way? I haven't seen him for ages, still keeping well I hope?" Tony and his father knew Piers of old. Perhaps a few years younger than his own father, Tony had guessed. Piers Easterbrooke was part of the old Dorset Farming community, infinitely wealthier than his father, he also guessed, as his estate seemed vast and had long turned its back on traditional farming practices. The series of six ponds he had inquired about had been man-made, dug out that is by a machine, but allowed to fill naturally taking advantage of the water table and streams feeding the

River Stour close by. Seen by many as just another wealthy landowner, with rights over a large swathe of Parley and into neighbouring wards, Piers was in fact a hard working guardian of his inherited plot. Much of his land was innovatively used and highly productive and, whilst he had a hard business head, he was mindful of the impact that his various businesses could potentially have on the environment. Most of them rather than being in anyway destructive would be by design in fact, complementary to the natural landscape, such as Turf growing and industrial scale composting.

"Yes he's fine thanks. Still working hard though," Tony replied, the latter part of the sentence implying that at his age, he thought his father shouldn't be.

"The foxes are having a field day though," Piers continued. "The visiting ducks have started to make nests around the ponds and some of them never seem to learn. Still it keeps them off my chickens for a while. Clever little buggers aren't they?"

"They certainly are," Tony agreed. "Mind you, I was watching some cubs up on Poor Common only yesterday. They're really cute. You know what I mean, all wobbly and large paws."

Piers nodded and a grin crept wickedly over his face. "Nothing that a good twelve bore couldn't sort out, eh?" Quickly adding, "just joshing," palms up in defensive posture as he registered Tony's smiling but furtive glances. The farming community's sense of humour Tony knew, was pretty down to earth and practical, so the joke was not unreasonable to his attuned ears, however, he wasn't so sure about some of the group surrounding them now.

"Having said that, these were a bit funny looking. Can't put my finger on what it was," he continued, "but they were still delightful to watch. I reckon they had only ventured out from the den in the last few days. I was just lucky to see them". Thinking about them reminded Tony, for some reason, of another brood of cubs he had seen the previous year on the common. "Whatever it is, must run in the family," he said "because I seem to recall cubs from last year bearing similar markings, and I don't know," he paused as if trying to summon up the image in his mind, "but these seemed more substantial than the average fox; broader maybe."

"Sorry," someone said from behind. "I couldn't help overhearing what you were saying." Tony turned and his heart fluttered.

"Hi Jenny," he said as casually as his accelerating blood pressure would allow.

"Ah Jenny," Piers greeted her warmly. A little too warmly, Tony felt as he noticed Piers's pupils dilate. *Right piss off Piers, you lecherous old bugger, I'll take it from here,* he thought; *she's mine.*

Before she was able to explain her intrusion on their conversation, Piers, a man used to being in charge, swung his confident charm into action. "Who's for a pint then?"

Of the ten left in the hall, three decided to leave, the other seven, two of whom were Piers' tenants, seemed it would be rude not to partake, bordering on insubordination even. To Tony's relief, Jenny had also said yes to a drink and he was back in with a chance. The little hall behind the United Reformed Church at

46

Longham was only a short walk from two Pubs; The Angel Inn, northwards on the Ringwood Road and Tony's regular haunt, or The White Hart Inn, also on the Ringwood Road, but South. Tony was glad that the general consensus had been the closer White Hart. He was not keen to be seen with the current crowd in light of the ribbing he was oft the butt of. Besides, he was less likely to be self conscious with Jenny, somewhere where he wasn't known.

Somewhat frustrated, on the short walk to the pub with Piers dominating the conversation, and further irritating Tony by seeming to monopolise Jenny's attention; he resigned himself to the back of the group and was last to enter the pub.

"All right Tone?"

Annoyed at the derivation of his name, Tony looked up. "Oh hi Gary, how's you?" he said flatly, *Could things get any worse?*

"Fine thanks mate," Gary chirped eyes darting to the floor nervously. "Off for a pint then?"

"No a dead dog actually, you twat!" he wanted to say with all the vehemence he could muster. But instead opted for, "That's right. You?"

"Off home me. Think I'll have a stroll through the common though. Never know what beasts you might see at this time of night." The jibe was not said obviously, as Gary made only fleeting eye contact. Tony, on the other hand, felt like punching his lights out. He had never taken to Gary and, in particular his incessant digs about the Big Cat Sighting at Moors Valley. They were always delivered from 'left field' or veiled in some way and took Tony a moment to realise he'd been had. Gary was not easy to talk to at the best of times and was often just a listener, awkwardly clinging to the periphery of a group, but he knew of Tony's 'expertise', and the constant inferences were not helping his cause.

"Yeah, very good," Tony said, as off-handedly as he could.

Gary, oblivious to Tony's hidden rage, pressed on through the pub door and disappeared into the night. Relieved that Gary wasn't staying, Tony went to join the others at the bar. He couldn't work him out. Right from their first meeting at the Angel some two years ago, Gary had jarred with him. Not many people in Tony's short life had annoyed him or got him wound up quite like Gary Brown did. In fact, Tony could happily say that he got on well with most people, young or old, even Gary's few friends. Perhaps it was because Gary often tried to make out that he too, knew a lot about nature and wildlife. On the rare occasions when he was forced to have a drink with him, Gary would tell him how he had stalked deer on Parley Common or lain camouflaged for hours watching badgers. It sounded like bollocks! Besides, when he was with his mates in the pub all they would talk about was computer games, or X Box live internet games. It was all really geeky stuff. "Yer, Call of Duty's awesome!" or "I reached the top level in Grand Theft Auto."

You want to get out more, Tony had thought. *Never seen him with any girls either.*

"What are you having Tony?" Piers enquired,

"Oh cheers, a pint of Forty-Niner please." Nudged from his angry deliberations, Tony's mood began to lighten.

Outside, Gary zipped up his combat jacket. He was missing the fire already. Setting off at a brisk pace, in an effort to keep warm, he walked up the Ringwood Road. Turning right after about a quarter of a mile, onto the track that would lead him past the entrance to Homewood House and on in to Poor Common. It was nine-forty-five pm, the street lights had been on well over an hour and the quarter-moon shone poorly, even in the cloudless sky. The path was unlit, the trees and bushes just dark shapes, and it was getting difficult to see his footfall. Flicking on his slim magnalite torch, the way ahead became instantly clearer. He kept up his good speed for a further 200yards. As the street lights of Evergreen Road began to cast some useful light in his direction, he switched off his torch. He continued to move quickly on the path as it snaked its way behind the houses that backed on to the common. Every so often he would glance over noting the familiar dwellings, some dark and empty but most illuminated in some way with security lights or just the warm glow of curtained windows.

Gary knew this little patch of land like the back of his hand and had first become familiar with it when he was fourteen and walking the family's Jack Russell. Though it had been a chore then, and it was as much as his mother could do, to get him out for some fresh air. One day though, that changed and nowadays he could often be found wandering on Poor common, even though his canine companion had died a number of years ago. But Gary had always been a bit of a loner and quite happy with his own company. He was generally a quiet lad, polite and self contained, and, almost confident when on familiar subjects: work, computers, games, films etc. He had grown up with just a few friends, like-minded kids happiest when plugged into some sort of electronics. Now at the age of twenty-four, he still suffered from bouts of low self-esteem but they had lessened; particularly having learnt his trade and becoming skilled at it. An avid electronics gamer and computer buff, Gary's room in his mother's bungalow on Dudsbury Drive was a shrine to all things techie. Not that his mother would know, she, had been banished on his eighteenth birthday. With his high spec computer, HD television, the latest gaming consoles and mobile phone, he could: contact his few friends, was able to surf the net, download films, go on ever more violent video games, watch porn if he wanted and emerge only for food, work or the pub. It was, he felt, absolutely ideal. His mother was reasonably happy with the arrangement too. He gave her some money for rent and food, and in return she got some company, occasionally.

Stopping once again, not far from the narrow path that would take him out on to Heatherlands Avenue, he looked back along the row of semi-detached properties. He checked his watch and, somewhat disappointed, decided it was too cold to hang around and made for home.

The White Hart has just one long bar, and the seating area not that spacious. A rare drinkers pub, though it did serve some simple food, but not much. With the usual array of traditional furniture: round wooden tables, upholstered wheel back chairs combined with long and curved bench seating, also fabric covered; it was cosy to say the least. They were still lighting the fire of an evening, the copper and brass ornaments that bedecked the walls and beams of the narrow Inn, reflected a fiery glow.

Tony's luck had changed, or so he'd thought, as he sat down at the table and realised he was next to Jenny. Luck had had nothing to do with it; she had made sure no one else sat there. Saying to all who tried, "I just need to speak with Tony, sorry do you mind?"

"Thanks for keeping the chair for me," Tony smiled shyly at her.

"Oh no problem," she said "I was getting a bit fed up with the old charm offensive." Her head jerked in Piers's direction.

"Yes nothing worse than, offensive charm," Tony shot back quietly. They stifled giggles as Piers sat down. If he was put out at being usurped, he didn't show it.

"So what were you saying to Piers back at the hall, about unusual foxes?" Jenny asked.

"Oh! Nothing really. I was just telling him that I had seen some fox cubs, yesterday, just up the road on Poor Common. Do you know it?" Jenny nodded. "There was something different about them. I can't say exactly what, they were just, well bulkier, you know sort of thick-set in comparison to others I have seen. Darker colour too and a sort of mottled coat, but that should change as they get older."

Jenny sipped her Chardonnay whilst Tony was speaking. "It's funny you should say that though," she said putting her drink down onto the table when he had finished. "Only, I was up that way a few weeks back and had a brief encounter with a fox."

"Oh yes," Tony's beer had been hovering close to his lips, and he took a swallow, before he too put it on the table. "What happened?"

For the next twenty minutes she told him of her job, and the call she had taken to go to Homewood House. "I couldn't believe it. American Pit Bulls! Can you imagine?" Finally relaxed, Tony was enthralled, perhaps not so much with the tale that was unfolding, but certainly with her. She was something else.

She told him how they had quietened the dogs down with food, enough to be able to separate them and catch them. She had also told him of the big fox, how it unsettled her, "And this during the day!" she exclaimed. He watched her closely, enjoying her animated face as it ranged through an unending repertoire of emotions; from the nonsense with James, the young Police officer, to the look of horror as she revisited the vision of Betty Thomas's mutilated body. "That poor old lady," she said sadly. The police had determined Betty had died as a consequence of a stroke, causing her to fall and hit her head, leading to massive blood loss. He had been a little shocked to learn that the body had been badly mauled, internal organs missing, presumed eaten by the local wildlife. "I reckon it was that fox," she said. "He looked more than capable." Tony was a little sceptical about this, although his mind jumped

49

to another possible culprit, one that had been reportedly sighted quite recently and, not that far away, but said nothing; conceding, he didn't know all the circumstances.

"Oi you two," broke the connection and both he and Jenny turned to the perpetrator, David Martin the local Butcher. The big man was on his feet towering over the table, a pint glass in each of his slab like hands and a grin from ear to ear.

"Oh you are with us then?" an obvious dig at their lack of attention, to the rest of the group.

"You're a bit slow my boy," he said in his fruity voice as he waggled one of the empty pint glasses, indicating the rest had already finished and he was off to get some more. Piers' tenants, obviously feeling they had done their duty, declined and bade their farewells. Jenny asked for another white wine on her way out to the toilets.

"Thanks David," she added. Tony glanced down at his pint glass, still half-full.

"Been a bit distracted have we?" David winked at Tony as he said it, his eyes darting to where Jenny had just left the room. The half pint that he had drunk was beginning to take effect and although he felt a gentle glow tinting his cheeks, Tony smiled back warmly. "Maybe," was all he was prepared to say, inhibitions dulling.

"Well?"

"Well what?" was Tony's fixed grin reply, realising as he said it, that it was not further interrogation of his obvious intentions, but as to what beer he would like. Now almost embarrassed at the off-hand reply he garbled,

"Forty Niner please. Sorry I thought…" his voice trailed off at the futility of continuing. He knew he'd been caught out, as the laughing David turned and made for the bar. Abashed, Tony hid in his pint, the rich and ambient beer, slipping down easily.

When David returned with the drinks the discussion had turned to the beer. Was it any different now, since the local Ringwood Brewery had been bought out by one of the larger brewing companies? The evening went by quickly it seemed to Tony, even though he hadn't monopolised Jenny. The chitchat between them all had been general and good-hearted. *Easy company* Tony had thought to himself, as they all made their way outside, ready for the short walk back to their respective cars at the church hall. All had made their second drinks last much longer and un-surprising to most the hands on the Clock Tower were just shy of eleven fifteen pm.

Jenny had fallen in step with Tony and, as they neared the church hall, he was wondering how to ask her out for a date. *Was she really only interested in the foxes earlier, or was there more to it?* The niggling little doubts threatened to go large and he fought to suppress them. He need not have worried.

"Do you think you could take me to see the fox cubs one evening?" she asked, grasping her Renault Clio's door handle.

"Yes I'd love too," he said, hoping that his reply didn't seem too eager.

"Ok. When's best for you?" she asked.

He was about to say Friday but realised that was the next day *Too keen* he thought, "What about this Saturday?"

"Erm..," Her eyes squinted slightly as she thought about any possible problems, "Yes sounds good to me."

The slight hesitation almost threw Tony off his stride.

"Shall I pick you up, say about six thirty, seven-ish? We should be able to get a couple of hours in before it gets too dark," and thinking, *Ok…. In for a penny…* "Do you fancy grabbing a bite somewhere afterwards?"

Chapter 13

Saturday 2nd May

"Your carriage awaits Madame," breezed Tony as the door to Jenny's ground floor flat swung open.

"Thank you kind sir," was her equally light reply.

Tony noted the tight jeans, walking boots and look alike sheepskin-lined flying Jacket; sensible garb for a chilly evening in the forest and a pizza later.

As they approached Tony's pride and joy he could see out of the corner of his eye she was looking somewhat quizzically at it, obviously trying to place what it was.

"What is it?" she enquired following up quickly with an unconvincing, "Looks interesting". She too had caught Tony's expression as he swept his arm theatrically to reveal the gleaming automobile and gathered he was expecting a bit more of a response.

"It's a Reliant Scimitar", he announced.

"Oh right, is that good? Sorry, I'm not very up on cars." She smiled.

The Scimitar had been his father's toy, a rare indulgence, and an uncharacteristic aspiration to be part of the farming 'smart set'. Registered in 1978 and bought second hand by his father in 1982, he'd looked after it with much love and attention and drove it with a quiet pride. In fairness, it hadn't been the most reliable car he'd owned but his dad was adamant, 'He wouldn't part with it'. Finally though, when it had let him down, 'for the last bloody time!' It was mothballed in one of the farms' many outbuildings. The plan was to do it up and re-build it at a later time. With its limited production runs he felt sure it might be worth something in the future. In essence, it was an elongated three-door hatchback but stylish and sleek, a classic sporting estate. It was different from all the other mainstream car manufacturers, in that, the body was made of fibreglass. But beneath the monocoque shell and astride two steel rails which just about everything was bolted onto, was a huge 3-litre Ford engine, and this was its main appeal. The car was not only gutsy and fast but also comfortable and smooth.

Growing up on the farm Tony had learnt many practical skills, of which tinkering with engines was just one. He took it upon himself during the summer break from college to have a go at rebuilding the car. His father was soon hooked as well and over the next two years they had restored it to its former glory.

It was why, as they drove off, he had felt the need to enlighten Jenny that this was more than just a car to him. It had been a labour of love. He had sweated, drawn blood and had cried in frustration with it. Jenny had been suitably impressed at all the practical skills learnt, from mechanics and paint-spraying to upholstery. As she sat in the comfortable front seat next to Tony appraising his craftsmanship, she viewed the car in a different light.

They drove the two and half miles from her flat in Bearwood back to Heatherlands Avenue, where he parked within a few yards of the path that led through into Poor Common. It was now six-forty-five pm and the sinking sun was still just probing the mixed woodland canopy, making the floor a patchwork of solid shadows and gleaming light. Only a few minutes had elapsed since leaving Jenny's flat, but the flickering low light and long shadows confirmed the need for their warm attire. On the short trek to the makeshift hideout, Tony had prepared Jenny for a bit of a wait.

"Need to let things settle down, too many dog walkers, still," he added optimistically, "once the lights dropped a bit more we should see something."

They had arrived at their hideout a few minutes before seven. It was now eight-forty-five pm. Their optimism had indeed been high when they had arrived and tried to get comfortable. But an hour and a half in, backsides numb from perching on uncomfortable boughs and legs aching with crouching, when not perched; optimism, like the sun, had all but disappeared. They had given it another fifteen minutes, but to no avail.

"Can you smell Pizza?"

"God, can I!" Jenny heartily agreed, "Let's go, I'm bloody frozen."

As they bundled back up the hill, all stealth abandoned, and blood once again coursing through their chilled veins, she turned and beamed at Tony.

"Don't ever let it be said, you don't know how to show a girl a good time!"

He returned the smile with a laugh of his own. "Not my fault they didn't show," he said, hands up in mock defence.

"Hang on." He stopped abruptly. "Whose idea was it anyway?"

"No idea," she giggled, continuing purposefully up the slight incline. "Last one at the car buys the Pizzas," she yelled back, already breaking into flight.

******

Five minutes after the Racing Green Scimitar had growled out of Heatherlands Road, heading for Bournemouth, Gary stepped onto the gravel path, aiming for the Angel Inn, through the common.

With his usual camouflage jacket and black jeans he was virtually invisible. The pale skin on his hands and face were covered by black Thinsulate gloves and a hat, the excess headband of which he was now rolling down, leaving only a narrow strip for his eyes, converting it to a balaclava. In the cold dark woodland, if he stood still he would at least be warm; warm and invisible. Just another dark shape amongst the myriad of tree trunks and dense bushes; not that he was planning to stand still, just at the moment.

Covering his left wrist with his right hand he carefully revealed his luminous Black hawk combat watch, a fake. No way would he spend nearly £300.00 on just a watch. It was five to nine, *I'll give it an hour,* he thought. *That'll give me time for a couple of pints later.* A few metres along the gravel track, he carefully walked off to the right and quickly found the inconspicuous path he used on regular occasions. One of the 'animal highways' Tony had called it. "What the hell does he know? I've never seen any bloody animals!" Not wishing to turn on his torch, Gary trod with deliberate care. Glare from some of the street lamps on Heatherlands Road just penetrated to where he was now. The trouble was, it was of little help; in fact it would play havoc with his night vision if he let it, but in an effort to try to combat this he kept one eye closed. A little tip he had gleaned from one of the lads at the pub, who was in the T.A.

For the next hour Gary patrolled at the back of the houses, moving stealthily back and forth over a 300metre range and some twenty metres away from the respective fences. He had successfully avoided a couple of late dog-walkers, spotting their movement well in advance and dropping like a stone to the floor. They had passed no more than 5 metres away. The dogs, luckily for Gary, had been on leads, otherwise they might have found him but like their owners they had been completely unaware of his presence. Pleased with his covert skills, he gently brushed the loose debris from his trousers and moved off, his heart still racing at the excitement. About halfway through the hour and almost back where he had entered the common, a light flicked on in one of the upstairs windows. The curtains were not drawn and like a beacon, it shone brightly out into the night. Gary held his breath. Movement now in the room drew his gaze - two people, both women, by the look of it. In a flash Gary had unzipped his jacket a quarter of the way down, taken out a pair of mini-binoculars that he had hanging around his neck and zipped his jacket back up. *Game on?* he asked himself.

With his two gloved hands holding the binoculars firmly to his face he focused in on the bedroom. *Bingo*, he thought. All around him the night was deathly quiet. However, a noise started up. To begin with it was so quiet it was hardly discernible, a soft thudding sound, but as Gary watched the scene unfold before him, it grew louder. Thud, thud, thud, it went. Unconcerned, Gary continued, he drew closer to a tree in order to steady his hands that were now beginning to shake. *Calm down! h*e advised himself. *There's nothing actually happening yet.* Drawing in a few deep breaths of cold air, the familiar sound of his pounding heart slowed as he tried to manage his growing expectations.

One of the women was carrying a younger child, cradling it in her arms as she moved towards the window. He could see she was talking, her mouth moving, it looked a little bizarre, the younger teenage girl wasn't saying much.

"Come on mum," Gary said under his breath, "Must be time for…." But before he had a chance to finish the sentence, "You bitch!" he breathed, sending plumes of warmed air out into the night. For almost as suddenly as they had come on, the bedroom lights darkened.

"You've closed the fucking curtains, you inconsiderate bitch!" More than a bit pissed-off at the sudden withdrawal of privileges, he quickly reconciled the situation, thinking to himself, *oh well, shit happens. Not the first time, nor will it be the last. Difficult Ops like these, you can't always rely on the target to do what you want. And let's face it Daisy,* he continued glancing as he did, to the dark house next door as if looking for confirmation, *your next door neighbour, is certainly not being very co-operative at the moment.*

But Gary was patience personified. He would wait. There'll be another time, he reflected. Indeed there had been hundreds of other times over the past few years and he had learnt that patience would win out. Besides he thought, *anticipation's half the crack.*

Chapter 14

They had decided on Pizza hut. Jenny suggesting there would be more chance of a table on a busy Saturday than the independent restaurants; quicker turn around she'd reasoned. And they had been lucky; a corner table had come free just as they had reached the greeter, after a short queue. With a Budweiser each, they soon settled into a relaxed questions and answers conversation. Knowing only a little about each other, was good, it was after all 'more fuel to the fire'. Physically they had been attracted to each other, 'the spark' being there long before they had ever spoken to each other; shy glances during previous wildlife meetings and events, a casual greeting, or a, 'See you next time,' the highlight of their communication for almost six months. Both had made discreet enquiries of each other, neither seeming to know how to coax 'a flame'. But, on the few chance occasions when they had spoken, the embers had begun to glow; frustratingly they just needed something more combustible, for it to catch. The walk had been useful kindling, a distraction to allow a further slow reveal of personalities, but now with curiosities truly ablaze and oblivious to the boisterous atmosphere surrounding them, they sat opposite each other, questioning, probing, exchanging details of their pasts and swapping hopes for their futures.

By the time the Pizzas had been demolished and the empty plates cleared away, and aided by two more Budweiser's apiece, they felt very relaxed with each other. Both had decided on and ordered a pudding. They were now in the first real lull of conversation. It wasn't however an awkward silence; it seemed like a mutual pause, a rest even and they took advantage to sip their drinks. In the past, Tony would have sat like this with previous girlfriends, enjoying their company, chatting making conversation, but like most men, one eye seemingly with its own agenda. Not always a conscious instruction, more probably a habit, but certainly programmed, to surreptitiously scan the possible talent. Tonight though, his eye still roved around the restaurant but it wasn't stopping anywhere particular, if anything he was watching the faces of the other men. Intrigued, and more than a little smug, he noted Jenny was attracting a lot of 'hits'.

Jenny too was enjoying a similar experience. With the benefit of conversational hindsight, she now had more of a handle on his character. *Apart from being a bit of hunk*, she thought, *he's funny, attentive, caring, thoughtful.... hark at me, I'll be saying perfect next, if I'm not careful.* The glances from neighbouring tables seemed to confirm her thoughts, the main one in particular; hunk.

"Tell me," she said, a slight mock challenge in her voice. "What's this I hear about you, being an expert on Big Cats?"

Tony's eyes rolled high and right. "Fer, fu… goodness sake," he faltered, a mixture of horror and disbelief swept across his face.

"I'll kill that Gary, so help me."

Realising that she hadn't so much touched, but probably severed a nerve, she quickly said.

"Sorry, I didn't mean to…"

"No no, it's alright," he said, now smiling sheepishly.

Feeling that the anger was more feigned than real, she attempted to re-work the question in the hope of avoiding any further annoyance.

"Look if it's an off-limits thing, then fine… but," she looked down momentarily as if studying the table. "No", a gentle shake of the head as her eyes came back to meet his. "I can't even remember who'd told me, but I remember they'd said that you had an interest in big cat sightings in the area. I was just wondering really. Like a lot of people I'm sure, who have seen the articles in the papers. It's quite exciting really."

"Well yeah, I think it's interesting. It's just this dick-head I see at the pub sometimes, Gary and his mates; they will keep on about it. Keep saying I'm some sort of expert. They're taking the piss of course." Tony relaxed a little. "To be honest with you, I don't know why I let it bother me. Normally I'd let things like that wash over me." Tony's obvious exasperation turned to resignation. "No, it's him, he just winds me up."

Desserts arrived and, as they began to tuck in Tony recounted the story of the big cat sighting at Moors Valley, the misquoted article in the paper he'd been involved in, and the knock-on grief effect. "It's funny, I can take it from everyone else, even now. It's just that little shit…. Sorry," he apologized, laughing now at his own stupidity, "I'll stop now…. promise". Jenny smiled back, reassured to see that he could laugh at himself.

"So how many do you think there might be, out there?" The question: a genuine response by Jenny, to continue the topic.

"Difficult to say, really," Tony mused. "Logically though, if there were thousands, there'd be sightings all the time. I think the general consensus is that there's probably not a breeding population. By that I mean there are not groups of them living wild, but individuals scattered around; unwanted pets and the odd escapee from private collections. Who knows how they get there?" Tony gave a questioning shrug.

Jenny could see that he was on a roll now, and was happy to listen.

"All I know is that once out, they would be like ghosts. Many people believe in them, some claim to have seen them. Most though don't even think twice about them. Why would they? They're so far removed from daily life. And you know… if you stop to think about it, we live in a well-populated area and yet there are thousands of animals out there: Deer, Badgers, Foxes, the big ones", he clarified with a cheeky grin, "Down to, rabbits, rats, mice… the little ones. I mean how often do you see them day-to-day?" He looked for her acknowledgment. "Very rarely," he continued.

"And, even if you know where to look, you won't always see them." Nodding in agreement, Jenny could see what he was getting at.

"For example," he continued. "Over on Parley Common, they allow a small herd, about ten to fifteen cattle, to graze during the summer months. It's not a huge area, a couple of square mile at most and mainly of heath, some mixed scrub and a few wooded areas. From one week to the next, I can walk through there and never see one." Jenny nodded", as he carried on. "Let's face it, they're not exactly small and it's not as if they need to avoid us. So a big cat, a Puma or Panther, I mean these guys are built for stealth and, as a threat, they'll want to avoid us." He gave her a knowing look. "If they don't want to be seen, they won't be."

"I can see what you're saying. It just seems a bit unreal to think I could bump into one on my next walk in the woods."

"Well believe me," Tony jabbed his finger at the table a couple of times in emphasis, "they're, there. Or at least, have been."

"You sound pretty sure?" It was a question not a statement. Jenny had picked up on the 'have been', the way it was said? There was more to it, she was sure. Staring at him she could see he was weighing up whether to say something or not.

"OK," he said after a short pause. Drawing closer and glancing involuntarily at the couple on the next table "I'll let you into a little secret."

Amused at the implied subterfuge, Jenny thought twice about a witty reply. Instead, not wishing to jeopardise the revelation, she settled for, "Sounds intriguing."

Chapter 15

The Angel Inn was packed. At ten-thirty-five pm, when Gary breezed in looking for a friendly face, he found it difficult to get to the bar, let alone find a vacant stool. The popular pub had a wide menu and it attracted an equally wide clientele.

He soon realised he had positioned himself behind three familiar heads. "All right Dave?" he called, and as if all were called Dave, the three turned to greet him.

"All right Gary?" said his boss Michael. "Slide in between me and Johnny here. We'll be going shortly anyway."

The Johnny in question was Jonathon King, a great hulk of a man, Gary's next-door neighbour and father to his best friend Miles.

"Time for a quick one before you go?" Gary enquired, eyeing the half empty packet of peanuts on the bar.

"No, we're all right thanks Gary," Jonathon smiled warmly. "As Michael said, we're off shortly, but thanks anyway." Noting Gary's stare and the subtle sweep of his hand across the bum bag around his waist, he quickly said, "Don't panic, I'll get rid of those," aware of Gary's long-standing allergy to all things nuts. Dave Fisher also refused as he was going to catch a lift with Michael.

"The Dockers are around the corner there," Dave said, the hand without the pint pointing to a part of the room, hidden from those at the bar.

"Oh right, I'll pop round and see them in a bit," replied Gary.

Eventually he got himself a pint and took a satisfying swallow.

"Daisy was telling us earlier," Dave started up again, "about their guinea pigs and the rabbits. Looks like a fox got them."

"They had my chickens the other day too," piped up Jonathon.

"What! Not all of them, surely?" Gary quizzed.

"Yep. All gone."

"Your hen-house is like Fort Knox. How on earth did they get in?" Gary looked truly amazed.

Jonathon finished his pint and made to leave, "I'll tell you what, they're either very clever little buggers or just plain lucky." His finger pointed in threatening stabs. "But the only place where the chicken wire was a bit dodgy is on the door, and, you've guessed it, that's where they got in. And when I say dodgy, the wire was actually ok, they just decided to rip away a corner from the wooden frame. Yanked out all the staples!" He continued in a more conspiratorial vein, "Dunno about you but I've got no idea what kind of animal would have that much strength? Bit more than your average fox, I'd have thought though." And as if to draw a line under it, hissed, "Bastards."

With that, the little group moved off from the bar, saying their goodbyes and leaving Gary on his own, feeling a little exposed and self conscious.

******

"I've actually seen one."

"Really?" It was Jenny's turn to move forward, eyes widening with heightened interest. "Where?"

"Mum and Dad's Farm in Bridport." Jenny noted the use of Mum and Dad. Not, the parent's farm. She used these words herself and it implied to her, his closeness to them still, and, a sense of family.

"I would have been about ten," Tony continued. "I was down by the lower fields. There's a stream that crosses the farm. Most places you can only get to it across the fields; our land you see, so few people ever go there. I was always there. Dad would probably tell you it's where I grew up, rather than the house." He smiled wistfully. "Anyway, most of the stream is lined by hedges except on the one field where he used to keep the cows. They had free access to the stream along the field's length. Got a bit muddy down there, I remember; all those hooves." He glanced up, checking that Jenny was with him! "Anyway the cows weren't there. It was milking time, and it was about six o clock in the evening. I can remember it, as clear as if it were yesterday. Gorgeous hot sunny day, blue sky, hardly any clouds, hardly any noise save for the sounds of the countryside: buzzing bees, chirping crickets the odd pheasant and me: shoes and socks off, paddling in the shallows."

Jenny's attention was well and truly caught, much like the minnows that Tony was now telling her about.

"I had just caught another minnow and was about to add it to my collection in the jam jar when I heard the screech of a Jay. I looked up. Their cry can often sound quite disturbing," he added quickly, "but this one sounded more so, somehow. It flew off from a tree a few metres along the bank, and as I followed its flight, it just skimmed the hedge and dropped behind it. But below where it had disappeared there was movement. I was maybe seventy-five metres away and the grass growing along beside the hedgerow was long and tussocky. With the glimpses I got, I could see that something was using the cover of the hedge and the long grass to make its way down to the stream." Jenny fidgeted forward. "At that point I had no idea what it was and wasn't really worried. It could have been anything; a fox, deer, one of our cats from the farm, literally anything. Obviously my mind was searching through the possibilities, looking for a familiar shape or movement, to give it away. As it drew closer to the stream, with only a few metres to go something was evidently not adding up. I wasn't concerned as such," Tony reflected, fiddling absently with his beer, "Probably more intrigued and excited I think, for I must have sensed some anomaly."

He paused, shuffling in his chair as if uncomfortable with his confession. "I have been over this in my mind many times and looking back, I think somehow, I'd realised that this animal was larger than those others. It was also moving in such a way that was unlike them as well." Tony wondered if Jenny might question these thoughts from a boy of only ten and felt the need to reassure her. "I appreciate your average child might not have the necessary skills to determine such subtleties, let alone have seen a fox or a deer, but I grew up with them, they're almost daily occurrences on a farm. So you see I was pretty astute when it came to our woodland friends, even at that age."

Jenny nodded in agreement, but was waiting now expectantly. "And?"

Seeing her eagerness, he decided to string it out, in devilment.

"Well… that was about it really."

She though, had begun to get the measure of his sense of humour and was not falling for it quite so easily.

"Fair enough then," she said dismissively, as if ready to move on to another subject.

"Ahh." he said, the grin returning. "Thought I had you then."

"Not this time sunshine," she laughed.

"Okay, okay," and pausing as if to remember where he had left off. "Well, when the animal broke cover to get to the stream about 40 metres away from me, I knew then exactly what I was looking at. A cat! However," Tony continued animatedly. "This was no moggy from the farm. More like something from the Zoo! - By this time my legs had turned to jelly so I just stood there frozen, watching this huge cat, lapping at the water. It had looked in my direction a couple of times, knew I was there." Tony was thoughtful. "I'm sure of that!" Jenny's face showed a mixture of concern and disbelief.

"But I wasn't scared exactly and nor it seemed, was it. I just remember being so excited and nervous, I reckon I had a lump in my throat the size of a small planet." Jenny giggled at the obvious exaggeration. "And at the same time, exhilarated, surely this would be something to wow my mates with." He looked encouragingly to Jenny. "You remember what it's like? I imagined them holding me in awe, not so much street cred, as field cred." Tony justified the joke. "You have to remember many of my friends were from the farming community." But it was unnecessary, Jenny had already cottoned on.

"Besides that, I couldn't wait to get home to tell Mum and Dad."

"After what seemed like an age, but was probably about two minutes, it left the way it came, disappearing half-way up the field through a gap in the hedgerow. I chased after it trying to see where it was heading, but by the time I had scrambled through, it had gone, probably into the little copse on the edge of the next field."

"What did it look like then?"

"I didn't know it at the time, but having looked at many pictures since, I am convinced it was a Puma. My mother, when I told her what I'd seen, was interested, you know as parents are, but I don't think she believed me. I think she just thought I was having her on."

"Can't imagine why," Jenny said in feigned surprise.

"Point taken," Tony laughed in acknowledgement. "Mind you I wasn't that bad then, and yes, before you say anything, I've obviously got worse since!"

"The thought hadn't crossed my mind," Jenny lied with obvious pleasure, "What about your dad, though what did he think?"

"Again, looking back on it, outwardly he was interested, we even went straight out to look for it, but I felt, that, unlike mum, he believed me. Although I realise now, that he didn't want to be seen to make too much of it," Tony explained. "Mainly out of concern, so I have found out latterly. You see the farming community had been aware for some time about other reported sightings and not just in Dorset, but also, all over the country. There had also been talk, of sheep and other livestock falling prey to vicious attacks by unknown animals. Dogs, was the official line, but evidence could not always back that up and so the rumours gained credibility and the reported sightings added fuel to the fire." Tony felt he needed to clarify, "Dad keeps an open mind, but probably wouldn't voice an opinion either way."

"So apart from that one you didn't see at Moors Valley, have you had any more encounters?" Jenny asked as the waitress deposited the bill. Tony grabbed it.

"My shout I believe," he announced before continuing. "No nothing, and that's why I was so sure of the one at Moors Valley. Mind you, when you were telling me the other day about that old lady having been savaged, I wondered if that might have been attributed to a big Cat, not that I would have said anything. The kids at school gave me a hard time, even back then. Unkind some of it was too; you know the way kids can be?" Giving the waitress his credit card to pay, he added with certainty and just a hint of sadness, "What with that and the recent Moors Valley incident I'd think twice about speaking out again, that's for sure."

******

Back at the Angel, Gary sauntered off in search of the Dockers. As he rounded a pillar into another area of the bar he heard his name being called. Ahead, seated on a small round table were John and Daisy Docker.

"Speak of the devil," Gary said under his breath as he approached the couple.

Grasping a spare chair he slid it to one side of the table and sat down between John and Daisy.

Turning to John, and with an uncertain smile asked, "How's it going Johno?"

"Yes fine thanks Gary," John replied politely. But as Gary turned, John looked at his wife and gave a look that clearly said, 'Well, you called him over.'

"You alright Daisy?" Gary asked, even more hesitantly, unable to meet her gaze.

"Yes thanks," Daisy smiled at him. "What about you though? I haven't seen you for ages. Still working hard?"

"Oh yeah, rushed off our feet," he replied eagerly, glad to be on familiar ground. "He's a bloody slave driver, that Michael Jones." Then changing tack he asked, "How come you guys are here? Night off is it, where are the kids then?" All the while Gary had been answering Daisy's questions with placatory words and then listening to her answers. In his head, his mind was rewinding like a DVD player and every so often stopping at points in time, notable moments of recent history that conjured visions he had been lucky enough, *no… that's not fair he chided, patient and cunning enough, to witness over the years. If only you knew,* he said slyly to himself, *you might not have seen much of me girl! But you'd be shocked at how much I've seen of you."* The inference lost obviously to her, but not to Gary, and he smiled inwardly.

Chapter 16

Wednesday 6th May

Peering out from their hideout in the rhododendrons, Tony and Jenny watched enthralled as the fox cubs provided the evening's entertainment. Tony had suggested, on their way home from the restaurant, on Saturday, that they should try to see them again. Jenny had been keen too, but work commitments and social engagements meant the earliest they had been able to arrange was the following Wednesday. Somewhat frustrated, they both had to accept this, knowing it was an opportunity to see each other again without having to use the 'date' word. What had become clear to both of them on Saturday, albeit that it was never said out loud, was the obvious mutual attraction. Although, on the one hand, Tony remained shy of any blatant over-attention, his normal reasons, the struggle within; irrational and debilitating *"what if she really is only wanting to see the foxes and I'm the means to an end?... Well, ok, I know she likes me as a friend that's obvious, but..? Anyway its early days yet, best give it a while.* Rejection, or at least the fear of it, he conceded, could be a right bastard at times!

On the other hand, Jenny was as sure as she could be... this was it! Always a positive character, when she set her sights on a goal, whether personal or professional she went for it with a quiet confidence, flawed only by the occasional 'blonde moments', she would joke. The first sighting of him had not been one of these, she was certain of that. Her resolve had been squarely tested though. Over the past few months, their paths hadn't crossed that often in fairness, but when they had; it was obvious he was attracted to her, *wasn't he*? "C'mon pull your finger out," she would curse at him under her breath, willing him to come over. Eventually she'd decided to extract her own digit and force the issue, at the pub the other evening

The sun was almost down now. They had not seen its departure from the sky, the thick Rhododendrons and tall Scots Pine at their backs, had put paid to that an hour earlier. Once again, the onset of darkening skies and its ill effects, had threatened to cut short their vigil.

But with the low light came the cubs; the vixen first, tentative and wary. She moved slowly and deliberately, sniffing and tasting the air, eyes scanning in all directions, her ears pricked and alert; pure caution attached to a hair trigger. There was no discernable call or signal, but as one, and in complete contrast, four fur balls with legs, barrelled out of the den. Immediately, two started play-fighting. One pranced unsteadily on to the back of its sibling, pushing and rolling over it before crashing into the vixen's hind legs; almost flooring her in one fell swoop. Had Tony and Jenny imagined it? The look of horror and indignation on her pointed face; as if she was saying, 'Hey, I haven't said you could come out yet!' Then that look of weary resignation, and a short bark, 'You wait till your father gets home!'

"They're probably anywhere between six to eight weeks old," Tony whispered hardly daring to speak.

"Like, how cute are you?" Jenny murmured, as if talking directly to them. It was hard to keep still and quiet, as they watched the antics no more than a few metres in front of them. It was difficult not to laugh at their naive stupidity when they climbed unsteadily up a fallen sapling or to want to cry out when they fell from the stricken trunk or point at them or jerk ones head in order to see where they had fallen.

The vixen on the other hand, as foxes go, was unremarkable. The dull orange fur, highlighted and tipped on the ears and feet, with darker hair, was like any other. Her white bib and tail end were as classic as one could get. Therefore nothing to set her apart from any of the thousands of foxes throughout the British Isles, and yet, here in her natural habitat and, perhaps, only just recovering from the ordeals of childbirth, she was magnificent; a creature of the living countryside, an animal of grace and poise, of warmth and nurture, a delight to see as she guarded her brood; a very rare pleasure and privilege to watch.

"Are they normally that colour?" Jenny's hushed voice, barely audible.

"To be honest, at this age it's difficult to tell what they should be. They do vary," Tony replied matching her volume. "They're normally almost black when born, growing lighter as they get older; so this is probably about right."

Looking like something straight out of a Disney film, the short squat furry bodies supported an equally furry head. Stubby, slightly rounded forward pointing ears protruded either side of the fluffy dome; and the face, like all young animals, cute and appealing. Overly large eyes, innocent but alert, aside a short snout that culminated in a stubby button nose; immature whiskers sprouting from either side. The vulnerability exuded is nature's protection plan, what right-minded and caring mother, could turn their backs on such defenceless charm and endearing charisma?

Purposeful strides, falter to wobbling steps. Aggressive lunges, in to ignominious falls and confident stances to rough and tumble. The playful biting and feeble pouncing are all signs that they are still young and poorly co-ordinated. But maturity will come, and quickly. Over the next few months their skills, practised and honed, will propel them well within the year, in to adulthood.

The cubs had been out for about twenty minutes and it seemed the ever-watchful vixen was growing twitchy. It was clear that she had begun to round them up and move them towards the natal earth, the mouth of which was in a bank beneath another huge rhododendron. From Tony and Jenny's hidden position they could just see where they disappeared into the undergrowth. The vixen reappeared in pursuit of the largest and clearly the dominant cub that evidently had slunk back out. Like a belligerent toddler that didn't want to go to bed, it plonked its bottom heavily on the ground, eyes on its parent, defiant and stroppy, daring her to act. A slap to the bottom or a nip to the rump; it worked the same way, the high-pitched yelp confirming… that hurt!

They were magical moments that had swept the earlier unpleasantness away, an experience that had threatened to remove the shine off just such a promising evening. With the show over they walked back to the car, deliberately taking a different route, they had no desire for a second viewing of the horrific scene that had greeted them on their way in.

From the moment they had walked onto the common earlier, Tony's senses had triggered. It was nothing perceptible, nothing obvious to the eye or disturbing to the ear, but he felt something non-the less. It made him uneasy and he tried to shrug it off, but couldn't.

As they had approached the 'animal highway', a mere parting in the low scrub, which they'd used on the previous occasion, Tony commented at how quiet the tiny woodland seemed. They had arrived at just after seven-thirty pm, almost an hour later than before. Following the same route, but with the light fading fast, there had been an eerie calm. No harsh cawing from the murder of crows, or gentle cooing from perched wood pigeons settling for the night. No road noise; the occasional car on the main road seeming to pass without sound. No voices or shouting; as if all human activity had been banished from this minute corner of the world. Tony spoke in hushed tones.

"I've never known it so still," he said, mirroring the disquiet around him and the strange atmosphere, thick with silence, "Might be unusual air pressure," he'd ventured, clutching at straws. "A front coming in, or something."

It was at the halfway point on the inconspicuous path that Tony had stopped in his tracks.

"Oh my God." His voice was filled with horror and revulsion.

"What?" was all that Jenny had managed to say before drawing up beside him and seeing the carnage that lay before them.

"Looks like a deer, well the remains of one," Tony corrected, as he'd fought the sickening feeling, rising from his stomach.

Concentrating on the animal, rather than the blood and the gore, he'd tried to work out what had happened. The deer was in a real mess. He could see that the head lay twisted away from the body, "Looks like the necks been broken. Can you see those marks on its throat?" He pointed at a number of what looked like puncture wounds.

"I wonder what they are," he mused to himself. The delicate creature's spindly legs were all still attached to the main carcass, but one only just.

"The body has been badly damaged." Again, he'd traced a finger along from where the chest and stomach should have been. He hadn't checked to see if Jenny was actually looking, but he'd kept up the running commentary anyway; it had taken his mind off his own churning stomach.

"Look at the ribs they're almost stripped of flesh, missing a few too, I think, and it's gone from around the flanks as well." He shook his head, "Internal organs, heart, lungs, stomach all appear to be missing too. Christ what a mess." He had seen enough dead animals in his time, on the farm, at college, and at Moors valley, none though had been quite so violated. His dad's flock of twenty chickens halved in number, dispatched by a fox in just one night in an orgy of destruction, seemingly clinical in comparison.

Jenny had been looking. "Not exactly pleasant?" The questioning understatement, a mild attempt at humour, her way of dealing with it, and, luckily not the squeamish type. All the same though! "How do you think it happened?" she'd asked.

He'd widened his search away from the body and noted the flattened undergrowth forming a rough circle around the body some two metres wide. There were broken stems of young bracken growth, saplings of pine and birch no more than thirty centimetres high, bent and snapped. Flecks of blood adorned some of the plants, smudged and smeared in places as if someone had tried to wipe them clean. On others, tiny droplets speckled the bright green growth, as if sprayed there by some bizarre artistic hand.

"Look at the plants all damaged around the body. I'm not sure but it looks to me like there was a struggle here." He'd glanced across to Jenny. "It's a small roe deer, probably one of last year's offspring, so about a year old." He stopped talking for a while, but all the time his eyes wandered over the scene, mentally storing it away.

"What you thinking?" Jenny had asked, studying his face.

"Again, I'm not sure," he'd said absently stroking his chin with thumb and forefinger, "but I don't think this happened very long ago, maybe even within the last couple of hours."

"What makes you say that?" A tiny involuntary shiver issued through Jenny as the idea that whatever had done this… might not be far away, made her uneasy.

"It's the blood, it looks fresh, and the ground is still damp with it. If it had happened some time ago, say this morning the blood would have dried more. But this is still sticky." He smeared a blood droplet over a leaf with his shoe, "No, I'm sure this is very recent."

"I wonder." Jenny's eyes widened in recollection. "Do you remember a couple of weeks back, in the paper, those kids that stamped a fawn to death, down in Upton Country Park wasn't it? You don't think this is a copycat thing, do you?"

"Yes I remember. That was really dreadful;" Tony's anger broke through.

"There were three of them. One actually picked the fawn up and hit it across the head, dropped it and they all took turns to stamp on it. I'd fucking stamp on them, "he'd growled, "given half the chance! Sick little bastards." Ordinarily, he would have apologised for the swearing, but felt somewhat justified, and let it go.

Jenny had forced a smile, saying. "I think you'd have to join a queue."

He'd shaken his head, "I don't know, might be." Looking around again at the damaged foliage his eyes returned to the torso. "Having said that, I'm not so sure. Why is half of it missing? And what are those puncture wounds around the neck?" He pointed. "Besides, this is almost an adult deer not a fawn, they would have been hard pressed to catch it, let alone stomp on it."

Another head shake, this time in certainty. "No this looks awfully like," he'd hesitated for a split second as if not sure whether to say it, "a kill to me. I'm no expert mind," he added quickly, "but you know those marks on the neck could easily be a bite." He'd made a jaw like shape with his open hand; fingers bent slightly inwards like teeth. He held it towards the animal's neck. "It's the classic place for an animal to kill its prey, once it has downed it."

"The question is…" Jenny paused. She had a suspicion where this might be going and had wanted to steer him away from felines large or small in an effort to keep it within her rationale. "What animal could have done this; a fox? That's the only animal I can think of."

"No way. A fox is far too light weight, not to mention lazy. Maybe a dog," Tony had pondered. "A big one mind, and fast. Even still, I doubt it could out manoeuvre a deer in full flight."

Jenny continued the train of thought, "I suppose the deer could have been sick or wounded."

"True." Tony glanced down at the neck again and then along the creatures back. There were scratches on its rump that he hadn't noticed before. "I don't know. Something's not adding up here," he'd said, head shaking once more.

"Right, come on lets go," Jenny had announced in a determined way. "Let's hope we find something more interesting… Take our minds off this."

Fortunately, the cubs had done just that and Jenny kept up a commentary about their every move as they walked back to the car, punctuated with asides like, "Oh but they were so cute," or, "Shame they have to grow up." Tony stayed relatively silent, his thoughts allowing the odd, "Yes they are," and, "It is," to absently answer her. He couldn't help but reflect on the possible events that had happened, potentially, only moments before they had arrived.

"You know that deer?" He said, as they made their way back to the car and ignoring the vibes that might curtail any further discussion. "The more I think about it, there's something not right there you know. As I say, I'm no expert." He had the good grace to smile at her, he'd said the 'E' word twice now. She giggled in response, de-railing Tony's train of thought and changing his mood for the better.

Undaunted, but in better spirits he pressed on. "I don't reckon that was a dog attack, nor do I think the deer was injured beforehand. I mean, there was obviously one hell of a struggle and I doubt a wounded animal would put up much of a fight."

"Depends I suppose, on how wounded," Jenny chipped in.

"True," he appeared to agree. "But the long scratches on its backside looked suspiciously like claw marks. That animal, I reckon, had been caught unawares. And whatever had done that could easily have lain in wait in the undergrowth, right next to that path and got lucky."

She gave a non-committal shrug. "I guess so."

"The deer would probably have tried to run but the attacker, jumping on its rump, would have brought it down very quickly," Tony added, his mind already made up, "finishing it off with a swift bite to the neck and breaking it… Wham, bamb, thank you Mam… Lunch." Adding in an overly exaggerated voice, "I rest my case, m'Lud."

A few steps later, and in a more reflective tone, he said soberly, "There's an awful lot of that animal missing you know." The inference wasn't lost to Jenny. Whatever it was had had a big appetite; implying, the attacker was not exactly small either.

On reaching her car, they stood either side of it. Gripping the door handle, she looked across to him from the driver's side, feeling a little uneasy. "Not a fox or dog then. What else is there? I mean, there's nothing else in our green and pleasant land, unless…"

In his eagerness to answer he almost cut her short. And she knew exactly what was coming.

Chapter 17

Cycling without lights was not easy but Gary's night vision had by now become well adjusted. He'd been back to see the Smiths in Dunlin Close. He hadn't been there for a week or two so he thought to pay them a visit. The decorating that he and his boss had worked on back in March had finished within that same week. Between the two of them it had only taken three days to paper and paint the walls plus prepare and paint all the gloss work.

It had been time enough though, and by now, Gary had got to know the family quite well. He'd enjoyed their company; the father Gerry, a familiar figure stomping about the house endlessly turning off lights. Mum, Linda, ever present: cooking, helping with homework, ironing and forever, nappy changing the baby; pretty little Jessica. Then there was the son David, a happy soul and not forgetting the gorgeous Samantha. A sly grin settled on Gary's lips as he rode away from where he had hidden his bike on Pompeys Lane. The familiarity however, was only one way. They, the Smiths, had not seen hide nor hair of Gary since departing in his boss's van on that last day. In fact their older daughter had, at the time, been out early and back late and had never even met Gary, or his Boss for that matter.

"Another successful mission," he said to himself as he avoided a rather large pothole in the gravelled road. The balaclava, now just a hat and binoculars stowed inside his jacket, meant he was ready to leave the unlit and unmade track and join the main Ringwood Road. *Oops better put some lights on*, he thought and with that, stopped the bike and reached behind for the red flashing light at the rear, and then forward to the bright light at the front. Satisfied that all was in order, and waiting until there was no traffic - he didn't wish to be seen exiting the small side road - he moved out on to the road. Just up ahead were the glaring outside lights emblazoning the familiar site of the Angel Inn. Glancing at his watch, Gary thought, *Nine twenty, Mmmm, just time for a swift one.*

"Orwight Gazzer." Dave's usual greeting to his long-standing mate and frequent gaming buddy. "What you gonner have, usual?"

"Yeah, cheers mate," was Gary's warm reply.

Gary turned his head and scanned the rest of the bar. "Eh yup, see the experts in." Winking at Dave and nodding in Tony's direction. "Allo, who's the crumpet with him?"

The pub was not particularly busy; a number of tables had diners and a few, just drinkers. The ambience was as usual, warm and inviting but the noise level only half that of a busy night. A few noticeable voices could just be heard above the general throng, but mainly though, the background noise was of lively discussions and polite conversations, creating a resonant atmosphere.

The nod had not gone unnoticed by Tony sitting at an alcove table and annoyingly in view of the bar, but he chose to ignore it as best he could.

"All I'm saying…" exasperation noticeable as he spoke, "is that animal, and let's face it quite a big animal, relatively speaking, has been attacked by something, and I hardly think it was super rat." He winced slightly at his own almost aggressive sarcasm. "I mean half of its missing, presumed eaten by whatever killed it. I'm just worried that if, and I know it's a big if, but if it was a big cat and it's found itself in a backwater, virtually surrounded by humans, it might feel a little trapped. And animals feeling cornered, often become aggressive. I doubt it would happen, but if a child ran in to it, well I don't know… I dread to think".

"Ok, I understand your concern, but really, how likely is it?" Jenny questioned, still sceptical of his theory. "Even in light of what you told me driving over here."

Tony had mentioned on the way to the pub that the reason he had moved so swiftly to blaming a big cat, was that there had been another very recent sighting of one. He was surprised she hadn't seen it in the local paper. The report had said that a big cat had been caught in the headlights of a car travelling through Holt Heath. The air traffic controller (his job mentioned to give better credence as a witness) had been going home after a late shift on Monday night, and had seen it dart across the road no more than fifteen metres in front. 'With no street lighting, the heath was very dark,' he'd said. 'But my headlamps picked it up perfectly. No question in my mind… it was a big cat; probably a bit bigger than a large Labrador, but with a cat like head and a long tail.'

Jenny had not been convinced even though she'd known Holt Heath was only about five to six miles away from the Common.

"Oh come on," she'd said. "It's pretty built up between here and there, surely someone else would have seen it by now?"

"I'm not so sure," Tony pondered and remained silent for a few moments. Then another thought occurred to him. "Don't suppose this is in any way connected to what was mentioned at the wildlife meeting the other evening, you know cats and dogs being mauled?"

Jenny, tiring of the discussion just shrugged. She was more than a little concerned that Tony was doing a really good job of convincing himself that this was a big cat attack. It wasn't that she didn't want to believe him; it was just that she felt there could be other explanations that he hadn't yet explored or, for that matter, entertained. Besides, with what he had told her about the grief he'd experienced from the last exposure at Moors Valley, she didn't want to see him ridiculed again. Deciding to change the conversation she challenged. "Why do you keep glancing up at the bar?" and with a look of mock indignation, "Am I not gorgeous enough?"

Amused and jolted off-course, Tony replied, in a voice heavy with sarcasm, "Oh just my mate Gary." He nodded towards the bar. "What's the betting he'll say something before the night's out!" The word cretin sprang to mind and almost became audible, but he stopped himself. It just wasn't worth the effort.

Fortunately for Tony and without saying a word, said cretin, upped and left at about ten-thirty, allowing him to relax.

Within ten minutes of leaving the Pub, Gary was checking out his usual haunts on Poor Common. He'd stashed his bike in the undergrowth by the gate ready for his eventual departure. Balaclava'd and gloved, he once again became invisible, ready to stalk his targets. With caution and stealth his watchwords, he would be unseen, unheard and able to carry out his 'black op' missions with impunity. Call of Duty (just one of the many games he and his mates played) was good, awesome, to use the modern vernacular, but it didn't come close to the buzz he got from his own, clandestine hobby.

Gary carefully picked his way along the route that ran behind the houses fronting Heatherlands Avenue and on into Fitzworth road. It was not well used, indeed, it wasn't officially a path. It had probably been hewn by the residents of the houses that backed on to the common, Gary had speculated. In reality, a good deal of the credit could probably go to Gary himself, keeping it adequately trod and just about navigable. It ran some twenty metres away from the fences and hedges that signified the end of the small gardens. As close as it was to the houses, the path would be in complete darkness to those viewing from inside. House lights, security lights and street lamps all glaring out towards the common seemed to stop at the bottom of each garden, blocked by the man-made barriers. The diffused half-light that managed to escape over would be quickly swallowed up, obstructed by rigid tree trunks and bushy shrubs casting further shadows and forbidding blackness.

Gary had travelled some 150 metres and was closing in on the entrance to the common, from where Heatherlands Avenue continued into Fitzworth. When through the gate and coming on to the common, he was just able to make out a figure. Dropping to a crouch he watched as it left the street lamp's aura and entered the relative darkness. Like an apparition it seemed to appear and disappear; hidden momentarily by features of the forest. Gary realised that whoever it was would pass quite close to him, perhaps ten to fifteen metres away; surmising they were walking along the gravel path. Keeping low and still behind a swathe of immature bracken growth Gary felt the familiar swell of excitement. It wasn't particularly dangerous, but the thought of it; of being caught, doing something secretive and furtive was exhilarating. The only downside, if he was caught in this 'innocent game' it could jeopardise his other more pleasurable pursuits.

Movement, some 40 metres away to Gary's left, caught his eye. He focussed hard on the spot for several moments, but assuming it to be a trick of the poor light, he turned back to his main quarry. Gary could see now that it was a man, and, judging by his steady gait, an older one, towing an equally elderly dog.

Gary's eyes shot left again. Something had definitely moved. *There*, he said to himself as he caught sight of it again, a fleeting glimpse moving low over the forest floor. It wasn't as far left as before. But whatever it was, was moving across his field of vision. Glancing back, the dog-walker was now closing from his right and would pass by shortly. *What the ...?* Gary strained his eyes, urgently trying to make sense of another dark shape. A shape that was moving stealthily and at an equal pace some 10 metres behind the old man.

Gary looked on, unsure of his own senses. Questions fired off in his mind trying to resolve the unfolding scene. *Perhaps he's got another dog following on? What was the other movement, a deer?* As the man went past Gary's covert position, the pursuing shadow took on form and substance. Gary held his breath, his heart was thumping, and fear seeped into his consciousness like liquid onto blotting paper. *What the fuck?* Moving deliberately, head low its body hunched as if ready to pounce the creature drew closer to the unaware walker.

Gary wanted to shout out but fear held his tongue. *I don't believe it, it's going to attack,* his mind racing. *What the fuck is it?*

At that moment, Gary became aware of what he thought was the other cautiously moving shape, also crouched, sliding forward a few metres to the man's right. Wondering if his mind was playing tricks, *two of them?* He thought. Even with Gary's limited knowledge of wildlife it didn't stop him from realizing - *this cannot be happening.*

It was then Gary had another disturbing feeling. He didn't know what it was or when he had become aware of it, but instincts had taken over. Probably irrational, but the sensation kept on coming, welling with every beat of his racing heart. Apprehension torpedoed to panic and dread. He so desperately wanted to look behind him. *Not three surely, he pleaded to himself.*

Before Gary had had a chance to summon even an inkling of courage to assuage his suspicions, the elderly dog let forth a savage and ferocious stream of barking; energetically belying his advancing years. Shocked by the sudden violent tirade Gary jumped, literally. His legs, already screaming in pain where he had been crouched for so long, shot him skywards, at the same moment twisting his body away from the danger, all fear overtaken by an overwhelming need to run away. As Gary ran the 150 metres back to his bike he could still clearly hear the mayhem he had left and it spurred him to unparalleled athleticism.

The old man had now joined in, shouting and cursing at the dark phantoms snarling and circling a metre or so from his feet. It didn't take him long to realise that it was the dog they were after. Pulling his stately golden retriever close he wielded his walking stick to positive effect and very quickly the assailants slipped silently back into the shadows.

Chapter 18

Monday 11th May 2009

The bright shiny doorbell with accompanying cheerful tone adorning the neat detached house on Carmel Drive belonged to Mr and Mrs Kennedy. The lively 'bing bong' sound lulled Jenny into a more optimistic mood. The fact that the report she was holding was a few days old had worried her. Somehow wires had got crossed at the council and the notification had not been passed to her until that morning. It was just after eleven am as a figure loomed large behind the frosted glass. The door opened briskly to reveal Cyril Kennedy wearing his usual scowl, assuming as he did, that all callers were trying to sell him something.

She took in the facial expression and summed him up in an instant. Trouble!

"Mr Kennedy?" Jenny enquired brightly.

"Yes," was the short, but not unpleasant reply.

"I'm Jenny Spader, From East Dorset District Council, with Animal Welfare."

Momentarily confused and seemingly unaware as to why anyone from the council should be on his doorstep, the light dawned. "Oh about the dog attack, come in, come in."

The hallway was not large, but at the top of the stairs was a large window making it feel light and airy. The hint of an artificial scent was evident, suggesting an air freshener or spray polish. The impression was certainly one of order and cleanliness, but the smell detected most, was one she was well accustomed to. She had smelt it many times before, even though it wasn't exactly the same -in every case, each property created its own version; undeniably it was the smell of dog.

Leading her through the hall to the lounge at the back of the house, he challenged her about the delay.

"I'm a bit disappointed that action wasn't taken earlier you know. This happened last week, Wednesday to be precise. I mean as far as I'm aware the Police did nothing."

He gestured towards a chair and Jenny took the cue and sat.

"Anyway you're here now," he said his face breaking into a warm smile and Jenny's harsh judgement, melted slightly.

She watched as he carefully lowered himself onto the rather garish sofa that seemed to complement all the other unusual nick-knacks and pictures cluttering the room. He was a tallish man, perhaps a little stooped with age, early seventies, she guessed, neither overweight nor skinny and his round face supported a pair of heavy rimmed glasses. The family photographs displayed on a sideboard beside her offered much younger versions of Cyril in various army uniforms. Some showed him surrounded by other soldiers in presumably far-flung postings Jenny surmised, taking in the lush vegetation, thick and jungle-like.

"Kenya," he said proudly. "And that one's me and the lads in Malaya. We got about a bit in those days." He smiled. Then, as if remembering something deeply unpleasant, the smile vanished. "Not that all of us made it back," he said reverently. "Stan and Johno there," he pointed to a group picture, "the two top left, we lost them to a mortar attack, they were inseparable as mates, a direct hit got them both. We had to bury them out in the jungle." Cyril stared vacantly, "Whenever I think of them now," he paused, "Rupert Brooke's poem, The Soldier seems to automatically come to the fore. Do you know it?"

"Yes I do actually," she acknowledged. "It's very moving." Suddenly aware to the possibilities of being sidetracked, Jenny spoke quickly and avoided the probable trip down memory lane.

"Yes, well, I am **so** sorry for the delay." She exaggerated the so, lengthening it just a fraction in an effort to emphasise the apology. It seemed to work, his face was intent but not unkindly.

"Perhaps you could tell me about what happened, I understand it was over on Poor Common. It's not a big area but it's ideal for dog walks". She had added the last bit to ensure that he realised she knew where he was talking about.

"Yes, right. Well as I said, it was last Wednesday just after ten-thirty in the evening. The dog had wanted to go out and she hadn't had a walk during the day as normal. My wife and I had been at the hospital for a good part of the day." He smile. "Often there you know at our age, all those ailments, if it's not one thing it's another. Ought to have got our own designated parking space by now," he said with a chuckle. Jenny smiled too, *perhaps he wasn't going to be any trouble after all,* she thought.

"Anyway, where was I? Oh yes. So I thought I would just give her a quick one on the common".

The dog or the wife? As the improper thought emerged, Jenny averted her eyes down to the report she was holding. The unintentional double-entendre would normally, and in the right company, have had her lively mind, firing off an aside of her own. *Stop it*, she admonished inwardly giggling to herself, *time, place… remember*?

"That gravel path is a godsend. Its surface is flat and even, so day or night it's easy for the likes of us old fogies to get around. Do you know where I mean when I say the entrance between Heatherlands and Fitzworth?" Jenny nodded, the nervous mirth subsiding.

"Well I turned left along the gravel path and as I came out of the trees, you know, into the clearing, I was aware of something moving to my right. The trouble is, although it's not ever pitch-black in there, when you come from out of the glare of streetlamps your eyes take time to adjust. Mine obviously hadn't, but I could detect the movement no more than 3 to 4 yards away and low to the ground. It made me start a bit, but I thought it was probably a fox or a badger that I had just stumbled upon."

"So you didn't get a clear look at it?"

"Well no, as I say, at this point it was just movement in the dark. It wasn't until I realised it was not going away that I became a little anxious. Then it just lunged behind me at Hattie, that's the dog," he said nodding his head towards the closed door. "She's in the kitchen poor old girl; her hips play her up sometimes. Still, she started barking her head off at whatever it was and it seemed to disappear. Then suddenly it was behind us." Cyril got up from the sofa and using his hands tried to show Jenny where the attackers had been, pointing in the relevant directions.

"I spun round and hit out at it with my walking stick. Got a closer look at it at this point," he said, looking over his glasses at Jenny. "And I'm almost sure it was a dog." Cyril twisted his body. "At the same moment, away to what was now my right something else moved fast in the undergrowth. Before I could get a proper look, something was coming at us again up the path," He turned again. "Remember, I'm now facing the way I had come. Caught it a beauty right across its head! It stopped after that, and then they just melted away. "Cyril looked a little non-plussed. "Then I just dragged the poor dog home. Funny thing was those dogs hardly made a sound, no barking, just a few low, sort of snarls."

"What sort of dogs do you think they were?"

"I don't know. It all happened so fast, I couldn't really see detail. I wasn't wearing my glasses and of course, it was dark."

"Could you make out size or shape? Perhaps colour or markings?"

"I suppose the one I got the best look at was probably Labrador size. The head was the wrong shape though and dark in colour." He thought for a brief moment. "D'you know, I thought about this for a while after, and the thing that stuck in my mind the most, was the movement." He looked at Jenny for affirmation. "You know, the way they moved. Somehow it didn't seem dog like, far more agile. When it was moving towards me, the first time I saw it, it was almost crawling, best way I can describe it is like an animal when it's stalking, keeping low to the ground moving hunched, ready to pounce."

Jenny stayed for a few more minutes taking down a few notes and personal details. She had though, pretty much, summed up in her mind that, although Cyril was clearly 'all there'; nothing wrong with his brain, other parts though, might be a little questionable; definitely poor eyesight, stiff military gait and slow of body and probably impaired hearing, all meant a less than reliable witness, particularly with the speed at which it all happened.

She would therefore check the common now, as she had promised Mr Kennedy and, gave him an assurance, to let him know of any outcome. Somehow though, as she waved goodbye, she didn't think that would be anytime soon.

Back in her van, clipboard resting on the steering wheel, she reviewed her notes. Deciding that this was probably one of those incidences (the soldiers poem flitting smugly into her thoughts) that would be laid to rest in some silicone chip, in a not too foreign corner, of a nearby council computer. She would certainly not lose too much sleep over it. Besides, through somebody's fault, it was old news anyway. Surely any self-respecting hungry dog would have moved on in search of richer pickings? Another thought flashed into her mind, *perhaps the pickings are rich?* She made a mental note to ask Tony, if he thought Poor Common would be a rich food source for a stray animal. That's what she would report this probably was. Someone's pet had escaped on to the common from the nearby estates; possibly even from the very road she was in now. And, having unshackled freedom in a familiar place, just wanted to play. The bit about lunging and crouching could just as easily be put down to a dog 'play bowing' to another of its kind, inviting it to, 'chase me', then running up to it, teasing and tempting them to make a move, in a catch me if you can sort of way. Apart from that, hadn't Cyril said there was no sound, no growling or noisy signs of aggression?

She hesitated before signing the document off, *just a dog then?* Inwardly she was cursing the finicky pensioner. *If it hadn't been for that one brief comment*, she reflected, *I might not be having this dilemma.* Now though there was an element of doubt. And all because he'd clarified his description of the animals' stealthy movement as… 'Cat like.'

Great, thought Jenny. *Tony's likely to wet himself, when he hears this!*

Chapter 19

Friday night seemed to take an age to arrive. Jenny had agreed to meet Tony in the Angel for a drink and supper. He had been away a few days to his parent's farm, helping out while his Dad had some minor surgery.

Two phone calls, she said to herself. *Away for five days and just two measly phone calls, what is it with him?*

At that moment, he walked in through the main entrance of the pub and all internal moaning vanished. Rising from her poseur stool at the bar she said, "Hello stranger," leaning over to kiss him. Not a great one for such public familiarity Tony accepted the greeting as warmly as he was comfortable with.

"How's you?" he asked.

"Better for seeing you," she enthused.

"I'll tell you what," he announced emphatically, and wearily plonking down on the adjacent stool. "I am bloody knackered. It'll be good to get back to work just for a rest." His boyish grin flashed and Jenny settled back on her perch, giggling happily.

They found a spare table, fortunately it was still early and "the great unwashed," as Tony's dad liked to refer jokily about the rest of humanity, or peasants, if he were really worked up, would be flocking in very shortly.

They caught up on each other's weeks. Tony explained the trials and tribulations of working at home again. He had found it really nice to be on familiar ground and having to do the chores and more besides: as he used to do when he lived on the farm. They had been long days, and recognizable as it all was, his dad had reorganised some areas since he'd left and it required a bit of detective work to find even the simplest of tools. He didn't really begrudge him though, despite the air being decidedly blue on more than one occasion as he searched, cursing abjectly; as his limited time was absorbed. All this was soon forgotten at the dinner table, tucking into his mother's home-cooked meals and the ever-present fruitcake that he was tempted to have with each brew of tea. "Go on," his mother goaded, "Looks like you could do with putting some weight on, I bet you're not eating properly." Ignoring the remarks, he conceded; yes, there was certainly something to be said for living at home.

It was on that particular reflection that Jenny reminded him, if he'd been still living under those circumstances, "You wouldn't have met anyone quite as exceptional as me!"

"True," he said feigning disinterest, "Although you've not had the pleasure of one of my mother's cakes, so as you would imagine….it's a real dilemma."

"Yeah, ha ha, you'd miss me really."

She was right. He had missed her. And it had only been a few days.

"Oh I know what I was going to tell you," she started. "Probably nothing but," she paused, unsure how to preface it, not wishing to steer him straight to where she had a feeling he might go. "Well, it's about Poor Common anyway."

She explained the visit to Cyril Kennedy earlier in the week and recounted what he had told her. She left the bit about the cat-like movements until last. Noting the subtle flicker of interest in his eyebrows, she pressed on; telling him her thoughts and conclusions on what had happened.

Surprisingly, Tony just shrugged and with little enthusiasm, agreed she was probably right, but added in his best mock horror voice, "Just one more thing to add to the strange goings on, around Poor Common."

As they laughed Tony caught sight of Gary sidling up to the bar, and he nodded in his direction, "Speaking of strange things".

It was eight o'clock and by now the pub was filling up.

Gary stayed at the bar for sometime appearing to be chatting with some of the regulars. However, the walk to the pub had set him thinking again about the encounter the previous week with the strange animals. Having seen Tony out of the corner of his eye as he had come in, he wanted desperately to pick his brains about I,t but without actually mentioning what had happened. Nursing a rapidly disappearing beer, he pondered on his approach and occasionally glanced Tony's way, to check he was still there.

Gary ordered another pint for himself and summoning up some nerve, aided by a large swig of his beer, moved away from the bar, head and eyes searching the large room as if scanning expectantly for a friendly face. The many alcoves and cleverly hidden parts ensured his route was subtly random and seemingly goal less. For Tony though, the sly glances in his direction had not gone unnoticed and so was half expecting the almost casual appearance, as Gary moved to pass by their table. Gary had forced the eye contact, continually checking his peripheral vision as he moved obliquely closer, waiting until Tony was definitely looking his way. Turning and with a quick upwards flick of his head, and eyebrows following suit, he acknowledged Tony's captured stare.

"All right Tone." He moved in for the kill.

"Hi Gary," was the monotone reply. With no welcoming offer to join them, Gary took it upon himself to pull up a chair.

"Sorry to bother you mate," and barely glancing at Jenny, "I can see you're with someone." There was an awkward silence as Gary waited to be introduced.

"Jenny... Gary," Tony's hand gestured back and forth as he made the enforced introductions. "Gary... Jenny."

"Hi Gary," was Jenny's warmer reply.

"What did you want then, Gary?" the question short and to the point, making it clear Tony was not looking for polite conversation.

"Yeah, right," Gary said self-consciously as if stalling, not knowing where to start. "I was wondering. You heard about Jonathon's chickens?" Gary indicated towards a bulky frame leaning against the bar.

"No," said Tony, "What about them?"

"He reckons the fox got them. He had nine, all killed in just one night. That's not normal, is it?"

"That's not unusual... once the fox is among them it makes the most of it," Tony explained, "It's called surplus killing. They'll bury and cache the excess somewhere to eat later. In fairness, it's highly unlikely to cache and eat nine; even if it did, other animals would get there first. But hey," Tony lifted his arms in a gesture of mock excitement, "in an enclosed hen house it'll make hay while the sun shines." He continued less animatedly, "I remember when it happened to my dad's flock. The fox didn't get them all but the scene the next morning was one of absolute carnage. It had presumably taken one to eat, feed its cubs, whatever; and left six others dead. They were pretty mangled and chewed up, blood everywhere".

"Yeah, well that's the thing," Gary leant forward tapping the table with his finger. "Apparently there were no corpses at all."

Tony looked puzzled. "Yes, I would say that is unusual."

"And the other thing is," Gary said excitedly, thinking he was getting somewhere, "Jonathon's coop and run, as I said to him the other day, is like Fort Knox. But he said they'd ripped a corner of the mesh away from the frame." Gary was enjoying his moment, "Well, I went and had a look at it. I'd just assumed the wood was probably rotten. But no way! Solid as rock! Whatever animal it was, had ripped all the staples out as it yanked the chicken wire. That must have taken some strength, don't you think?"

Still puzzled Tony nodded in agreement. "You said, whatever animal it was. You don't think it was a fox then?"

"I dunno. Just wondered what you thought, you being an..." Gary's voice trailed off, as he caught the flash of annoyed expectation in Tony's eyes. Realising very swiftly any chance of help was likely to be cut short if he pushed that particular button, he began again. "Sorry, I just thought, y' kno..." Gary struggled to find the right words. "You know more about these things than most people round here."

Tony recognised Gary's diplomatic effort by letting it go, but although still a little perplexed, he decided that these things happen and it was difficult to comment, without knowing all the circumstances.

"I can't think of anything else other than a fox," he said, even though his mind had made another connection; one that he certainly wasn't going to suggest, in front of Gary.

"Let's face it," he said realistically. "Chickens get attacked by foxes all the time, it's hardly breaking news."

Gary was a little put out by the off-hand remark. "Yes but what about all the other incidences? Daisy's guinea pigs and rabbits just disappeared; some friends of Mum lost one of their cats recently. Loads of people I've talked to in here seem to have had pets go missing and the funny thing is; they all live within spitting distance of Poor Common. Then you've got that bloke the other day, attacked when he was walking his dog."

Tony and Jenny exchanged knowing glances.

"How did you hear about that?" Jenny queried, somewhat askance.

"Same way as you I should think," he fired back, unaware of her involvement and annoyed at what seemed like a challenge; as if he shouldn't know about it.

"News travels fast you know, especially in here," he clarified defensively.

"All I'm asking is," he continued. "Could there be anything else out there stronger than a fox? I dunno… a rabid dog or…" he had the good grace to look a little sheepish. "You know what I am trying to say… a cat. A big one, like you've talked about in the past."

"Well as you say," Tony's answer was carefully constructed and belied the growing feeling of excited agitation, "I have mentioned them in the past, and I suppose anything's possible, but to be honest with you I'd want a bit more evidence: paw prints, sightings, pictures, that sort of thing. Missing animals tell us nothing really and the official line, I heard, was the old chap was bothered by a dog just looking for some fun. So frankly I'm saying nothing."

Gary stared at Tony for a short while, almost as if he didn't believe what he was hearing. When nothing else was forthcoming and it was clear Jenny was not going to say anything either, he lifted his glass from the table and took his leave, still unsettled that he hadn't come away with anything more positive.

Glancing down at his watch, he noted the time and sank the dregs of his beer, "Right I'm off," he said to himself. "Not hanging round here till it gets dark." However, as he emerged from the warmly-lit pub to find his bike, at just before nine-thirty, the sun had already retired to bed. As he stared out from the harsh lighting of the car park into the near distance and towards the black hole that was Poor Common, he gave a little involuntary shiver.

"Shit!" he breathed. The forbidding dark shapes of the distant trees loomed large in his mind's eye and, the thought of riding into the blackness sent twinges of anxiety through his alcoholically affected brain. Usually a couple of pints would have buoyed him up, such irrational and childlike fears washed away, as his inhibitions were suppressed; but not tonight it seemed. Whether he had hoped for an answer from Tony about what he had seen the other night, something that would have explained it away, made it right, something he could understand and then be able to move on from, he wasn't sure. All he knew was… he was annoyed with himself, and for some pathetic reason wanted to avoid his regular run home. A route he reasoned, he was so familiar with day or night, *particularly night*, he corrected, through a patch of land he felt confident in, at home even; an area, in fact, he likened to an extension of his own back garden; safe, secure and normally without incident. "Better pull yourself together soon," he told himself in no uncertain terms. Then, with a hint of a smile breaking on his lips, "Hate to think I was missing anything."

81

As soon as Gary moved away, Tony's enforced blank expression changed to one of eager animation as he stared across the table at Jenny.

"Told you," he said with more than just a hint of triumph in his voice. "Definitely something strange going on over on the common." Carrying on and not wishing to sound too dogmatic, he held his hands up in a defensive submission. "Look I am not saying it is a big cat, but since our run-in with the dead deer, another bit of evidence nobody else knows about, I might add, I've been thinking and, what I just said to Gary stands. There is no positive evidence to suggest a big cat, but you have to admit there's a fair bit of unexplained and related activity around the common that could indicate a predatory animal, whether that be a big cat, super dog or a stoat on steroids."

Jenny was watching him as he spoke and realised that with all he had just said and particularly the last few light-hearted words, that although Tony was in earnest about this subject, he was also prepared to not be too blinkered, or indeed, take it too seriously. *And that...* she thought *was fine by her.* So without wanting to appear committed either way, she said, "Well, whatever – I'm sure it will prove to be relatively normal and have a rational explanation."

"Yeah, you're probably right," Tony agreed, but she could see by his expression, that he wasn't convinced.

Chapter 20

28th May

Once again, the "hardcore", Dave Martin had quipped, about the little group now sitting round the table; having retired after their wildlife meeting, to the pub. Along with him were his wife Janice, Piers Easterbrooke, Jim Bennett from the little nursery up the road (a rare appearance) and Tony and Jenny. The warm atmosphere of the cosier White Hart Inn had beckoned as usual. The conversation, also as usual, was led as often as not by Piers and David; their social skills benefiting from advancing years, although the oldest by far, Jim Bennett, bucked the trend. He was a quiet man, friendly but not given to speaking out in groups. None-the-less it was easy to see that he was enjoying the company. The small nursery where he worked by himself meant his was a lonely existence, and such gatherings a rare treat.

The topics had swung from football and the Cherries (the nickname for Bournemouth F.C.) the prospects of future games and outcomes, to the closure of the small town's only hardware shop, another casualty of the massive DIY stores. Janice and Jenny, disinterested in all things football, had started up a conversation of their own.

Tony was aware that Jim only seemed to speak when asked a direct question and, having met him once before, was happy to find out a little more about the shy man. Sitting next to him he was able to enquire how business was going and what effect the two big garden centres just up the road were having on his trade. Tony noted he seemed pleased to have been asked and chatted for a few minutes. Even so, Tony felt a little awkward, he wasn't entirely sure they had much in common to talk about and the age gap probably didn't help. Jim had quite a slow and deliberate delivery and was softly spoken which didn't help. Consequently the conversation began to wither. Trying hard to keep it going Tony enquired about whether he walked on the common at the back of the Nursery.

"Oh yes, Cockles and I often are up there," he said almost animatedly. The ever-present dog seemingly conjoined to Jim's heel raised its head at the mention of its name. Tony gently ruffled the downy head as Jim continued. "We're really lucky to have such a useful bit of space."

Seeing the man's positive response, Tony pressed on.

"Have you seen that family of foxes living up there? Actually, I think they're just behind you, certainly not far away"

"I have seen the odd fox, mainly in the field next door, but they don't come into the nursery. Probably the dog puts them off. Can't say that I've seen any more than one at a time though"

"Jenny and I have been out a few times to watch them over the last month or so. There are four cubs, it's incredible how quickly they change; they were little fur balls when we first saw them about six weeks ago. Now they are getting lankier in the leg and becoming just miniature foxes."

"Have you seen the mum and dad?" Jim asked.

"Yes, we've seen the vixen every time. Ever watchful, y'know. Seems like a good mum. Mind you, she seems to have a number of helpers, about three we reckon. One of them must be the dad, and we think it's the biggest one. And when I say big he's not so much taller than the others but thick set, although in fairness, the helpers don't appear that much different. The vixen, the mum of the litter, seems quite small in comparison although to be honest I think she's actually quite normal size."

"So these helpers, you're assuming, are the big dog fox's siblings?" Jim interjected, "What do you reckon probably a year, or two years old?"

"Yes I should think so. The mortality rate for urban and country foxes is pretty high so if they are all siblings they've done pretty well," Tony mused.

Jim picked up the thread, "What's interesting though, we often think of the fox as a solitary animal, but apparently that's not the case." He paused, shifting in his seat as if uncomfortable at having so much to say. "Given the chance they're very sociable animals, living in family groups often with older siblings from a previous litter and some hangers on, that used to be dominant, but now just follow the pack, as you might say."

"That's right and I believe the size of the group will depend as much on the amount of food available as anything," Tony added. Jenny had overheard Tony telling Jim about the foxes and both she and Janice now listened in. Within a few minutes the rest of the little group had given up on their conversations and were intent on hearing about the foxes.

"Nature's way of limiting the population," Janice acknowledged. "Plenty of food means healthier animals, and more of them I suppose, logical really; scarce food and the population declines."

"Well this lot seems pretty well-fed, don't they Tony?" Jenny smiled and he returned it with one of his own. The simple act confirming, once again, to the others what they had guessed, a few weeks back. These two were an item.

"Ah well," said Piers half jokingly, "I reckon they must have been round my ponds then, because," he looked over to Tony, "you know I was telling you about the ducks nesting in stupid places around the edges? Well they've practically all gone. There are one or two pairs out in the little islands and that's it."

Tony looked amazed. "But there's usually... what fifty or sixty birds on that stretch of water?"

"I know, and it's not just them, the moorhens, coots and the little tufted ducks, all gone. I even found one of the great crested grebes floating in the pond, dead; and all their other nests are empty or still partially built out on the water."

"Any evidence of predation?" Tony quizzed.

"There were a few feathers scattered in an area that would suggest something had got one, or perhaps two. But whatever it was I guess has just spooked the rest of them." His head shook gently as his mouth turned down, "No it's weird, I mean the foxes have always had the odd one or two… that's normal, but this is definitely out of the ordinary. Looks like they're giving Costa del Easterbrooke a miss this year." He brightened.

"Yes perhaps they have paid you a visit then." Tony looked mystified, "But, as you say, they should be used to a bit of collateral fox damage. It always happens." Exchanging a quick look with Jenny he added, "So I wonder what's changed?" The little group were quiet for a few seconds all trying to come up with an answer.

"Although I'll tell you what," Tony began again on his earlier reflections. "That vixen is pretty feisty, never mind her size. She caught Jenny and me in our hideout. Don't know why she saw us. We were pretty well hidden. Anyway she did. Flew across the clearing towards us; it was quite alarming. There was literally about two metres between us when she squared off on the edge of the bush we were hiding in, baring her teeth and hissing forcefully at us; she was having a right paddy."

Jenny cut in, "And although there was an obvious barrier between us she didn't seem frightened in fact she seemed pretty bold if you ask me."

"That's when we decided to leave, hoping not to jeopardise any future visits."

"Did I hear you say they're bigger than normal?" Dave Martin chipped in. "Only I believe they can vary in size quite a bit. Think I read it somewhere. Something to do with their circumstances." Janice nodded in agreement, whilst he continued. "If the area has all the right conditions for a long period of time, abundance of food, lack of human intervention, no roads or culls, etc. then over a number of generations, they become more robust; not fatter, just stronger and healthier."

"That seems logical too, although I wouldn't have thought the conditions around here were exactly ideal: too many roads, too many people," Tony said. "Anyway, I know I said they were bigger but it's difficult to tell. It's not like you can get them all to line up next to each other and compare. I mean you either see them curled up fast asleep or trotting off somewhere on their own. And anyway what is normal? Look at all of us," his voice questioning.

"Better not," Dave chuckled.

"No you're right there," Piers joined in. "Very dangerous!"

They all laughed at the harmless nonsense and Tony finished off with a, "You know what I mean," accepting that his point had been curtailed, but enjoying the banter.

As the jocularity died down, the momentary pause in conversation triggered a spate of regrets and time to go comments and, soon, Tony and Jenny were left on their own.

"I was thinking the other day," Jenny said. "About their colour. Now they're older they still aren't showing much signs of getting their red coat".

"No you're right, but then, in fairness, fox colour can be highly variable. You can, I believe, get all black ones, not that I've never seen one, and albinos of course."

Tony looked thoughtful. "Having said that, if the big one is the father you only have to look at his coat, I mean, he has very unusual colouring. African wild dogs spring to mind, that sort of mottled effect, of blacks and browns. Our boy though," he smiled playfully, "is just a dirty dark brown with some grubby red bits and a hint of filthy white bib, nowhere near as defined as the wild dog. On second thoughts," he chuckled, "nothing like an African wild dog. Forget I even mentioned it."

"Actually," Jenny said, still amused by Tony's back-tracking. "I'll tell you what it does remind me of." Her mind flashed back a couple of months and intrigue spread across her face. "Do you remember that old lady who died, just up the road? You know," she said jerking her head northwards, "at Homewood house, and her two American Pit-Bulls?"

"Oh yes, I remember."

"Their coats were similar colours to Foxy boy," she continued. "When I looked on-line, there were loads of pit bull pictures showing a wide variety of colours. But the one I'm thinking of was a mottled brown with flecks of black, virtually all over." A quizzical look crept over her face. "Funnily enough they too had white chests. Seemed to be quite common with that particular breed."

Jenny lifted her white wine and sipped; her thoughts racing. Tony followed suit with what was left of his pint.

"A dog and a fox can't mate, can they?" she blurted out.

The amber liquid shot to the back of his throat as he tried to laugh and swallow at the same instant. "Hardly!" he managed to say between choking fits.

"Just a thought," she said looking a bit ruffled.

Seeing his dismissive reply hadn't gone down too well; he paused to think about it, "I don't really know, I don't think they can?"

Jenny wasn't about to give up. "Well, they are part of the dog family, Canidae to quote the Latin," she said, the smile challenging and a little smug.

"Aren't we the clever clogs," he laughed.

"I'll Google it," she said determinedly. "When I get a chance."

"Yeah you do that. Right now though," he looked over to the bar searching for the clock. "Right, it's Nine-thirty near as dam it. Another drink?" But before she could answer he added, "Have you eaten by the way? I haven't if that influences you in anyway."

"No, nor me."

"Fancy a curry then?"

Chapter 21

Unbeknownst to them, as they headed off to Tony's car, and not that far away in the murky shadows of Poor common, the vixen was arranging new sleeping quarters. As the evenings had lengthened, walkers and dogs ranged longer and later. With the cub's spraint freely spread it drew unwanted attention, making them in some respects more vulnerable now, than when newborn. With the danger growing daily, the ever protective vixen's instincts had told her it wasn't safe anymore; the cubs needed to be away from the potential harm above them.

Two hundred metres west of the natal earth was a secondary den. Smaller and hidden beneath the remains of an old summerhouse, it had once been old badger excavations, deep, but for some reason abandoned and unfinished. The dilapidated wooden structure above, was itself, all but lost at the end of a large garden; the bottom half of which was drowning under a green sea of dense wild rhododendrons. The aged owners had left; like their property they had become somewhat run-down and had sold up. So as human activity waned and the garden succumbed, nature moved in.

At eleven weeks old, a definite pecking order had been established, the two larger pups, coincidently the males, being more boisterous at play and at feeding. They began to forage in the immediate area for some of their own food, anything from earthworms and berries to small rodents and opportune carrion; the dominant cubs throwing their weight around in a well-established feeding hierarchy, grabbing the lion's share as the vixen and helpers deposited their offerings, or simply stealing from their weaker siblings any scraps they might have caught or foraged.

Though still cute and cuddly and evidently young, the cubs have learnt much already. Their mannerisms, body language, and facial expressions are developed to almost adulthood. The erect ears, tail held high and stiff legged walk, much practiced by the males, throws off a confident air, whilst their sisters are more submissive with low to the ground movements, tail under body and mouth agape. To all intents and purposes, these 'teenagers' are adults in waiting and will, very soon, be ready to join the grown-up pack.

At the same time as the vixen was moving house, and on the other side of the common, Gary was wending his way home from the Angel. Unusually, wary of his surroundings; it was as if he was moving through the common for the first time. Not only picking his way through the undergrowth as carefully as always, but also this time, he had to cope with a rising tide of irrational panic. "For fucks sake!" he breathed, his voice admonishing and hard. "Get a grip. Tony said it was just a dog." He'd replayed the incident over and over in his mind during the past few days and he had almost convinced himself, it was a dog. But now in the cold dark of night his mind was backtracking and he didn't like the conclusions it was drawing.

He'd just hidden his bike by the gate and was gingerly picking his way along the path when he noticed lights flooding out of two bedroom windows about 50 metres up the track. Wild thoughts of cats and beasts were suddenly cast aside, *surely not a double whammy* he thought. His heart began to change pace, quickening with every step as he drew near to his usual vantage point. In his mind, he assessed their relative positions by counting the darkened houses. "Yess," he almost said out loud, as un-curtained windows shone their beacon lights out into the blackness, luring Gary just as surely as any moth.

Once he had realised that not one but two rooms were stealing his gaze, he quickly climbed the tree that he had gone straight to. He had chosen this tree one afternoon on a supposed walk not long after he had begun this new hobby. Its position was almost ideal, a clear view to both windows, plus the short stubs of broken lower branches created footholds, enabling him to reach up to sturdier limbs and haul himself up. About three and a half metres up he was able to perch, legs astride a substantial bough. With the main tree trunk directly behind, it offered a back rest and screened him from the path. Unless he moved violently, it would be unlikely that anyone could see him from any point on the gravel track as it traversed his position in a wide arc some twenty metres away. With his camo clothing and tree-hugging posture, he would blend in and be as one with the dark trunk. He made himself comfortable and mentally prepared for a bit of a wait. *Patience is everything,* he thought excitedly. With deliberate movement he concealed his mobile phone inside his jacket, shielding the screen's brilliance whilst tapping a few icons with a proficient thumb; and setting its camera to video. As he watched for movement in the rooms, he checked the focus on his Olympus binoculars, holding them up to his eyes and carefully adjusting them to obtain the clearest vision. At ten metres away from the fence and just over twenty metres to the bedrooms, he was as close as he felt comfortable with. In other words, not to be seen from the windows even if they had turned the lights off and peered out into the dark tree line, providing he kept absolutely still of course. He was though, close enough that the powerful binoculars brought everything into sharp clarity and right up close, particularly when the lights were full on.

He looked first at Daisy's house, where both upstairs lights were on and incredibly the baby's room. Here the curtains were almost wide open and, next door, in Daisy's room they were sort of half-heartedly closed. Training the lenses on to the kid's nursery, he could easily see the frieze stuck onto the wall directly opposite the window and above the child's cot. Familiar images of well known nursery rhymes: Humpty Dumpty lying beneath the wall, Kings Horses and men charging in, Little Bo Peep, Ring a Ring o Roses. *You won't want to know about the real meaning of that one*, he thought, remembering, he'd read somewhere that most of these so-called children's rhymes all had historical, and usually unpleasant origins, and particularly that one*, with its black death and all.*

He was surprised that the light was on at this time. *It is dimmed a bit,* he noticed, *compared to the main bedroom.* He would have guessed that they'd put little Martha to bed much earlier. As he mused, his eyes were right inside the bedroom, scanning for signs of life, subdued movement or flickering shadows that told him, someone was in there. Suddenly Daisy stood up and virtually blotted out his view. It made him jump, she was so close. It seemed, he could have reached out and touched her. "Daisy, Daisy, Daisy," he breathed, his heart accelerating with the shock and it was now, once again, thumping in his ears and head. "Don't do that to me." A thin smile stole onto his lips and broadened rapidly as he calmed down, "You wouldn't want to make me fall off, now would you?"

Daisy dimmed the lights to a glimmer and moved out of the room. The brief flash that he'd seen was of Daisy from behind. He suspected, she'd been stooping over the open cot dealing with Martha whom he couldn't see. This particular vantage point was high enough to get an excellent close and level view right into the rooms, which meant effectively anything from waist up, was fair game. However, it did have its drawbacks, and, unlike other perches, it did restrict his pleasures… somewhat.

His eyes remained glued to the window, like watching one of his computer screens go blank in front him for no apparent reason. He stared in disbelief, expecting the image to suddenly flicker back to life. It didn't. "Bitch!" was his final comment on the matter and with that he turned his attention and the binoculars to the house next door.

After twenty minutes had elapsed, and for no good reason that Gary could see, the light in the room just went out. "What nothing…? Not a sodding thing? His hushed voice, incredulous, "I don't believe it,"

High expectations now in ruins, he clambered down in a hurry from his lofty seat, one pissed-off bloke. He managed to snag his ever-present wristband and jacket on one of the gnarled branch stumps and he cursed as the wood grazed his flesh. The pain was vicious and, as he stood rubbing his wrist with the other hand, his anger exploded. He looked across towards the houses and mouthed obscenities at the unsuspecting women whose fault, it surely was.

With his mind cussing and dealing with residual pain he made a beeline for the gravel path, the waist-high bracken and twisted heathers, intent on slowing his outraged gait. Stumbling on the uneven ground and flaying his hands to sweep aside the bracken he moved as if a man possessed. Twenty seconds later he stood upon the gravel path smoothing and manipulating his pained arm, the burst of concentrated activity, all but subduing his indignation. Half-heartedly toying with the idea of going for another pint to calm down, and unaware of the damaged buckle loosening at his every move, he decided on an early night and headed off along the path towards his hidden bike.

In no more than ten steps, Gary felt the hairs on his neck prickle; he'd heard a soft rustling noise behind him, much like the sounds he himself had made through the underbrush, only much, much quieter. He was aware now, although he hadn't turned around, of a feeling that something was behind him. Emotions fired, his brain perversely began to enjoy its free reign, partied with his senses and led his mind in a forbidding dance. Terror stricken, the thoughts of earlier, gate crashed and he knew what was behind him. Gary tried to turn his head, hoping that a glimpse behind might assuage his reeling mind. Almost rigid with fear, he willed his neck to respond as images of a huge black cat, had a ball with his imagination. It was behind him, and yet in his mind's eye he could see it; sitting bolt upright, looking straight at him. Its head a metre from his own and its evil eyes, black elliptical slits against a fiery glow, burning into his soul.

With a supreme effort Gary turned his head until he could just see out of the corner of his eye. The strained periphery was not perfect or clear, and still partially night-blind from the lights, it conjured swirling patches of grey and black, blurring further the distorted vision. The more he strained the more his eyes played tricks and he thought he saw something. With his head almost fully turned and shoulders following suit, he could now peer more easily through the darkness. Slowly, shapes and shadows sharpened, revealing to Gary, as he grew accustomed to the murk, an empty pathway where his mind had told him the creature should be. His stiff body relaxed and he had to check it from slumping all the way to the gravel.

Then just as he began to turn back, he saw it, about three metres back up the path.

"What the"… his eyes were not playing tricks this time. It was not as big as he had imagined, but the dark black shape sat squarely on the path and occasionally light just glinted from two points on its head. The size and shape told him it was a dog, *wasn't it*? He could make out the upright ears like a…. cat, or an Alsatian he reasoned, but it was not quite as big as that. Its head must have moved imperceptibly, because as it did so the reflected light burned out, and Gary's heart skipped a beat as the vertically slit pupils from his imaginary phantom, became real and were now focussed on him.

"I've had enough of this!" His voice was level, normal, but it sounded louder in the dark and he drew strength from it. "Get away, go on…" He raised his voice and threw his arms forward in an aggressive shooing manor. Whatever it was, stood its ground.

Gary took a step forward and repeated the shout and the actions: Nothing, not a flicker. It was a living thing, he'd seen its head turn and he thought…. *those eyes.*

Unnerved again, Gary backed off and still the implacable creature stayed put. A few more steps widened the gap and with the black shadow still immobile Gary continued to back away. Even though he hadn't taken his eyes off the black form, it eventually merged with the surrounding inky shadows, as he moved further away.

He kept his eyes as close to the spot as best he could, but the path was now curving gently around to the entrance where he'd left his bike. Behind him and about twenty metres away, a dim light shone from Heatherlands, up the little path between the houses and it gave Gary hope. It indicated the way back to normality away from the recesses of his own wild imagination but more importantly, away from the shady, unlit world of Poor common, and with that he turned on his heels and fled, unable to glance back.

Chapter 22

Monday June 1st

"So far so good," Daisy said quietly to herself as she plunged her hand back into the soapy water to retrieve the baby's cup. It had been a relatively peaceful start to the day. Martha content to sit in her pyjamas had toyed with a banana, John, Daisy's other half, hadn't rowed with Ben over the fact his favourite bowl was still dirty in the dish washer. In fact, their six year old, had taken it pretty calmly really. Normally, stubbornness and sheer bloody-mindedness prevailed on both sides, although, for different reasons, and sparks often flew.

Staring absently out of the kitchen window as she washed the cup, then placed it on the drainer, the relative peace in the kitchen allowed her mind to wander. She liked this view. The postage stamp garden with Sunday's mown grass, dew-damp like a fresh coat of green paint, was still unblemished by daisy dots or dandelions. Her eyes drifted off further down the garden to the new shed that John had erected over his long weekend; its coating of red wood preserver making the six-foot high fence that surrounded the garden, tatty in comparison. *He'll need to paint that as well,* she thought and at the same time made a mental note to go and shut the gate on to the common later. But it was the trees behind the back garden that she appreciated the most, although pretty much all pines with the odd Silver Birch sapling optimistically vying for space, it gave a hazy bluey-green back-drop to the end of the garden. They were fortunate to live on this side of the road, the houses across the street were not so lucky, as their outlook was, effectively, the rest of the estate.

It had been a great weekend too, she reflected. The weather had been good, John had had the extra day off, they'd worked in the garden for a bit, played with the kids and had a barbecue Sunday evening; the sun smiling warmly all the time. Ben, kitted out with an old Bob the Builder hard hat, had helped John with the shed construction. Martha too, had enjoyed time in the garden. Involuntarily, Daisy cupped a hand over her mouth as she laughed, and remembering John's face as he realised that his, now, very mobile young daughter was also capable of digging. She had cost him half an hour to replant the begonias he'd put in only last week, the little monkey. But the laughing little face said it all, as her daddy had chased her falteringly around the garden, tripping and stumbling, chubby hands and arms flaying uncontrollably. Now though, the break was over and reality was kicking back in. The long sunny days of the weekend, relaxed and un-pressured, changed as Monday dawned, and time, became someone else's: stress and anxiety, the weekday norm.

A movement two gardens down caught her eye. An animal lazing on the flat roof of another shed was stretching out and evidently enjoying some early rays. At first she thought it was a cat but with the flick of a strangely dark but bushier tail, left her pondering; but not for long, for the clear powder-blue sky and ascending yellow ball smacked of a good day to come. *Lucky bugger*, she thought, as turning to Martha, she lifted her from the high chair. The remains of a half-eaten banana still lay on the tray, "Mummy give you proper brek brek", she said with a huge smile, "after we say bye bye Ben." The childlike speech, annoying in anyone's book, was beginning to irritate her. "Time mummy got out more," she said to the small person toddling at her feet. Martha evidently couldn't care one way or the other as she stumbled determinedly towards her favourite toys from the past weekend, a bright red bucket and yellow spade.

John had been determined to go in early that day and had left at seven-twenty saying, "It's always a nightmare in the morning trying to get across town after a half-term holiday." Just five minutes later Ben descended noisily down the stairs. He was breakfasted, dressed and ready in his uniform early, copying his father.

"I'm ready Mum," he yelled down the hall. "Shall I wait in the porch?"

"Ben you've got ages to wait yet, Auntie Mel won't be here for another forty minutes."

"Oh, is that very long then?" he enquired. And without waiting for a reply asked, "Can I put the telly on?"

"Yes go on then," was his mother's resigned response. "It goes off the instant I say. OK?"

Knowing there was unlikely to be a reply; Daisy tied-off the bag of rubbish, opened the back door and took it outside to the bins. Distracted by thoughts of her morning's itinerary she came in the door and swung it, to close. Hearing that the telephone was ringing she dashed into the hall without checking that the latch had caught.

It was her mum on the phone and crouching down, rested her back on the cupboard door under the stairs, ready for what she knew, would not be a short chat. *Amazing,* she thought *I have actually got time today.* Content in the knowledge that Ben wouldn't be going for a while yet, and Martha was busy playing, she slumped all the way to the floor.

"Hi Mum… no we're all under control here, I've got a bit of time." She listened for a short while as her mother checked the family's health status.

She'd called wanting to check that they were still on for lunch at the local garden centre. Daisy kept an eye on the clock as the conversation moved on from the proposed time of meeting, to the other things they might do after lunch, a bit of shopping in the store and a walk to the park with Martha, before going on to pick up Ben from school. She still had a good twenty minutes before Mel came for Ben. It was seven-twenty-nine am.

Some ten minutes earlier, and a hundred metres away from where Daisy would soon be happily chatting, the big male fox and its sibling vixen had moved along the rear boundaries on the Poor common side of the houses on Fitzworth Road. The other dog fox preferred to sun-bathe before going back, despite the fact that he was hungry and the night's hunting had not been very forthcoming. By seven-thirty, the radiated warmth was of a strength to be absorbed by an eastwards sloping felt roof; perfect for a little foxy R and R. The air was still and calm; no gentle breeze ruffled the fur that covered his tired limbs. Even the tufts of loose hair, from the summer moult, teased out by the sand paper like surface and snagged on the roof, didn't twitch. Stretched out so that his stomach took the full force of the sun's rays and with feet facing down the small roof, he languished; eyes half-closing with contentment.

Seven thirty-two the clock told her, after scanning it for the umpteenth time over the past five minutes. Although she knew she had time in hand, it didn't feel, right. It was great to talk to her mum, but a constant nag slipped in and out like a snake through grass, *surely I should be doing something. What have I forgotten? Ben's lunch...done. School bag packed and ready to go...* "Probably about three I should think Mum"... *Mel's taking him in today so Martha can stay in her jammies... John's gone.* Try as she might nothing untoward sprang to mind, and all was under control. Despite this, her brain continued to nudge and doubt. A glance to the kitchen confirmed Martha's whereabouts.

Ben was busy, engrossed with Dennis the Menace on CBBC. Television was usually limited to an hour or so in the evening, today's early allowance seemed reasonable, he had been a good boy to get ready early and without any problems, so it had seemed only fair to Daisy.

Martha, all this short time, had been busily arranging some wooden blocks on top of her bucket. The bright colours, attractive and fun, shot across the laminate floor as she bashed the small tower with the yellow spade. The novel action accompanied by a high pitch scream of pleasure. After a couple of wobbly attempts at stacking and the bricks skidding noisily over the practical flooring, Martha's attention was drawn to a wayward block that had been overlooked, by the pedal bin. Tottering dangerously below the kitchen table she crossed the kitchen in her padded slippers and bent to retrieve it. The slow forward descent with outstretched hands caused podgy knees to bend and shake, her fast growing brain compensating for the uneven weight distribution. Stubby fingers on an outstretched hand gripped the block, and in doing so, the concentrating mind, lost its control over the vertical plane and the heavily-nappied-bottom sank to the ground with an unassuming thud.

Undeterred by the setback, Martha pulled herself up to standing with the aid of the pungent bin casing. Her eyes swept the area by the back door as her little body endeavoured to keep pace. Stumbling forward her other chubby hand slid its fingers around the edge of the door. The door swung limply and a gap appeared. The brick tumbled to the floor as both hands gripped the door jamb. Carefully sidestepping up to the raised threshold, her weight and balance aided by the solid frame, she hoisted a leg up and over the five-centimetre ridge. Her determined little body swayed unnervingly as the other leg followed. She'd attempted this manoeuvre repeatedly at the weekend but protective hands had checked her before success had been tasted, and her eyes had blazed with annoyed defiance.

93

Now though, escape was possible, the errant guards distracted, and her little eyes beamed with innocent excitement. The concrete path into the garden was flat and smooth and through beady eyes she saw, a means to the familiar play area of the garden. If she had been aware, Daisy would have watched in horror, the sinking stomach feeling welling in-side, as the little form teetered close to the splintered edge of the fence post then on towards the jagged edge of the path. Stepping confidently on to the grass, the tiny tot gathered pace, as if remembering that this was soft and safe but her eyes were swiftly drawn to a new goal; the half-open gate at the end of the garden.

Chapter 23

Out beyond the neat back gardens, the two foxes move only another twenty metres before a familiar call pricks their sensitive ears. Highly vocal at times, although not often heard by man, their range of calls is wide and varied, from the guttural shouts that pierce a still night, to chirps and squalls, conveying who knows what? Their hearing, also highly sensitive, attuned perhaps more to the lower frequencies, noises like the rustling of prey moving through the undergrowth. But on this occasion, the meaning of the broadcast is evidently clear to them. As one they turn, tired paws padding silently back along the route that their finely tuned battery of senses has given the 'all clear to'. At fifty metres from their cohort up on the shed roof, and without any visible communication, they part. The dominant male, continuing on his course beside the hedges and fences, is undeterred by the noises of households on the move, just a few metres away. The high boundary of wood and brush muffles the surrounding sounds: car engines labouring to start, garage doors opening and people calling their farewells. Like a guided missile, on its pre-determined course towards its target, all other factors and considerations become irrelevant to it; the eyes searching ahead for movement, ears alert to the minutia of sounds, the nose, perhaps its deadliest of senses, sifting the warm air flowing across the mouth and nasal linings, in an effort to detect prey.

On parting company with the male, the vixen too seems to power-up her array of scanners, her head alert and moving quickly to survey the route ahead. She trots obliquely away from the male but, by picking up the pace, she keeps in line with him. Brambles and heather, grass clumps and trees slide by as her sylph-like body silently weaves and wends, around and over the uneven ground.

The male on the roof is crouched and watching something intently. Sliding on its belly, it oozes towards the highest corner to improve its line of sight. He has alerted the others but is unaware, as yet, that they are near. Nervously he drags his eyes away and shoots a glance out into the woods, looking to catch familiar movement on the ground around him. On the third attempt, and without losing his view of the prey, he sees them. The dominant dog fox is almost directly below him and already crouching, assuming a waiting position. Some thirty metres out, through the well-spaced trees, he catches a glimpse of the vixen taking cover amongst the stubby gorse. Once still and hunkered down, her blotchy brown coat blends in to the dull heathers and grasses nestling against the gorse; camouflage at its very best.

The male on the path has also melted into the scrub; stock still and flat to the ground, his broad head slightly raised and watching intently. Even if you had seen them move into their hiding places, it would only take a moment's distraction to lose them. Only those with the keenest of eyes might determine the wisps of hot breath condensing in the slight chill of the shadows, where the sun has yet to penetrate.

It is obvious something has caught their attention, and by their tactical positions, it is easy to assess that it is probably an animal. Certainly it is one that will require stealth and caution to entrap and, for that, this skulk of foxes is well equipped.

Chapter 24

"Look, I better go Mum," Daisy said as the clock ticked to seven-thirty four and the dubious feeling getting the better of her. *There must be something I need to do,* she thought guiltily. It took another minute or so to say good-bye and putting the phone back on its cradle, noticed a figure in the porch through the glass door.

Not far through the open gate, and just a short distance away, keen senses were fixated as the foxes lay in wait. Their attention rapt, head movements slow and deliberate, but eyes wide and alert, flicking between others in the pack and the point at where the closing prey was likely to appear. Pricked ears were gathering in sounds, some familiar – movement, the rustling of plants and the soft pattering on grass - and some not, requiring caution and vigilance. The distant sounds of humanity on the move were being selectively faded out as if the foxes possessed their own internal mixing desk; focusing on the target, nothing else now would be allowed to distract them.

Up on the roof, the dog fox, with its elevated vantage was innately aware like some self-appointed lookout, of the unfolding scene below him. His eyes moved from the hidden hunters, checking for activity, over towards their potential quarry that from his perspective was now unseen in dead ground; then onwards to the brick and tarmac landscape, ever mindful of the different dangers encountered there and the threats they now posed.

"Blimey Mel's early?" she said questioningly and peering round the lounge door to see the clock on the television, just to confirm the hall clock was right. She threw the door open in the expectation of seeing the warm smile of her friend from five doors down; but was greeted by the blue shirt and shorts of the miserable young postman, who always seemed to begrudge delivering anyone's mail.

"Parcel for you," the unsmiling postie said, and proffered a small package barely bigger than a letter, but thick. "Sign here," he said holding out a pen and pre-printed form with John's name on it. She signed. He took it, stepped back out of the porch and made to go.

"Thank you," she called; the intonation pointed and heavy, almost challenging. He didn't look back. *Miserable git,* she thought, and not for the first time.

Seeing one of her neighbours on the opposite side of the road getting into his car she called, "Morning Michael," and waved. Turning to go in, she spied Mel coming up the road, buggy in front of her, with Amy her youngest in it, jiggling about as if possessed. James, Ben's friend skipping along beside, stopped and took aim with an imaginary gun at the gnome's adorning the front garden a few doors down.

Daisy waved, the smile and open palm communicating much, a warm greeting and acknowledging a good friend's imminent arrival; then changing to a pointed finger at the house and the intention of getting Ben from indoors.

"Ben?" she called turning to go into the house. "Telly off now, auntie Mel's here."

"Aaw mum, it's not finished yet."

"Well I'm sorry, but Mel's here so you need to get your shoes on. Come on hurry up. Turn that off." She advanced on the television with a pointed finger bound for the on/off button.

"No! I'll do it." he shouted moving like a rugby player to block his mothers' way, but all the time watching the screen.

Daisy changed tack, "Where are your shoes then?"

Her question was met with silence, save for the Menace's dad on the TV, yelling **Dennis** at the top of his voice, the cartooned anger implied, but amusing and unthreatening.

"**Ben!**" Daisy's voice, raised with irritation, made him jump and look away from the television. "Turn it off, NOW."

"Aaaw mum."

Daisy found his shoes behind the sofa and dangled them in front of the young man's eyes; bright orbs that were still wide as they moved closer to the screen, desperate to try to capture every detail of the final image, as the button is pushed collapsing it to a singularity and then blackness.

Outside, at the back of the house, and some thirty-five metres away on the common, the vixen lay. It was cool and damp in the shadow of the stately pines, but in places shafts of bright sunlight pooled, burning the film of moisture still clinging to the vegetation and sending wisps of swirling vapour into the high blue sky like a hundred boiling kettles. In this microcosm, the air felt charged and expectant. The foxes, in tune to the electric atmosphere, sensed the moment was upon them and fidgeted with growing tension; paws imperceptibly lifting off the ground in a subtle war dance of agitation.

At the end of the garden, Martha was clinging to the rough gate post. Still swaying slightly as each leg took its turn to take the weight. She stopped to study her left hand, a tiny splinter had sunk into the fleshy pink skin and it prickled enough for her to examine the new sensation. Then her eyes gazed out in wonderment across the rough track and into the trees; tall shapes, an array of colours, light streaming through and catching dew drops clinging to the bracken so they sparkled like diamonds. This magical landscape, new and exciting, held no fears; it could not, for she knew none. Young and uninitiated to man-made horrors whether fictional or real, the stuff of nightmares or waking phobias, none as yet had been allowed to tarnish the expanding canvas of her naive and angelic psyche. She had of course, experienced physical pain, new hunger and the need for comfort and contact, basic needs and reflexes. But she had yet to make rational connections between these and the world around her. Like an innocent abroad, an adventurer or explorer, she was breaking new ground but unlike those wanderers, her mind would not be handicapped by irrational thoughts of bogey men and Zombies or worries of physical harm, tripping and falling, or even the very imaginable dangers found in a parent's worst nightmares.

With the sun's warmth caressing her fair skin, happy, smiling and willful she let go her mooring arm and launched herself out into an expanding and colourful new world.

Shoes now on and the television forgotten, as soon as James had called his name, Ben grabbed a Buzz Light Year rucksack and headed towards the front door. Meanwhile Mel was been explaining why she was, in fact, a bit early - needing to have a quick word with James's teacher.

"Well we were ready anyway, John went in early," Daisy said and bent down to kiss Ben good-bye. As she did she threw another look down the hall to the kitchen, *I wonder what that monkey's up to she thought, it's a bit quiet.*

Not too concerned, she waved to the little group as they walked and wheeled off down the road. Going back inside Daisy glanced at the digital readout of the television. Seven-forty-three.

"Right young lady. Time for your breakfast... and mine for that matter." As Daisy took the five steps up the hall, her demeanour underwent a seed change, from bright and breezy to one of unadulterated panic, as the half-open back door hove in to view.

"Oh Shit," she said under her breath and, as she moved across the floor, another two steps, she swept the kitchen to confirm what she already knew. Martha was not there. Stepping through the backdoor, time seemed to slow her movements so they were deliberate and laboured; it was like entering a portal to another dimension, fearful of what lay beyond. Another step into the side passage... A barrage of potential garden related dangers exploded into her head and the panic balled in her throat. The left-out mower, the barbecue tools, the folding chairs, the wobbly slide, "Oh fuck!" the splash pool.... She let out a crescendo of curses, "Shit, shit, shit," not in volume but in vehemence. Then she remembered... the gate!

Another step took her to the corner of the house and the view she now dreaded, a view she had just conjured into head a split-second earlier.... an empty garden. Her breathing threatened to stop as she gasped for air. The violent charge of emotions that had assaulted her over the past ten seconds nearly broke her. She knew in her heart that something had happened and, fearing the very worst, tears welled, stinging as they threw themselves down her whitened cheeks.

She covered the distance to the gate in another few seconds, a twinge of hope made a valiant effort to throw aside her consternation, swelling as she made it to the gate. As swiftly as it began, it was violently crushed, Martha, was nowhere to be seen. Daisy stood for a short while, wildly searching through the trees. Close up, the randomly planted trunks were three to five metres apart, but by the time her eyes moved further into the distance they appeared to be closer, and even further away, closer still, until the impression was almost of a dense forest, albeit that its other edge was only 40 metres away. Her eyes darted from trunk to ground and back to trunk as she desperately searched, trying to catch a glimpse of the familiar baby grow material.

In desperation she shouted her name three times, the words difficult to say as she choked back the tears. Suddenly a thought emerged, and as if a revelation had dawned, she ran back into the house. "I bet she's in here, just hiding somewhere, where I can't see her." The positive idea and the swift movement forced her in to taking deep breaths and she began to calm a little. However the feeling of dread did not fully leave and it kept stabbing at her as she inspected likely hiding places; behind the sofa, in the cupboard under the stairs, behind the closed door of the downstairs toilet. As each possibility proved negative, the panic began to rise again until in desperation she started opening the kitchen cupboards; finally she ran upstairs knowing it wasn't possible for her to climb stairs yet. Was it?

Madly throwing open the doors to each room she became aware of a knocking sound, *that's downstairs* she thought, *the front door.* Her mind raced through the possibilities, but latched on to, *one of the neighbours, they've found her!* The bedside clock read seven-forty-six as she charged out of the upstairs room and down the stairs. She recognised the figure through the half frosted front door as Sandra from next door, her tall frame and blonde hair a give-away. In the few seconds it took her to get to the front door Daisy assessed that there was no child in her arms and she wasn't stooped, as if connected to a little person. Never the less she flung the door open with failing expectation, the speck of hope that remained was once again, swept away.

Sandra, a mother of teenage children, instantly read the distress on Daisy's face, knowing something awful had happened.

"Daisy love, what on earth's the matter? Is it Martha? I heard you calling for her."

It spilled out, fast and panicky, "She's gone. I can't find her. She was in the kitchen playing, Mum was on the phone. The back door must have been open, I only left her for a moment!" she added defensively.

"Come on love," Sandra's voice comforting and reasoned, "She can't have got far, let's go and have another look," and moved to the back door.

Daisy shrieked, "She's gone, I tell you," the outburst angry and challenging, as if accusing Sandra of not believing her. Sandra stopped, momentarily shocked at the violent change in the normally happy girl. But it spurred her on, aware that something was very much amiss and that action was what was needed. However, her confidence too was dented by Daisy's certainty and defeated attitude.

Moments later Sandra came back in to find Daisy slumped on the stairs and sobbing uncontrollably. Sandra desperately wanted to comfort her, the pain in her own heart rising and reaching out for the poor girl. But ever practical she ran out of the house and started to alert the other neighbours. Within a few short minutes those that she had found in were throwing on shoes and clothing and rushing out of their houses in a spirited response to the crisis. As soon as they arrived outside Daisy's house Sandra was barking out orders, sending a group to check all the neighbouring gardens, another on to the common. Satisfied that all possibilities had been covered she went back in to the house and began to systematically search it. Not because she distrusted Daisy in any way, but *maybe just maybe* she thought *the little devils here and Daisy's just missed her*. As unlikely as that was, she felt she needed to satisfy her own mind. The house was not large and the rooms and furniture easily checked, on finding nothing she went back outside to wait for returning searchers.

As eight o'clock ticked over on Sandra's wristwatch, and shouted information had been exchanged with people now looking further afield, she made the decision to call the Police; going into her own house to make the call in order not to distress Daisy any further. After not much convincing, the police control room acknowledged they would be sending some one over. Whilst she had been talking she had been searching through her address book for another number. When the call was over she dialled it.

"John Docker," was the business like and breezy reply.

"Thank god," breathed Sandra on hearing his voice.

"John its Sandra… from next door."

"Hi Sandra." His voice quizzical, but guarded as he wondered why on earth she would be calling him.

Struggling for the right words, in order not panic him, but failing in the tenor of her voice, "John, I think you need to come home, there's a problem…."

"Daisy?" his voice worried now.

"No, it's Martha. She's missing."

"What?" His voice almost disbelieving. "Where?"… He stopped. It was almost as if he didn't believe her, "I mean have you looked?"

"Trust me John," she said forcefully, "half the neighbourhood is out there, as we speak."

The tone was enough.

"I'm on my way".

Chapter 25

June 1st 8:45am

"What number Pat?" asked DS Thomas Connelly, the Inspector's regular chauffer, reliable colleague and, outside of work, good friend, as they turned into Fitzworth Road.

"Twenty-seven Heatherlands Avenue, but just look out for the crowd; it'll be a way yet. This road curves right round and then continues into Heatherlands Avenue. There's no obvious break," he said having just consulted the A-Z map booklet. Patrick watched as the bunched up, neat houses went by. It was a modern estate, the houses all similar styles, detached and with small front gardens. Most had integral garages, others just a parking space in front of where the garage used to be; the valuable space, more useful now as a dining room or a playroom. The road was not wide and because there was little off-road space in the front gardens, many cars were parked roadside; a number of them half on the pavement. The resultant thoroughfare was more like a series of chicanes and Thomas had to repeatedly give way, to the on-coming traffic.

"That looks like us, up ahead, Sir."

Patrick viewed the road ahead; the patrol car, an obvious give-away. Around it though and on either side of the street, groups of people huddled. It was nine-thirteen by the dashboard clock.

Drawing up a few doors away, Thomas followed the residents' lead and mounted the pavement to park.

"Right let's see what we've got," said Patrick as they got out of the car.

PC Grover strode towards them, looking troubled and concerned. "Morning sir, this is not looking good."

"Ok, how long have you been here Grover?"

"We got here, PC Barnes and I, about eight -fifteen, so about an hour."

"So you've had time to assess things and speak to a few people, yes? …We've got the basics." Patrick nodded towards Thomas, ensuring that the PC understood he meant both of them. "So give us a brief rundown on what's happened and what's been done so far."

The experienced PC ran through what he had gleaned so far from Daisy and the others.

"She's very upset so it's been difficult to get exactly what happened, her husband returned from work about forty minutes ago. He's pretty distressed as well, obviously." The PC glanced at his note-book to confirm a name.

"I have spoken with Daisy's next door neighbour though, Sandra Baker. She seems to have done sterling work in getting the other neighbours involved in the search. They'd covered a lot of ground before we'd even got here."

"What's your take on it Grover?" The Inspector fixed him with a questioning look. He valued the man's input and was genuine in his reasons for asking him. "You know the way these things work, there's only a few possible scenarios."

"Abduction sir, no question: They're a happy family, no problems according to the neighbours, both children are theirs, so no wayward father or mother laying claim. I'm pretty sure the child is not hiding or trapped anywhere. The neighbours have done a good job, they've searched gardens and houses close by and they've been onto the common." The policeman fixed his gaze on the Inspector. "Bearing in mind this child has only just learnt to walk, she ain't going far under her own steam. Besides which, by the sound of it, she only had literally a few minutes to go anywhere, and Linford Christie, she's not."

"Point taken," Patrick said with a grim smile, "which is why the desk sergeant called us in so quickly. He trusted your judgment. Right let me have a word with the neighbour," he tried to recall the name, "Sarah?"

"Sandra Baker, sir. She's in here with the Dockers" he pointed to the house beside him.

"Is that the Dockers house?"

"No. That one there is." The officer pointed to the house to the left of Sandra's.

"Ok, can you bring her in there please? But give us a few minutes, I want a quick look around and it's useful that the parents aren't in there."

Standing in the hall of the modest house, with the stairs at his back, he noted the telephone table beside him, remembering that that was where he had been told Daisy had last viewed the missing child. Ahead of him was the door into the lounge, and he stood in the doorway. The room appeared normal; sofa, chairs, children's toys stacked in, and on, a basket in the corner and a coffee table, with nothing of any import on it. Patrick quickly noted that all knick-knacks and photos were cluttering the mantlepiece, on high shelves or furniture, and guessed the room had been hastily sanitised to accept a newly mobile little person. Behind him, and to his right was the front door where she had seen the other child off. He wondered how the little boy would react when he found out, particularly as the parents were likely to be so distressed. As a father of two, he couldn't imagine what they were going through, and indeed, what they would have to cope with in the weeks to come. He swept the thoughts aside. To his left was the kitchen where the child had been playing.

He walked in, saw the strewn coloured blocks and, suddenly, the enormity of it began to hit him. He'd caught sight of a picture of Martha on his way in, on the hall table, but it wasn't until seeing the bricks; that he flashed back to when his children had had the same toys. He could see them clearly in his mind's eye, and he silently thanked god for his good fortune.

He turned to look out of the kitchen window, hiding the welling emotion as his colleague, DS Connelly joined him in the room. Thomas had worked with Patrick for the last four years and they had built up a close working relationship. He felt comfortable to convey his innermost thoughts about a case to the solid-framed and tough Sergeant. He was a good listener and quick to catch on but even Patrick was still coming to terms with the heavy responsibility of it all.

"You do realise Thomas," he said gravely and without turning. "If this is for real, we're going to be under an awful lot of pressure in the next few days, weeks probably," he reflected. Then he continued in utter disbelief, "This is Ferndown for God's sake! We're like all the other places nobody has heard of, normal, run of the mill, nothing ever happens here, sort of town… Now this?"

"I know what you mean Pat, hard to take in. Still," and trying to sound more positive than he felt, "early days yet. Although, if we do think this is an abduction, do you think we should action the Child Rescue Alert system? From memory, it would meet all the criteria. If we can get it to the media it can be on the television in probably less than an hour."

What DS Connelly had mentioned, was an initiative that allowed Police Forces to forge a loose Partnership with the press, quickly alerting the public, with the details of a missing child. This would mean publishing on internet news sites, breaking into radio and television broadcasts, mid-flow if urgent enough, and all newspapers. By getting the information out quickly to the public, and enlisting their help, it was deemed that there was more chance of obtaining useful information relating to the disappearance, rather than any detrimental effects it might have.

"I think you're right, but let's just talk to the neighbour, and perhaps get our own thoughts on the parents, before we jump the gun. OK?"

As they went outside into the Garden, PC Grover and Sandra followed them out.

"Mrs Baker Sir,"

"Thank you Grover;" said the Inspector as he quickly cast his eyes over the forty-something woman in front of him. Almost as tall as he was, s*limmer, but that wasn't difficult,* he thought, involuntarily resting a hand on the not unsightly bulge above his waistline. She had a kindly face, motherly even, but at this moment, one that was in earnest and shocked.

"I understand from PC Grover, we have a lot to thank you for, organising the neighbours so quickly, I'm Inspector Stimpson by the way." He held out his hand, and very briefly, they shook.

"Not that it did any good Inspector, we haven't found hide nor hair of her. It's like she's just vanished into thin air."

"Mmm… you know the family well I take it?" He walked towards the gate as he said it, not wishing to meet her eye. She followed a couple of feet behind.

"Since they moved in, about four years ago now. They only had little Ben then, of course. He would have been about two, I should think. Why, what are you getting at?" Her head craned to see his face looking for visual clues.

Standing in the gateway and looking at the little woodland, he turned slightly towards her

"Sorry, but I have to ask this, you understand, was everything okay with the family? I presume Daisy is a good mother and the dad… I think you know where I am going with this?"

Aghast, and under Thomas's vigilant stare, Sandra spoke, "For God's sake Inspector, just come next door and see for yourself. They're absolutely distraught in there. No way they're faking it."

It wasn't quite what he had meant, but let it go. On the remote chance of either being involved, from a mental breakdown or similar, the grief could well be genuine. He just wanted a bit more about what they were like as people.

"Again my apologies, perhaps you could just run through from when you became involved. You heard her shouting I understand." They moved, as a little group, to standing on the path and, for the next ten minutes the officers listened to Sandra's version of events, both of them asking questions and checking any significant points, D S Connelly taking notes.

"So we're thinking, that Martha has managed to get this far or probably not much further and then…." Patrick Stimpson struggled for the right words but settled uneasily on, "gone."

"Look Inspector," Sandra began hesitantly, "I know it's not exactly my place… I mean, you're here now, but if somebody has," she lowered her voice and looked back through the gate as if worried she might be overheard, "taken poor little Martha, God forbid…. they could have made it away over to the road." She pointed south towards the Christchurch road. "There's a path to the road over there, it's not far, and another one over there on the other side of the big houses." She moved her pointed finger westwards in a direction roughly towards the crossroads where Christchurch Road met the main Ringwood to Poole road.

"And," she said thoughtfully, "there's another path that runs right down to the Ringwood Road. It comes out in that little lay-by just down from the Angel."

"I know it," Thomas acknowledged. "But it's quite a long way to go, particularly with a struggling child, I mean, I know the place isn't crawling with people, but he'd have to get lucky not to be seen."

"True," the Inspector agreed wistfully, his eyes taking in the fairly open woodland and noting the points of vegetation and scrub and the waist-high bracken. "However, if you wanted to get from here to let's say over there." He pointed to where Sandra had initially indicated. "The road. Just look at all the cover. There's some fairly substantial bushes and swathes of bracken to hide behind, or in. And, with the trees well spaced, it's pretty open and you'd be able to see people coming from a good way off. You'd have enough time to hide."

Unconvinced, Thomas continued his earlier train of thought. "Yes but you're carrying a struggling, frightened and probably noisy child. You'd be taking one hell of a risk, don't you think?"

"Yes, but what if the child wasn't struggling," Patrick said, his voice quiet and distant, his mind already working on another theory.

Connelly's face changed as the implication dawned on him. "Oh right, somebody she knew."

Uncomfortable now that they were moving into areas that perhaps shouldn't be discussed in front of a possible witness, even, dare he say it, a potential suspect, Patrick directed Sandra back to her role as parent support.

When she had disappeared back inside, Patrick turned to face Thomas. He looked as if he was searching for an answer in the face of his trusty sounding board but in fact he had just made his mind up, "Fuck it, I'd better take this upstairs, let the chief know his budgets blown for the year. Oh and while I'm calling him find out how we go about implementing this child alert initiative, I have a feeling we're going to need all the help we can get."

Chapter 26

"Patrick, I'm told you might have something brewing down there?" his immediate superior asked from the other end of the phone line. "What's your assessment?"

"It's still early days sir," he began. Using the common expression, deployed in this case somewhat defensively; after all, he was about to make his pitch for untold resources and on, so far, relatively sketchy evidence. And there was always the possibility that the child could turn up any minute, leaving him with egg on his face. *Despite that,* he thought to himself, *the point is a child is missing and I need to act, now.*

"My gut feeling is, it's abduction," he said into his mobile phone. "The trouble is, we have no witnesses who saw it happen and we have no physical evidence, as yet, to support it. We do have two very distressed parents and a worried neighbourhood. We haven't searched ourselves, as of yet. We'll need manpower for that, although the neighbours have rallied round, and I'm sure if the child was anywhere close, hiding or trapped, they would have found her. She has literally just disappeared."

"Oh Christ!" was the only reply.

"I think we need to go to the Press really quickly with this. I doubt very much it's abduction for money. They're not wealthy as far as I can see so I don't think we have to worry about pissing off any kidnappers hoping to keep it low key. We're going to need help from the public and, as I say, we're going to need bods on the ground for house to house and searching the common and, I'm afraid, as soon as we can muster them."

"Okay," was the accepting reply. "I'll get on to it at this end; see who we can call in."

"About the media Sir, Thomas has suggested we use the Child Rescue Alert Initiative and I'm inclined to agree. This could be in the public domain within the hour. I can get photos of the missing child and the information we have so far, back to base, but it might need you to actually communicate it."

"Ok, let me speak to the media liaison department and see if they know how to activate this alert system." There was a pause.

"God Patrick," he could hear tension and trepidation in his superior's voice. "You do realise, don't you," it wasn't an accusation aimed at Patrick for laying this at his door, it was just a grim statement of fact. "The whole of bloody hell is about to descend on that quiet little street. Media wise, we are going to be catapulted, onto the front pages of every newspaper and TV station throughout the country.... I am not," he said forcefully, "happy about that." Then as an afterthought, "We need to do this right Patrick. We're going to be under a microscope and there's going to be an awful lot of people staring down it."

Chapter 27

After Patrick and Thomas had interviewed John and Daisy, they went back onto the common. It had been a fruitless task; the distraught couple could add nothing to help. What it did confirm though, was that it was for real and there was no untoward information that would lead them to suspect the immediate family.

With more officers now beginning to arrive and being detailed tasks by an efficient Sergeant, the two CID officers began to chew it over further.

"Right," began Patrick as he ran through things for both their benefit. "The chief is going to start that Rescue alert system but he'll need all the info and a photo. Perhaps you can whip that over to him now. Also when you're back at a computer screen do a quick check on the immediate family, grandparents, where they live etc, we'll probably need to pay them a visit soon."

"Paedophiles, local or of interest?" Thomas interjected.

"Yes my very next point. See what you can dig up. I'd like to get to them as soon as possible. You never know they might not be the end user, if you catch my drift, but they might know something and the sooner we ask, the more rattled they'll be."

Thomas moved to go.

"Oh I tell you what, get somebody back there to run a check on mothers who have lost a young child recently, either in child birth or a bit older, like Martha's age. Keep it relatively local for the moment, go back a year maybe, but ask for national figures as well. We might have to widen the search later."

Wheels in motion, he wandered off into the woods, absently searching, for what..? He had no idea. He quickly came upon the gravel path and decided to see where it went; it would give him time to ponder. With the small wooded area behind him coming alive with blue uniforms he walked through the small clearing eastwards, aiming eventually he hoped, for the little path that Sandra had pointed towards.

He continued to work through the possibilities. Could she have been taken by somebody she knew? He made a mental note to try to get a list of people that Martha would be comfortable with. From the parents; that wouldn't be easy in their current state. Anyway, he said to himself, even if she did or didn't know them, how did that person know that Martha was going to be there and alone. That smacked more of opportunism rather than a planned abduction; after all, that child shouldn't even have been there, let alone in the garden on her own.

He toyed with the possibility that the family had been targeted in some way. The common at the back of their house would provide a relatively discreet observation point, and means of escape, particularly if you could get to the road. Noticed, or unnoticed at that time of day, you would be out on to a main artery, taking you then on to the dual carriageway up to Ringwood and be out of the county in forty minutes, although, that time of day, not great for a speedy getaway; the traffic would have been building by seven forty-five. Alternatively of course, there's safety in numbers, just another car amongst thousands.

Following the path down the slope, he could just make out a small field, and the road beyond. *Christchurch Road,* he thought. He wondered how many houses, if any, had access directly into the woods. The clearing someway behind him had become open woodland once more and the houses partially screened by the overgrowth along what he thought must be the fence line. *You could come and go from these houses and few people would know.* The thought broadened his scope of possible scenarios as it opened up further opportunities for evasion and escape. He hadn't held out too much hope for any eyewitnesses, local or otherwise, and the ease of access to the area wasn't going to help, still, you never knew. The Child Rescue Alert would be firing up any time soon and the national media energised. He wasn't too confident either about that bringing in results either. She seemed like a tiny needle in an enormous haystack. Who on earth was going to notice a young child amongst thousands nationally?

Arriving at the busy thoroughfare, he wandered westwards. The pavement ran along the southern boundary of a little field then past a tiny garden centre. After this, a number of large detached houses were set back off the road, their front gardens sloping quite dramatically up the carefully selected plots, affording them a sweeping vista over, the wide flat Stour Valley and beyond, to the back end of Poole and Bournemouth. *They'll all have to be questioned,* he thought, noting, *their gardens must back on to the common.*

Beside the front garden of the last house, he found the other entrance to the common that Sandra had mentioned; it was a little muddy and a bit more overgrown than the other. He might have missed it save for the green wooden signpost pointing up the side of the property, but it did have a better place to park. Next to where the path led off was a short narrow lane, hidden by high hedges and leading to a gated field. The gate was well hidden to traffic going east, but anyone west-ward bound would have seen the gate up the track. *You could easily park a car in there,* thought Patrick, *not completely hidden, but not far off.* The grassy enclosure led on to other fields and, away off into the distance, he could see a stable block and behind that, he reckoned, was the big house he had visited earlier in the year. *What was it? Oh yes, Homewood House.*

Taking the overgrown track beside the house back up on to the common to rejoin the main circular path, Patrick felt he had mastered the layout of the immediate area. *All being well,* he surmised, *this should take me around to where I set off from, at the back of the Dockers' house.* Striding out now, through the open woodland and past more adjoining fields, he came to the back of a housing estate, confident that, if he kept the houses to his immediate left, he would be okay. As the high boundary fence to his left stopped and turned a corner enclosing the last house in the block, the woodland scrub to the right became less. The glimpsed view between the sparser plants showed that the area behind was more open. As he rounded a corner he understood why the trees were further apart. Between them, a series of large depressions in the ground held water, creating a series of ponds and boggy areas. The largest of the ponds was perhaps thirty or forty metres across. *I wonder how deep that is*, he considered and tried to work out how far away this area was from the Dockers' back gate.

It didn't take him long to figure it out. As the path circumnavigated the ponds, past another entrance, onto Fitzworth Road, he made the connection...*That means the Docker's place must be up ahead some way.* Sure enough a few steps further and he could see the stooped blue figures about a hundred and fifty metres away. He stopped and looked back, and across, in the direction he presumed the ponds to be. Undergrowth again obscured a direct view, but it wasn't very thick. Turning towards the Dockers' back gate he tried to guess the distance, *two hundred – two fifty max,* he thought, *no way could she have got there on her own; not in that short time.*

For the moment, he could not think of any other scenarios to be found on this patch of land, nothing that would make sense anyway, *no, she must have been taken it's the only option.* The recognition that she would probably not be found here on the common, and, that it was looking increasingly like she had been snatched led him to darker thoughts. He didn't really want to entertain the whys but it was one of the questions that would have to be posed. What had she been taken for? The mention of paedophiles earlier was the obvious answer, and the most upsetting.

Christ, he thought, *please let it be some misguided or disturbed woman who had got her, at least that way she would be loved.* The thought brought an emotional lump to his throat and nearly overwhelmed him, his mood suddenly despondent, and the question that had been troubling him for the past couple of hours resurfaced yet again....

"What if we never find her?"

Chapter 28

Dipping under the police tape, Patrick took in that Sergeant Ball had obviously cordoned-off an area in a rough semi-circle about fifty metres around the Dockers' back gate and was busily directing the movements of the officers, some on hands and knees, checking the undergrowth. It was going to be a painstaking job and the row of some ten Bobbies looked pathetic against the immediate expanse they had to cover. *How far are we going to have to push this perimeter?* Patrick wondered.

The Sergeant, as if reading the Inspector's mind, reassured him that there were another eight officers on house-to-house around the common, plus CID, some on the immediate roads like Fitzworth and Heatherlands and others moving further into the estate. Patrick advised the Sergeant that there were houses on the Christchurch Road, and a little garden centre that would need to be canvassed as well.

"Yes, that's in hand sir. I've also got a car with a couple of bods in, checking out the Ringwood Road properties, I know they are some way off, but you never know. And apparently, SOCO's just arriving, not that I'm really sure where to direct them."

Patrick's mobile phone rang in his pocket and, on retrieving it, saw it was Thomas calling and that the time was five minutes past eleven.

"Hi Pat, it's me."

"What have you got Thomas?"

"Right, well the Rescue Alert broadcast has already happened. About fifteen - twenty minutes ago."

"Blimey that was fast!"

"Yeah, the chief got it sanctioned from on high really quickly, and, he wrote up the necessary blurb. So that, plus the photograph, was on the TV, as I say, not long ago. So I should think any minute now you should be seeing your first journalist."

"Thanks for that piece of joyous news."

"Look, I've also got a couple of names, local nonces. Do you want me to go and see them or shall I swing by and pick you up for a more pressurised approach? One of them's pretty close to the incident."

"Yes, come and get me, I'm feeling like a spare part just at the moment. It would be good to feel like I was doing something useful. SOCO will be up and running soon, but to be honest I am not sure that they are likely to find anything, I mean, we're not even sure where to advise them to look. Anyway, Sergeant Ball seems to have got things organised round here."

"I'll be there in fifteen," Thomas announced.

As Patrick slipped the mobile phone back into his pocket, he heard a shout from one of the searching officers. This time it sounded more urgent. The rough ground immediately behind the houses had given up much already: the inevitable soft drinks cans, plastic supermarket bags, fag packets, the odd used condom, all discarded amongst grasses, heathers and partially buried builders detritus from when the houses had been built. It wasn't to say that it was a litter-strewn wasteland but inevitably the close proximity of humans ensured a reasonable amount of wind-blown and direct deposits, particularly along the fence line.

"Sarge, I think I've got something?"

"This time," the experienced Sergeant agreed, as he bent to take a closer look, "I think you might have?"

Patrick arrived to find the two men gingerly trying to remove a miniscule piece of fabric from a vicious tangle of brambles, snagged at knee height on a spray of shoots at the base of a large clump of bracken.

"This fits the description of the baby-grow material, don't you think Inspector," said the Sergeant somewhat triumphantly.

"Well yes, although it's so small, I mean barely a few strands, it's difficult to be sure. And if it is, what does it tell us? …She went this away?" His arm traced a line from the gate to the offending bramble, and on to point into the distance.

"It's the right height for a toddler," interjected the young PC.

"I'd be amazed if she got this far on her own though," said the Sergeant, a father of two youngish children, as he looked back over to the gate some eight to ten metres away. "If she's only just learnt to walk, this uneven ground, brambles, tree stumps an' all, she wouldn't have stood a chance."

"Yes I'm inclined to agree with you Sergeant," Patrick acknowledged. "But if it is the right material then possibly whoever grabbed her perhaps took cover here behind this bracken. So keep your eyes peeled young man, look for any other signs. Well done." He patted the crouched and pleased officer on the shoulder.

Chapter 29

Four miles away, in the historic and bustling Market town of Wimborne, Jenny Spader was climbing back into her specially equipped Vauxhall Combo Van and in a right strop. She had been lucky to park just off the main square, so that she could nip into the bakers to get a sandwich for lunch. While she had been waiting for her tuna and sweet-corn roll to be made, the quarter jack clock on the ancient Minster had not long chimed ten-thirty. Staring absently, but deliberately, out of the shop window, lest her eyes feasted upon the tempting home-made cakes, she watched the folk of Wimborne from her narrow-framed but sweet-smelling hide, as they went about their business. After a few minutes, an elegant woman on the other side of the road drew her gaze. Carefully she placed her hand-held Chihuahua on to the pavement. Her other hand was clutching another portable device into which she was speaking. The conversation was not long, but all the time she was completely aware that the diminutive animal was fouling the pavement. Watching as the woman walked off without retrieving the mess, Jenny was incensed and was determined, as part of her job, to rectify the misdemeanour.

"Excuse me," Jenny called as she negotiated the traffic, headed the harridan off and moved in for the kill. Dressed in her official green sweat shirt with East Dorset District Council emblazed on her left breast, she smiled and said, "I don't know whether you noticed but your dog has just fouled the pavement."

The face below the beautifully coiffed hair was unflustered. "Has she? I obviously hadn't realised, must have been when I was on the telephone." *Oh she's good*, thought Jenny, the shocked face seemingly pretty genuine. Knowing that the next question would be the acid test, Jenny asked politely, "I wonder if you wouldn't mind going back and picking it up?"

The change in the facial expression was almost as if Jenny had asked her to bathe in it.

"What!" was the disbelieving reply.

"I'm afraid Madame, you are legally required to clear it up."

"How can you be sure it was my dog?" the reddening face displayed her true colours, but the voice became challenging and superior.

Jenny was aghast, "I watched it do it, and I believe you saw it too, while you were on the phone." And at that same moment, Jenny knew, she should not have been quite so confrontational, but the woman's off hand manner had been too much. Consequently, it was not handled as diplomatically as it ought, but Jenny was not going to give in. However, after a while of threatening the woman with a fixed penalty fine and with the help of a passing copper, the now ruffled sixty-year old stormed off; up-market shopping bags rubbing shoulders with a not so fragrant, but well knotted little package.

Although she had won the battle, Jenny was still annoyed. Apart from the woman's attitude, she was cross with herself. She really shouldn't have let the stupid bitch get to her, it served no purpose. Switching the engine on, she manoeuvred the little van out of its parking space and headed off, a favourite tune from the radio changing her mood. The song though, stopped abruptly mid flow, "We interrupt this broadcast with an urgent appeal." The grave intonation in the broadcaster's voice seized her attention and she turned up the volume.

"At approximately seven forty-five this morning a thirteen-month-old little girl disappeared from a home in Ferndown, Dorset and the Police have requested that we alert the public."

Ferndown? On a national broadcast? Jenny was once again gripped and pulled over, ignoring the double yellow lines.

"Dorset Police are appealing for any witnesses to, what they believe is an abduction of the child, which happened on a housing estate in West Parley. The estate and in particular the child's home, backs on to an area of common ground, known locally as Poor Common".

"Jesus!" she said, as two more familiar names emanated from the tinny speakers. Her skin crawled with an excited thrill.

The announcement continued, requesting members of the public throughout the country to be vigilant and to report any suspicious sightings, enlisting neighbours to be alert for unusual appearances of a young child in a household that had none. A number was given and a repeat of the title message.

Jenny's heart had already skipped a couple of beats at the familiar places. Out of nowhere, she found herself marrying them up with something Tony had said, after they had seen the ripped apart deer on the common, and it fluttered again; 'Cornered animals become aggressive... if a child found it, well I don't know, I dread to think'.

She didn't know why she had immediately jumped to link the incidences; the Police had said it was abduction, *hadn't they?* Then remembering - they had used a word and she said it out loud, understanding at the same moment all the connotations it could imply, "Disappeared".

Chapter 30

"So what did you make of our Derek, then? asked Patrick as he and Thomas drove away from the shabby little bungalow, housing two tiny flats and where the convicted Paedophile was living.

"Well he lives close enough, the common's probably only about half a mile from here, however, it does sound like he's got a good alibi for this morning", confirmed Thomas.

"Yes, and to be honest, looking at his file, Mr Hanson didn't like them so young." Patrick didn't like the way he'd just said that. It sounded more like he was discussing what food Derek liked, rather than the depravity listed in his record sheet.

"Anyway will you check with the hotel, Thomas? I'm sure they would have missed their washer-up at breakfast, if he hadn't been there."

After a fifteen minute drive they pulled up outside a small block of flats in the nearby community of West Moors. Phillip Carver, seemed to Patrick a more likely candidate. His record showed he was 34, but had been convicted of a bungled child abduction back when he was 25. "Unbelievable," said Patrick as he read the details. "Did you read this? He was caught whilst actively putting the child, who was just eight months, in the back of his car. Apparently, instead of just whipping the child out of the pram and chucking it on the back seat to make a quick getaway, he was caught trying to fold the pram up as well. He said he had found the child abandoned and was about to take it to the Police station. He might have got away with it as well if it hadn't been for the fact that the mother, and the people in the shop she was in, watched him walk off at high speed with the pram and followed him to his car around the corner. The images found on his computer didn't exactly endear him to the judge and jury either. He did three years and, by the look of it, is working at a scrap metal yard. Doesn't appear to have been in trouble since."

"We'll be the judge of that," said Thomas raising his eyebrows, "once we've had a look on his hard drive."

They waited for a few minutes after they had rung the doorbell for the second, and more forceful, time. The thug of a next door neighbour stuck his shaven head around the door and informed them he had gone away for the weekend. "Something about mates in London."

"Well its Monday now," Thomas asked, in a voice that clearly said, so where the hell is he?

"How should I know? I'm not like his dad or nuffing."

Back in their car, Thomas asked for control to send a car, to Phillip Carver's address later, to pick him up. "Tell the duty officer to keep sending a car every hour or so until we've got him okay, and then let us know."

Pocketing his mobile, Thomas's face looked almost animated, "Well, he's a possibility. I wonder who these friends are he's visiting."

"Let's not start jumping to conclusions, but as you rightly say," Patrick looked across to his square jawed colleague, who reminded him so much of an all American quarter back, "a definite possibility."

On their way back to the scene of the crime a call diverted them just around the corner, to a possible eyewitness who lived on Linford Close. The bungalow, they both noted, backed on to Poor Common. The PC who had called in the information, whilst carrying out routine house-to-house interviews, had moved on further down the road.

"A Mister Anderson, is who we're after. Seems he saw, or has seen, a suspicious character," Patrick said, standing on the doorstep, peering at the notebook at the end of his outstretched arm. *Could this be the break we've been looking for,* he thought, the anticipation growing with every second that they waited for the door to open.

The chain rattled and a bolt slid across before the door was pulled slowly back by a frail, grey-haired woman.

"Mrs Anderson?"

"Yes."

"We're from the Police. This is Detective Inspector Patrick Stimpson and I'm Detective Sergeant Thomas Connelly."

"Oh yes, please come in, my husband is through here." As she shuffled ahead of them, Patrick found himself wondering how reliable such an elderly couple might be.

As Thomas closed the solid front door behind him, the narrow hallway dimmed and became quiet. The ticking of an ancient carriage clock, the only sound to break the hallowed silence, created a sense of aged reverence. Opening a door at the end of the corridor she led them through into an unexpectedly bright room at the back of the house, the drawing room. This not insubstantial room had long since been opened up to a huge conservatory and the French doors spanned its entire width. Seated at the far end of the glassed structure in a high-backed and well-cushioned cane chair, sat an equally small, but quite dapper-looking old man.

"Detective Inspector Patrick Stimpson and Detective Sergeant Thomas Connelly," she repeated clearly to her husband.

"Thank you for seeing us, Mr Anderson," Patrick said formally. "I understand from one of our officers, who called earlier, that you might have some useful information for us."

"Would you care for some tea?" asked his consort before an answer could be given.

"Actually, that would be great," said Thomas, realising that he hadn't had one since he'd been at the station earlier. Patrick who hadn't so much as had a sniff of one since breakfast was in full agreement. So Mrs Anderson excused herself and left the room to make tea.

"Well I'm sure it will be of some use," Mr Anderson replied, looking to Patrick a little aggrieved that his wife had actually spoken before he had even said hello.

"So, I understand you saw somebody hanging around the common?" Patrick continued.

"Yes, a man. I have seen him a few times, perhaps, acting strangely."

"When you say strangely, what exactly do you mean?" Thomas asked quickly.

"I have seen him come onto the common, sometimes from the Fitzworth entrance, and sometimes up from the other direction. He often has a bike, and the peculiar thing is, he must go and leave it somewhere because one moment he has it and then in a few minutes, he hasn't and then walks off into the bushes."

Thomas looked at the old man quizzically, "I presume he hasn't seen you, so how do you see him?"

"From our gate in the back hedge, it leads on to the common, but it's pretty well hidden and I often stand there looking out, usually early morning or anytime in the evening. You'd be surprised what stalks this little piece of land in the wee small hours."

"So what makes you sure it's the same man?" Thomas asked sceptically. "I'm assuming you're seeing him in poor light all the time."

"My dear Sergeant," the old man's voice became a little admonishing, "I may be old, but luckily, most of me is still in working order, and particularly my eyesight. He always wears the same clothing, you see, a camouflage jacket, like the army has, dark trousers and, I think, a black hat."

Thomas added the description to his notebook.

"How many times have you seen him?" continued Thomas, still frantically scribbling.

"About maybe five or six times over the last, perhaps, three years." Concerned that this might not be significant, he became flustered and the words came out fast and almost apologetically. "It's quite sporadic, it's not regular, I mean, I'm not out at the gate every night you know. But it is, usually, just when it's getting dark."

"So he goes off into the bushes, about where?" Patrick asked, intrigued.

"Well that's it you see, not far from where that poor little girl lived." Looking upset, Mr Anderson continued, "The thing is I haven't really taken much notice of him, well not up until now of course. I suppose," he stopped as if reflecting on his actions, "I suppose I'd just thought he lived in one of the houses over there and dismissed it. But now, I don't know, and I thought I ought to mention it to someone, and so when your officer came this morning it seemed prudent to pass it on."

"Quite right, quite right" Patrick acknowledged and, mentally crossing his fingers, asked, "Would you recognise this man or know who he is, by any chance?"

The tea dutifully arrived, once again disturbing the head of the household's flow; china mugs on a tray with milk in a jug and sugar in a bowl. Patrick's practised eye had swept the tray and his stomach seemed to groan inwardly reflecting his immediate disappointment, *what no biscuits?*

"Unfortunately Inspector," his irritation barely concealed as he flashed a look at his wife, "that is where I fall short, I'm afraid. The poor light just isn't good enough to pick out much detail and it's jolly difficult to see his face, in fact, come to think of it, I don't think I have seen any skin showing at all, you know flashes of white hands or face."

"Could you show us the back gate and where you saw him?" Thomas asked without looking up, updating his notes with the additions to the description.

"Certainly," he said rising quite sprightfully and opening the doors to the conservatory. "Oh bring them with you," gesturing toward the mugs that they were both coveting and somewhat reluctant to put down.

The meticulously well-laid-out garden was about fifteen to twenty metres long and ended in an immaculately clipped Photinia hedge; its leaves burnished a stunning red in the bright sun. The eight-foot-high hedge had a neat door shape cut in it, rounded at the top to accommodate the arched tongue-and-grooved wooden gate. It opened directly in to the tree line, and Patrick noticed the parted lower vegetation and bare earth leading out to the gravel track some twenty metres away. They were standing looking out over towards the flashes of blue movement within the clearly discernible fluttering police tape.

"What's that about a hundred metres from here?" Thomas said, pointing at where he thought that the Dockers' gate must be.

"Yes, about a hundred yards, sorry, still on old money Sergeant. That's where he usually disappears just over there, off the gravel path." He pointed to a spot on the vegetation line, some sixty-five metres away. There was no discernible feature or landmark to be seen.

Seeing the detectives' searching and questioning looks, Mr Anderson hastily added, "I think if you go over there you'll see a gap through the bushes. It's not obvious but there is a sort of pathway."

"So did you say you'd seen him this morning by any chance, only the information I've got is not clear?" Patrick said trying to read his handwriting and holding the notebook away to help focus

"Oh, no Inspector. I haven't seen him for a couple of weeks actually. Sorry," he added as he saw the two expectant faces, exchange withering glances.

"Okay, not to worry Mr Anderson," Patrick smiled reassuringly. "It's something for us to work on, but if you do think of anything else, be sure to let us know. You can never tell whether something is relevant or not. However, I do feel this might be, so we're grateful for your help."

They drove the quarter of a mile or so back to number 27 Heatherlands Avenue to find cars and vans cluttering the available spaces along the already narrow and congested estate road. The hastily erected cordon around the Dockers' small front garden consisted of white tape with police printed on it, hanging limply from metal stakes that were already falling over, as if the tape weighed half a ton. It wouldn't have held back a fart let alone a serious attempt by the swelling media pack.

"Christ they were here quickly," said the disbelieving Thomas as they ducked under the tape.

"Your fault I think," said Patrick with a friendly glare. "Tip of the Iceberg, I should think."

Catching up with Sergeant Ball they were given a run-down of what they had found of possible significance. Depressingly, it was very short.

"The divers are here by the way," the Sergeant informed them. "They arrived about half an hour ago. I found out that Moors Valley Country Park oversees this bit of woodland and they have sent somebody with keys to unlock the gates and get the vehicles in off the road. I've also taped up all the entrances onto the common. Hopefully that might keep the area clear for a while."

"Okay, well done," praised Patrick as he and Thomas moved to go. "Mind you, lots of houses have their own gates and direct access. Better tell your boys to be sensitive if they find any people wandering around," adding quickly, "Oh, unless they're Press of course."

Patrick glanced at his watch. It was nearly two-thirty and except for a miniscule bit of fabric and a possible unknown male, they had nothing. The search teams had nothing to show for their breaking backs and the house-to-house would continue on into the early evening, attempting to mop up those households that had not been in.

"Come on Thomas. Let's go back to the station, grab a sandwich and a coffee, talk to the chief, see if he has any bright ideas."

Chapter 31

"No, I haven't heard anything. Why what have I missed? Tony said, looking a little non-plussed at finding an agitated Jenny on his doorstep at just after four in the afternoon.

"And, eh hello, by the way," he teased, taking in the fact that she was still in her work clothes and that, evidently, this was an unscheduled visitation, particularly as they had planned to meet later.

"Oh yeah, hi," she said, her excitement barely contained, and gave him a peck on the cheek as she swept past him into the open-plan living area.

"What planet have you been on all day, not to have heard anything?" Her expression incredulous, "I mean, it's been on the news all day, and there was a special bulletin this morning! It broke into the radio station I was listening to, and, as I understand it, most TV channels as well."

"Someone died...? The Prime Minister's taken a dump..? What?" Wide-eyed and grinning, he feigned innocence, adding by way of an explanation, "I've been in a pond all day."

"Lucky you," she said smiling at his nonsense and then explaining how she'd heard the broadcast in the morning. "At first, I couldn't believe it when the announcer said 'Ferndown,' I had to pull over, which was just as well, otherwise I'd have crashed the van when he said, 'West Parley' and 'Poor Common'. Let's put the telly on, see if there have been any updates." Tony moved to switch his old Sony television on, while Jenny continued, "I caught the news at lunch and, although they were speculating that it was an abduction, they didn't seem to have any clues or evidence. The press are saying she's just vanished, disappeared, you know, all sensational like, as if she's been taken by aliens."

"She's probably just run off. They'll find her somewhere," said Tony reasonably.

"Thirteen months they said, not thirteen years, Tony. She's only just learnt to walk." Jenny wondered whether Tony had either just misheard her or had some wild delusions as to how quickly children grew up.

She could see by the awakening facial muscles he was making connections, a light was dawning, like one of those energy saving bulbs, slow and dim for just a few seconds and then brilliance as the power kicked in.

"What, you think this might be connected with all the other things that have happened around the common?"

"Er, Well, yes," aghast at his sluggishness; "you said it yourself - a cornered animal, a big cat, what if a child came across it?" She looked into his face, her own was intent and expectant waiting for him to arrive at the same conclusion as her. She didn't wait long.

"Shit!" he said running both his hands through his hair and holding them on his head, as his mind tried to grapple with the idea. "Surely there'd be some evidence left at the scene?" He was looking at Jenny but not really talking to her, as he weighed things up in his mind. Then he corrected himself, "Not necessarily. A big animal like that could probably carry off a young child and, of course, you know what panthers do with their prey once they have caught it?"

"No," said Jenny, although she didn't feel it was necessary for her to have said anything.

"From a very young age, black panthers develop fantastic climbing skills and they drag their kills up into a tree. It's a natural place for them to keep their prize from other predators, as most of them can't climb."

"Clever."

"Yes, but thinking about it," Tony was on a roll now. "Supposing it was a big cat, a panther, you know an escaped pet or the like, they're incredibly stealthy, I mean they're hardly ever seen in the wild – ghosts of the forest they've been called in some places. If it doesn't want to be seen it won't be. And I bet you money, any searching done by the Police or whoever wouldn't be looking up a tree." With Tony's childhood experience heavily influencing his determinations, he pressed on. "Besides, that creature could cover a lot of ground. It could be miles away by now."

"Not in daylight though and not in such a built up area, surely?" Jenny reasoned. It would have to cross a busy road somewhere to get out of Poor common."

"Yeah, true," Tony looked thoughtful. "Which means, if nobody has sighted it, and I'm sure we'd know if they had soon enough, be in the papers tomorrow or internet any second," he glanced at his laptop. "Ought to check the web news, see if there's anything. If there haven't been sightings today or any that gets reported tomorrow, in the Press," Tony's face brightened, "then it's quite likely the animal could still be around."

"The thing is," Jenny countered, with a meaningful stare. "If we wait for the Press tomorrow, and there's no coverage, it still tells us nothing, and by then our black pussy cat could have high-tailed it out of here under the cover of darkness."

Tony felt an uneasy weight of moral responsibility under Jenny's gaze. He understood what it was implying and he fretted for a while about what he should do. He didn't want to draw attention, like last time. Okay, it had been amusing at times but downright unpleasant for the most and he resented being hailed as an 'expert'. He discussed it with Jenny, who up until now had been quite protective, understanding that the incidence at Moors Valley and the so called Beast of Dorset had for a time, been quite disturbing for him. From the outset of these 'goings on' she'd been sceptical, even arguing against the probabilities of a big cat, in an effort to dampen his zeal, but right at this moment she was erring towards him making the phone call.

"Look Tony, I know we don't have much physical evidence to present, but when you take into account all the circumstances that we know of, it does add up to some unusual happenings around the common and this missing girl…" She was perched on the edge of his sofa, open palms imploring reason. "Might just be the culmination.

I'm sorry," she paused, looking down at her feet, "I really think you should speak to the police, if nothing else, just to alert them of the possibility. I mean if there is something out there, and the child hasn't been abducted, then they could be looking in all the wrong places. Perhaps speak to the detective in charge. At least, if you explain your reluctance, he ought to be able to keep things quiet for you."

Tony knew she was right, so with heavy resignation, he called, asking to be put through to the detective in charge of the missing child case.

A little tongue-tied and nervous he recounted his theory to an Inspector Stimpson. It did not go as well as he had planned.

******

At number twenty-seven Heatherlands Avenue the mood was funereal; Daisy's parents had taken charge of their daughter, after thanking Sandra for all her help. David, her brother, had rushed round as soon as he had heard from his mother. He too was shocked and silent. Once inside the familiar surroundings, cocooned from the outside world and the ever-present media, they could allow their grief free reign; tears of sadness and shock, of worry and frustration, tears of guilt and self loathing. The five of them took their turns with all of them; whatever the time, grief was incessant and cruel. Visions of little Martha, so vivid in their minds eye, only added grist to the delusion of her presence. Before being snatched away again in grim realization; the trauma replayed and relived.

Grandpa staring out into the back garden, in a moist daze, had brooded on the idea that she was already lost. David, tearful that he could do nothing to help his sister, had also visited the dreadful notion. John though, alone in the nursery, fixated on a christening card, one that now sat on the cot-side chest of drawers, it was a simple embroidered card of a lit candle, with the words, 'To a new Light in the World'. The significance had touched him deeply at the time, but the tears, now, were uncontrollable and he glared at the card and hated it. In a blind rage he scrunched it and threw it at the bin, the sentiment had become irrelevant, and the light of his world, extinguished.

Nobody knew what to do. They sat in the living room absently watching the silent television. The WPC assigned as liaison officer, dutifully made tea, and could offer little more than the usual platitudes. Don't give up hope, they're doing all they can, I'm sure the public will come up trumps. None of them really listened.

Daisy's guilt was extreme and unwarranted, but she couldn't see it. She kept going over it in her mind and occasionally felt the need to say it out loud, punctuated with sobs and heart-wrenching wails. "I only left her for a few minutes, Mum, while I was talking to you. I could see her in the kitchen. I know I shut the back door. How could she just disappear? Why didn't I shut the gate? It's all my fault. Who would take her Mum? Who?"

The debate on what to do about Ben brought a fresh burst of tears. She had barely thought about him and immediately felt guilty about that. Fortunately Mel had come to the rescue, offering to have him overnight. She had collected him from school, on the promise of a sleepover, bangers and mash for tea and ice cream to follow. He had suspected nothing, albeit his grandma sounded a bit strange on the telephone. So in the household, just four doors down, Mel and her husband Mark kept things light, the television put to good effect distracting and concealing their hushed and shocked conversations in the adjacent kitchen. They, like many, could not begin to fathom how such a thing could have happened in their quiet and unassuming little neighbourhood.

The team on the common kept quartering the ground through into the late evening, trying to cover as much of it as they could before nightfall, and without rushing. By eight-thirty, the light under the trees became gloomy and unreliable and, without any further useful evidence, Sergeant Ball dismissed the officers. Some CID officers carried on with the house-to-house enquiries, covering all those missed in the day, but again no further information was forthcoming. It had been fruitless and depressing and few went home with any great optimism for the next day to come.

As the long, long day slipped into night, the residents of the estate, and particularly those that had answered the call to search, remained stunned and wary. Parents, protective and nervous, wondered what sick mind was at work and more importantly, were they still around? As unlikely as this was, the barely seen neighbours around Daisy's grieving world would, from this point on, become closer knit. A community thrust together under a common cause, now throwing watchful glances, through chinked curtains out into the night.

And, of course, the television news was full of it. If they'd told the facts once, they'd told them a hundred times. They'd dragged up old news, similar cases and compared them to this. They'd postulated on the Police's next moves and skirted around the topics that nobody wanted to hear, just yet. Throughout the country, it would not be possible to remain immune from the events of that morning; but all in the immediate vicinity, would be, without question, fearfully aware. And those feelings of concern and disdain would ripple out like shock waves from the tiny epicenter of West Parley and would be felt, almost instantly, throughout the country and very shortly after, on into the wider world.

Chapter 32

It was eight o'clock in the evening when Thomas dropped Patrick off at his house, at the northernmost end of Ferndown.

The Inspector felt that the afternoon spent at headquarters had been marginally more profitable. They now had a list of females they wished to talk to, all of whom had lost babies or young children. Locally there were not that many, but collectively, and on a national basis the numbers shocked him, and he realised the impracticality of trying to get to them all. If none of the locals fitted the bill they would have to build up a set of criteria with which to sift through the others countrywide. The trouble was, his thoughts kept alighting, rather depressingly, on the old adage, 'not shitting on your own doorstep.' It was crude, but in this case, he could somehow see it being apt. If you were going to snatch a child and keep it, or whatever, he reasoned, you wouldn't pop next door, or indeed, grab it from the same town where it might be recognised. No, you would want to be as far away as possible, wouldn't you? Mind you, he corrected himself, that's assuming you're in your right mind, of course. And in some ways, hoping for the latter, he opened the side gate to his house and wandered down the narrow passage and ignored the back door. Turning the corner onto the patio that stretched across the back of the house, he waved his presence through the window, to Marjorie in the kitchen, and then the kids at the table doing their homework.

"Dinner's in the microwave," Marjorie called through the kitchen window, knowing that a few minutes in the garden would help him switch off.

"Okay, be there in a minute," he called back as he inspected his runner beans. The spiralling stems were now charging up the canes and would be at the tops in another week to ten days. He wondered where the case would be in ten days time. Would something turn up to change things or would they still be completely clueless as to where little Martha was? He knew he would have to work for a while tonight, having called a team briefing in the morning at 8.30am and, just at this moment, didn't have much to say. He would need to get some ideas down on paper, try to think about what needed to be done, and who would do them. Police forces throughout the country were on high alert for this child and perhaps he could speak to other officers who had been involved in similar cases.

With his mind beginning to find new avenues to explore, his mood became more positive. *You never know,* he thought, *with all the coverage in the press... that ought to light a few fires. It only takes one vigilant soul or nosey parker to come forward... and we could be off.* Now a little more buoyed up, he passed the blackcurrant plants, pleasingly laden with fruit. Evidently the hastily erected netting had done its job in foiling the birds. However, the far more substantial cherry tree, unable to be covered, would once again fall foul of the pigeons. He couldn't recall ever actually eating one of his own cherries from this tree. They never had the chance to ripen; stolen before his very eyes. Some copper eh!

"All right my girlie?" he said resting his hand lovingly on his fifteen-year-old daughter's shoulder as she pored over her English homework. The simple gesture saying much; dad's home, he's there, he's seen me, still loves me; the gentle squeeze, a father's awkward caress for a near-adult child. She still gave him big child-like hugs, but more often these days it was cupboard love, when she was after something. Usually though it was a cursory clasp, as daily routines sprinted by. It was normal, but today he could have done with a trip down that particular lane; annoying texting, the inappropriate clothing, face-booking, all forgotten. She was there and he thanked his lucky stars.

Without looking round: "Yeah fine dad." The usual, almost off hand reply. He wondered if she had heard yet; wondered if she knew he was involved. After a moment, she turned and gave him a kiss. "Sorry, got to finish this, in tomorrow, bloody woman (referring to her English teacher)" With the cheeky smile that said, I swore, but hey… that's okay, you do it, she returned to her work. Patrick smiled too.

"You okay, big man?" His son had risen to greet him and gave him a hug. He usually still did, but today Patrick was grateful and he held him a bit tighter and perhaps a bit longer.

Without directly answering his father's greeted enquiry, he launched into… "Match on Saturday. Can you come? It's against Christchurch. We stuffed 'em last time." Hopeful eyes implored expectantly, "Oh go on please try?"

"I'll see what I can do. What time?"

"Dunno… Ten usually."

He kissed his wife as she retrieved his meal from the microwave.

"I had mine with the kids. I wasn't sure what time you'd be back." She gave him a sympathetic look. "I imagine it's been a difficult day?"

He sat at the breakfast bar to eat his meal, so he could chat with Marjorie as she finished clearing up. He spoke before she was able to turn back to her chores. "The trouble is, we have got zilch to go on, so short of standing around postulating theories, Thomas and I have done," he mouthed the last bit, "bugger-all."

"She can't have just disappeared into thin air," exclaimed Marjorie, lowering her voice in a disbelieving almost accusing tone; also aware, of the children at the table.

Marjorie's tone riled Patrick slightly, like the chief's comments had earlier. They seemed to imply he hadn't been working hard enough or looked in the right places.

"Well if there'd been anything to find, we'd have found it," he countered prickily. "We've no witnesses, save for some old boy who's seen a man," Patrick held up both hands and made quotation signs, "'acting strangely' on the common. God, if we picked up all the blokes who were, 'acting strangely'; half of them'd be coppers." The frustration through his smile, was obvious. "So really, all Thomas and I have physically done, is visit a couple of the usual suspects, if you know what I mean, and one of them wasn't in."

Half expecting a call from work, he began eating his meal in near silence; Sally was still finishing off her homework on the kitchen table and so he didn't want to disturb her, preferring now to brood rather than chat to Marjorie. Simon, he could hear, was now in front of the television in the lounge next door, watching Master Chef or something similar. He hated these evenings, the trill chirping of the kitchen telephone, becoming a sound he dreaded whether it turned out to be the station or not. Marjorie finished wiping the surfaces, put away the cleaning spray and rinsed the dishcloth.

"Right I'm going to join Simon, you coming?" she said. Her hand hovered over a tray, and wavered in expectation, while she waited for his reply. "Yes?"

"Thanks," he replied as he took the handed-tray. Perhaps the television will take my mind off it, he thought, following Marjorie into the lounge.

Settling down on the sofa, the tray balancing on his splayed out legs, with his meal sliding precariously on the plastic surface, he attempted to eat whilst vacantly watching the television. His mind, though, was elsewhere.

Often in the evenings, at this time of the year, he would have had time, after an early supper, to get out in the garden for an hour or so. But it was too late now. The light outside had almost gone and the darkened windows served only to reflect, dully, the family at rest. He stared at the window and watched his ungainly and reflective double, mirror his every move. Transfixed he began to ponder.

Taken then? ... But by whom?... Someone just happened to be walking past the house when this tot appears and they think, I'm having that, as if it were a commodity, something they could use or sell on? A rare coincidence, of course, but possible. Just suppose it did happen that way. So, you've grabbed it, Patrick tried to detach himself from emotion, the child becoming just a thing, another item of stolen property and not some devastated family's living nightmare.

So this child is struggling... maybe? But because of its size it's easy to restrain. How do you stop it crying? You can't. A hand over the mouth would do it, for a short time, but you would have to use a fair amount of force, to stop it keep flicking and pulling its head away. Yes quite a lot of restraint then. And what's that going to do to the babe's anxiety levels? It's going to struggle like it has never done before, and that, subconsciously Patrick became the abductor, *is going to make me nervous. I'm going to need to get out of here. Let's say I know the exits. Why am I here at this time of day? Where am I going...? To work...? Home from work...? Maybe I've just been out for a walk? Whichever, I must be local, why else would I be here?*

Right! I need to get home, hide it. But if I take any one of the formal exits off the common no matter how short on a road, I'm going to be seen. Hang on though, what if I had a personal entry on to the common a gate, one that was well hidden, like old Mister Anderson across the way there? I could be in my house, keep the child in a room, feed it, wait till the fuss dies down, and then move it. Dangerous though, the police are bound to go house-to-house. No... probably only doorstep enquiries, not a complete search, particularly if I was deemed far enough away from the scene of crime. I'd have to keep my nerve though. However, if I live that far enough away, then I've still got a good deal of open country to cover and there are bound to be people on the common, walking their dogs etc... You might get lucky I suppose. Patrick made a mental note, *to do another house-to-house in the morning, as early as possible, of all the adjoining properties to the common, checking whether they had gates, and being a bit more forceful - not just asking if they had seen any suspicious persons hanging around, but really delving. We want to search their gardens again; we need to check their outhouses, garages, even, dare he say it, their houses. Effectively they must be treated as suspects. Anyone refusing to allow their house to be searched would be advised that a warrant would be issued. It may be bully-boy tactics but a baby's life was at stake. Any reasonable person with nothing to hide, and with everything to gain by helping, might not like it, but surely they wouldn't refuse?*

As Patrick's mind explored the possibilities as logically as he could, each step threw up new questions and new lines of enquiry. He often likened an investigation to a river; as information was gathered in from various sources, Scenes of crime, forensics, house-to-house - the catchment of the high ground, it flowed into open water. The evidence and clues assimilated by the team, all pointing in a general heading, downstream. But no sooner did you have all this gushing data than it hits the wide delta of one's reasoning mind. A thought - which way did the abductor go? - It slows, as multiple possibilities open up and, like a silt deposited plain, the river divides again and again, as different scenarios open up - before finally reaching the sea. Naturally, the more specific evidence; clues, testimonies and information you have to feed into the brook at the beginning, the faster the case's momentum and the rivers direction clearer and more carved. And, like many rivers, they seem to just spill out into the sea, no low alluvial tract of land or muddy waters, just a clear run through; in other words a swift conviction.

However, Patrick's river was in danger of drying up. Facts and evidence were negligible, leaving only the uncertain precipitation of supposition and guesswork to trickle into the murky watercourses down-stream. It was a bit overwhelming. He just hoped for a downpour tomorrow.

A frog emerged from the patio pond and distracted him momentarily. He watched it as it hopped slowly and deliberately off into the damp, and bug filled, undergrowth of his garden.

Okay, if not an opportune snatch, then what? ... A deliberate and premeditated kidnap? That's going to mean planning, surveillance and targeting, and probably not just one person. Assuming you aren't doing it in your own neck of the woods, you would need to find a good place to start. Why here? Maybe they aren't from too far away, Southampton, Dorchester, or wherever? Perhaps they have a contact here. Patrick sought to dispel the reason, the purpose, for why she had been taken. He wanted to just work out how. The reasons might have some bearing but, just at the moment, he felt they might cloud, rather than clear his thoughts. He still felt there could be a chance, albeit slim, that the child might still be close by.

So you've settled on this place, Poor common, *why...? Because you know it! You've realised that the open land behind the houses will afford you some cover while you watch. You can come and go as you please, another rambler, dog-walker perhaps...? Of an evening, the houses could easily be viewed from the trees, particularly with lights on. You've assessed that the estate of houses are first or second buy properties... will be inhabited with younger families, and the potential for suitably aged targets. You can study their movements, gauge their routines, note opportune moments, and check the neighbours too; making sure the coast will be clear. Small gardens with back gates, ideal, a short run in whilst the parent is distracted at the front of the house, an unlocked back door, you could be in and out in a matter of seconds.... Still got to get across the common unseen, but you'd have a car nearby, or perhaps,* Patrick revisited the idea he'd had earlier, *you live in, or rent, or have access to, one of these houses backing on to the common.* Patrick's mind started spinning again, *any number of those big houses on Christchurch Road would be good, even if you didn't own it, but you knew the owners were away, or at work. You could park a car in their secluded drives and nobody would be any the wiser. Christ, all you need is access to their back gate. That's got to be how it was done.* Convinced now, in his mind, he would brief the team in the morning and press home a more aggressive house-to-house search. He would need to write up a list of information he wanted gathering, houses with back gates, houses rented or empty, movements of all the people in these house. As the list gathered pace in his mind, he placed the tray on the carpet and went to his study.

Chapter 33

The first thing he did was to make a call to the station and speak to one of the duty officers. He asked them to contact the CID team and any other uniformed officers destined for his deployment, to inform them that the briefing time had changed from eight-thirty am to six-thirty am. Protestations from the constable on the end of the telephone, about the fact it was now nine-thirty pm, did not break Patrick's train of thought. He wanted those guys out knocking doors by seven-fifteen, if he could. Catching people in before they set off for work, the school run, or whatever, was paramount. The more properties they could get into, the better. His mind was set and he was not about to argue the toss with anyone.

"Look, I know it's late, but this is urgent, so please get on to it right away." The determination in his voice drew a curt reply.

"Sir."

The list, when he finally finished it, was comprehensive and not too long, but it would give his team some useful pointers in what to look for, and what questions to ask.

Earlier thoughts, about Mr Anderson's camouflaged man on the common, re-entered his mind. *And we need to find out more about our mystery man with the bike. If he lives in one of the houses close by, we should be able to eliminate him quickly. Alternatively, if he doesn't, then we need to find him. He could be the watcher, collecting all the necessary info about the family.* He added another couple of lines to the list.

Tilting back in the cushioned office chair and staring once again out through the diamonds of the imitation leaded pains, into the night, he was aware of two piercing orbs with vertically slit pupils observing him disdainfully. "Bugger off cat," Patrick said quietly to himself. "I'm not your servant. Use that bloody expensive cat flap I put in." No way was he getting up to let it in, although clearly the contemptuous gaze felt he should do otherwise. Turning away from the window, and ignoring the scrutiny, Patrick was reminded of the telephone call he had had earlier at work.

"A Panther? What will they think of next," he said, smiling to himself. Often direct appeals to the public for help seemed to give an official stamp of approval for every nutter to postulate their wacky theories.

He'd taken the call from Tony Nash at about five o' clock, just before the evening press statement. In fairness, the guy had sounded quite sensible, well-educated, and when he'd that he might have some information that might be relative to the case, Patrick's heart had lightened. Anticipating a breakthrough?

Sadly though, as Mr Nash laid out his theory, reaching the part about Black Panthers, Patrick had quickly switched off. After that, he half-listened whilst reading something on his desk.

"…animals going missing" said Tony's digitised and tinny voice.

"Yes I see."

"…half-eaten deer."

"Aha."

"…possible big cat on Holt Heath a few weeks back."

"Right, and this is relevant how?" Patrick's voice was verging on the bored and uninterested

"Cornered animals can be dangerous."

"Yes, well we shall have to keep our eyes open, sir, and, if we see anything, rest assured, we'll be careful." He'd realised the caller was speaking again, something about 'up in trees', but he quashed him quickly with, "Apologies Mr Nash, I have to go, Press conference to attend… Yes thanks again for your concern, we will look into it." He had put the phone down quickly and left his office. "Fucking nutters," he had said under his breath as he turned into the corridor outside his office.

Despite the lack of information to expound to the press, the conference had gone well. The questions had been fended off easily, early days yet, etc, etc. And indeed, it was early days, just under the one in fact and Patrick new the pleasantries, such as they were, probably wouldn't last past tomorrow morning. And for some reason, which he couldn't explain, he wished he hadn't made that off-hand remark to the local echo Journalist Brian Maidment, but surely it had been harmless enough? He'd known Brian for some years now and he wasn't a shit stirrer like some he'd met. But…? There had been a slight glimmer in Brian's eyes, when he'd said it, almost an acknowledgement of some kind, as if he'd picked up on something, but wasn't going to let on. It niggled Patrick and he tried to remember exactly what he had said.

He remembered that after the formalities, he had been cornered by the experienced journalist who was still hoping to extract anything that might be of use, something that hadn't been mentioned earlier. Patrick naturally was not wishing to give anything away, and was slightly embarrassed by the fact that it was unlikely he would let anything slip, because he had bugger-all to let slip in the first place. So he had said as much to Brian, although a bit more professionally and along the official lines, finishing up with "Let's hope the appeals bring in more than some nutter called Tony and a Black Panther on the loose." It was at that point when Brian had reacted. It was almost as if he was going to speak, then thought better of it. They'd said their goodbyes and Brian had scuttled of pretty quickly.

Patrick's thoughts were interrupted by Simon slipping into the little room, giving him a quick peck on the cheek and a swift "Night dad," before spinning on his heels to go. Patrick glanced at the clock on the desk. It was ten o'clock. "What are you still doing up, you rascal?" he asked, amused at his son's attempt at saying goodnight without actually drawing too much attention to himself, or, by the look of it, the time. "Mum said I could stay up."

"Yeah I bet," he said scornfully. "She's probably fast asleep on the sofa."

A muffled giggle from the stairs, in the hall, told him he was right.

He too had had enough, and was contemplating turning in as well, reasoning with himself that he would be getting an early start. So with his optimism higher than it had been earlier in the day, and buoyed up by the action plan he had just set in motion, he went to find Marjorie and then to bed. However, the niggling feeling about Brian wheedled its way back in to his thoughts as he lay down. Fortunately it didn't rob him of his much needed sleep. Well not this night any way.

******

Gary had been in the pub since nine p.m. and was, like most of the punters, engaged in conversation. The main topic, of course, was the missing child. A number of the regulars knew the family well; Roy, Jonathon and Miles in particular were there, sombrely piecing together their version of events. Some of the other customers mentioned it as they bought their drinks. "Dreadful business with that little girl," or "Has there been any more news, do you know if they've found her yet?" It was as if the bar staff were expected to be the font of all knowledge and in fairness, they probably did know a fair bit more about the goings-on locally and around the popular hostelry. They were, after all, everybody's mate, a welcoming listening post, a human facebook wall. They absorbed comments divulged by every visitor and then, posted them freely and publicly; part of their expected bonhomie, to all who wished to know and those willing to listen.

Collectively, the bar staff knew that Daisy's family had often drunk in the pub. They had, in fact, been in only a few weeks ago. This, of course, was information gleaned that morning from a customer, but they didn't actually know Daisy or John. However, by the end of the evening it was highly likely they would know more about them and the family than probably Daisy's' own mother. They would speak about the little family, in an authoritative but non-committal way, the cute kids, how Daisy was a good mum, how the dad was a bit of a workaholic etc etc, or so I've been told. And then, as sure as one day follows another, the stories would change as gossip spread. 'I heard she left that child alone in the house for half an hour. Talk about irresponsible!' One thing was sure, pub regulars needed to learn that all information acquired in such surroundings should come like crisps of yester year, with their own little packet of salt. Some would use the condiment wisely, others wouldn't, and as a result, rumour and tittle-tattle became a very moveable feast.

"I wonder if Davesss with her?" Gary slurred. It was an enquiry of the three men propped at the bar, about his mate, the brother of Daisy. Unusually for Gary, he had managed to down three pints in the space of an hour and was well on his way to finishing his fourth. Consequently, he was feeling the effects, the inrush of alcohol messing with his head; words garbled, emotions heightened and fragile, movements were becoming exaggerated and clumsy.

"Oh I should think so, don't you," said Jonathon. "She's gonna need all the help she can get, poor kid."

"Do you think there's anything we can do?" Gary asked rather loudly, but with an element of genuine concern. I mean I've known Daisy, and of course Dave," he quickly said, his face colouring heavily, "all my life pretty much. We were at school together."

Jonathon noticed the flash of embarrassment and, in an effort to inject a bit of fun, said, "Rumour has it you fancied her at school. Bit of a crush was it?"

"Crush? Juicer more like," added Miles, with a broad grin and a devilish twinkle. "Never seen so much drool."

Trying to cover his discomfort, Gary struggled for something witty to say back. But "Piss off," was all he could muster, his smile false and chagrin. "I just meant, well y," the gaseous lager made a pathetic attempt to escape and he belched noiselessly into his balled-hand, "you know, Daisy's always so much fun, don't think I've ever seen her upset about anything." His face visibly sank. "Dreadful to think she's at home right now worried sick." This was a side of Gary the others barely knew and they too felt awkward, appreciating their comments might have been a little inappropriate under the circumstances.

"What about John?" Gary continued questioningly. "He'll be devastated," saying it in a way like the enormity was only just dawning. "And Martha." Gary took a swig of his beer quelling the lump that was rising in his throat.

"Oh come on, we're all talking as if she's gone for good. She might turn up tomorrow, for all you know." It was a good attempt by Miles to give it a positive spin, and outwardly all agreed. Deep down though, each man held their own belief and, unsurprisingly, negativity was the driving force in all.

Chapter 34

In his flat on Glenmoor Road, Tony was inflamed. Jenny looked on, feelings of guilt and embarrassment surfacing as Tony alighted on the subject once again.

"What did the bastard do? Put the phone down on me and shout ECHO?" The bastard he was referring to was Inspector Patrick Stimpson.

He had been regaling Jenny, off-and-on, for the past three hours, ever since the phone call from one Brian Maidment had ruined their evening. It had made Tony's mind up for him and he'd elected they stay in and have a take-away with a bottle of wine. Jenny had duly responded by driving over to him rather than the other way around, as planned.

The call had come in at seven-fifteen pm. Five minutes later and he wouldn't have been there. That annoyed Tony as well.

"Hi, Tony?" the voice was warm and familiar. It had the suggestion this was a friend, a mate, someone you conversed with every day. The trouble was, Tony couldn't quite place who it was. It wasn't anyone from work, or from down the pub, or his badminton group, or Dorset wildlife members, Piers, Dave, his mind was running out of people. It didn't matter. He evidently knew him well to be so casual, sounding like an old pal just calling to arrange a pint.

"Yes 'tis me," Tony said lightly and with pleasant expectations.

"How are you matey?"

"I'm fine thanks," *Who is this?* He thought. And, without thinking, he automatically asked.

"You?"

"Yeah, I'm good too."

Tony was a little irked that he couldn't work out who it was, and he didn't want to ask him directly. That might be embarrassing if it was somebody he should know. And by the familiarity, he did. The trouble was, he did recognise the voice, that's to say it was recognisable as somebody he knew, or had known... and well, by the sound of it. There was though, another part of his brain that was beginning to send little packets of doubt, *you know this voice... you've spoken to him in the past... it's annoying he hasn't said who he is... Why?*

"Is this a good time? I mean have you got a minute?" asked the voice.

"Yeah... no I'm," Tony fumbled, he was just about to go out to see Jenny, but he was confused now. *Whoever this is wants something and, by the sound of it, not just a quick answer.* The little packets were piling up now and one or two were displaying warning signs. "Actually, I was just about to go out..."

"Oh right, so it's not good at the moment then?" There was a moment of hesitation, "Only, I just wanted to ask you a quick question, really."

"No, it's okay I can be a bit late." The words were no sooner out of his mouth than the bomb dropped on his cerebral doorstep, exploding Brian Maidment into his mind's eye.

"Sorry, but who is this?" Tony's voice hardened. Brian new he'd been rumbled, picking up the elements of a sudden awareness, of disdainful recognition tinged with caution and a hint of anger. These vibes were expected and, to be honest, Brian was amazed he'd got past 'Hi'.

"Yeah, sorry it's Brian at the Echo, Brian Maidment, you remember?" Brian was very aware that Tony had remembered, and, evidently not favourably, but he kept up the pretence.

"I did that piece a while back, on the big cats. You helped me with it. Yeah?" A bit of flattery never went amiss.

"How could I forget Brian." The warmth had gone completely from Tony's voice. "I got a lot of grief from that, you know?"

"Really?" The incredulity was feigned but it didn't show. "Why what happened?"

"You, that's what happened! You just blew it up out of all proportions."

"No surely not," he said aghast, "I told it the way you said it to me, I'm sure of it."

"It was plastered three foot high across the front page Brian, it was a nothing story and you elevated it to nuclear meltdown, for Christ's sake."

"Okay," Brian sounded genuinely hurt now, "I appreciate that, in itself, there wasn't much of a story, but after you had given me the run-down on all the other sightings around the country I did a bit of digging. Besides, we've run stories about these cats before. It's not the first time you know. I just thought it would make a good story taken in context with all the other evidence."

"Yeah, but what evidence? A few dodgy pictures of black cats wandering across a field and ancient reports from way back when, which, I reckon you cribbed off a website all about them."

"That's as maybe, Tony, but you yourself said they were out there. All I was trying to do was raise their profile a bit, you know, in an 'inform the public' sort of way, make them aware of the possibility."

"Yes but did you have to make it… actually me, did you have to make me so public? A front page picture, 'expert says they're here'."

"Oh come on, it's not like you were the headline or anything."

"No, but there were other pictures inside; of me and the woman, quotes from her like I never heard, twisted out of all proportion I've no doubt, and ones from me for that matter."

"Look I don't print anything unless it's been said. I don't make it up you know." His voice wounded and shocked. *God I'm good*, he thought, as he heard the subtle change in Tony's speech.

"I know, I know… but you do embellish it, you can't deny it."

Tony was climbing down a bit from his lofty irritation. He knew he'd said those things, just not in the way Brian had reported them. How could anyone make, "I'm pretty sure they're, there," into **'expert says they're here'** sound so sensational, he couldn't imagine.

"Anyway Brian what is it you're after? I need to go."

"Oh yes, well I've just been up to the press conference about that poor little girl that's gone missing. Dreadful thing. Now that will be front page news tomorrow. Like me though, you'd want to help the poor family any way you can, I mean they were too distraught, to even talk to us!" Brian sounded amazed, as if the Bournemouth Evening Echo actually counted for something.

Are you surprised? thought Tony.

"As I said to Patrick, he's the Inspector in charge... Oh, I think you spoke to him, didn't you?" Brian didn't wait for the answer. "We really want to help if we can Pat, anything the paper can do, just say the word." The egging sounded sincere, but like Patrick, Tony suspected it was a real double-yolker.

"Look, where's this going Brian?"

"Tony, I know it's my job, obviously, to report everything, but please don't assume I'm here to try and catch you out or just grab a headline... I've got kids you know, one about the same age as little Martha," Brian paused and Tony thought he had heard real emotion at the other end of the phone. "I can't imagine what I'd do if it was one of mine."

Still ruffled by Brian, but perhaps more by his own naivety, Tony continued to listen.

"It's just that Patrick said he'd had a call from you, worried that this might have been another one of those incidences." Brian didn't want to use the words 'Big Cat'. Incidence' sounded so much better, less inflammatory, somehow. "He was very complimentary of you, by the way."

"Oh yes?" Once again the flattery was a little obvious but it had an effect. "How so?"

"Well, how you hadn't wanted to waste his time any more than necessary, as you knew he would be busy etc, with the case, and what you had to tell him was probably nothing, but you felt it your duty to call in."

Brian had, in fact, only got the one throw-away line from Patrick and he was now guessing how Tony would probably have broached the subject.

"Oh yes, he obviously took in all that you had said. Presumably, you're worried that it might still be there?"

"Well, yes, that was a concern. Not that I necessarily think this has anything to do with that little girl's disappearance, you understand," Tony said a little too hastily.

"No, No, of course not, but you must have felt there was something, otherwise you wouldn't have called the Inspector, right?"

For a moment Tony forgot whom he was talking to. "Yes, it's just with all the other things that have happened around the common, it just seemed more than coincidental."

Brian willed himself not to sound too interested, or indeed too excited.

"Oh yeah what's that then?" he said sounding almost bored, and hoped he hadn't overdone it.

Tony told him about the pets and animals that had been going missing, all around the common over the last few weeks, the attack, such as it was, on Cyril Kennedy, the dead deer, the Big Cat sighting up at Holt Heath, which he reminded Brian the Echo had covered. As he recounted them it didn't sound so impressive, but then added, "But now this has happened... I don't know. It all seems too coincidental."

"So you think this Big Cat might have taken her?"

The direct question sounded almost challenging and Tony stiffened. He had a very nasty feeling he'd just been had again.

"Come on Tony Give it a rest," was Jenny's imploring request. "What's done is done."

"I know, but all those questions that Brian bloke asked me. Why I didn't just put the phone down on him is beyond me," Tony agonized. "He was like this the last time. You'd have thought I'd have learnt my lesson by now!"

Tony had told Jenny, earlier that evening, that this was the same reporter that had written the piece on him and the Moors Valley story.

"Somehow that twat of an Inspector must have given him my name and old Brian, the devious little shit that he is, is probably going to drag it all up again."

Once again, Jenny felt a pang of guilty responsibility. After all, she had helped him come to the decision to make the call.

"Come on," she said. "There's nothing we can do about it now. Sticks and stones as our parents would have said."

She knew that wasn't going to cut it. Razor sharp words and weighted pictures could be almost as damaging mentally, as any physical violence. Such was the unrelenting world of fast news, Facebook, twitter and blog.

The television had done nothing to take his mind off it and, although the ten o' clock news was still mainly about Members of Parliament and their expenses scandals, a close second was the unfolding news of the missing child, Martha Docker. Even though the story had broken with the alert that morning, the journalists and press corps had been caught in the midst of other stories, and were slow to catch up, but by now were frantically searching for information. As little was forthcoming from official sources, it was reported without much depth. Access to the immediate family was still some way off. But the media machine was unstoppable and their insignificant and ordinary life was being picked over. Public records were being looked into, the neighbours would be questioned, the school where Ben attended would be found and the parents quizzed, as they took their children to school the next morning. Few stones would be left unturned. Stunned, shocked and with reluctance the Dockers would find themselves being inexorably propelled into gratuitous significance.

The sad fact of the matter was that the army of journalists and the informed populace would all come to realise, that after 'exhaustive' and 'in depth' investigations, the footprint that the child Martha Docker had left on the world, her stamp, her presence, indeed the provenance of her being was next to nothing. Her life so short, that apart, from birth and medical records, little detail about her existed. No school achievements or sporting triumphs, no work record or credit history, no mobile phone or internet presence. For her grieving parents there would be a few snapshots, a few video clips, digitised and filed to prove her real. Of course, little Martha would be 'hardwired' into their memories, painful and permanent and only fading as they grew old. But in the great scheme of things her actual being would be but a pixel on a universal screen. About her, therefore, there would be only scraps to tell… blonde, blue eyed, a sweet child, full of life, happy, wilful… but sadly…. gone. Save for the last three words it could have summed up any one of a million kids countrywide.

It was a Monday evening and they were into their second bottle of wine, unheard of in Jenny's book.

"Don't they just love it," Tony said, his voice filled with derision for the industry that was, news. "Why can't they just report it factually, tell us what happened, not what might happen or what could happen, or what they think is going to happen. It really winds me up."

"Well turn it off then," was Jenny's practical advice.

But, as if the effort to press the little red button was all too much, Tony just "harrumphed," and it remained on.

The news on the television turned into weather, and then to an uninspiring film. The couple lounged and snuggled up on the well-worn sofa; a hand-me-down from his parents. Tony's deadening right arm lay beneath her. His mind, now dampened with alcohol, was less outraged and the sense of a great injustice well and truly spent and it left the way open for baser thoughts.

"I take it," he grinned, looking down over her upturned head, his eyes playfully meeting hers in mock disapproval, "you're not going home tonight? AGAIN!"

Chapter 35

Tuesday June 2nd
Day 2 of investigation

It was eight-ten, when Inspector Stimpson and DS Connelly arrived to chaos on Heatherlands Avenue. Cars and light vans, some with network names on them, were parked haphazardly in every available space. Others, still trying to park, were cruising the narrow street with menacing intent. The media storm had arrived.

"Right, I want this fucking lot gone... yesterday," Patrick growled as he opened the door and made to get out. "Find somewhere to park, Tom. I'll have a word with whoever that patrol car belongs to." He nodded in the direction of the swamped police car outside the Dockers' house. "Get him to throw his weight around and clear this lot."

By the time Thomas arrived back at the Dockers' house, having parked the car around in another road, a few hundred metres away, Patrick was looking smug. He had found the PC lurking in the back garden, had detached him from the warm brew proffered by Sandra from next door, and instructed him to get the road cleared pronto.

"All right for some?" was Thomas's mildly sarcastic acknowledgement of the brimming mug.

They had come back ostensibly to try to speak to Daisy and John again. However, they felt it was still a little early to be knocking on their door and, so, decided to go through the back gate and on to the common. Patrick wanted to follow up on the theory he had thought about last night; chew it over with Thomas. As they walked in silence through the garden, towards the gate, the abandoned toys sent sobering messages to the two detectives and for a short while they were both lost in their own thoughts.

Patrick was reflecting that the briefing earlier that morning, back at the station, had seen most of the team there. Evidently, one or two could not be contacted late last night, hence their absence. After thanking them all for their attendance at this, 'ungodly hour', which drew a few acknowledging grimaces, Patrick had gone through his concerns and the reasons for the actions they were about to undertake, briefly explaining what he felt might have happened yesterday.

He'd concluded with, "Unfortunately, I don't hold out much hope that the child is still in the area." It was a realistic statement and it reflected what most of them already thought. "However, those re-visiting the houses today, you must be vigilant. You must question everything you see or hear that seems out of place. Don't allow yourselves to be taken in by what looks normal and mundane. See past it. Get under the skin of these people. Don't be unpleasant or rude, but be prepared to push them a bit. I want you to gain access to the grounds and gardens of these houses, I'd like," and he'd looked up from his notes at that point, to gauge his audience's reaction, "for you to coerce them, enlist their help, appeal to their better natures… whatever, into allowing you in to their houses. Explain that it will help to eliminate them quickly from any further investigation, the implication being, they're under suspicion. Tell them it's urgent and vital, that we satisfy ourselves, that their house is not implicated in any way."

He had stared out, this time making eye contact with as many as he could, in the hope that determination might be transferred by look alone, adding, "But remember, should anyone kick off, remind them a warrant can swiftly be arranged."

"So don't forget, I want to know," he'd raised his voice as people began fidgeting, some standing up as if to go, sensing the briefing was coming to an end, "houses with Gates. Who is the Guy in the Camouflage jacket? Empty properties and anything you're not happy about. Time, ladies and gents," he'd been almost shouting, "as always, is of the essence, and that is why we are going back now."

The office calmed a little, so he'd dropped his voice. "Just suppose that child had been taken by somebody in one of those houses." The readying movements had stopped and he'd seen a few questioning looks. "Forgetting the whys, for the moment, but maybe, just maybe, they haven't moved her on… we cannot afford to overlook that possibility…" He'd shot another purposeful look, "can we? Ok, go… Sergeant Ball I believe you are coordinating," and as a loud aside added, "and try not to ruffle too many feathers!"

Thomas broke the silence as they exited the troubled little property, the curtains still drawn, the insubstantial material helping to hold off a new day for the depleted Docker family.

"I spoke to the diving team late yesterday, just before they left. They hadn't found anything, but they still had another two smaller ponds to check today. They said they would be finished by lunch, easily."

"Right, that'll rule that out then," said Patrick, his mind still elsewhere.

"The more I think about it, Thomas, this has to be a planned abduction. It was all so quick… clinical. Anything else and somebody, somewhere, would have seen something. There's just too many people close by. They'd have made mistakes, and there'd be more of a trail." Shaking his head, he continued, "No somebody knew exactly what they were doing, and to have done that they needed to work out the most opportune moment. Which means - they were watching the Dockers."

As he spoke, Patrick was staring out into the trees, his eyes slowly sweeping the area at the back of the houses. "That would take some time, and where better to do it from than out here; the road's far too busy. Okay, let's put ourselves in their shoes."

For the next twenty minutes the two officers inspected the trees within a reasonable viewing distance of the Dockers' house. They were looking for something easy to climb and that, potentially, had a good view. They soon gathered that most of the tall pines were deficient in low branches, the race to have the dominant canopy seeming to have energised their sap at the expense of all else. After a few abortive attempts at scaling even the lowliest of heights, and with self conscious thoughts as to how their subordinates might view their antics, they were beginning to give up hope. All of a sudden though, Patrick came upon a tree that met all the right criteria. The once-lower branches were now just stubs and all but hidden by the lofty scrub through which the trunk had grown. Thomas very quickly climbed it and established that there was a perfect position from which to view three houses, the middle one being the Dockers'. The blue haze of foliage was not dense and Thomas guessed that' from his close perspective, any gaps appeared quite large, thus offering the almost expansive view, while from the houses, these would appear as narrow gashes in the canopy and would probably provide excellent cover for anyone sitting still.

"How do you feel? Exposed or concealed?" Patrick called.

"To be honest, I'm not sure? I feel a little obvious at the moment… night time wouldn't be a problem though. But during the day I would have thought you'd have to stay really still in order not to attract attention to yourself. It would be interesting to see what this would look like from say the kitchen or a bedroom. The gap I am looking through is not that wide, so it might afford enough cover."

"What if you were camouflaged in some way?"

"Of course, our mystery man with the bike. Well it could only help," agreed Thomas.

Aided by the knowledge of the various woody outcrops, his descent was more confident than the climb up and his powers of observation less distracted.

As he jumped from the last foothold to the floor Thomas brandished, with some triumph, a fragment of green cloth.

"I think I might hazard a guess as to what this is," Thomas said as he approached Patrick with the inch long piece of material dangling at eye level between thumb and forefinger; and adding, "snagged on a twig halfway up."

"Bingo" said Patrick in a self satisfied way. "I think you might just have confirmed our theory, Thomas."

"Right," Patrick was fired up now. "Tom, leave me to the Dockers and you get yourself round to the local Army surplus stores, there can't be that many. I want you to see if you can get a list together of anybody who has bought camo gear and, with a bit of luck, they might be able to identify what type of material this is. The design or pattern might narrow it down a bit and tell us how new or old it is. It's a bit of a long shot, many will pay cash, but some won't. Besides, a lot of these guys are probably regulars, let's see if we can get some names. When you have done that get it off to forensics."

"Might just be kids climbing trees, you know," Thomas said reasonably, but trying not to dampen any enthusiasm.

"Yes it might, but somehow, I doubt it. It's just too coincidental."

"Ok boss." Clutching the now encapsulated find, Thomas strode purposefully through the gate back into the little garden, pleased that, at last, he had something positive to chase down.

Chapter 36

Patrick reasoned with himself after checking his watch, "I know eight-forty five is still a little early but this has got to be done sometime, and the sooner the better."

It was highly likely the family wouldn't have had much sleep, if any, and what they had managed to snatch would've been fitful and next to useless. But he had to get on with it, they might not thank him now, indeed they might not have cause to thank him at all, but if he was going to have any chance in stopping this nightmare he needed to act now. Steeling himself for an interview, that would almost certainly be one of the worst he'd ever have to deal with, and wishing there'd been something positive to give them, he paused at the back door ready to knock.

It opened before he'd got the chance. The observant police liaison officer now entrenched with the family had seen movement through the frosting and, fearing the press might be getting restless, was on the attack. She quarter-opened the door and used her body to obstruct any view into the room. Quickly assessing that the need for such a shield was unnecessary she drew back, revealing to Patrick the huddle of people around the small table at the dining end of the kitchen. Patrick wondered if they had been there all night; as drawn, tear-stained eyes looked expectantly at the tall police officer moving self-consciously into the kitchen and the door closing behind him. They still hadn't given up all hope, Patrick judged, and that was clear by the flicker of animation as they laid eyes on him; faces dulling at his unchanging demeanour. Nobody spoke, the silence awkward and unnerving.

Patrick exchanged a glance with the female PC, before turning to the family.

"Look… I'm really sorry to disturb you so early," said Patrick finally, "but I was wondering whether I could speak with you all, individually…. I'd like to try and go through the events of yesterday just to see if anyone has anything new to tell us, or, maybe I can help jog a few memories with one or two questions." Patrick caught Daisy's eye and stretched his arm out gesturing towards the connecting door. "Perhaps we could go through into the living room, Daisy."

The liaison officer, Tracey, followed the Inspector's cue with a cocooning arm around her shoulders and a positive note, "Come on love. Let's see what we can do to help the Inspector, eh."

Patrick was grateful for the constable's warm professionalism, despite having had her work cut out for her and probably, *she too having been up half the night, as well,* he thought.

"I'll come with you," was John's flat response.

Daisy sat at one end of the three-seat chesterfield and tucked her legs under her, visibly shrinking back into the soft cushions as if trying to withdraw completely from the world, like just another lost item down the back of the sofa. Tracey sat next to her and John took the armrest, next to his wife. Patrick took the adjacent armchair, perching on its edge and swivelling to face Daisy, banished all thoughts of being a complete heel and concentrated on the young couple in front of him.

"Look Daisy, John, I won't deny it, but we are struggling on this one. We have very little to go on, and so anything you can think of, anything at all which might be relevant, you've got to tell us. We are working on the theory that Martha has been taken and, if there is any chance of getting her back, we have to act quickly before any trail goes cold." *Trail? You've hardly got a starting point,* Patrick reflected scornfully. Adding, "We are following up a few lines of enquiry as we speak so let's keep our fingers crossed, eh?" and hoping he sounded more positive than he felt.

"OK Daisy, I know this is going to be difficult for you, but do you think you could go through what happened yesterday again? Right from when you got up in the morning, through to when you realised Martha was missing."

Falteringly, Daisy recounted the events leading up to the moment she knew Martha had gone. It took her all of five minutes. Patrick watched her closely, *poor kids on automatic pilot,* he thought, but on reaching the fateful moment she broke down. She wept uncontrollably burying her head in her hands and turning to her husband's swift embrace. "I only left her for a couple of minutes," she wailed, her voice distorted; thick with tears and spittle. "I could hear her playing in the kitchen for God's sake!"

John tried to comfort her, but his unshaven face, Patrick noted, was a picture of bewilderment. Was it that he was unused to dealing with such raw emotion, or was he inwardly in turmoil at his wife's public guilt? Had she left the child for too long?

Patrick tried a different tack. "Try and think John... Daisy, was there anything unusual yesterday, out of the ordinary, did you see anybody ... somebody you know or don't know, perhaps, somewhere you wouldn't or shouldn't have expected to see anyone? In the street, when you went to work John, or before that, in the woods behind, when you drew back your curtains in the morning? .... Anything, no matter how trivial."

Patrick was aware his words had taken on a pleading tone and that he sounded almost desperate.

The couple shook their heads and remained resolute. "It was just an ordinary morning like any other," they agreed.

"I wonder," said Patrick a little hesitantly, cautious of the couple's possible reactions, "I wonder... whether we could talk to your son, Ben. You never know, he might have seen someone, kids are good like that."

As he half-expected, it brought on a fresh bout of tears. "He doesn't even know yet, Inspector, I mean how...what are we going to tell him?"

"It's Okay," Tracey clasped one of Daisy's damp hands, "I'll help you. We'll do it together, perhaps later when he's back from school. Yes?"

Once again, Patrick felt indebted to his colleague, having little idea as to how to answer that one.

"Tell me," he started on another pressing question, "Have either of you ever seen any one hanging around, walking, or cycling perhaps, on the common and wearing a camouflage jacket, say, within the last six months or before that even?"

The question seemed to spark something in John. "Why so specific? Have you got a suspect then?"

"No, nothing like that, but an old boy across the way has reported seeing such a person coming and going into the undergrowth on the common, not far from here."

The couple searched each other's drawn faces like some bizarre staring competition, each hoping that the other might remember something, a scrap of detail that might just be significant. Daisy lost, tears welled and she buried her head in John's fleece.

"We haven't seen anyone like that Inspector," croaked John, his throat tight with emotion.

"Okay, let's leave it there for the moment." Patrick glanced over to Tracey, "But if you do think of anything that has seemed strange, out of place in the last few days, somebody staring at you in a shop or at the pub, for example, anything at all, you let Tracey here know."

"Actually that's a point," John looked quizzical, uncertain perhaps whether to say anything.

"Go on."

"No, it's just," John hesitated again his mind weighing up its relevance. "Well we do know somebody who wears a camouflage jacket, only…"

Daisy lifted her blotchy red eyes towards her husband and it was clear to Patrick, by her questioning look, that she hadn't cottoned-on yet, as to whom he was referring.

"Please John," Patrick held the worried man's gaze and, in a kindly but determined voice, "allow me to sift through what is and isn't important. Who is this person?"

"He's a friend… actually a friend of Daisy's." Patrick noted the clarification. "We see him down the pub occasionally; he's been here a few times. Daisy used to be at school with him, same year, same class I believe. Always in a camo jacket. I don't think I've ever seen him in anything else."

"Yeah but Gary's a friend, John, as you said?"

It was difficult for Patrick to read the poor girl's expressions through the mask of despair, but he did feel that she was being somewhat defensive. And he got the distinct impression that John was not altogether in agreement with her thoughts.

"He's harmless," she continued. "He wouldn't do anything like this."

"Okay, perhaps I could have his full name and address just so that we can eliminate him from our enquiries?" With that Patrick scribbled the details in his notebook.

As John and Daisy left the living room to rejoin the others, still hunched around the table, Patrick caught John's eye.

"Just one other thing if I may, John," and he indicated to Daisy for her to carry on.

143

When they were alone Patrick spoke in hushed tones, "This Gary Brown, I got the impression you perhaps don't approve?" It was a leading question Patrick knew, and he had asked it somewhat provocatively, hoping to get some sort of a reaction.

"No, no, it's nothing like that Inspector." John's mouth tried for a smile and only just made it. "It's just that, I think he was a little sweet on Daisy back at school, he's a shy-ish bloke mostly. He's okay with Daisy now, known her a long time, I suppose. I don't see him as any threat, if that's what you mean. No, as Daisy says, he's harmless, a bit geeky and a pain when he latches on to you at the pub; can't get rid, if you know what I mean."

"I don't suppose when he visited here, he used the back gate did he? Only, the chap who reported seeing a man in combats said he'd seen him quite a few times heading in this direction."

"No, front door," the bewildered expression from earlier crept on to John's face. "Well, not when I've been here, I mean... I'm not aware that he's been here when I haven't."

Patrick could almost see the thought processes whirring in the man's head, eyebrows drawn down and wrinkles appearing on his forehead. Patrick could have kicked himself. He had no idea that the question, asked in all innocence, would set the poor man wandering down a different road, as co-incidental as it surely was, and, especially with everything else on his plate.

By eleven-fifteen, Patrick had finished talking with the rest of the family, with no significant advancement to his quest.

They'd seemed a tight-knit group; very close, and open with each other, and had not appeared to hold anything back from him either. He doubted there would be any skeletons in their cupboards. Despite this, discreet checks were already underway, back at the station, just to be sure.

He wandered back out, on to the common, and surveyed the scene. The search perimeter had been extended out since yesterday, the police tape stretched left and right of his field of vision and was now out to the gravel path, hugging it in a wide arc from the entrance at Heatherlands to the one at Fitzworth, a distance of nearly three hundred metres. The path was still accessible to the public but a uniformed officer patrolled along it, a token, to hold the flimsy plastic line. All the houses backing on to the common in this small area had also been taped off, nobody would be allowed through their gates for a while yet.

He called Sergeant Ball, on his mobile, who gave him a run-down of the significant finds from the house-to-house. Not that there was anything particularly significant. Depressingly, there were too many gates, and still a number of people out, although, they had taken liberties with their gardens and one empty house over on Christchurch Road. A car parked on the same road, by the field, had revealed that the horses' owner was there every day at about seven-forty-five am, to feed them, he had seen nothing. *Great!*

The feelings of frustration began to gnaw at his focus as he called in to the station, to see if Phillip Carver had returned home or been picked up yet. The negative answer did nothing to help.

"Get a search warrant organised for his flat will you? Let me know as soon as you have it".

As he finished the call, out of the corner of his eye, he could see the lead diving officer approaching. The head shaking was enough for Patrick to guess they too had found nothing. Good news?

He wasn't that sure.

Chapter 37

Day 2 Afternoon

"Shit," Thomas cursed loudly to no-one but himself as a rather large dollop of tuna, mayonnaise and red onion parted company with the bread, smearing his tie and looking like a well-aimed bird dropping. He had been en route back towards Ferndown, having visited the four local Army Surplus Stores and had pulled into a car park to consume the coffee and lunch, grabbed in town.

He dialled Patrick's mobile number and licked the tie clean while waiting for it to connect. The digital read-out told him it was near enough twelve-thirty.

"There's a lot of names here, Pat. I've asked those that can to send the information digitally as well. At least when they're on the computer we can try and prioritise them more easily. I have had a quick flick through them. Nothing jumps out at me though, no Phillip Carver or anything."

"Okay, speaking of which, I have organised a search warrant for his place. Come and pick me up and we'll go and pay his flat another visit."

"Righto boss, on my way."

Patrick was on his way back across the common heading for the Docker house again. He had taken a walk earlier, over to the vacant house on Christchurch Road, hoping that he might have spotted something to back up his theory of somebody just using it as a convenient and secluded parking space, with access to the common. The large bungalow had been in a bit of a state, he'd noted, as he'd peered in through the windows. The empty shell had been neglected both inside and out; loose roof tiles and falling gutters, flaking soffits and fascias, a couple of broken windows where the rain had entered, internally dampening wall paper and ceilings. The detective constable who'd called it in had done some homework calling in the estate agent, whose broken board he'd found. Gaining access, there had been nothing in the constable's opinion to suggest any suspicious activity and, apart from the two broken windows the integrity of the building remained solidly intact. He'd also learned that it had been sold to a couple returning to the country from working abroad. Nobody had set foot inside since they had viewed it some four to five months ago, with their architect. They were due back for good in about ten days and they had already got planning permission to drop the building and resurrect it as a two-storey, five-bed roomed, luxury home.

The driveway was secluded. Once anybody had turned in off the busy Christchurch Road, any car would have been well hidden. It was the last house in the row before the footpath he'd walked yesterday and the fields beyond. The house next door the other way was effectively hidden by an out-of-control Leylandii hedge.

Despite this advantageous aspect Patrick had found no obvious signs on the degraded, weed-infested tarmac of any recent traffic, motor or otherwise.

Around the back, the garden had been overgrown and it had been difficult to discern where the boundaries should have been. The long grass of a once-proud lawn, blurred at the edges by engulfing shrubs, was nearly knee high and spread throughout with scores of yellow dandelions beaming triumphantly. At the end of this colourful meadow was a wall of Rhododendrons, which at first glance seemed to signify the end of the garden. On closer inspection, Patrick had found a gap, an old path almost engulfed by the green invader. It had lead to a derelict summerhouse. Standing in the clearing in front of it, Patrick had been aware of the smell of damp wood, and mustiness associated with long forgotten items of humanity.

He had also been aware of another strong odour, pungent and foul. And looking around he could see evidence of what looked like dog or probably fox droppings. *Lovely*, he'd thought… but no gate. If there was one, it had long since been buried. Bang had gone that theory. *Still,* he had reasoned, *I suppose they could have used the driveway to park and then gone up the path at the side of the house.*

He remembered the secluded spot had been quiet and warm in the rapidly rising sun, and yet he'd felt cool - actually… chilled if he was honest about it; brought on by a strange sensation, like he was being watched. Whether it was the decrepit summerhouse, broken and lifeless, or the imposing plants looming high around him, menacing and, in a way, threatening, he hadn't been sure. But when he couldn't find the ragged tear in the foliage that had been his way in, he had begun to get a little flustered; the difficulty discerning it causing mild alarm. It was as if it had just closed up on him. When he finally spotted it, he was more than glad to push on through and swatting damp leathery protrusions away from his face, he'd moved with rising speed. He also remembered though, somewhat disconcertingly, the irrational need to be out of there, growing and became paramount. *Green's supposed to be calming* he'd remembered thinking, as a mild swelling in his throat galled like the first signs of imminent, *don't be ridiculous…* panic! And had he seen movement in the twisted wood and vegetation? There'd been brief glimpses and snapshots of something, as the sunlight flickered and strobed through the shadowy interior, but he couldn't swear to it. He'd burst out onto the meadow like lawn, the repulsed vegetation noisy and unsettling behind him and he hadn't look back until he'd reached the road. With nothing more positive to show for his efforts and still inwardly concerned at his over-reaction, he had decided to go back to the Dockers' House, where he would make contact with Thomas and cadge a lift back to the station.

On reaching the main gravel path and its flimsy Police barrier he could see, further up, the patrolling officer in conversation with an elderly lady accompanied by a yapping Jack Russell. Before he could duck under the tape, Patrick became aware that the officer was calling for him.

"**Inspector Stimpson**"…. Even though the common wasn't exactly hushed, the words still jarred the relative peace… "**Sir…. Over here.**"

"What's up constable?" he asked as he drew near, having covered the 100 metres or so at a brisk pace.

"This is Mrs Stone,"

Patrick gave an acknowledging smile in her direction and dropped his gaze to the noisy animal at her feet.

"My word, he's got a lot to say for himself."

Ignoring the persistent barking, the officer continued, "Mrs Stone has just handed this bracelet in. It's a medic alert. She says she found it early yesterday morning when she was walking her dog along this path."

"I see. Where exactly did you find it?" enquired Patrick. He wasn't overly excited. In fairness, people lost or dropped things all the time, much as the search yesterday had found: a couple of gloves (not a pair), a mobile phone, a pair of glasses, pens, a pen knife, not to mention all the usual detritus of litter from uncaring people, and all within the relatively small area they were combing. All had been bagged, and would be checked, but you could see from their condition, they'd been there a while, so it was doubtful they were connected to the case.

Mrs Stone was short and slightly stooped, had a pleasant smile and a kindly twinkle in her eye and was obviously pleased with her find.

"I would have taken it to the station next time I was in town, but what with all this going on, I thought to take advantage, you being here already. I don't suppose it has anything to do with what's happened, although," she hesitated, looking expectantly at the two policemen, "you never know, I suppose?"

"No, you don't," Patrick took the bracelet, allowing it to be dropped into an evidence bag he was holding open, "but we will look into it, rest assured, and thank you for being so diligent."

Her duty done, she pulled on the lead and made to go.

"Sorry, you didn't say where you had found it?" Patrick queried again.

"Oh it was just up there," she pointed with a bony finger to a spot, a few metres away, just off the path and in the direction of the exit on to Heatherlands Avenue. "It was in amongst the bracken. George found it really," and looking down proudly said in an exaggerated voice, "Who's a clever boy then?"

Time to go thought, Patrick. "Thank you once again," he said, and ducked under the tape.

Twisting the plastic bag around in order to read the tiny metal shield that held the details of the owner's vital medical condition, the name Gary Brown struck a chord, as Patrick remembered the conversation with John Docker earlier that morning.

"You again…. Coincidence?" Patrick asked himself. He was more than happy there were such genuine occurrences and, ordinarily, might have not paid much attention. Let's face, it loads of people walk here, why not the watch or the gloves they'd found, they could be equally as interesting. But no, if he hadn't heard that name this morning and the fact that this particular artefact looked recently lost (not weatherworn in any way) would it have raised the element of doubt in his mind.

Perhaps have a little chat with him later, find out if he knows he's lost it. He ought to, it's pretty important to him. Wonder if he has reported it missing yet?

Ten minutes later he was flopping gratefully into the front passenger seat of Thomas's car. The reporters clamouring outside the metal cocoon were ignored, as they drove off.

"Right, he said. "Back to the station, collect the warrant and then on to West Moors and our friend Mr Carver. And, depending on how long that takes…" Patrick sucked in some breath as if about to issue bad news. "You're not on a promise for an early night at home Tom, I hope?" Patrick said with a teasing smile on his face, "only I'd like to pay a visit to a Gary Brown later. His name has cropped up twice today. He's a friend of Daisy's… but probably not John's," he added as an after-thought. "His medic alert has just been handed in by a sweet little old lady who found it on the common, not a million miles away from the back of their house. It's probably nothing but we'll follow it up."

"Actually," Thomas looked surprised and excited, "I'm sure that name is on one of the lists I've just picked up. He's obviously into military stuff."

"Oh, did I mention he wears a combat Jacket as well," said Patrick with an annoyingly smug expression on his face.

"Talk about, wasting the best part of a morning," said Thomas somewhat aggrieved.

Patrick placated him, "I wouldn't worry about it, I've no doubt this Gary bloke is nothing to do with it, and he's supposedly a friend, after all. I'm sure those lists will come in handy."

Patrick went quiet for a few seconds, seemingly lost in his thoughts, then turned to his colleague with an expression of concern.

"You know Tom, three times his name has come up today. Is somebody trying to tell us something?" And grabbing the medic alert from his pocket he added, "In my book, three strikes and you're out. Let's go and pay him a visit right now, I'm sure Mr Carver will wait."

Chapter 38

The call centre operative at Medic Alert was naturally cautious about giving out any information as to Mr Brown's address, although the facts about his allergy to all tree nuts and his propensity to anaphylactic shock, was there for all to access, obviously.

"Mr Gary Brown?" Thomas asked, craning his neck up towards the ceiling, of the young man atop a sturdy ladder, with loaded brush in hand and concentrating hard on cutting in a warm yellow paint.

No-one had been in at his home when they had called but, fortunately, had found him through speaking with his next-door neighbour, who knew where he was working.

"Yep, that's me," Gary said without turning around. He wasn't being rude, just engrossed with the tricky job in hand. Indeed, he hadn't really taken in the formality of how his name had been said, so wrapped up was he. "Give me a sec. Just let me get to the corner."

It seemed to take forever to finish the last six inches, but finally he turned and viewed the two men gazing up at him. He looked to Patrick like some errant children's entertainer in his baggy overalls. The white all-in-one was heavily flecked with a frenzy of colour and around his ankles he had gathered in the trousers with elastic bands. The narrowing effect made his equally decorated and trainered feet look huge, like a clown. The bulky clothing had the opposite effect on the young man's head making it look unnaturally small and almost comical.

"You need a steady hand for that job, I imagine?" said Patrick as Gary descended looking a little perplexed.

"You from the council then?" It was a logical question. His boss had secured a contract with the local authority to repaint a number of their houses before being re-let.

"No... Police!" Thomas advised him with warrant card on full show at the end of his outstretched arm.

"The painting's not that bad, surely?" Gary said sheepishly, deploying a nervous grin, in an effort to engage the straight-faced officer in front of him.

"Looks fine to me," said Patrick acknowledging the joke with a smile. And holding up the bag with enclosed bracelet he asked, "Is this yours?"

"My Medic alert. Where did you find that?"

Genuine surprise thought Patrick; he doesn't seem to be worried that we have it.

"It was handed in to us," was Patrick's limited reply, not wishing to volunteer all the information. "When did you lose it?"

"I'm not sure… couple of days ago, sometime over the weekend anyway." He paused. "Trouble is, I hardly know I'm wearing it. I only ever take it off to have a shower. Actually," realisation lit up his face, "that would be it. I had a shower Saturday morning, didn't have it then. I must have lost it on my way back from the pub Friday night and didn't realise."

"Had a few had you?" The question from Thomas seemed somehow threatening to Gary.

"No, just a couple," was Gary's defensive reply, looking at Thomas in a way that clearly said what the fuck's it to you anyway.

"Look, Mr Brown, it's okay," Patrick began, holding up a hand, countering the hostility of his Sergeant. "We just want to know what you were doing on Poor Common."

Gary looked mildly aghast and the tiniest flicker of worry flashed in his eyes. Both officers caught it.

Gary composed himself quickly and looked quizzical. "What do you mean?"

"It's a simple question Mr Brown," said Thomas with eyes that didn't seem to blink as they bored into him making Gary look away. "Your bracelet was found on Poor Common. We just want to know how it got there."

Gary didn't like this hulk of a man; he was way too aggressive for his liking. *Where was he going with this? Why send two coppers about a missing bracelet. Shit,* do *they know about me? How?* Gary's insides were doing somersaults as he grappled with the thought he'd been found out. *Stick to the stock answers,* he reminded himself, *the ones he had worked out in case he ever got caught.*

"I expect," he said hesitantly as if trying to give it some serious consideration, "I must have lost it on the way back from the pub. It's a short cut. Y'know - through the common - from the pub to my house on Dudsbury Drive."

"Which pub, and what time were you there?" asked the unsmiling Thomas. Patrick had backed off, he'd seen that his colleague had touched a nerve and was happy to see where it went.

"The Angel, bout half nine…ten maybe. I'm often in there."

"And where were you Monday morning between the hours of seven and eight?"

"In bed I should think," he gave a snort of indignation, "if I'd got any sense." Seeing that yet another attempt to lighten the proceedings wasn't going to win over the big bastard, Gary added quickly, "Uhm, I got up at seven-thirty had a quick breakfast and was out of the house by about eight-fifteen."

"To where?" Thomas asked curtly.

It was dawning on Gary pretty quickly, by the fresh line of questioning, that this had nothing specifically to do with him - as yet, and all to do with what had happened to little Martha. Losing his medic alert on the common had brought them to his door; obviously they were just looking at all connections around the family and of course, their house backed on to the common, as well he knew. He'd need to be careful. Don't want to give the game away with offering too much information. On the flip side, though, he wanted to be seen helping Daisy in any way he could. That ought to deflect any nasty suspicions.

"To work, here," he said looking around him relaxing visibly. "It takes me fifteen minutes on my bike."

"I see," said Thomas, "Can anyone vouch for you before you got here?"

Gary looked worried again. Well, my mum was at home before I left. She'd tell you I was there."

What had occurred to Gary was that his mum had had a few the night before, and had not surfaced before he'd gone out. Surely she'd have heard him getting up and moving around. He bloody hoped so!

They would check his alibi shortly but Patrick tried a different approach, "So you're often on the common then?"

"Well, like I said, it's a quick route home from the pub."

"Wouldn't it be easier by road, assuming it's dark when you leave the pub?" Patrick reasoned, "I mean there's no street lighting on the common. The gravel path might be flat enough but that first part would be very tricky."

"Yeah, well," he paused as if he didn't have a valid answer for this. "I've got lights you know," and as if to prove his point he said more forcefully than he meant to, "Bloody good ones as well."

"Is this yours?" Thomas swiped the jacket from the chair it was draped over and held it up for Patrick's benefit, as if displaying some piece of evidence in court.

"Yeah, so?" Gary was becoming wary again. *Why are they asking about my jacket. What relevance has this to Martha's disappearance?*

"The thing is, Mr Brown," Patrick peered purposefully at Gary. "We have a witness that claims to have seen a man wearing camouflage clothing, and probably riding a bike, and on numerous occasions too, coming and going into the undergrowth on the common just behind the house where that little girl went missing yesterday. Who's to say that isn't you?"

"Wh..what!" Gary blustered. *I don't fucking believe this*; they were actually connecting him with the taking of Martha! *How the fuck did that happen?* The windows in the empty room were wide open to dissipate the paint smells but Gary became uncomfortably warm. He felt his cheeks flushing, as he realised that, despite all his cautious planning, he was in deep shit. Casting his eyes over the array of decorating equipment on the floor, as if searching for something, he avoided the two officers' persistent gaze. He was going to have to be careful what he said. Turning sharply, and knowing he was still under scrutiny, he looked at Patrick, believing him to be the softer option.

"Oh come on... I know Daisy," eyes widened with a wounded innocence, "we've been friends since school. I'm gutted for her, like everyone else round here." Adding, more defiantly than he felt, "You can't really think I had anything to do with that, surely?"

Meanwhile, Thomas had lifted the jacket to eye level and twisted it around, examining the sleeves and pockets and hems. He couldn't see any obvious damage, but they would let keener eyes at the forensics lab see if they could get a match.

"So," Thomas said, drawing Gary's imploring eyes away from Patrick. "If it's a short cut home why waste your time climbing trees?"

Shiiiit, thought Gary, shocked at the certainty of the statement. He flustered again, "I... I don't know what you're talking about."

Both Patrick and Thomas had felt there was a whole heap more to the story than Gary was letting on and the barely concealed panic on the young man's face had sent a look between them. A knowing glance that clearly said, this could be it....

They took him back to the station to formally interview him. Piling the pressure on whilst he was still reeling from their initial approach, they had found out he had no previous convictions or indeed any run-ins with the police at all. Not that that meant anything, but if he hadn't been inside a police station before, that extra strain might just tip the balance in their favour.

Unfortunately though, the short car ride had given Gary time to think. He wasn't daft, and the fact that Thomas had asked him, in the car, why a piece of his camouflage jacket had been found in a tree, very close to the scene of the crime, left him in no doubt they were just fishing. Nobody had actually seen, him, he was sure of that and, besides, that jacket wasn't damaged. He knew that too. But it was cold comfort; he was about to be questioned by these two morons and it could get bloody tricky from here on in. "Keep calm," he told himself. "They've got nothing on you and, if you stick to your stock answers, they still won't have."

Chapter 39

Tony already felt somewhat at a disadvantage. Not only was he knee-deep in foul-smelling water, the colour and consistency of crude oil, but his rubber gloved hands were tight around a substantial branch beneath the vile water line. His two Ranger colleagues were similarly engrossed with the watery obstruction, when the unsuitably dressed pair started asking questions from the water's edge above.

"Hi there," one said, his sharp fashion shoes already suffering from the waterlogged surroundings.

"I'm sorry, you shouldn't be here. You need to stay on the path over there," John the senior ranger pointed.

"Oh Right, only we were looking for Tony Nash."

"That would be me," Tony said warily and feeling like he wasn't exactly dressed for, whatever occasion this was going to be.

"We just wanted to ask you a few more questions about the Echo article."

Something in the way they had said it, told Tony this was not about the story two years ago and, fearing the very worst, asked forcibly, "What article?"

With that, the other held out a copy of the local rag they had brought with them. Tony started climbing out of the ooze, slipping and sliding on the partially submerged bank. He peered at the article and glanced up at the date in the corner of the page, confirming it was that day's.

"Oh great!" he sighed, resignation heavy in his voice. Not thankfully front page, he noted, nor a whole page, but halfway down page four was a two column piece with the old picture from last time, suitably cropped to a headshot with the mini-headline. 'Big Cat Danger, warns expert ranger.'

"You've got to admit, it's catchy, Tone", smirked John.

Far from amused, Tony speed read the article. It didn't actually say that the child, Martha, had been taken by a big cat but it might just as well have done. It read…

Moors Valley Ranger Tony Nash has warned of a possible danger to the public, particularly young children, from what he believes are big cats, such as: puma, lynx and panther that are roaming the British countryside.

Over the years, the Echo has reported such sightings and, indeed two weeks ago, we reported a sighting on Holt Heath. The Ranger asserts, "They are here. How or where they come from, no one is sure." He went on to explain his worry that the close proximity of these sightings to a major conurbation should be taken far more seriously.

We also have it, on good authority, that the Ranger was concerned enough, in light of the recent tragedy of missing toddler, Martha Docker, to contact the police yesterday, advising them, that he believed her disappearance might be the result of just such a possible scenario.

Understandably, the officer in charge of the investigation, Inspector Stimpson, would not be drawn to make a comment on this particular point, but he did say, "All 'creditable' information would be followed up by his team."

"What makes you so sure, Tony, that little Martha was taken by a big cat?" the shorter of the two asked.

Tony gave them a quick once over, and the image that sprung to mind was a likeness of the entertainers Morecambe and Wise, only in reverse; the shorter and scruffier bespectacled one with the cheerful and engaging smile, opposite the taller, neater and more dapper, also with an equally pleasant smile. Remembering how he'd been taken in by Brian Maidment at the Echo, and guessing that these two were also press, Tony's intended mindset was clam-like. He wouldn't be rude or get angry; he'd just ignore them and get back to work.

"Look guys," Tony said in a way that he hoped would appeal to their better natures. "As you can see, we are right in the middle of shit creek," smiling as he said it and gesturing behind him to the inky pool, still bubbling as pockets of trapped gas made it to the surface. "And so, I'm really not interested to talk. OK?"

"No, absolutely fine. Perhaps we can catch up with you later, after work maybe? Buy you a drink? Presumably you live around here?"

"No, Parley," Tony answered; a little thrown by the fact they were not going to try to extract anything further.

"Oh, not far from the common where the girl went missing, then?" the 'Wise' look-a-like asked.

"Where do you recommend we can get a decent pint over that way then?" the other half of the double act enquired with apparently genuine intent.

Without stopping to think Tony said, "The Angel's good," knowing as the words left his mouth, he'd just dropped himself in it, yet again. He turned away, cursing under his breath and vowing not to go in there for a few days. *You're not gonna catch me that easily,* he thought.

Chapter 40

After a two-hour session with Gary the feeling that he was hiding something grew stronger in both the detectives' minds.

"It's bloody frustrating. There's something he's not telling us," Patrick railed at Thomas. "I know it. I can feel it in my water, same as you".

"Yeah, it's surprising what three mugs of tea will do to ones intuition." Thomas smiled ruefully as he knocked on the door of sixteen Dudsbury Drive, Gary's home.

"Mrs Brown?"

With the introductions and formalities taken care of by Patrick, Trisha Brown led the two officers through into the lounge at the back of the house, worry written all over her face.

Patrick had told her that they had Gary back at the station and that he was helping with their enquires. The stock line did nothing but heighten her concern.

She confirmed what Gary had told them about the morning of the first of June. Although she hadn't seen Gary yesterday morning, she'd heard him get up and go to work; her timings she explained were a little fuzzy.

"Bit of a hangover." she grinned coyly at the hunky looking copper. "A night out with the girls so, as you can imagine, not quite 'with it', if you know what I mean."

Both men had been somewhat taken aback when Trisha had opened the door, not that they had any preconceptions as to what 'Gary's mum' would look like but they weren't ready for the vision that confronted them. At 41, still relatively young, and despite a none too healthy lifestyle, she had kept her figure. Mature, but curvy in all the right places. Heavier than she would like, but in reality only a little overweight and, at 5' 10" she carried the extra 'naughty pounds' extremely well. Naturally a strawberry blonde, her shoulder-length shiny hair framed a still pretty face. Clearly, time had taken a gentle toll but with her usual care and much practiced skill with make-up, at best, she could have been one of those more mature models in Vogue or Marks and Spencers, and at worst, your local buxom barmaid, offering an attractive distraction, to the male population of all ages. Although Patrick had seen this obvious 'danger' he was determined not to be diverted, unlike his Sergeant whose attention was evidently being toyed with.

The conclusions they'd come to after what Patrick had felt was an unnecessarily long chat with the fulsome Mrs Brown, was that Gary was still very much in the frame. Not only was his mother probably an unreliable alibi but, also, the picture she had painted of Gary's life, to them, seemed narrow and warped. Unintentionally, she was doing him no favours.

Patrick's initial summation would show a profile of a quiet man, aged twenty-four, five-foot-ten, stick thin, single and still living at home with his divorced mother.

And, by the sound of it (they hadn't been able to get into his room to verify this yet), a bit of a geek by all accounts, with hobbies of computers, electronic games like Playstation and X Box, watching television and films. Not exactly reclusive, he seemed to have a couple of friends, but evidently comfortable with his own company for a fair amount of the time.

Thomas had expressed a wish to check out the computer later, saying, "Should make for interesting viewing. I bet you any money he has an extensive porn collection." Patrick was more than inclined to agree.

The locked bedroom was an annoyance. Trisha had explained it allowed Gary his privacy, as if he had his own flat.

"He's got everything he needs in there, pretty much," she'd said with more than a hint of pride.

Clearly there wasn't a lot coming into the household, Patrick assessed, but between them they had managed and the house was clean and tidy.

"En-suite shower-room, telly, kettle, fridge, he eats with me though... sometimes anyway," the bubbly dialogue momentarily wistful and sad. "It's nice to have the company," she'd concluded.

Frustrated by the locked door, and the fact that Gary, didn't see why his mother should have a set of keys, meant that entry would be a top priority for Patrick and Thomas. Both were certain the security was way over the top for just a bedroom. Surely it would reveal all, just as soon as a search warrant could be issued.

They'd also learnt that Gary's father had walked out on them when Gary was sixteen. Jack Brown, "Jack the lad, huh, Jack the bastard!" Trisha had revised with spiteful derision born of half a lifetime of abuse. The bullying, both mental and physical was fuelled by booze and both of them had suffered over the years. When Jack had left for a younger model, she could not believe their luck.

It was a few minutes past six when Patrick and Thomas rolled back into the station. The summer sun was still hanging in there, spreading warmth and light, as expected from the still lengthening days. Despite the early start and full day, the two detectives were still buoyed up, a credible suspect in the hold, and with a prospect of a night in the cells to soften him up. By morning, forensics should have matched the fabric and with help from the eye witness (maybe?) yes, hopefully they could be getting somewhere? For some reason though, neither felt that Gary had actually snatched the girl, although they hadn't discussed it greatly. They were, however, certain he was involved. Information gatherer perhaps, lookout even, his local knowledge a great help to those probably from further afield.

The thought of others, reminded Patrick somewhat annoyingly of another sicko. "You up for another excursion Thomas?" determination clear in his voice. "Phillip Carver."

Chapter 41

"I like it," Jenny said, a playful smile lighting up her face, in marked contrast to the misery guts sitting opposite her. "Ranger Danger. Catchy…don't you think?"

"Oh don't you start," he said rolling his eyes dramatically.

They had decided to meet in a pub at what Tony had described as 'a suitable distance away'.

"The Echo does reach the depths of outer Wimborne," she'd said sarcastically to him on the phone as they discussed the choice of hostelry.

He had briefed her about the run-in with the two reporters and the Echo piece, suggesting. "We need to keep clear of the Angel for a few days, let things die down a bit."

So they'd met in an out-of-the way place about a mile, as the crow flies, from the centre of the little county town. It had a spacious bar, which, at six-thirty was unsurprisingly empty, save for a group of noisy lads playing darts and making a very good attempt at creating a lively atmosphere.

They had found a table outside in the sunny garden. Tony had flopped dejectedly into the solid wooden chair, stretching out his long legs and letting his bottom slide to the edge so that he was angled to make the most of the early evening rays. Jenny read the article that Tony had chucked in front of her, listened to his gripes and whinges, made a few attempts at gentle ribbing and, after half an hour, had told him that it was probably best if he left it alone now, particularly as the meals had just arrived at the table. With the benefit of some time away from the subject, and swapping pleasantries about each others' day, Tony lightened up.

They chatted on for a while, Jenny about a couple of cute stray dogs that she had picked up recently and Tony about his propensity for mud baths and the fun he had had clearing the stream earlier in the day.

"Oh I know what I was going to tell you," she said animatedly, suddenly remembering it. "I did a bit of googling the other day, when I had a few moments free at work,"

"Oh yes," Tony managed, looking perplexed.

"You know!" she said, exasperatedly, struggling to get a piece of paper out of her pocket. "Dogs mating with foxes. I said I would look it up to see if it's possible."

"Oh yeah," he said. *That was bloody days ago, surely he wasn't expected to guess from such a casual thread?*

"To be honest, I had the usual dilemma, what's the best way to phrase it? It seems to me, you type in what you think is reasonable, hopefully getting right to the point of your query, only to find, that it appears the first pages are way off the mark and there are billions of hits."

Tony cut in, "So, not much luck then?"

"Actually, it wasn't too bad. I typed in the question, 'can dogs and foxes breed?' and got back specific answers, trying to deal with it. However... bear with me, my notes are not that brilliant... I was hoping for some sort of definitive answer." She began to unfold a sheet of A4 paper. "Perhaps, from a renowned scientist or David Attenborough, even. But all there appeared to be was loads of attempts at answering it through media sites and chat rooms, wiki answers and the like. So as you might expect, the answers ranged from: the ridiculous and bizarre, to genuine attempts, albeit probably unsound."

Tony looked a little puzzled, "So did you reach any conclusions?"

"Well, after reading through a lot of this nonsense, I did come across a site that seemed to be more authoritative; indeed a number of people on the social forums had referred back to this site. Even still, it wasn't a scientific institution or university, and the name," Jenny paused trying to remember, "something like 'Messed up world' or 'Messed up animals' Anyway," she giggled, hands flying out as if owning up to one of her 'dippy' moments, "I forgot to write that bit down but, as I say, it did seem to know its stuff and it, too, referred back to 'legitimate' references. Basically, it said there was anecdotal and unconfirmed evidence, of dog-fox hybrids, termed 'dox', and that Gamekeepers of old used to claim that Terrier bitches could produce offspring with dog foxes, and that these hybrids were stronger and more vigorous than either parent."

Tony's quizzical nature was beginning to perk up. "Gosh, that does sound interesting. Anything else?"

"Yeah. Hang on though," she said in an attempt to quell his excitement. "There were other links and sites, some saying it was possible, some adamant, it wasn't. One link I went to, was written by a Senior Fellow at a Department of Molecular Biotechnology, it didn't say of where, but his area of science was Genetics. Quoting a reference from Mammalian Hybrids, he seemed to suggest that all species of Canis have been known to hybridise in captivity and, although the fox and dog have diverged greatly over thousands of years, and their respective chromosome levels are different, something like 78 for dogs and 36 for foxes; that, in itself, wouldn't necessarily be a barrier to breeding. He did however sum up 'that a dog-fox probably isn't viable.'

At this point, Jenny showed Tony her notes, saying, "See, that last statement to me," she carried on, "sums up all the information I've found and read. Nobody seemed to give a definitive yes or no. I couldn't find any scientific journal or paper specifically about this and the Biotechnologist, himself, said he wasn't aware of, or had found, a general resource for this dilemma. So maybe it is possible?" She looked at Tony, shrugging in a, 'what do you think', sort of a way.

"So what we're saying is... that the old lady over at Homewood House... what was her name?" Tony looked to Jenny for help.

"Mrs Thomas".

"Allowed her dogs to mate with a fox and bingo we have a new animal, a dox."

"Well, a hybrid, yes. But I think the point is that - as according to that last bloke I quoted said, the artificial conditions created, had to be just right. In this case, the foxes being fed by her and probably alongside the dogs, for some time; possibly years, might have allowed it to happen."

Tony's eyes lit up as he picked up the thread. "And that walled garden of hers, secluded and private, with hardly any dangers to growing cubs, would be an ideal melting pot of conditions for the natural order to be..." he struggled for the right word, "interfered with. Let's face it, occurrences in the wild would be very, very unlikely. Foxes only have a narrow window to be in season, so mating with a domesticated dog just wouldn't be feasible."

"Exactly," Jenny agreed. "Most dogs are closely controlled by their owners and besides, physically, most are too big or too small. But her pit-bulls, by coincidence, were not that much bigger than a fox and you'll remember the gamekeeper folklore about terriers." She paused to let Tony find his way to the answer, and said as she could see it registering. "Pit-Bulls are Terriers."

Tony was hooked and was barely able to contain his excitement, feeling this could be something really exceptional. Besides, discovering such a rarity, he imagined, might go a long way to settling some old scores.

Jenny had continued, reminding him of the similarities between the fox cubs, or doxes she presumed they had seen, with the Pit bulls of Betty Thomas. "Their mottled brown coats are so like her dogs, and that fox, the one I saw on the wall when I was collecting them, his was the same, I'm sure." She paused, trying to replay the moment in her head, but as if the clip had been time sensitive, she could only conjure a somewhat corrupted version. Frustrated, she added, "I do remember at the time, though, commenting on how big he was; actually, not taller necessarily, just more solid, perhaps."

"Mmm," Tony said absently, only half-listening to her last sentence.

"Ok," he said, as if finalising some inner argument, "here's what we're going to do. Tomorrow, you and I are going to track these doxes down and get a really good look at them, get some photos if we can. We need to get some hard evidence. What happened to the dogs by the way?"

"They, I'm afraid won't be any good to us, put down a few days after, just too wild." As if reading his thoughts, Jenny added, "Cremated. So what time shall we meet up, six-thirty, seven maybe?" she asked.

"No, we need to be earlier than that."

"Well, I don't finish work tomorrow until..." her voice trailed off as Tony raised his eyebrows, playfully.

"**You** have **got** to be joking," she said slowly and deliberately, eyes wide, her face distorted in disbelief. "Mornings are bad enough at seven-thirty, let alone some other ungodly hour."

"Sun-up's at five," Tony confirmed with a smile, he was enjoying the moment. "We should be on site about then."

When it finally sank in that she would have to get up at four-thirty am, Tony said, "We'd better go and pick up your jarmies…" and laughing, added. "Cheer up girl, you've pulled!"

******

An unpleasant nightmare involving his daughter and a huge black cat had woken Patrick Stimpson from an already fitful night. As he slipped back into sleep, his dream's other tormentor, Tony Nash, was trying to coax a reluctant Jenny out of bed.

"Five more minutes" she implored sleepily nuzzling up to the warm body next to her. "Come on. It won't take us that long to get ready." She slid a naked leg over his thigh and rubbed sensuously, "I'm sure you'd really rather stay here?"

"I would," agreed Tony, a wicked grin just breaking on his lips, "but this is probably the best time to see those foxes. So shift your butt." And with that, he threw back the covers exposing them both to the cool air, and clambered out.

"Tony!" she exclaimed, taken aback by the sudden loss of warmth.

What is it with him, she thought, *he's not normal. I'm offering it on a plate, but he'd rather get up in the middle of the night and watch some mangy animal!*

Chapter 42

Wednesday June 3rd

Tony was still smiling as, resting their backs against a substantial tree trunk, they sat down on the plastic-backed rug. Their slightly elevated position overlooked the series of ponds on Poor common. He was full of anticipation and in excellent spirits.

"If we sit still here, and watch the ponds as the sun comes up, I reckon we might see them," Tony explained.

Jenny, however, was not looking that impressed. Outside of the sparse tree canopy the inky sky was already being replaced by a dull grey half light.

"Not exactly warm," Jenny commented dully.

Tony glanced at his watch.

"Five minutes past five," he said. "In theory the sun's already up, but I suppose with the trees behind us it'll seem darker for a few minutes longer. Anyway you've got your thermals on."

She ignored him; the boyish optimism wasn't generating any warmth in her direction.

Imperceptibly the view he'd promised was revealed, capturing her attention by degrees. Shapes sharpened and dark masses became more obvious as the shadows were chased away. Trees, bushes and clumps of grass became discernible and recognisable for what they were; pine, birch, rowan and holly, or the bulrushes and flags in the black voids of the ponds. By night the hidden depths were sinister and moody, but as lighter tones eased across the calm surface, they became mirrored and reflective.

It had rained continually through the night, stopping only a few moments before Jenny and Tony were leaving his flat. Consequently the morning felt damp but refreshed. As more of the picture unfolded Tony began pointing things out and Jenny's eyes were opened to a world she hardly knew.

"The early morning is such a magical time," Tony whispered; his eyes filled with a passion for his subject. "You never know what you might see. I often wonder at the similarity of this scene, to one in Africa or the rain forests; the water holes an attraction for almost every living thing. You could almost imagine wildebeests, Zebra or Gazelles drinking cautiously at the edge…. Not here obviously," he grinned, "mores the pity, but I've seen deer, badger, foxes all manner of birds, all doing exactly that, coming down to the watering hole to get a drink."

They stared out quietly for a few minutes, in hushed silence, savouring the stillness and in wonderment that humanity was stirring less than a hundred metres away. The only real noise was the occasional patter of water hitting the ground as a bird leaving the canopy disturbed the retained moisture. As the light prompted further awakenings so came the bird song, choruses heralding the new day becoming noisy and dominant. A squall of urgent squawking and flapping of wings burst onto the scene as a blackbird chased another through the wet undergrowth. In the rushes of the pond there was another squabble and the dark brown spikes shook unnaturally.

By six-thirty the sun was almost quartering the sky and stabbing the watery clearing with shafts of gold. Jenny looked across the main pond, and the broad strip of land surrounding it, to the fences some seventy metres away. She could see now, how close the houses were, and yet, this little oasis was alive with life. And she guessed, most of it would remain unseen by the occupant's just metres away; shuttered behind their artificial barriers and busily getting on with their own lives. If it hadn't been for Tony, she would still be one of them. *The poorer for it,* she realised.

"Can you see up there on the trunk of that tree?" Tony pointed to a huge pine some ten metres away, "That's a little tree creeper." The tiny bird seemed to be hugging the bark as it made short hops, climbing higher as it probed the deep wrinkled crevasses of the conifers protective layer, searching for insects.

"If you could spend twenty-four hours here, just watching," Tony continued his near silent commentary, "It would be fascinating as to what you could, or might see."

"A fox would be good," she said smiling. "Or a big cat," she said half-jokingly.

"Yeah, I'd forgotten about them," Tony said, looking thoughtful for a moment, all vagaries of newspapers, journalists and phantom felids swept aside by this new quest. "Let's forget them." Tony swiped a hand in front of him as if sweeping them aside, "I tell you what though, it would be quite something if we had proof of this dox creature," he whispered, "particularly if, as you say, it has never been proven in the past and nobody really knows if it's possible or not."

"Well we've got to see one first," she said scathingly and thinking, *just whose going to be brave enough to tell the world?*

As they chatted, more birds flew in and around the pond area: a spotted woodpecker drummed a few trees down, wood pigeons perched high in the branches cooed and flapped their wings noisily, a crow squared off against two magpies.

Suddenly, there was a loud skaaaak, literally a few metres off to their left; the witch-like shriek shattering the gentle tranquillity. Jenny, jumping a mile, gripping Tony's arm and looking suitably perturbed, began, "What the f-?"

It had taken Tony by surprise also, only because the harsh sound had come out of nowhere, but he knew exactly what it was.

"Jay," he said before she had time to finish her expletive. "Look there it goes." He pointed at a buff coloured flash as it flew straight and level, from their side of the pond to the other, alighting on a spindly Rowan sapling, still covered in creamy white flowers. A second Jay followed, bending the twiggy plant and forcing them to fly off again, their bright blue wing patches in stark contrast to the dull brown.

What Tony and Jenny hadn't realised was, the Jays had originally been sitting on a low branch and had been startled by a movement on the damp ground below. A few seconds later, Tony caught in his peripheral vision, the exaggerated swish of bracken as it was shoved to one side, beneath the now vacant perch. The tall plant was amongst lesser specimens and so stood out above the swathe of green. The movement was not natural. Something had definitely brushed into it as it passed. Whatever it was could not be much more than half a meter tall, the stand of bracken giving lush cover.

Tony raised his hand slowly pointing in the general direction saying, "Something's coming, over there." The hushed and excited voice sent shivers up Jenny's spine as she too saw more shoots sway positively. She tensed, even though knowing it was probably something innocuous.

"What do you think it is?" she asked, hardly daring to speak.

"No idea yet," replied Tony without turning, his eyes fixated on where he expected it to break cover. But nothing happened.

After about a minute, Tony breathed, "There."

A brown snout, barely visible just inside the vegetation, was ever so slowly easing its way out. The animal was clearly sniffing the air, its senses alerted to the unfamiliar smells it was detecting.

"Fox," Tony said, and although barely audible, Jenny could hear his excitement in that one snatched word.

Transfixed now, they sat willing the animal to come out. The unseen vibes seemed to coax it forward. In reality it had given the area the all-clear despite the earlier agitation. It moved swiftly, followed by two others, in an oblique direction away from them, as if to move around the main pond.

"Look at the colour," Jenny almost squealed. "It's them."

Tony got the impression that the lead fox was aware of their presence and seemed unconcerned. As if to confirm this, the fox stopped, the others immediately following suit. His body was still pointing in the direction of travel, but angling his head towards where the two humans were sitting, gave them a long contemptuous stare.

Thrown a little by the belligerent attitude, and the almost challenging glare, Tony had to force himself to focus on the creatures, taking in the detail, searching for differences that might separate them from the norm. This, he found was a difficult task. Apart from the colour, which was different - a mottled brown; dark, dirty looking; the different shades flecked with black rather than red-brown, like one might expect - it still had a bib, albeit a filthy white. The shape of the body was perhaps chunkier, but the low slung tail as it moved, the pointed ears, the sharp snout tipped with a dark button, all said fox. He wished he had a normal fox with which to compare it. Outwardly, and somewhat disappointingly, Tony couldn't see any earth-shattering anomaly that would shout out 'I'm different'; no sabre-tooth-like fangs or giveaways as to an alternative parentage. He managed to capture a few pictures on his digital camera, although he knew they wouldn't be much good. The zoom was naff, not like those he'd researched, and had promised himself he would get, one day.

The skulk moved off. Their warning had been given. Tony and Jenny sat compliantly routed to their spot; neither having the urge to move anyway. They watched as the little group trotted off through the sparse undergrowth. As they passed a fallen tree, its trunk fully prostrate on the ground Tony registered that the animals were much the same height as the thickest part. From where they were sitting, he judged the tree was on ground, almost at the same level as them. With that knowledge he made a note to go and check what sort of height this might make the fox, intending to use the trunk as a point of reference.

"Wow," said Jenny, as they both relaxed, their stiffened and more upright bodies, sliding back in unison to rest against the hard wood behind them. "Did you see the way it looked at us?" she continued. "It was as if he was saying 'I know you're there. Stay put, or else.'"

"Yes, I think I got that impression too," he said thoughtfully. Then something else registered. "Listen."

Away in the distance, they could hear, the dull sound of traffic, background noise, the occasional faraway shout, a light aircraft whining overhead.

"What?" Jenny looked perplexed.

"Where are the birds?"

She turned her head to listen. Unable to detect any, she peered out across the pond and up into the sparse canopy overhead. It was as if someone had pressed a button; no twittering or chirruping, nor cooing or screeching. It was uncanny.

"When did that happen?" she asked.

"I'm not sure; I've only just noticed it."

With that, Tony got to his feet. "Cmon," he said holding out his hand to offer support to Jenny. They walked over to the fallen tree and, lining himself up at the point where the animal had passed, Tony gauged the height, holding his downward-facing palm against his leg at the same level. "Its shoulders a bit below my knee" he said. "What do you reckon? About half a metre... maybe?" thinking... he would need to check on the average height of a normal fox to see if it had any significance. Despite that, the impression he was left with, when he looked down again at the point on his leg, and using the estimated dimension to try to assess in his mind's eye, the creature's length and width; *dox or fox, if this measurement is right, that's some bulky animal. The idea played in his head for a while ... and definitely bigger than a normal fox I'm sure*, he debated with himself. He was aware now of muted birdsong. It was a notch above the subliminal, and on the increase, as a twinge of anxiety crept in, and he said to Jenny, "I reckon," he paused momentarily, as if still trying to work something out, "it **is** bigger than the average fox, and you know what..." He spoke deliberately, choosing his words carefully. "I'm not sure I would be wholly comfortable, around a wild animal that size."

Chapter 43

"Pat?" The Inspector knew that voice and winced inwardly. "You got a sec?"

On Turning, Patrick glanced at his watch and pulled a face to suggest he didn't. He was on his way down to interview Gary Brown, armed with a newly issued warrant to search his room and was keen to get on.

Undeterred, Chief Inspector Jonathon Bryant held the door to his office open and waved Patrick towards a seat. The door closing gave Patrick the distinct feeling it was not going to be as swift a chat as he would've liked.

"I know you want to get on Pat but just give me an outline of where we are. A quick progress report if you like."

Patrick gave him a run-down of the activities of the previous day, his gut feeling about the suspect in the cells, and their hopes of finding further evidence at his house that might be able to link him in with a wider ring of probable paedophiles.

"Speaking of which, we were able to search Phillip Carver's flat last night. He's a local nonce that seems to have gone missing over the last few days." Patrick shrugged. "Coincidence?" Shaking his head, he continued, "Who knows? We didn't find anything specifically at his flat. There was a wireless router but no desk top PC, which suggests that he has probably got a laptop. So I think we can safely assume he's able to connect whilst mobile and so could easily keep up with a like-minded community. His previous, shows the young Martha could fall into his target range," Patrick shifted uncomfortably in his seat, "But whatever," he continued, "we need to find him and rule him in or out of the equation."

"Okay," his boss nodded in agreement. A look of concern spread across his already serious face, "But what you've got so far on this Gary Brown, sounds pretty thin, Pat"

"Yeah I know that, but Tom and I are of the same opinion. He's hiding something. No question, he's involved. We've just got to prove it. As you know, we don't have much to work with, very few leads, and just one or two lines of enquiry. So, unless something else crops up to say otherwise, he is our main and only suspect."

"Understood."

The tone was one of agreement, underlying it though, Patrick detected a hint of negativity, and said quickly, "There's a but coming, if I'm not mistaken."

The chief threw him a newspaper, folded to display an article about Big Cats of Dorset. Patrick noted it was the Sun and it was page 5. He read the half-page article whilst his boss looked on. Apart from picking up the name Tony Nash in the text

166

beneath the Rangers picture, his eyes, were also drawn even more quickly to his own, including his rank. The article had started off asking the question as to whether these creatures might exist, based on the recent article in the Bournemouth Echo about the sighting on Holt Heath, just over a week ago. It included other such sightings from around the country and mimicked, pretty much, the original article that Brian Maidment had written in the Echo after the sighting at Moors Valley Country Park. The last two paragraphs though, neatly diverted into the current investigation, suggesting, that the Ranger was concerned enough to call the police, speaking with Inspector Stimpson and warning him of the potential dangers to the public, and particularly young children, of a big cat attack. And, as in the Echo article, which Patrick noted was also on his superior's desk, that this notion was a possible explanation for the disappearance of the little girl Martha Docker.

"Load of crap," Patrick said dismissively, unsure where his boss was going with it.

"I've no doubt Pat, but it only goes to prove that we have to be careful about what we say to the press. It," he said pointedly referring to Patrick's eloquent description, "sticks as well as mud remember!" With a half-smile flitting on his lips, and vanishing as quickly, he added, "Before you know it, they'll be saying that we think this is a viable line of inquiry and are organising a big game hunt."

"I know," Patrick said in full agreement. "Bloody tabloids - they really know how to whip up a story."

"Exactly Pat. We need to dampen this sort of nonsense down; it's no help to us. We want the local people focussed on this investigation, not worrying about some fictional black panther at the bottom of their gardens."

Patrick left the office feeling peeved. He felt like he'd just been told off. *Still*, he thought, *it could have been much worse*, his boss being somewhat unpredictable at times. Admittedly the remark to Brian at the Echo had been his, but that story had come from nowhere, apart from Tony Nash's name and his questionable mental state, he hadn't given anything else away. Still aggrieved, he went in search of Thomas.

In the near empty, open-plan, CID office, he found the Sergeant at his desk and just putting the phone down on to its cradle. "Just chasing up Forensics," Thomas said with little emotion. "See if they had anything yet, and before you ask…no they haven't." Patrick shook his head, as if he couldn't believe it either.

"Right, Tom, let's go and inform our friend, we are about to go and search his room. See how that affects him?"

As hoped, Gary looked mightily unhappy about this fact, as they bundled him into the back of the car. It didn't help that on the fifteen-minute journey, Thomas kept gently probing, "I expect you're on Facebook or some other social chat sites. Oh and don't think that just coz, you've deleted something we can't find it."

Gary knew this and was going greener by the minute. Besides this, he wasn't looking forward to going home; his mother was likely to go ballistic. He'd never been in trouble with the police before. He didn't even know if she knew where he'd been overnight, not daring to call and tell her. Although that probably wasn't a problem, quite often he didn't see his mother from one day to the next if their shift patterns clashed. *Hopefully*, he pleaded, *she'll be out now.*

Patrick noted the look of absolute horror on the young man's face, as, unlocking the solid front door to his home, it suddenly swung open, and with more pleasure than he knew he should have, watched as the look turned to one of shamefaced embarrassment finding his larger-than-life mother, glaring at him. Her eyes bored into her son as she began to speak, reluctantly dragging them away to settle on Patrick's.

"So what's all this about then?" the anger in her voice apparent.

But Patrick felt it hollow, put on perhaps, for it had a tremulous quality as if she might burst into tears at any moment; the question posed about Gary's movements yesterday clearly rattling her. The connotations had been going round her head ever since. It would seem obvious even to the bluntest tack as to what Gary had been dragged in there about. What she couldn't understand was why.

"I'm sorry Mrs Brown but we have a warrant to search these premises and in particular your son's room." Thomas informed her, ignoring her original question.

"I have a right to know what this is all about," she said defiantly. "You're not going anywhere until you tell me."

Thomas gently moved her to one side, saying, "All in good time Mrs Brown, but this piece of paper gives us the right. We have no desire to add obstruction to any charges we might bring."

Crestfallen, and frightened, she looked wildly at her son and shouted accusingly, as the group moved to the locked door that hid the stairs to his room. "What on earth have you done?"

Gary would not turn back. He too was in a state; shocked by her words, they felt like betrayal. He unlocked the door with shaking hands and pushed it open. The two policemen guided him up the steep flight in to his room and took in the layout. It was a good-sized bedroom Patrick thought, five metres square he reckoned with two dormers facing east and west. He had also realised that this was the only room upstairs in the chalet bungalow. The solid panelling of the balustrades either side of the stairs ended in the middle of the room, bisecting it and creating three distinct areas. On one side was a small bedroom, just two metres wide and, mirroring it on the other, a sort of living space with a large TV on the end wall and enough room for a single armchair facing it. Opposite the stairwell they'd just come up, and effectively linking the two areas, was an array of equipment dominating the room just in front of them. This was his working area, or play area? At this moment, Patrick could not decide which. The sloping eaves all around gave the room a cramped and oppressive feel and made all three of them, at times, stoop to avoid banging their heads. The colour scheme too was drab; it took Patrick a few minutes to understand that there was or had been at sometime a distinct theme. But by the look of it, the scuffed olive green walls, plus poorly hanging curtains in camouflage material, meant that this military makeover was some years old. An interesting feature, he thought, was the dartboard hung on a target, one of those charging soldiers clutching a rifle to his chest, the type they used on army ranges. It was positioned next to one of the dormer windows. Patrick also had the distinct impression that this was probably the most people Gary had ever had in the room. Everything seemed to be geared up for one: a single bed, a single armchair, one-office style chair on wheels at the long desk which spanned the room and held all his electronics.

Thomas homed in on the computers. "Nice set up," he said genuinely.

At home he and his wife shared a laptop either perched on knees or on the small dining room table. This was pretty awesome. Gary noticed the interest and was quick to recover, seeing potential common ground.

"Yeah, it's not bad is it?" he said with a swelling pride. "I've got a Playstation 3, an X Box 360, a Nintendo Wii, a high-end gaming PC, this one here," he pointed to the black box under the table and the huge 27inch monitor, "and an older one I use for working out my finances or word processing. I've got DVD, video and blu-ray players and of course you can get the television on-line now, as well. The printers and scanner are wirelessly connected. Yeah I've got everything I need here."

"Not cheap though," Thomas began, and as if remembering why he was here, followed up in a brusque tone. "Where'd all the money come for all this?"

"What?" Gary said angry at being slapped down again, "I earned it," he challenged, indignant at the unjust inferences.

"Well I'm afraid," Patrick countered, "earned, or otherwise, we'll need the mainframes and any external hard drives unplugged and ready for our guys to take away and examine them. Oh, and your laptop if you have one? Now, you can either do it yourself, the safe way, or I let Thomas do it, your choice."

Reluctantly, Gary got under the desk and began pulling out the mass of cables, finally disconnecting the wireless router.

Meanwhile Patrick began looking at the shelves neatly stacked with, computer and console games, videos and DVDs, from the latest blockbusters to obscure cult horror movies; he inspected each of the titles. He noticed with some envy that they were grouped by genre and then in alphabetical order. He could never find anything at home. The kids left them all over the place. There was nothing pornographic that he could see on the shelves, just a lot of violence, blood and guts, particularly in the games section.

So you've got it well hidden then, Patrick thought to himself and started assessing where such a collection might be stored.

Thomas meanwhile had finished rummaging through the drawers full of clothes and the wardrobe, finding nothing. He too looked around somewhat perplexed, *Ok he might have it all on his hard drives, I suppose, but somehow I doubt it, that would take up a huge amount of disk space.* Almost at the same time they spotted the doors cut in to the plasterboard walls and leading into the loft spaces under the eaves. Either side of each corner of the room there were two doors, except one corner, which had only a single entry point, the unusual Dartboard covering the space where the eighth one should be.

The two policemen managed to access each one, finding all manner of clutter, dusty and damp-smelling; boxes of old clothes and shoes, redundant board games, an ancient sewing machine; accumulated junk basically. With every receptacle and storage space checked, Patrick gave Thomas a withering look suggesting, what now? They scanned the room one last time, looking for inspiration, but decided that it was 'clean'.

"Right, let's get this stuff to the station, see what we can find on it," Thomas leered threateningly in Gary's direction.

"Ever thought of joining?" Patrick asked Gary casually, pointing to the target behind the dartboard. "The army - looks like you're into it?"

"Can't because of my allergy."

Patrick nodded as he picked a dart from the board, took a few paces away and threw. It bounced off the wires and fell to the floor at the cut-outs feet. "As you might gather," he said abashed, "I'm not in the squads' darts team."

On collecting the dart he turned back to look at the other Dormer with the two small doors either side. It had struck Patrick that the room was very symmetrical, a perfect square, two dormers on opposite roof aspects, and yet only seven cupboards, by rights there should be another. Peering along the wall in an effort to see behind the target and how flush it actually was to the surface, Patrick could see that it was actually fixed in what looked like four places and there was a discernible gap of perhaps one to two millimetres. Gripping the edge of the targets mounting board with just his fingertips, he pulled hard. Unexpectedly the target swung violently.

Turning to look at a horrified Gary, Patrick said, "Clever." Glancing over to Thomas, explained, "It's fixed to the original door behind. Someone has removed all the surrounding architrave so it lies almost flush, and from most angles it looks just like it's attached to the wall."

Patrick felt a bit like a treasure hunter who'd struck lucky. On the floor under the restricted eave space was a wooden wine box that held the gold. There were a number of videos and about ten DVDs and stacked in piles outside of the box, were porn magazines of every persuasion and interest.

Fixing Gary with an acknowledging palm to stop him speaking, Patrick raised his voice, "Don't..." he glared, "even think about saying they're not yours, young man."

Chapter 44

A full English, half-eaten, soon became a chore to consume, as Tony concentrated on the Newspaper left on one of the café's tables.

The morning's early start had, by eight-thirty when he'd said goodbye to Jenny, made him ravenous. His shift would start at ten so plenty of time to grab some food. However, feeling that he'd earned something more than the usual cardboard flakes topped off with fresh fruit, the lure of the cafeteria, and a fry-up at the country park beckoned; and dressed for work already, he'd been able to drive straight there.

Despite the girl on the counter, who he hadn't seen before, giving him a strange look, he wasn't aware of anything to worry about. Hunger had narrowed his consciousness and needing to eat, the heady aromas as he waited for his meal to be plated; distracted him further. He chose the table with what he assumed was a discarded newspaper on it; something to absently peruse, whilst polishing off his plateful. It was that morning's copy of the Sun; the headline suggested Prime Minister Gordon Brown was being pilloried as normal. Inside, the first two pages were dedicated to the disappearance of little Martha. He noted with interest, the paragraph that announced the Police had a local man in custody for questioning, and wondered who that was. There was a whole section given over to reporting that two known paedophiles were living in the area and were being sought out for questioning. It lead on to the familiar debate of 'The right to know' whether convicted paedophiles were living in your area and should these monsters be allowed to remain at large, helping to create a culture of fear for parents and guardians. *Christ, if you lot would leave it alone, instead of being so quick to report every detail, there wouldn't be a fear culture,* Tony mused as he continued to read with growing annoyance, at the zealous and almost gleeful reporting.

By the time a good deal of his heavenly breakfast had disappeared, he turned over to page five. It took him a moment to register. After a swift glance to check no one was near, he flashed back to the old photograph of him in his Ranger uniform and the article that accompanied it. Rapidly, his appetite diminished as he picked over the remains, all the while scanning the columns and assessing the National's take on the subject. A thought flashed through his mind, *God, I hope it's only the Sun.*

He grabbed his mobile and punched the number for Jenny, from his recent calls list.

"Hi it's me," he said without giving her a chance to speak, "have you seen the Sun?"

"Yes it's gorgeous and so hot."

"Jen!"

Surmising Tony was not in the mood, "I'm guessing here, you mean the newspaper. What's up now?"

"I'm in it. Page five. Same old photo, same total garbage as the one in the Echo from yonks ago."

She could hear the disgust in his voice.

"I'll tell you what Jen I am not sticking my head above the parapet ever again. I don't care what happens. They could string one up by the balls for all I care."

"So no more big cats or black panthers then," Jenny confirmed. There was a well-timed pause. "Probably see one tomorrow now," she said, laughing.

"Yeah," he agreed. "Probably."

"Anyway, changing the subject, I was thinking about our foxes and I managed to find the address of Mrs Thomas's housekeeper; you know the lady who had the Pit Bulls. I was thinking, why don't we pay her a visit this evening and get a bit more background information. She's bound to know something."

"Good idea," agreed Tony. "Mind you, I won't be finishing until about seven tonight, so seven thirty-ish?"

Jenny gave him the address, which was in Ferndown, so they agreed to meet there.

Chapter 45

The search of Gary's room and a swift look around the rest of the house, with only one cup of tea proffered, had taken the two detectives way past lunch. Depositing Gary back in the cells, they headed to the canteen to rectify the situation. They took their time, in the knowledge that, although the techies had been instructed to check the computer drives immediately, they had only picked them up that morning at about eleven-thirty and it was only two-fifteen now. They doubted just over two hours was going to reveal much, and so sat in Patrick's office to eat their sandwiches, enabling them to continue discussing the case.

"Is that a forensic report in your tray Pat?" Thomas asked, his head skewing to try to read it upside down.

"It most certainly is, my friend," he replied, his eagerness sagging on catching sight of the results. "Bugger! No match. Apparently, the piece of material did not come from that jacket, and, there were no deposits on it with any DNA potential." Patrick continued, "D'you know, already I can feel this little shit slipping through our fingers. The porn, on its own, will mean very little. Let's hope the geeks can come up with some juicy chat room gossip or damning e-mails, otherwise we're going to have to let him go shortly."

Patrick started flicking through another file on his desk containing some background information on Gary.

"Not much in his bank, no big finder's fees, or anything out of the ordinary for that matter, credits good, only one card and a bank card. Seems to live within his means."

"Bit early praps, for any kind of payoff, for services rendered I mean," Thomas said thoughtfully. "Having said that, it might not be cash these sicko's are after."

"Yeah, doesn't bear thinking about," said Patrick, knowing with some certainty, that these were horrors he would have to endure if they drew closer to their quarry. Holding the file's outer cover ready to close, he finished off. "No criminal record, cautions or anything, he doesn't have a car, not even sure if he drives. Correction, he hasn't passed his test yet, he has a provisional license." He let the flimsy cardboard cover fall and looked up at his colleague "Outwardly, he seems to have kept himself whiter than the proverbial."

"Well let's hope the tech guys find a few black marks embedded in his data," Thomas added cynically.

After they had finished their lunch, and had had a second coffee, they felt more like tackling the likes of Gary Brown again. The technicians had made an initial report, finding a fair amount of pornography stored on one portable hard drive. The large mainframe appeared to hold more electronic games than Amazon, according to the officer, who seemed to be in some awe, sounding more like he'd made some breakthrough in particle physics, rather than finding some fatuous pieces of software.

"There are games I've never even heard of," he said clearly impressed and continuing as if this were more important.

Patrick had rolled his eyes and calmed himself, and said with muted sarcasm, "Well, I'm pleased for you. But have you got anything we can hang him with? Pictures, e-mails, the paedo's good sex guide, anything?"

"Sorry... yes," he flustered, "and eh... probably no."

The irritated and barely whispered, "F' fuck sake," by Patrick at the other end of the phone, sharpened the reply.

"The stored porn on the separate drive covers a lot of genres but there doesn't seem to be any preferences. Looks like he just hangs on to clips and films that turn him on, and yes, there is a very small kiddie porn section and I do mean small in comparison to the rest, literally three in number, four and five minute clips. The kids are not that young though, could be anywhere from, I dunno, eight, nine maybe. I'll tell you what though," he added, the reverence in his voice making a comeback. "He's made our job very easy. All the titles are listed in a spreadsheet, alphabetically, and genres noted. Click on the title and a hyperlink starts the clip. Amazing."

Patrick's first thought was eight or nine's young enough, then moved on to Gary's seemingly obsessive cataloguing. *This boy needs to get out more*, he thought, but on reflection couldn't help feeling, it wasn't just Gary this statement might apply to. "And what about chat rooms, e-mails, etc?"

"We're still searching those, although it doesn't look very promising. Whatever conversation we've found it's been predominantly centred around his online gaming friends. Still, we've got some deeper searches going on as we speak, but they could take quite a bit longer."

"How long?"

"How long's a USB cable?"

Patrick sighed wearily, *like I care*. "No idea."

"Right answer, we'll let you know."

On their second formal interview with Gary that afternoon, he'd been non-committal, not unhelpful or obstructive, just not giving anything useful away. He'd sat in the chair opposite them seemingly calm and collected, although his body language said something else. For most of it, he leant slightly forward in his chair, the balls of his hands resting, sometimes gripping, the seat just behind his knees. It gave the impression he was eager to oblige, keen to want to help, but perhaps a little on-edge; the tension being released through his hands opening slightly as they relaxed, and body moving back to a more natural posture whenever he realised that the question being asked was undemanding and answerable. Patrick had commented to Thomas, when they'd had a break, that Gary's answers seemed trite, rehearsed, but not necessarily for what they were asking him.

"That moment's hesitation before answering, it's almost like he's running down a list and seeing which one suits the question best."

Thomas pointed out that "he'd obviously used the time in the cells, well."

"I don't know," Patrick said thoughtfully. "He obviously knows the mother, Daisy, quite well, being at school together… but he didn't like your question about whether they had had a relationship."

"Whether he did or not, it's hardly a motive for abducting the child," Thomas said reasonably.

"Unless it was his, or wanted to get back at her for going off with someone else?"

"No," Thomas shook his head. "I don't see it. He hasn't got it in him. Too shy, too nerdy, ugly's probably too harsh; I mean he's no looker. When I spoke to his boss earlier, he was less than complimentary about his speed of work, lack of ambition, not taking any responsibility. A good timekeeper was about the only positive thing. No I don't think he's got it in him to do anything off his own back."

"Sadly, I'm inclined to agree with you. However, we go back to, accomplice, watcher, the eyes and ears of others. That's where I see him at the moment and that makes it easier for him to deny complicity…. But he is hiding something, I can feel it."

By the end of it, Patrick was all but ready to kick him out. When five o'clock came, and another quick call to the boffins working on Gary's computers had still turned up nothing of any real use, he instructed the custody Sergeant to release him.

The day was turning into doom and gloom as all lines of inquiry were drying up. Discreet investigations had not led them to suspect parents or close relatives. There appeared to be no desperate mothers, well, none damaged enough, to pull off such a crime. The other police forces nationwide had nothing to offer, even the specialist units were not aware of any 'snatch squads' operating in Dorset, or indeed anywhere. According to them that wasn't usually how they operated. They were more devious; insidious. Often, no one knew anything had happened till some time, years possibly, after the event. And their other on-going investigations did not fit this one. Despite two television appeals, and the initial, alert there had been no useful calls from the public, not even on the last one, with the shattered parents barely able to keep it together and Daisy, finally breaking down and pleading, the tears uncontrollable and her husband looking on in stunned bewilderment.

Once again, the weight of responsibility was crushing and the frustration at all their efforts amounting to nothing, was more than disheartening, it was debilitating. As Patrick sat alone in his office, he thought about going home, see the family, but it was difficult to get motivated, even for that. Instead he brooded, annoyed with himself for feeling so dispirited, ashamed and guilty even, and, staring out of the window, asked what had now become an all too familiar question, except that this time, he sounded desperate, "What more can I do?"

Chapter 46

"Mad as a box of frogs," had been the way Dave Martin, from their wildlife group, had summed up Julie Hoe, and so far, the description was hitting the mark, Jenny thought. She had telephoned the Hoes during the day to see if they would agree to see them. The white lie about needing some background information on Betty's dogs, just to finalise the paperwork, seemed to work, and the bonus had come when Julie had said, "Why don't we meet at Homewood house? I've still got a key. Neil, that's my husband, still looks after the gardens and I keep it clean and tidy; not the garden, you understand the house," Julie continued, and it seemed without the need for air. The rapid fire words kept coming and Jenny was sure she didn't hear any intake of breath throughout the one-sided exchange.

"It's still empty you know. Whacking great house. My daughter's husband is going to rent it for six months - well the company he works for is - when they come back from living in America at the beginning of August... I can't wait. Mind, I can't imagine anyone wanting to take that on full-time. Neil would, he loves it. The garden was his baby, he and Betty spent hours and hours designing it and planting it. He's got his own business see, gardening. What time shall we meet? Is seven o'clock okay?"

They'd settled on seven-thirty and by seven-thirty-five Tony and Jenny were exchanging looks across the weathered kitchen table, the surreptitious messages confirming Dave's opinion. Not a big woman in size but what she lacked in stature she more than made up for with her ebullient personality. If there was a size larger than life, then that would be Julie's, Neil had managed to say on introductions. It was pretty much the only thing he would say, not that he seemed concerned at all. For all her extravagances Julie had a good heart, kind, caring and fun. The round face reflected her jolly nature and the silver-white hair swept back into a bun looked like a knot of spun sugar. A box of frogs maybe, but not a hint of bitterness.

Jenny wore her East Dorset uniform, helping to further the deception. They had thought it best not to come clean about the real reason for their visit. The idea didn't seem that daft to them but others might not take it in the same way, and particularly in light of Tony's new-found notoriety. Jumping in at a convenient nanosecond of silence, Jenny started asking the questions that she had, sensibly, thought to write down.

"How long had you worked for Betty?"

"Thirty-nine years. Would have been forty, next month." The pride beamed forth changing quickly to a near hysterical guffaw, "I can remember..."

Jenny shot the next question.

"Sorry," she said smiling her apology to Julie who seemed unconcerned, as if such interruptions happened all the time. "How long had Betty had the dogs for?"

"She's had them for as long as I've known her... not those dogs obviously, that would make them ancient, 'specially in dog years" She laughed loudly. "Older than all of us put together, I shouldn't wonder." The laughter subsided but a fixed and wide smile remained, threatening a new outburst at any time. "No, those dogs were about five or six years old, but she has always had the same breed, her and her husband, no children see."

"So she's always had two, or perhaps more, before they were banned?"

"How do you mean banned?" Julie looked quizzical the smile shrinking, and gave her husband a similar look.

"You mean you don't know?" Jenny's voice was incredulous. "Those dogs were regarded as Dangerous dogs, as passed in the government act of 1991. They should have been registered. Strict conditions applied for owners, to be allowed to keep them. In theory, Betty should not have been able to get hold of these dogs since that act was passed because it's illegal to breed from them." Jenny had to think, trying to remember the act as near verbatim as she could. "Or to sell them, abandon or give away such dogs."

"What a load of rubbish," Julie sneered. "They were as good as gold those dogs, nothing dangerous about them."

The withered smile changed in a flash, it was now broad and jovial again, but it didn't quite hide her concern. It wasn't right to speak ill of the dead, was it? And besides Betty wouldn't flout the law, surely?

"I think if you'd seen them when I had to take them away you might think otherwise. That Police officer was badly scarred," Jenny looked suitably stern.

Julie's defence was less determined. "Well that's as maybe. Mind, they were starving by all accounts, and with us being away..." For the first time, Julie's face looked sad. "If only we hadn't gone on holiday, none of this would have happened."

"Granted they hadn't been fed properly," Jenny acknowledged. Then, thinking it through... "In fairness, I suppose, being kept in this walled garden all their lives, protected them from coming into contact with the outside world."

"I don't think so," she said indignantly. "She often used to take them for a walk," Julie's defiance rallying somewhat. "Well only on the common there," she added, pointing towards Poor Common.

"Muzzled, I hope?" Jenny said.

Julie gave a little mixed up laugh and a snort, "You'd be lucky. She hardly had need for a lead either; those dogs were so well trained. One word or command from Betty and the response was immediate - jump off a cliff and they'd do it."

"What about people who came to the house, what were they like then?"

"Noisy, obviously, but you wouldn't want a quiet dog, no security there. But when Betty shouted 'quiet', believe me, they shut up. We all jumped a mile of course. God she could shout. Army wife see. But they were good with people, interested, but not over the top, like some."

177

"I understand Betty used to feed the wildlife, especially foxes." Jenny changed the tenor of her question making it seem just a casual and conversational sort of remark. "That must have been something to see?"

"Oh lord yes. She's fed them, for years too." Julie cast her eyes toward the back door trying to remember. She made another sound similar to the one earlier but with the mirth removed. "Hmph! I don't know how many years now, there've been pups born in the old sty there. I reckon half the foxes round here are Betty's off-spring." She sounded for a moment like she didn't approve.

"How did the dogs get on with them? I'd be surprised if they tolerated them," Tony asked and speaking for the first time.

"Shy is he, your boyfriend?" Julie winked at Jenny with a grin so broad it looked impossible. Jenny sniggered at Tony's mild discomfort. "The foxes have always been here, same as the dogs. You see, Betty and her husband always brought puppies in as their old dogs got to be about eight or nine, so there's always been..." she struggled for the right word, "continuity. The old dogs passed on their traits to the puppies accepting the foxes in and around the garden, feeding together and playing with them like they were family. It was actually quite charming and funny at times."

"You didn't sound like you approved, earlier?" Jenny asked wondering if Tony was actually going to say anything more. He was still looking flushed.

"No, well," Julie fidgeted in her chair looking uncomfortable for the first time. "It's not right is it... you know... what she allowed them to get up to?" It was Julie's turn to colour up, her round cheeks looking like sun blushed apples. "You tell em, Neil, I can't."

Neil was implacable, a man of the Dorset sod, down to earth and basic.

"Copulating, rutting, shagging whatever you want to call it."

There was a wicked glint in his eye and Jenny wondered if he wasn't enjoying his wife's discomfort just a little too much. "I couldn't see the harm in it myself her dogs were only doing what came naturally. That's if they got lucky, but the vixens usually gave them short shrift. They're only in season for a very short time of the year you know, usually early part of the year, I think."

Tony gave Jenny a look that clearly said, Wow.

"Course, when the vixen's pups grew up they all played together, the cubs not being able to get out of the garden for some time."

"They had pups?" Tony could not contain himself.

"Oh yes, almost every year," Neil started, but Julie had got over her embarrassment, had obviously been quiet for too long and guessing what Tony was insinuating, cut in.

"I doubt they were the dogs', if that's what you're thinking."

"What makes you so sure?" Tony asked, trying to hide his disappointment.

"Well, chance in a million isn't it? As Neil said, the vixens only in season for a short while,"

"Yeah, but it's no different to humans," Jenny countered, and looking at the confused faces around her, qualified it with, "Surely, it only takes one mistake?"

The conversation stalled for a short while, as all seemed to be digesting this morsel of wisdom; Julie and Neil appearing to be weighing up the idea as if the thought had never crossed their mind.

"I suppose it's possible," said Neil adding, "Come to think of it some of those little devils had similar colouration to the dogs. Not that that means anything. Animals can often stray from what's normal."

Tony nodded in agreement.

Julie, back on form, made one of her noises again, it could almost have been a laugh, before saying, "Oh yeah, there's been a few queer ones right enough. Quite a few years back though, some runty little things." Her face lit up, as if suddenly remembering something else. "And, that big bugger a few years back, Christ he was almost as big as her dogs... mind he didn't last long."

Tony had been hanging on to every word, his excitement growing until the last line. "What died?" He couldn't believe it!

"Noo!" She looked at Tony as if he was daft, "I mean he was off over that wall, the first chance he got."

"So how long ago was this?" Jenny asked, her curiosity, also piqued.

"A few years back I s'pose." Yet another irritating snorty laugh issued forth. "Mind, I'm bloody hopeless. I don't know about a sieve, my brain just doesn't seem to work like everybody else's."

Never a truer word, thought Tony. Picking up on the last few comments he'd been rapidly wondering if the big fox they were talking about was any of the one's he had seen with Jenny at the ponds that morning. Although the time frame Julie seemed to be indicating, made it sound unlikely.

"No," Neil cut in positively, "He was last year's litter, and he was a blinking nuisance, digging up the veg patch and the like. Chased him off a few times, I can tell you." He smiled as if remembering the antics of a grandchild, or favourite dog, adding wistfully, "I haven't seen him since poor old Betty died. Funny thing is, well it's not that funny, the coppers said, when they found her body in the garden, where she'd been outside for so long, the animals had got at her. Rodents, badgers, etc but most likely foxes and I tell you, I wouldn't put it past that bugger to have had a nibble."

Chapter 47

At least they hadn't taken the telly. Gary was looking around his now electronically denuded bedroom and feeling like his world had been tipped on its head. Just over twenty four hours ago, he'd been at work and, within that time, they had dragged him off, accused him of god knows what, chucked him in a police cell over night, pinched his computers and left him to find his own way home. *Fucking bastards*, were he felt, the only adequate words. And besides those major irritations, he still had to face his mum, and Michael his boss. "Fuck it!" he said out loud, as the thought widened and the enormity of having to get back into normal life dawned. *Who else knew?*

It was a little after eight o'clock when he heard the front door slam into its frame, the shock waves reverberating through the bungalow, announcing the arrival home of his mother and the bearer of the answer to his question.

"No it doesn't say your name," his mother shouted furiously, holding up that evening's edition of the Echo, and shaking it in his face. "How long do you think that's going to last, eh? If Michael knows it'll be all round the Angel like wild fire by now, let alone Ferndown."

He managed to fend off her attack, pleading innocence and ignorance, explaining they had found his medic alert on the common not far from where Martha had gone missing. "Putting two and two together the cretins had come up with five - me. It's not fair I haven't done anything," he whined looking suitably chaste and knowing exactly how to get round his mother.

Whilst in police custody, he'd quickly assessed that everything, was deniable and readily excusable. Naturally it hadn't taken long to persuade his mother of the like. What concerned him more, though, was that most other people would see the smoke and think, fire. As if that in itself wasn't bad enough, people locally recognising him, pointing him out and inadvertently raising his profile and maybe... he would be under police surveillance? He glanced out of the window; ultimately, it would mean he would have to lay low for a while. No more nightly activities, it wouldn't do to be caught at it, so soon after the event. *That wouldn't be good for anyone*, he thought, managing a smile, the first genuine one in the last twenty-four hours.

******

If he'd had any inkling that Gary was getting it in the neck, Tony might have felt somewhat happier, as he attempted to buy some drinks at the White Hart. However, their choice of bar being influenced, yet again, by the media and Tony's reluctance to be the butt of any more ribbing, friendly or otherwise, meant that the opening comments by the regular barman, on what he had judged as more civil ground, had once again, really pissed him off.

"Look, I might have said some of those things, but they weren't meant to be heard by everybody," he said defensively, to the member of staff who was pulling his pint and the other, casually hooked by her elbows on the back bar. "But, as usual, the bloody press have just blown it all out of proportion."

"It's true," Jenny said shrugging one shoulder. "You know what they're like, one sly fart and they report a hurricane!"

Tony winced inwardly, not sure how the ridiculous exaggeration would be received by the non-committal bar staff. He needn't have worried, Jenny's smile and accompanying look, daring the two people not to laugh, won them over.

"No you're right," the girl said, unable to suppress a giggle, "But it's been a hot topic in here, this evening. Earlier, I had two people in asking for directions to Poor Common. They weren't press, I'm sure of that, but they had cameras and binoculars and were dressed for a walk." She pushed herself off from the rear counter and picked up a cloth to mop up a spill on the bar, continuing, "That prompted the debate between the regulars about how they were probably looking for the big cats which led, of course, on to a discussion about whether they were real. It got a bit heated at one point when a couple of women said they wouldn't be allowing their kids out to play on the common and one of the blokes telling them to stop being so daft. As you can imagine that didn't go down too well."

"No probably not," Tony agreed and feeling mildly responsible.

"Your name was mud though," the barman added. "That bloody Tony Nash, I heard one of the women saying, as they were leaving."

Tony had the distinct feeling the barman might have been winding him up, but he wasn't sure as he and Jenny went to sit at one of the few vacant tables. They chatted for a while about their day's work, but the conversation soon turned to the recent visit to the housekeeper.

"Imagine waking up to that permanent ray of sunshine?" Jenny said scornfully, "I could have happily slapped her, and that was before she'd said hello."

Tony smiled at her irreverent reflection.

"Yes she was a bit much. Mind," he mimicked her expression, "What old Neil said about them being a bit free and easy, it could just be another piece of evidence to prove our dox theory."

Jenny nodded in agreement. "Thing is Tony, how are we going to prove it, short of catching one?"

Tony thought for a while and, not coming up with anything that might prove definitive, apart from capturing one, said, "I think all we can do now is to get some more pictures, better ones, close-ups, maybe some video footage. And, if we could find a way of accurately measuring its size, that would be useful. I mean, we keep saying that it's bigger than the average fox, but we're not sure." He lifted his glass and glanced over the rim, "Judging by what I saw this morning, I reckon it is, but I go back to, without a normal fox to compare it with, and I'm assuming the other two with him were not normal, probably siblings, then it's difficult to compare. The thing is, if these guys are bigger, then they still seem to be displaying fox-like proportions. I'll see if I can borrow a camera or video from one of the guys at work. I'm sure they won't mind."

"Yeah, she agreed, devilment playing in her eyes. "Just tell 'em you want to photograph a black panther."

"I know somebody else who'll be in line for a good slapping, if she doesn't shut up," Tony countered good-humouredly.

Chapter 48

Over the following three weeks, Tony and Jenny managed, on numerous occasions to visit Poor Common armed to the teeth with a super-duper digital camera with a lens that would not have been out of place amongst the reporting Paparazzi.

"Point, zoom with your left hand and click with your right, it's really that simple," John, his boss at work had said. "No need to worry about light…and by that I mean… there does actually have to be some."

He'd seen the surprise in Tony's eyes at the statement.

"Christ Tony, what have you been using? A box Brownie or something?"

Tony looked sheepishly aggrieved "No but… mine is digital, it's just not a very good one. Obviously I know you can't take pictures in the dark." Adding as an afterthought, "It would have been useful though."

Initially, they had struck lucky. After only three attempts, they caught the doxes early one morning, as before, down by the ponds. They had watched with some concern, but mostly with amusement, as the mallard parents, who had nested on one of the tiny islands, defensively manoeuvred their eleven unsinkable balls of fluff, as the doxes had circled the pond. Not that they had any real hope in catching one, Tony had said to Jenny. "They might be able to swim, but it's very unlikely they would be bothered to." Tony had managed to get some good close-ups, even from the other side of the pond. As luck would have it, the dominant male dox stood, on a brief occasion, beside a short stretch of two-railed fencing enclosing the small viewing jetty, posing in just such a way as to ensure that height and length measurement could be assessed against the known fence dimensions.

What had also struck Tony was that they had very rarely seen the animals singly, nearly always travelling together.

"That's another oddity," he said. "Most foxes, according to all the bumph I've read, are usually very solitary. They aren't given to pack behaviour. These guys seem to be forever in each other's company… strange admittedly and, one could argue, perhaps a dog-like trait, but hardly earth shattering."

For nearly two weeks subsequently, their early morning and mid to late evening vigils came to nothing. It seemed that the fox group had disappeared. Tony and Jenny postulated a number of theories; perhaps one had been killed in a road accident, or the like, and the others were just laying low. Maybe they had caught some disease, or perhaps, they had moved off the common, choosing to centre their range on the golf course to the south of the road.

However, it was just as likely, Tony reminded Jenny, that these were wild animals and if they didn't want to be seen then they could slip through the landscape like a shadow. "It could also be as simple as us being in the wrong place at the wrong time. I'm sure they'll turn up."

******

Meantime, the investigation into the disappearance had, as the Police had chosen to inform the press, stalled; the specific term coined to suggest that there had been some initial momentum, when in reality there had been little forward movement. This, in fairness, had not been for the want of trying. The investigating team, led by Patrick Stimpson, had been unable to detect how or who had abducted the child and had few leads with which to postulate her whereabouts at any given moment. As the likelihood of ever finding Martha or, indeed, solving any part of the mystery faded, the officers involved grew hardened to that fact. And as each took on new work, a burglary at a local electronics store, a suicide, a glass attack on a young man in the local rough house pub, the missing child became even more distant as life moved on.

The forensic team too, had spent hours laboriously looking for clues taking finger prints and examining fibres either from the house and on, out into the garden and the area just outside the back gate. They had studied the articles and items found from the ground search. None, apart from the Medic alert and the swatch of camouflage material had offered up any reason to dig deeper. The basic problem, right from the outset, had been where should they look? Unlike most crimes they were asked to attend, this had no point of reference, no obvious crime scene, like a broken window at a break-in, or a body. It was often this department that clarified and confirmed what the detectives suspected, and they knew just how much store was put upon them, to come up with the goods. But up against it from the start, no one could feel more impotent than these specialists.

There had been a couple of brief days of excitement, a very positive sighting in Essex led two of Patrick's officers a merry dance for twenty-four fruitless hours. Then came a disturbing report of a child's body, matching the age and sex, being found in Scotland and the community held its breath, another day's wait, only for the autopsy to confirm it wasn't her. And then there was a retired couple in Cornwall who had miraculously just got a toddler. The age guessed at, as Martha's, by the well-meaning village busybody. An inkling of hope was trashed in seconds by a local WPC who had been sent to the cottage, only to verify the child as the woman's granddaughter staying for a few days whilst her parents had a break.

Of the Dockers, suffice to say their lives would never be the same again. Daisy's guilt would be endless; assisted by seemingly uncaring and self-righteous interferers, expressing themselves publicly and fuelling speculation about her suitability as a mother. And somewhere, hidden deep in John's mind lay the whisper of a suspicion, an unanswerable question of his wife's culpability; a thought he would never consciously want to entertain, as to do so would ruin the remnants of his life. Indeed, for Daisy and John, whatever the future held it would be tainted at every juncture by the loss of their precious little miracle. Whatever the occasion, at work or leisure, a social gathering or a trip to the cinema, she would be remembered… 'Martha would have loved that film.' On high days and the lowest days, she would slip into consciousness at a meal or bedtime… they would never be allowed to forget her.

As the month of June drew to a close and summer established itself, the people of Ferndown normalised. The hysteria at the start of the month had led to panicked communities, and not just those local to Dorset. This touched the country and beyond. The culture of fear whipped up by the twenty-four seven news-hungry and technology driven media would always remain. Consigned perhaps for most, to the back of one's mind, but it would never be far away. The fact that a child was still missing was bad enough, but more disturbing was no one had been caught. The question of whether the perpetrator, a paedophile surely, and of the worst kind, was still at large, would be on parental lips for weeks to come. Society's modern monster, hidden in the fabric, biding its time and waiting for the moment to once again, soil innocence and defile vulnerability, would never, be far away.

Life though, is nothing if not resilient. Dangers, real or perceived, would always be there and parents and families might become more protective, closing ranks, minimising risk and being over liberal with cotton wool for a while. Eventually though, blunted by the daily grind, people would become unwary, not necessarily complacent, but less attentive, caution nudged gently into the wind and their hurly-burly lives once again becoming almost… careless.

And on the last weekend in June, Tony and Jenny were witness to a rare treat. Not only had the adult doxes appeared but they were joined by their now gangly offspring. Sitting once again amongst the vegetation of Poor Common, now luxuriant and summer lush, they were well hidden and able to play the animals at their own game.

185

Chapter 49

It had been a long, hot, lazy Sunday. Tony had taken Jenny to meet his parents and show off the farm. A home-cooked lunch of roast potatoes and all the trimmings, had just about set the two of them up for an evening in front of the telly, and an early night. It had been on the drive back from Bridport, a journey of usually about forty-five minutes, summer traffic notwithstanding, that Jenny had pondered on another visit to try to see the doxes. They were using this expression more and more now, although not in company, but it was useful. They needed to clarify these supposedly different animals, to the average everyday foxy. They hadn't seen the doxes for over two weeks, nearly three, and were beginning to wonder if they had seen the last of them.

"What I don't understand is, where the cubs have gone," Jenny said, her seat reclined a few notches allowing her head to nestle comfortably on the plump headrest. "We haven't seen them since, what was it, end of May, I should think? I mean they're hardly likely to move away. The adults could, obviously, because they can, but surely the cubs wouldn't be able to travel far?"

"No, I'm sure you're right, I should think she's moved them... somewhere she thinks safer. When you think of those huge rhododendrons stretching for tens of metres, possibly even a hundred metres, there must be loads of places for her to hole-up in. She might not even go to go ground, depends on the weather of course."

"So what are they now?" she had to stop and think, "... about ....fifteen, sixteen weeks old?"

"Yes, sounds about right. It won't be long before they start to move away, find their own territory... or get run over."

"Oh don't, Tony," she said, her voice taking on a higher pitch and imitating distress, before changing to one of action, "Right, if you think you're falling asleep in front of the telly tonight, then you've got another think coming." Tony glanced away from the road and caught her playful look and fired his own broadside; a grin that clearly said, "Well I'm up for it."

"And before your dirty little mind gets overheated," Jenny advised, "I meant we should go and have another look for the doxes tonight."

So here they were, surrounded by bracken and brambles, not the most ideal combination, but at least the thorny plants were not as abundant. The natural hide was only a few metres from the tree, by the ponds where they had first watched the doxes. In fact, it was virtually where they had appeared from. It was eight forty-five. They'd been there since seven-fifteen and the brightness of the day was fast fading. Warmth was still evident though, in the gentle breeze that agitated the slender rushes and flags protruding from the water. On the far side of the pond, and walking on the path at its edge, was a man. Walking might have been too gentler a word for it, as rummaging and pulling in different directions, but generally ahead, were two lively retrievers, their leads straining and slackening as the chap fought genially to control his charges. They heard his admonishing coaxing, "Leave it Alfie… no this way… come on Arturo… no you're not going in the water."

Tony and Jenny exchanged a glance, who calls their dogs Arturo? "God help us," Tony whispered and Jenny giggled.

"Hang on," Tony stiffened, "I think we might be in luck. Look on the path up ahead of that guy."

She saw what Tony was pointing at. And then, just a little way into the underbrush at the side of the path, there was movement. "There," she said. "There's more of them."

"Oh yes, must be the other two." They watched as the animal on the path, having registered the advance of the two dogs, began to hunker down, half crouching at first, then fully prone on the ground. It didn't look disturbed, even though the human-led pack was only thirty metres away; it seemed to be bobbing its head.

"Looks like one of those dogs on a parcel shelf," Jenny said finding it mildly amusing. "What on earth is it doing?"

The movement in the bushes settled and, apart from the man and his dogs, everything seemed to stop. The random surges of the retrievers, persistent, almost violent, as they smelt blades of grass and snuffled fence posts, meant their leads seemed to be constantly at breaking point with their owner trying to rein them in.

In the failing light Tony watched as the dogs moved closer to the dox on the path. Amazingly they hadn't smelt or seen it. They were about ten metres from drawing level to where the other doxes presumably were hunkering down. Tony wondered where this was going. Were the doxes regarding them as friend or foe? Outwardly, the animal on the path looked like he was just waiting for some doggy mates to play with. Some of the moves, Jenny had said, looked like play bows, the sort of greeting often seen between dogs; like a sort of canine manners, a courtesy perhaps, before they chase each other silly.

"Why are the other two in the bushes though? They don't appear to have moved," Tony pondered aloud.

"No idea," said Jenny scanning back down the path. "But I'm not sure there's two in those bushes, look… down the path almost back to the jetty on the pond."

"Yes, you're right that must be number three."

The words had no sooner left his mouth, than the hushed and still evening air erupted, the two retrievers going ballistic, barking, snarling and charging at the dox ahead of them. The man went flying forward, losing his grip on one of the dog's leads as his hands went forward to break his fall. He cursed loudly as the sharp gravel stones tore through his palms; the other dog, eager to join the fray, yanked hard again and was rewarded with freedom, its lead flicking madly behind it. The doxes scattered in all directions followed closely by the large pets, clearly excited at the prospect of the chase.

"That won't last," Jenny laughed. "I doubt those dogs will have the stamina. Come on let's go and see if we can help that poor bloke."

"What happened there?" he said, clearly embarrassed in front of the two younger strangers and not really expecting an answer. He was sitting on the floor studying his hands. They were grazed and bleeding.

"Here," said Jenny handing him a pack of travel tissues she'd got in her pocket.

"Thanks. Bloody dogs," he said sheepishly. "They're a bit of a handful. Wouldn't harm a fly." He said it to reassure the couple; not everyone was a dog-lover after all.

"Oh I know," said Jenny smiling. "Retrievers are lovely dogs. Don't worry on our account though. We both love dogs. Can we help you get them back?"

"That's kind of you. To be honest, give them a few minutes to realise they haven't got a cat in hell's chance of getting that fox, and I'll give them a call. They'll soon wander back for a treat. Funny though, I saw that fox before they did, and I swear it wasn't worried. It even looked like it wanted to play."

"Yes I got that impression too," agreed Jenny.

"But what about the others," Tony asked, sounding puzzled, "What were they up to?"

"Others?" The chap said, echoing Tony's puzzlement. "I didn't see any others."

"Well, believe it or not, there was one in the bushes just there," Tony pointed to a clump of mixed foliage about five metres up the path. "And there was another one back down there, coming up the path."

"What following us? That's weird." Looking around for his dogs, he yelled, "ALFIE, ARTURO!"

Weird or not? Tony thought, wincing at the name and stifling a laugh. He was thinking though, of the doxes and their relative positions to where the man was walking. The path, at this point, had left the ponds twenty metres or so away but was continuing to hug the high wooden fences of the houses backing on to the common. Had the doxes been following the dogs in the hope of 'joining the pack' and just wanting to play? Somehow, Tony felt, it didn't seem to fit. Clearly, the fox on the path was waiting openly, obviously wanting to be seen, but the others, particularly the one in the bushes, he was hiding. What was he hoping to achieve? *Perfect place to jump out from as the guy drew level*, he considered, *and was the one on the path bringing up the rear?* It didn't take a genius, nor indeed, a tactician, to work out, these creatures could just as easily have been closing in, preparing to trap the man in a three-pronged attack. Tony shook his head in disbelief. He was crediting them with way too much intelligence.

Five minutes later, all was tranquil again. The dogs had duly taken their master back home and Tony decided that, as the light was nearly gone, they might as well call it a night. They moved to go along the path, following it back around the ponds to where his car was parked, on Heatherlands Avenue. But as they did, and seemingly out of nowhere, the skulk returned, boisterously tumbling over each other, biting and snapping some twenty metres up the path. Tony and Jenny stopped dead in their tracks, surprised at their reappearance so quickly, and intrigued by their behaviour.

"Hang on," whispered Tony, peering into the gloom. Was the low light playing tricks? "I think there's four of them now."

"It's the cubs," Jenny said excitedly almost under her breath. "Look! They're just mucking about, and they haven't seen us yet."

"God they've grown. No wonder I didn't recognise them in this light."

The vision of nearly four weeks ago, when they were just balls of fluff, was well and truly blown. They were still young, no question, but if they had been pre-teens back then, these long-legged and lithe creatures were now adolescents, not far off fully grown. The fact that they were out like this, without an escort, although Tony suspected the vixen wouldn't be far behind, meant that they were beginning to forage for themselves.

"They've grown quickly," he said, "I wouldn't have expected to see them on their own just yet, I'm sure the vixen must be close."

They watched for about another eight minutes, as the boisterous group tumbled over each other, continuing to play fight, stopping occasionally, to listen, ears pricked, heads turning, as they heard an unfamiliar noise from the houses behind. One of them, its attention drawn to movement a metre or so ahead, shrank slightly on its haunches, eyes and nose fixated, wriggled its backside just slightly and then pranced forward, its body seemingly rising equally off all four legs, like a spring Lamb, and landing in much the same fashion. Its head darting to one side as it tracked the sounds and caught the movement. Pushing off, this time, with its hind legs, the momentum long and low, it pinned the tiny creature to the floor. A swift stab with its pointed jaws and the unfortunate frog or mouse was no more.

These guys are pretty street wise already, Tony reflected, seeing the way the youngster had expertly dispatched its prey.

A few moments later, as predicted, the vixen appeared. Her experienced nose had sensed the two watching humans and was quick to collect her brood, leading them off into the undergrowth and away from the danger.

"Amazing," said Jenny, in whispered awe.

Chapter 50

Wednesday July 1st

Still fresh from birth, the fawn, eager for life, nuzzles its mothers belly desperate for "the stuff" that will fuel its existence. It is frail and vulnerable but determined and driven; instincts so base that all new and emerging life is inexorably dependent on. The doe is weak from birth and she too is vulnerable. Her instincts, now, are of protection and safety for her new-born. The task before her is great but not insurmountable. Luck will play a part; either placing her fawn in harm's way or not. Her first good fortune, not that she would be aware of it, was to have been born in the relatively benign British Isles. There is danger for her though, but not from predation. No active hunters stalk the diminutive heather covered plains that are the unique Dorset Heath lands. Exuberant dogs, cars and all human paraphernalia pose probably the greater threat. Even these are distant if she remains in her own habitat. The very worst Mother Nature might throw at her are the natural opportunists like a badger or fox. These creatures though, would also have to get lucky. An unattended fawn might be tempting but its natural flight instincts would kick in quickly. The cumbersome badger would not stand a chance and the lazy fox, well, probably just couldn't be arsed. However, these retiring animals would soon take advantage of an abandoned and injured fawn, and, in this unlikely eventuality, they would be disturbingly remorseless.

Some thirty, to forty minutes after the birth, very carefully, the doe stands. She needs to move her young away from the birth site and into hiding. In that first half an hour she has cut the cord and eaten the sac. She has licked the fawn clean of the mucous clinging to the fur that up until a few hours before had protectively enveloped her baby; a simple necessity but one that cements a bond, with strength like no other. The soil around the fawn is damp and the vegetation slick with the discharge of afterbirth. Instinctively, the doe knows that to stay would be to court danger; the aromas wafting on the warm summer breeze would be heady to all the natural scavengers large and small. Gently she nudges the fawn, encouraging it to stand; it takes its first jittery steps and very soon, it has mastered the art and is ready for the off.

The morning bird song seems to herald in the new life as the fawn follows its mother. Dawn, at this time of the year, is just after four-thirty am and, by five-thirty the sun has risen above the tree line on the eastern edge of Parley common. This much larger area of mainly heath, just over a mile to the east of Poor Common, is already warming up. The coarse heathers and long wispy grasses, now brown from the early summer's heat, cover the ground like a massive dirty carpet. Every so often, just poking above this scorched shag pile, new life is struggling to find the light.

Bright green ferns and tiny fir saplings stud the landscape like scattered emeralds sparkling as adorning dew droplets just catch the sun's rays.

A magical time to be up and breathing in the fresh morning air. The doe and her fawn take a few tentative steps, the tussocky grass proving difficult for the tiny creature, although eventually, it finds a path between and around the mounds. The purple moor grass, the heathers and the bracken provide a soft playground for the young creature to find its legs, tripping and falling, brushing and scraping, all part of its meteoric learning curve.

In an effort to widen the range in which to forage, the doxes of Poor Common have been pushing their boundaries, and the month of June has not been wasted. As the pups begin to forage for food on their own, the adult group has less to do, but more time for themselves. Nosing their way through the leafy gardens of West Parley, each night extending the time away, they come across the wider expanses of Parley Common. Occasionally they over-morning, using abandoned badgers sets on the chillier days or sleeping rough amongst the gorse and heather. This morning is one such occasion and the east-facing slope, on which they have huddled, is soon bathed in the warmth of a brilliant sunrise. They will be safe here, with only the occasional wayward dog, well off track, likely to disturb them, if unlucky. Their bed amongst the heather is on cushions of washed out lime green-coloured lichen and springy moss that smothers the ground. As they sleep and laze the gentle breeze wafts a scent, which quickens their hearts and brings them to movement, momentarily stretching, but soon on their feet, snouts raised in salute to the air, and tasting the promise it holds.

The doxes moved swiftly, their low slung bodies almost invisible as they cover the ground to the source of the smell. Excitedly they fall upon the scrape where, only a few minutes ago, the doe gave birth. Instinctively noses sweep the area and discern the residue left on the vegetation, and it points the way to go. They catch a glimpse of the doe just fifty metres ahead, she is looking down at her new born struggling with the unfamiliarity of life; breathing air, using legs, staying upright. They are only a few metres from respite in the scrub up ahead, where the doe is hoping in to leave him, hidden from view and in relative safety, whilst she feeds close by.

Behind them, and closing fast, the three doxes fan out, the big male in the centre. The ones on the wings pull forward and soon they are level with the unsuspecting deer. With ten metres to go the male dox deliberately strikes his colours, jumping on to a nearby log. The doe is momentarily spooked; but at nearly twice the height of her pursuer, the roe deer is comfortable with her stance. Moving, so the fawn is behind her, she squares off to the threat, barking three or four times at the familiar creature. She is confident in her size and ability to wound, and the influence this will have on the normally lazy and reticent animal. The warning shouts should be enough to send this intrigant opportunist on its way. Undeterred by its arrogance; the doe moves a step closer stamping the ground, expecting her aggressive display to win through, and for the startled animal, to turn and slink away.

But the bleat from the young one behind draws her gaze to the side and to the unexpected danger closing purposefully on their exposed position. Agitated, and sensing her predicament, she swings her head around, checking for the relative dangers and to view escape routes. Spotting the third dox coming up on her other flank, it's instinctive. She knows the time has come to cut her losses. With a warning bark to her defenceless offspring, she runs at the big male in front of her, hoping to catch him off guard, sure in the knowledge that she can outrun him; her other less obvious intention was to entice the others into joining the chase. It's a vain hope.

The dox dog makes to follow the doe as she veers off, but the rustling noises behind him tell him there was no point; the young one has already succumbed to a merciless joint attack. At a little less than twenty metres away, the doe stops running. She turns and, unconcerned for her own safety, watches helpless and forlorn as the tiny body, so recently inside her is dragged off; the big dox leading his triumphant procession back to the temporary lair, the lifeless fawn trailing from its powerful jaws.

Chapter 51

Monday 6th July

"I don't understand," said Gary looking at his boss in the seat next to him.

It was Monday morning. He'd accepted the offered lift with uncertainty, the proposed destination easily within biking distance for an eight-thirty start. Michael had brought the van to a stop outside a boxy little bungalow; a new job, to paint a bedroom for an elderly couple. Knowing that Michael wouldn't have to concentrate on the road any more, Gary twisted his body to face him.

"Why am I doing this one?" Gary asked, not unpleasantly, but he was still suspiciously perplexed as to the explanation his boss had given him. "Only, you said the other job had a hall, staircase and landing to do."

"That's right," Michael said warily. He had given Gary a couple of weeks off, because as Trisha, Gary's mum had feared, the rumours had spread like wild fire. Gary's name had been linked to Martha's disappearance. Fortunately, his notoriety, as such, remained fairly local and, as he had been released quite quickly from the law's grip, he'd gone virtually unnoticed by the press, at large.

The fact that nothing had come of his time in the police station, and his name had not appeared in any paper, nor his likeness displayed in print, didn't stop the Chinese whispers. With the papers shouting about abduction, and of paedophile gangs, big cats and monsters, this person whom the police had interviewed was but a name. Close friends and relatives would know, but most would keep quiet, not wishing to draw attention to the fact that they had anything to do with this Gary Brown.

Indeed, Michael had been in two minds whether to take him back at work. The first week after it had happened had seen him fending off a few questions from recent customers and associates. He explained and assured them of Gary's worth and that there was nothing in the rumours flying around.

"It had just been an unfortunate set of circumstances," he had said, "that had brought the police to his employee's door."

The second week, it seemed it was business as usual, not one mention or remark, and it had swayed him into accepting that the unsubstantiated murmurings were just that - rumours.

"But you normally give me, those jobs," Gary persisted, "The ones with ladders and working up high, 'cos of your Vertigo."

"I know," Michael said uncomfortably and beginning to get shirty. "Look you've just got to accept my decision. You can either like it or lump it."

"You just don't want me there because they've got kids," he challenged. "Have they said something?"

"For God's sake, Gary. What if they have or they haven't? It makes no odds. You know as well as I do, your name's as close to mud as it's going to get at the moment. I'm just trying to be careful. I've got a good business and I can't afford to lose it, so, if that means you lying low for a while and not doing some jobs that might be…" he faltered searching for the right word, "unsuitable, then I just think it's sensible to be prudent about it."

Pissed off at the familiar advice, Gary shook his head. "It's not bloody fair."

"Life isn't, Gary," Michael said predictably. "Just get on with it."

******

Jenny had been in for an eight o'clock start at the council offices at Furzhill. The small animal welfare team, part of the Public Health department, shared an open plan office and it was slowly filling up. The flexible shift arrangements suited the differing requirements of her job. With the longer days and better weather, dogs and their owners were out and about in greater numbers and at all times of the day. Between the five of them it was not possible to cover every waking hour throughout the week and then have on-call cover for the weekend. Some days Jenny might do a sort of split shift, going out early on patrol until about ten or eleven, have a few hours off and then go out again in the afternoon. At least, that way, they could be available at the peak times.

Trouble was, animals didn't work by the clock, which meant any strays in that 'off' period, in the middle of the day, could mean she got a call, if staffing was thin, like holiday times or training days. It could be a pain at times, but overall Jenny was happy with the arrangements and her supervisor Jill, and her other colleagues, played fair and were conscientious enough to want to make it work for all of them.

Jenny collected a range of forms that she would need to carry, and her clipboard, before heading off to her vehicle. As she got to the door Jill reminded her to swing past the Tricketts Cross Estate, to the north of Ferndown and around the airport, keeping an eye open for some missing dogs.

"The owners reported them missing on Friday, both early evening, hence we've only known about them this morning from the answer phone messages. Evidently," Jill said with an edge to her voice. "Whoever had been on call in the department had either not picked them up, or they just couldn't be bothered to pass them on to one of us."

"What am I looking for then?" Jenny asked. Pen poised to jot the breed down.

"A Yorkshire Terrier, at Tricketts, and a Westie, over by the airport."

"Could you not find anything smaller?" Jenny joked sarcastically, eliciting a smile from her boss and a quick reply.

"I'll see what I can do."

Tony too was gearing up for a busy period at Moors Valley. Within a week the private schools would be breaking up for the long summer holiday, and two weeks

194

after that, the state schools. The park would be full to overflowing. With access to the Park not restricted to just cars; bicycles and walkers entering via the many paths and bridleways that ran through the well-managed area, from other neighbouring plantations, would swell the numbers still further. They were also frantically trying to finish the back-log of clearing ditches and streams, replacing a whole section of fence, repairing others and, on top of that they were running a programme of tree planting at one of the other satellite sites that they managed.

With the weeks seeming to fly past, work commitments heavy for both, plus their non-work activities, and family obligations; meant the moments they were together, they were happy to just chill. Cinema, meals out, a drive out into the country for a walk, or staying local, wandering the other Heaths and woodlands, it didn't really matter, as long as they were together.

For Tony, the spectre of big cats stalking the land had died down by mid July, the ribbing at work almost non-existent and only the occasional jibe in the Angel. Conversations in there still cropped up about little Martha, and although it had been assumed by the authorities that she had been abducted, most people spoke of her in the past tense, as if accepting her demise.

Life on Poor common had also returned to normal. Dogs walked, mums pushed buggies, and kids played around the ponds or rode their bikes down the slopes and jumps from the higher ground. The vegetation was in full summer ware, bright greens of the brackens, stands of purple on the loosestrife and foxglove, yellow flames of the gorse and broom. If one chanced upon this randomly wooded patch of land, passing through it for the first time, one would delight in its intimacy, marvel at the proximity of dwellings whilst wondering at the peacefulness and acknowledging the few who cared to use it; the sort of everyday activity found on open spaces and parks throughout Great Britain. But unbeknownst to all, this little slice of geography nurtured a difference, an anomaly that would become evident as the summer progressed.

Chapter 52

Saturday July 11th

It had been one of those long hot days, expected for the time of year but not always experienced. At least not as often it seemed, by those who looked back to halcyon days of youth when the sun shone all day, every day and life was measured in endless hours, rather than the seconds of today. Jim Bennett fell into this breed, his age allowing him to remember days of the late forties and early fifties; a special time, post war relief and the promise of a new world. Doubtless though, subsequent generations, in spite of life rocketing away, would be no different, and those formative years from early teens to adulthood would always be unequalled.

The good weather hadn't necessarily helped his takings for the day at the nursery but it made him feel better. At eight o' clock, after having had a bite of supper, he decided to leave the security of his own little world to venture out for a walk. It was far too pleasant to stay cooped up. He felt like taking the dog for a walk. But more than that he'd realised, he wanted to feel part of the world again and talk to someone; he wanted company. To this end, he planned his route to include the Angel, taking him on a circuitous route via Poor Common. A couple of pints, maybe? Then, through the estate, past Tesco Express, back down Dudsbury Drive and home. *A reasonable distance*, he thought, looking up at the sky and assessing the need for a jacket, *Ach, it'll still be warm when I get back.*

The spacious double bedroom in their detached house, overlooked a well-stocked and neatly trimmed front garden, denoted by a four-foot high fence, similar to the other properties on Dudsbury Drive. As an older couple, David and Sarah Marsh, had forgone the king-size bed some years back and now slept in two luxurious small double beds, for which they were readying themselves

Over the years, David's restless sleeping patterns and vivid nightmares had created a hostile sleeping environment for his wife, Sarah. But she had flatly refused separate rooms. They had only been apart on a few occasions in their married life and now, as things might be... she hesitantly put it at a doctor's appointment, "drawing to a close," she was not going to be out of touching distance with David, even if that had meant him being accused of domestic violence. She'd winked at the physician as she said it. So, the decision had been separate beds, close enough for some intimacy but far enough to create a sort of fire break when all hell let loose. It had seemed to work. The nightmares had perhaps diminished; at least that was Sarah's view from her nocturnal domain. More importantly though, she slept and, with generous rest, her own health had returned. And tonight she would sleep like a log, her joints weary from the day's exertion.

Jim hadn't felt so positive in years, helped by the two pints of Forty-Niner - delicious and refreshing - and as luck would have it, good company; young Tony Nash and his girlfriend and Dave Martin, the butcher, and his wife. The first few mouthfuls had worked their magic and it had felt like he was amongst old friends. Cockles, his old spaniel also seemed to have a spring in his step, the fuss people had made, appeared to lift spirits and ease the aged frame. They were on the homeward stretch a third of the way down Dudsbury Drive and the old dog faltered slightly, "Not far now boy," Jim encouraged in low tones. The cooler air was welcome, as they sauntered on. The odd car went past them on the wide leafy street, flanked on both sides by dwellings of substance, their mature gardens boasting high fractions of an acre.

Unhurried, and a little light-headed, Jim looked down, watching with almost childlike fascination, as their shadows seemed keen to overtake; the orangey pools of artificial light from each lamp as they passed beneath, cast a fluid perspective. Moving towards the next light he looked back to see his rear shadow grow more defined as the front one diminished. As he brought his head round, something caught his eye on the pavement, some ten metres behind him; another shadow, a fleeting movement that all too quickly disappeared. Unconcerned, Jim tugged on the lead a little, "Come on cockles, past our bedtimes."

A few more steps taken and Jim looked back again, intrigue getting the better of him and knowing that, as like as not, it was a cat or a fox out on its nightly prowl. He peered into the shadows and glanced quickly into the half-lit openings denoting the end of each driveway.

"Gone," he said to himself with a knowing little smile, accepting that no self respecting cat, was going to come near a human on the move, particularly one with a dog, irrespective of age.

The next lamp post saw the old dog linger, sniffing deeply at the plethora of little messages left, some from friends, some not, but all still needing to be read. The lead became taut as Jim tried to walk on, the resistance forcing him to turn again whilst waiting for the dog to finish. *Strange*, he thought, there was something moving on the other side of the road now. *It must have moved very quickly?*

Through the flickering shadows, cast by the overhanging trees, he saw the animal, a fox, trotting purposefully towards them. The relatively bright corridor of road created dark voids of the unlit front gardens laid out behind the walls and hedges flanking the pavements. And set some way back, along block and tarmac drives, were the darkened windows, discouraging and hostile.

Unaware they were being followed, Cockles shuffled on, but Jim kept his head turned, watching with some amusement as the creature seemed oblivious to their presence, its reflective eyes flashing momentarily, although staring straight ahead. Movement again, but on the other side of the road, Jim glimpsed something through an open driveway gate.

"Got a friend have you?" he said quietly to the advancing fox, now only metres from him. "I should disappear up that drive before Cockles sees you," Jim chuckled.

He had no sooner finished the sentence than it dawned on him; it wasn't going to, and that, from across the road, the second animal, had covered the distance at shocking speed and was getting ready to jump.

Jim stumbled back letting out a cry as the animal hurtled into him. The impact took him totally by surprise and he was shaken to the core. Terror and anger rose in equal measures as the second animal came at him and he lost his balance. He lashed out and shouted again, losing grip of the lead. Like a formula one racing engine his heart went from idle to red lining in a beat. A younger model would have coped, but the vintage shell it was fitted to could not hope to stand the surge, and his rapidly failing eyes stricken with pain, stared helplessly as the leathery grip slid menacingly out of view.

"Leave the windows open David. It's baking in here."

"Ok dear, It's been a fabulous day hasn't it?"

David too was ready for bed and he felt hopeful of an undisturbed night. He was bushed. The long days, extended even longer, it seemed, because of the hot and sunny weather, had rewarded him with a back breaking day in the garden.

"Fantastic," he reflected as he drew the lightweight duvet over him. "I'm going to pay for that in the morning" he joked.

"Well I told you to come out of the sun at midday, but would you?" Sarah chided gently and, as she said it, turned her bedside light off.

The room darkened. All was still, save for her husband's fidgeting, the duvet proving too warm for him. With the windows open to the road, the occasional car passed, its headlights casting swift shadows around the room as it pierced the chinks in the heavy curtaining. They had got used to it over the years and it was a quiet road with low traffic levels. Not that it mattered to David. He was drifting away quite quickly amidst pleasant thoughts of another day in the garden, what needed doing and when; the loose schedule forming dozily in his mind and accompanying him to sleep.

As so often happens on long summer days, it takes forever to bring true night and darkness to the world. Safe to say anyway, pitch and inky blackness are rare in towns and cities across the country, the glow of artificial light from a variety of sources pervading all but a few places. Dudsbury Drive was reasonably well lit. But fortunately for David and Sarah the streetlights fell some way either side of their property and the high hedges and trees from the neighbouring front gardens shielded them further. Outside their front garden, the pools of light from the not too distant lamps barely touched, their diffused aura reaching out in a desperate attempt to seamlessly light the way.

Suddenly, the cry of a man's voice shocked the night. It woke David from a near deep sleep and, in his groggy state, was instantly confused. *Was I dreaming,* he thought? "Not tonight please," he implored, whispering lest he wake Sarah.

"GET AWAY!" the voice snarled loudly again. David was now waking and focussing rapidly. *That came from out in the road.* He glanced at his bedside clock.

The glaring green numbers said twenty-two-forty-five. A bare twelve minutes had passed since he had slid into bed.

"Bloody hell," he whispered, somewhat forcefully.

His wife now stirred.

"What's up now?" she said impatiently.

"I don't know. Some bloody drunks outside shouting his head off."

"Ignore it," was the weary reply. "He'll soon go."

There was a heavy thump as if something soft, but bulky had fallen to the floor. Then a feeble groan barely reached their ears. They listened intently for a few moments more, the silence palpable; straining to catch any stray sounds that might issue.

David whispered but was cut short "Sounds like he's collap…"

The silence was severed. A short high pitched and pained wail assaulted the room, and outside, all hell broke loose.

The hairs on the back of David's neck jumped to attention, as very quickly did David. The sound outside was of a violent struggle, snarling and growling, then the scrabbling of shingle, a beastly fight between…

"Dear god it sounds like animals!"

At the window, David could see nothing. He bobbed from side to side in an effort to get a better view around the low growing Sumach. As quickly as it started, the mayhem stopped. It lasted no more than twenty seconds; time enough for David to be pulling on his dressing gown.

"I'm going out to investigate," he announced.

Chapter 53

Dudsbury Drive was looking very different now, to when David had emerged from his drive fifteen minutes earlier. The flashing lights from the attendant ambulance and two skewed police cars were illuminating the road in bright blue pulsing streaks. The faces of neighbours staring out from their drives were barely recognisable in the strobing effects, but David waved anyway.

"Looks like a heart attack," the Paramedic advised the Police Sergeant standing at his back.

"My god he was only, I don't know, 67 or perhaps 68" David looked on somewhat aghast.

"You've known Mr Bennett a while then?" the Sergeant asked.

"Well, not as a friend, although I have shopped at his nursery on occasions, you know, the little one just round the corner. Often see him about, walking the dog, or in town, that sort of thing. He was always willing to give advice about the plants and happy to chat. He struck me though, as rather lonely, particularly since his wife died a few years back. Actually that's strange." Puzzled, David started looking around. "Where's his dog? He never goes anywhere without it."

"You say you heard a fight or struggle?"

"To be honest with you, I'm not sure what we heard. We heard Jim shouting, 'Get away'. That's what woke us. Then there was a dreadful howl, of what sounded like an animal in pain followed by blood curdling growls and snarling; the dog presumably. But not for long though. By the time I had got out into the road, all was quiet. That's when I saw him lying in the drive opposite."

As he'd been talking, David's mind had been making some connections and it dawned on him, "Oh my God! It was the dog! That's what made that awful wail. What on earth could have happened to it?"

"Sarge, over here." The call diverted their attention to the officer crouching down on the pavement, a few yards down the road.

"Looks like blood," he said shining his torch at the glistening patches on the tarmac. Widening his search the beam picked another dark patch a few feet away. It was long and narrow.

"Hallo," he said quietly to himself, and then louder for the benefit of the others, "I reckon something's been dragged off here, or dragged itself, the dog I mean."

"That would seem to confirm your theory Mr Marsh," said the Sergeant looking somewhat perplexed. "Not that it helps make any sense of what happened. The dog will probably turn up sooner or later," … *one way or another.*

David looked down at the streak of blood and followed its implied direction of travel. Another smear was just perceptible halfway across the road, then another. The trail appeared to be heading for David's next door neighbours' drive.

"Anything for me Sergeant?" Patrick Stimpson asked as he ducked under the police tape stretched across the road. "I was on my way home, heard the attendance request and thought I'd show my face."

"I don't think it's a CID matter. We've got an old chap, late sixties, a Mr Bennett, who seems to have suffered a heart attack whilst, we think, walking his dog. It looks to me like he was scared by something, enough to give him the attack and for the dog to run off. Mr Marsh here," the Sergeant moved his hand to indicate the man standing beside him, "Lives in the house over there." He pointed across the road. "And the body is just a few steps into the drive over here."

He led the Inspector over to the lifeless form sprawled across the shingle.

"Did you hear any other voices?" Patrick asked directing his question to David Marsh.

"No, just Jim's"

"Are you sure it was Jim's and not somebody else's, perhaps threatening him?"

"Look officer," David countered, unsure who this un-uniformed policeman was, "I might not have known him that well but, it was so still out here, the sounds we heard might as well have been directly outside our window. It was definitely him."

"Okay. Have you seen anything unusual tonight, people, kids hanging about, anything out of the ordinary?"

"No nothing like that and we'd have noticed,"

David pointed to his wife standing at the end of their drive, dressing gowned and arms folded. "Been in the front garden for most of the day, well up until six-ish I suppose, supper in front of the television, from eight and bed at just after the news, so what's that about ten-forty?"

He shrugged eliciting agreement form his wife. She nodded as he suddenly remembered, and added with an amused little snort, "No nothing unusual apart from that fox. Nearly gave **me** a heart attack, cheeky thing, sitting outside our open French doors, bold as brass, watching us eat our meal. He just appeared from nowhere. Took a bit of shooing off, I can tell you. The little buggers, well big bugger, in this case, are getting so bold these days."

Patrick just nodded and looked at the Sergeant fiddling around in the dead man's pockets.

"It doesn't look like a mugging or anything," the Sergeant added keen to get things wrapped up. "His wallet's still there, so's his credit card, money, nothings been touched. As I say, it looks pretty straightforward; something scared him and the poor bugger's heart couldn't take it."

Patrick looked down at the attending paramedic.

"You happy with that?"

"Yeah, I reckon. I mean, he seems outwardly to be a healthy enough bloke, but then without checking his medical history I can't be sure, and if that's the case, then

201

whatever it was must have been pretty scary, to do that. But, for all we know, he might have had a weak heart, so anything that got his pulse racing might have done it."

"Okay Sergeant," Patrick countenanced, "I'll leave it with you."

Glancing in his rear view mirror at the receding and intermittently blue lit scene, he couldn't help but wonder, what would be scary enough around here to frighten a man to his death, dicky heart or not? The wide tree-lined road, with the houses set well back in large plots, told him, even in the dark, that this was a wealthy area, the houses probably twice or three times the value of his own reasonably sized property. Not the typical stamping ground of the town's wayward few, either. The little shits, whom he regularly rounded up for such offences, usually hung out in the much larger town centres of Poole and Bournemouth. However, he thought, the town's you often felt above this sort of thing, Wimborne, Ringwood, Christchurch and the like, nice rural market towns, were all suffering their share of anti-social behaviour, drink fuelled and loutish. Somehow though, he reflected, this just didn't feel like one of those incidences and, if he was honest, the Sergeant probably had it taped. An old boy... a poor heart, bit of a shock, and, curtains. It was hardly unusual. *Still,* he thought, *it makes you wonder what sort of a shock? I mean they come in all shapes and sizes, it's difficult to imagine... a disturbed roosting bird flying out noisy and flapping, or a dog jumping out from its driveway defending its territory, drive by thugs threatening and menacing people for kicks, or as Mr Marsh said, 'a fox at the window? Could've been anything like that.... except of course... all the aforementioned were noisy, and the old boy would have been alerted to it... wouldn't he?*

202

Chapter 54

Monday 13th July

"Take a look at this Jen," Jill called out as soon as Jenny entered the office at a bleary eight o' clock.

"Ooh, let me get in first," Jenny said pressing a thumb to her temple and gently massaging her brow.

"Heavy night," Jill teased. "Better grab a coffee, and make it two."

Through a forced, but none-the-less, genuine smile Jenny replied, "Most sensible thing you've said so far."

She busied herself making the coffee whilst fending off Jill's breezy interrogation.

"How's it going with ranger man then, be getting married soon, I should think?"

Jenny gave her boss a withering look.

Undeterred, and enjoying the gentle teasing, Jill continued, "Judging by your glowing mug of a morning, you've obviously accepted a few indecent proposals." She gave a crude cackle whilst staring pointedly.

"Yeah, well, you're only jealous," Jenny fired back but not really feeling like making the effort. "So what you got?" she asked, placing Jill's coffee on her desk and then walking around behind her colleague to get a better view of the computer screen.

"Well it might be nothing specifically for us, depends where it was shot. But I presume it's local to us and that's why he's sent it in." Jill clicked open an attachment whilst continuing to talk.

"This was sent in by a cameraman who, by all accounts, was getting some footage for a report on the Dorset Heaths. Anyway, the note on his e mail said," and she began to read and paraphrase it, out loud, "Having just taken off from the airport, intending to fly down towards Poole, and on to the Purbecks, when we spotted something that we thought would make a good clip, providing we could get close enough and not scare them away. But, what should have been a nice gooey shot of mother and child, turned out to be about as far from that as could be imagined."

"Intriguing," Jenny said bending in towards the screen as the Windows media player flickered into life. "You've seen it, I take it?"

"Yes. I warn you it's not very pleasant. But I can't make out where it was taken. It's not somewhere I recognize. I mean, I don't even know if he took off from Bournemouth airport. I'll have to e mail him back and find out a bit more about it. Look there's the deer."

For the next few minutes the two women remained transfixed watching the short video clip play out. From the outset their comments had been sparse,

"That's so sweet," Jenny muttered. "She's so careful with it,"

Nearly a minute passed.

"I just can't work out where it is though," repeated Jill, before falling quiet again.

"What's that moving at the bottom of the screen?" Jenny puzzled, not really expecting an answer. "And there?... Shit, another." A few seconds later, she spoke again. "Shi-it," she said, lengthening the vowel for effect.

In the last few moments, as it became clear to Jenny what was just about to occur, she cupped her hand to her mouth saying, with a look of shear horror, "Oh my God."

Chapter 55

Five minutes later, and with the video clip now on a memory stick, she sat in her van frantically dialling Tony. When it rang to answer phone, she left a message, asking him to call her urgently. Waves of frustration spurred her into action.

"Bloody Moors Valley signal," she said, turning the key on the ignition and saying absently, "If Mohamed won't answer his mobile, looks like I'll just have to go to Mohamed." Adding belligerently, "I bet he's not got it switched on any way."

It took her twenty minutes to drive to the country park and another twenty-five to find him at the Tree Tops Trail, after collaring another ranger for directions.

"I might have known it," she said under her breath as she spied him some way off, and some twenty-five feet below the elevated board walk. Waders up to his armpits and mud almost as far. He was grubbing around in a pond, occasionally lifting a net and studying the contents whilst a group of families watched with keen interest away on the bank. Evidently his net had caught something to show the group on the sidelines and he waded over looking pleased with himself.

She felt guilty at the thought of dragging him away; it was his job after all. But equally, the video clip couldn't wait either. He caught sight of her and waved, surprised but happy to see her.

As soon as she had explained about needing to see this video clip, he'd guided her back via a short route to the park's offices which, he assured, would be empty of staff, as everyone was out in the field for most of the day.

Tony plugged in the memory stick to the nearest computer and waited. "Oh come on!" he moaned, glaring at the screen. The power light flashed repeatedly in recognition of the processing involved.

"Ah, here we go."

Once again, the familiar windows media player filled the screen and the clip started.

"Can you see where that is? She asked excitedly.

"Give me a chance, it's only just started. Besides, the cameraman hasn't focused properly yet, or the helicopter is still moving, one of the two."

"I knew it almost immediately," she said, her voice vaguely triumphant. "We've walked there quite recently."

"It's obviously a heath, but where?" Tony said, almost under his breath, and then it came to him. "The pylons; that's Parley Common." He turned to Jenny as he said it. "I didn't get it at first, never seen it from that angle before. It's a bit shaky though."

"Yes, but it settles down soon. But now look, watch the deer and her fawn, there in the middle of the screen."

"He must have a good Zoom. I can't imagine him being that close, the noise would have spooked them surely"

"I'm reckoning, he's hovering somewhere above the main path that runs across the Heath, you know on top of the hill." She looked at him expectantly.

"Yeah, I think you're right,"

Tony's head nodded gently, eyes glued to the image. "Okay, it looks like they're making for this patch of scrub, here." Tony waved a finger along a line of dense bushes and low saplings on the screen. "That fawn looks pretty new, its movements are still jerky. Mind you, it's difficult to tell at this range."

The creatures could be seen clearly enough on the computer's standard monitor, and it was evident that although they were the focal point of the camera's image, the angle it was taken from meant there was an expanse of foreground, and a good deal of background, which included the woodlands some hundred metres away in the distance.

"So what am I...."? He moved to tip his head back to speak to Jenny, watching over his shoulder, but something caught his eye before he finished the question. "What's that in the heather, just coming on to the screen?" He pointed vaguely at the bottom right-hand corner. "Moving towards them."

"Give it a minute. The cameraman gets a close up. "

Tony didn't need to wait. Something was registering in the back of his mind. Was it the movement, the colour, the shape? He wasn't sure, but he knew he'd seen the animal before, granted not from this angle. And then the close up came. "I thought it was," he said turning again to Jenny, a faint smile perched on his lips. "It's our old friend the dox, by the look of it." As two more moving animals appeared from out of the screens silver trim... "Correction, doxes. That's brilliant."

"Yeah," she said flatly, "although as you'll see, not so friendly I'm afraid."

He watched a few seconds more.

"That's an interesting manoeuvre," he commented, as the three animals split and, looking back quickly at Jenny for her reaction, saw in her face that whatever was coming next was not going to be easy viewing. With a mixture of fascination and dread, his eyes returned to the screen. "My God," he said, "She's just charged at that dox." Then in pointless frustration, almost shouted, "No... the fawn, you've left it wide open."

He knew, in that split second, the fawn was doomed and watched, riveted, as the other two animals fell on the helpless creature. He stared with morbid interest as the three animals moved off and noted that the doe was also watching. Did he imagine it, or was her posture different? Not stiff legged and neat but now, somehow, slumped and heavy.

"You have to wonder what that poor creature is feeling right now; there must be a huge sense of loss." His head shook imperceptibly.

Jenny too was shaking her head. She still couldn't believe it either. "You do realise where this takes us," she said. "I appreciate you've only just seen it, but I've been thinking about it for the last hour."

"Not sure I follow you just at the moment," Tony said, looking still a bit nonplussed by the all too real horror, he'd just witnessed.

"Don't you see Tony?" she said somewhat incredulously... his processing about as swift as the sluggish office machines. "Think back Tony." Her eyes implored him to speed up. "Our first trip to see the cubs on Poor Common.... the deer."

Halfway there at the beginning of the sentence, the recognition was in full swing by the end, "Shittt," he breathed.

"Exactly," she said.

"Christ." Tony's face drained. "Whilst I've been banging on about, panthers and the like, the answer's been right here, under our noses all the time. Those pets and animals, the deer all killed by these... things."

Continuing to stare, neither dared speak, each lost in the same thought. In a half whisper, Tony broke the silence. "And the little girl?"

Jenny gave an exaggerated shrug.

Chapter 56

Later on, and with work-days over, their minds were still on overtime; struggling to make sense of the conclusions they had drawn whilst trying to carry out normal duties. Their focus on the day-to-day interrupted as they kept drifting back to the events of the past few weeks; events that had brought them to the final grim determination.

They sat either side of the breakfast bar in Tony's flat, Jenny on the kitchen side, Tony in the living room. A bowl of pasta and sauce in front of each, a meal that they'd thrown together purely for something to eat rather than to satisfy any wanton taste buds. But it was passable and they both picked over it as they sporadically aired their thoughts or quietly contemplated the various implications and outcomes. The television was on in the background but they weren't watching it.

"You know, I don't know what I find harder to believe," Tony said leaning his back against the stool's cushioned rest. "A big cat, something that we know to be real, but shouldn't be here, stalking the suburbs, or a creature from folklore that we have no proof of." He gave a little shrug acknowledging his uncertainty. "Yet we have footage of said creature, carrying out a savage hunt and all within spitting distance of a major town. Which is more likely, eh? It's so fantastic that I'm struggling to believe it myself." He shook his head. "I don't know about you but I've been thinking about it all day."

"I know!" Jenny agreed. "And there's a perverse injustice really. We've gone to the police in good faith with the big cat idea, only to have it ridiculed. And now!"

They fell silent, chewing this one over. After a while, Jenny broke through the back ground chatter of the television.

"So, what are we going to do now?"

Tony looked thoughtful for a moment. He had been wondering just that when she had spoken. A rough idea was taking shape but it wasn't exactly dynamic.

"To be honest with you I think we should let it go for a while."

Jenny looked surprised.

"What do nothing?"

"Well no, not nothing exactly, I mean, we just don't tell anyone."

"So what... wouldn't we be doing, exactly?"

This was the part he was having difficulty with. *What could they do?*

"I think," he hesitated. "I think all we can do at the moment is to gather more evidence."

Once again, Jenny gave him a hard stare, implying she was more than unconvinced by this rather passive response.

Tony threw his fork down angrily, "Christ's sake Jen! What do you expect? You said it yourself." He stormed off, slinging his plate into the sink. "Who's gonna listen now? Look," he said sharply, ignoring her shocked expression, "I reckon we've got to gather all the stuff we've got so far, get it into some sort of order and then when the times right… we go to whoever."

Jenny's eyes were glistening with moisture but the look was still defiant. Tony softened. "So things like the statement you took from that guy, what was his name, Cyril somebody, about being attacked. Talk to people who've lost pets. Our photographs we took and this video clip, that's what's going to matter. Unless you've got any bright ideas, Jen? I think it's all we can do at the moment."

He looked across at her, appealing for some support. The blank stare and a slight head shaking, plus her continued silence, in a bizarre way, gave him some comfort. He thought of something. "You know, I don't necessarily think that the police are our only port of call, for example what about your own office's, 'animal welfare.' Might not this fall under their jurisdiction? Dangerous dogs and animals or exotic pets, etc"

"I'm not sure that it would," Jenny said, looking thoughtful. "Our department dishes out licences for pet shop owners, zoos and the like, but the dog wardens only handle dogs and cats. We wouldn't normally get involved with trapping or catching other animals. But you're right though." Her face brightened a little as the positive thoughts began to flow.

"There's the RSPCA they handle a much broader range of animals, although, I'm not sure this would even be in their remit. There's DEFRA of course. They cover a lot of areas, farming the environment, invasive species, the control of plants and animals. Although," she hesitated, "I'm not sure about rounding up dangerous wild animals. Tell you what," she said more optimistically, "I'll make some discreet enquiries at work."

"Yes, well." Tony's mood still un-lifted, "I do think we need to be discreet. Not just because of being humiliated again, but more from the point of view of causing alarm or panic. If any ones going to do that, it should be the authorities. But, I suspect, even they might wish to keep it quiet; dangerous animals on the loose? Christ, you'd have vigilante groups taking the matter into their own hands."

The conversation lulled; tension still apparent, as they cleared the remaining plates. A brief debate whether to wash up now, or not, resulted in water being drawn and Tony taking poll position at the sink. As Jenny dried the few items that they had used to make and consume the meal, she pondered on new considerations.

"You have to wonder at just how dangerous these doxes are. I mean, look at their heritage: one half we are assuming is a fox and the other a pit bull terrier. Independently they are not particularly dangerous to people."

Tony picked up on the thread.

"Yeah, I see where you are going with this. The fox by nature, is a wily predator, and a superb hunter, but also very adaptable, and will forage wherever food is abundant. And, of course, its diet is hugely varied from small animals: like rats and mice, to worms, fruits and berries," Tony let slip a smile, "the odd take away, fish and chips whatever it can find. As I've said before, they're a bit lazy, preferring a well stocked bin than running a prey to ground."

Jenny quickly fired off a thought of her own as Tony finished speaking. "I suppose you could argue, that, although the Pit Bull, as a 'domesticated animal' would not be regarded as any of those things." Jenny stopped rubbing the plate she was drying and gazed down at the floor whilst summoning the information to the fore. "What did the website say?" Oh yes, "The American Pit bull has been crossbred to produce a versatile working dog: guard duties of herds, flocks, whatever... against foxes, here, or cougars in the states, they've been used for rounding up cattle, or as catch dogs for semi-wild livestock."

Glancing back up, she continued.

"But what I was getting at is, you can't get away from the fact that the animal's basic instinct from way back, before it was domesticated, would be to hunt and, of course, in more recent years, some owners have cross bred to produce highly aggressive dogs used for fighting."

"And," Tony acknowledged, reiterating one of Jenny's own much vaunted rulings. "Any dog can be aggressive, depending on its circumstances and treatment."

"Exactly. And so, given the right circumstances, as in Betty's dogs' case, they became violent because of the conditions they experienced, almost like reverting to type, back to default as you might say."

As the washing up chore ended they sat down on the sofa, half watching the television but continuing with their deliberations.

"Assuming we're right about this crossbreed animal," Tony continued. "It's likely to draw upon the traits of both sides, and, throwing in for good measure the wider dog family's basic instincts, so we're talking: wolves, coyotes, jackals etc. etc, it has the potential for being, at best, a lazy but clever lap dog, or at worst..." he paused to pool the right terminology, "an ingenious, powerful and adaptable, hunter killer... Is that about right?"

Jenny was nodding in full agreement and added, "I guess so. And let's factor in these particular animals' circumstances. Partially raised by humans, so plenty of food, keeping them healthy and strong, an enclosed environment within the walled garden so plenty of interaction between the dogs and foxes, and, even if some of the traits didn't pass through the genes, they may have learnt them through familial contact."

"Yes," said Tony as a new idea hit him. "Presuming our big male dox is the father of the cubs of the vixen we saw, once Betty's free food dried up, where would he find it...? Wherever he could is the answer. All around Poor common and beyond, by the looks of it."

"They appear to be reverting to default as well," chipped in Jenny. "Hunting as a pack, and not on their own."

"And judging by what we've seen, they're pretty efficient too," Tony added prophetically, leading to another pause in the conversation.

A few moments passed and Jenny fixed Tony with a troubled stare, as she reflected back on the day when she had been called to Homewood House. "That day, when I went to get her dogs, you know she'd been found dead in the garden." Tony nodded again, "Well, she'd been there for some time, by all accounts, but the thing is, the police said she looked a lot worse than she ought to from the injuries she sustained, because the local wildlife had got to her, namely badgers and rats but most likely... foxes."

Tony looked very thoughtful, "Looks like they got the taste for it." And as if to clarify, added, "Human flesh I mean."

Jenny looked down at her shoes.

"It does make you wonder though," Jenny said rather blandly. "If..." and hesitating, as if she oughtn't to say anything, "if this animal is real..." She paused again, "Well, we know it's real, don't we?" She sought confirmation from Tony, who nodded his response. "Is it just co-incidence then... Martha, I mean?" Frustration swept across her face. "You know what I'm trying to say... did they kill her!"

And there it was. The big question that they had both avoided, was now out in the open. Disturbingly it didn't seem the better for being there.

Tony didn't answer, preferring to brood on a depressingly familiar dilemma, a place somewhere between duty and obligation.

Jenny decided to lose herself in the local paper, and curled up into the crook of the sofa's armrest. She found little to capture her interest, scanning the pages and speed-reading the headlines. Page six held her gaze for a moment, an issue close to home - local authority cut backs affecting staffing levels in Dorset Councils. *Whatever!* She thought, determined not to let it worry her. But the adjacent column, next to that article, held a number of familiar phrases and she was strangely drawn. They seemed to stand out from the others. 'West Parley' was one, 'Nursery owner dies from shock' was another and then, 'pet dog feared dead'. All relatively innocuous to ninety-nine point nine percent of the Ferndown populace, but to the minuscule representation on this particular sofa, it would be glaringly relevant, and so, with an urgent trepidation, they read the article together.

Chapter 57

Sunday July 19ᵗʰ

A luxurious lie-in, had led to confused digestive systems. The flimsy 'plastic' toast eaten in bed, with mugs of tea an hour earlier, meant that, by twelve-fifteen, both Jenny and Tony were starving.

Neither had to go to work and they debated on a Sunday lunch at a pub, followed by a walk somewhere, perhaps in the New Forest, or over on the Purbecks. Still scantily pyjama'd and taking it easy, in Tony's flat, the television providing background distraction, they sat on the sofa with a weeks' worth of information that they had gathered about the hybrid foxes, spread over the coffee table. Tony had suggested that, later, when they got back from their walk, they ought to start collating it.

"Get it into a folder, probably in date order, I think."

Jenny had agreed with building it chronologically, and absently shuffled the sheets picking the odd one up and reading it through, but had been less than enthusiastic about giving up her Sunday evening.

"Oh come on," she'd said. "We're both in work tomorrow. Let's just have a quiet night in, get a film, bottle of wine, and who knows." a wicked grin lit up her face, "I might not be in a fit state to drive home again."

He'd laughed along with her and warned that the neighbours might be getting a bit pissed-off, as her car was conspicuously hogging a much coveted space on the limited forecourt.

They'd worked hard all the past week, both at their respective jobs but also in the evenings too, writing up the documentation that would help them in any future presentation; feeling it needed to look well put-together and professional, and, not just the ramblings of a couple of local nutters. This was their big fear, getting people to take them seriously, and not just anyone, but those in authority from whichever agency they decided at the time, it should be. They had written statements either about their own experiences, or others, who were part of the story. This had proven tricky, because they couldn't afford to let on why they wanted the information, or indeed, what it was going to be used for. Jenny's trump card had been her uniform on most occasions, explaining that she was with animal welfare, which seemed to cover a multitude of possibilities. Tony had needed to be more circumspect, his already tarnished persona leading to outright suspicion from some, or poor humoured cynicism from others, particularly the Angel's fraternity.

It made him wonder though, at just how they might react if he was right. When might they realise that their safe world had overnight become perilous. Animals they knew, familiar and comforting, part of the British wildlife's gentle persona now deemed hostile, menacing and dangerous. Foxes – so common and yet normally so shy, now emboldened and, seemingly, lurking in wait for that one chance opportunity to exploit; a child at a lonely bus stop, a shuffling pensioner in an empty park, or even to a simple solitary stroll in the woods. How long would it take for them to realise this green and pleasant land was no longer harmless and that, in time, few places, might not be really safe again?

Tony's brush with Gary in the pub one evening had turned out not to be the annoyance he had feared it might. It had, in fact, been a lucky strike; Tony's initial irritation at being collared by Gary, waning when he realised who he was sitting with. Tony knew that Sandra was Daisy Docker's next door neighbour and an opportunity to, perhaps, elicit information about that fateful day could not be passed up. It had been common knowledge that Sandra had been a driving force at the time, and subsequently, as the furore had died down she had endeavoured to keep it alive. Tony had stayed for much longer than he'd intended, but had come away with a modicum of extra grist to add to their tenuous mill. Unfortunately the results had been gleaned through general conversation, somewhat tedious, but eventually gently steered by Tony to discuss what had happened.

Sandra had not been suspicious. It seemed only natural that acquaintances and people she'd met would want to ask her about it; after all, it would be much easier than any tortuous conversation with Daisy or the family. Gary had given him a funny look, when after some time of chatting about the events, and the conversation possibly drawing to a close, Tony had casually slipped in that he and Jenny had often been on the common.

"It's a nice walk, not far from my flat, and we've been watching some fox cubs. Seems to be a lot about at the moment. You seen any?"

The question had been directed at the both of them and Gary had duly piped up about his next door neighbour's chickens, and looking even more quizzical as Tony probed, as innocently as he could.

Sandra had been half listening, appearing to join in with a few nods and murmurs in near silent placation, but Tony could see she wasn't really in the conversation. And then suddenly out of nowhere, as she was gazing up at the ceiling, as if trying to escape the lively din, she said, "There was one that day you know."

Tony had had to reign in his excitement; he knew exactly what she was saying. It had taken a great deal of effort to tease out where she had seen it and keep it casual.

"It was on the roof of next door's shed; not Daisy's, the other way. Cheeky beggar, sunning itself, I was watching it through the kitchen window. Disappeared a few minutes before everything kicked off, when I heard poor Daisy."

Admittedly it didn't prove much, Tony knew, but the coincidences just kept on mounting and, sooner or later, they were going to break the surface. He just hoped the stack wouldn't get much higher before they could prove anything.

When Sandra left, Tony moved to go too, but Gary waylaid him with a question of his own, one that Tony hadn't expected at this early juncture. Resting a hand on Tony's arm and mouthing, 'Hang on,' as Sandra turned.

But as she moved out of earshot, "You're thinking it's maybe the foxes then?"

Tony felt himself go cold. "What do you mean?" feigning as much ignorance as he could muster.

"All those disappearances. You know what I'm talking about, the animals and the like."

Tony could only guess as to what he meant by, 'the like,' but if everything else was classed as an animal, that left only one option… Martha. "What?" Tony had given an incredulous laugh, which, he hadn't felt, was very convincing, "What makes you think that, for goodness sake?" and trying not to over-egg it.

Gary had stared at him with little emotion, giving nothing away.

"Well you seemed to be asking a lot of questions about them, that's all, and when I asked you in the pub that evening whether you thought a big cat might be responsible for all those chickens going missing and other animals, you were right off-hand about it. I reckon you know more than you're telling, that's all."

Tony, put on the back foot, was sure Gary had just made a simple leap and was testing the water with a notion that had just popped into his head. He didn't believe that Gary had actually given it much thought. However, believing that attack was probably his best defence, he had deflected giving his reply by asking Gary what, he felt, might be an awkward question for him to answer.

"How come you were taken to the police station?"

"Simple misunderstanding, which, I might say, has given me a good deal of grief."

"Oh, what misunderstanding was that then?"

It had been Gary's turn to feel uncomfortable and unlike Tony he didn't hide it too well, shifting uneasily in his seat, avoiding eye contact by starring into his quarter empty, pint pot.

"If it's any business of yours" he said aggressively, "I lost my medic alert," Gary had hauled his sleeve up displaying the bracelet, "on the common not far from Daisy's house and of course the bastards put two and two together to make five. They thought I must have been part of some paedo ring." He snorted heavily. "Bloody cheek. I wouldn't mind but I've known Daisy for a long time. We were at school together, she's lovely," he looked mildly wistful, "I wouldn't wish what happened to her, on my worst enemy."

"No, you're right, I'm sorry I shouldn't pry," Tony said genuinely apologetic.

"Bloody pigs," Gary continued. "Luckily I never got mentioned in the papers or anything like that, but it soon got around."

"Just be glad you never had your picture in the paper," Tony said empathising with Gary's unwanted notoriety.

The beer had evidently had an effect on both of them, Gary becoming maudlin and stroppy and Tony, backing off, beginning to feel sympathy for the guy.

"So things settled down for you now?" Tony asked.

"Yeah, been back to work a few weeks now. The dusts just about settled."

Tony wasn't quite sure, why he had pursued the conversation, he could have left; but knowing what it was like to have enforced attention from unwanted sources, he had hoped to show a bit of solidarity, appreciating what Gary had gone through.

When they had parted half an hour later Tony had felt pleased he'd stayed to talk, not exactly a burgeoning friendship, but at least he felt he had made some effort to try.

After seeing the video with the deer losing her fawn, and during their subsequent discussions, Jenny grew to suspect a connection with the two dogs that she was asked to keep a watch for, a few days back. The places where they had gone missing were both in close proximity to Parley common, indeed both bordered the area, one to the north the other to the south and west. And, as it was clear that the doxes had widened their range to include Parley, so, she had reasoned, it was a distinct possibility that they might be to blame. With her official hat on, she had visited the owners. Their addresses recorded at work had been easy to come by. Both tales had contained a similar theme - walking the dog over on Parley Common, losing them in the trees and the gorse as they followed scents and trails; the owners unconcerned as the animals in familiar surroundings would often reappear somewhere further on. On both occasions though, neither returned and, despite lengthy searches, nothing was found. By the time she had met up with the owners, the incidences were nearly two weeks old; neither dog had subsequently been picked up. This fact led Jenny to assume the worst. A lost dog was usually picked up within a few hours, and maybe worst case a day or two; often shopped by worried members of the public restraining them from certain death on some busy road.

Whilst she realised the finger of suspicion was pointed the doxes way, yet again, it would need a lot more to convince anyone. The only real evidence, and it was compelling, there had been no doubt in her mind, was the doxes hunting in the video clip. But even that wasn't definitive; it didn't mean that all the other suspicious events that they knew of, and indeed probably those they didn't, were necessarily down to them. Especially Martha - that particular tragedy would require a minor miracle to confirm.

She had also found that on following up an incident it could often lead to another occurrence and a new lead. The sprightly pensioner who had described the evening when wandering down her garden to shut her free-ranging chicken up for the night, had sent Jenny in two further directions.

In her case the seventy-eight-year old had gone out into the late evening gloom, as she did every night, but was aware immediately of an unusual stillness. "No soft chuckling of chooks fidgeting on their roosts," she clarified, "nor frogs splashing back into the pond as I went by. It was like;" she'd stared wide eyed fixing Jenny, "like the devil himself had just passed by!"

From anyone else Jenny would have accused them of hamming it up, but this outwardly capable old lady was genuinely on edge. The upshot had been, out of the nine strong flock, all but two, found clinging in some high shrubs, were gone. "A few scattered feathers, but no carcasses." She advised, shaking her head and adding, "That's not like any fox kill I've seen before." When she'd called to warn friends, like-minded souls who kept chickens and ducks, to be on their guard, it had revealed two more exterminations; one, nearly three weeks earlier, with the loss of ten Bantams from a converted shed over on the Dudsbury side of the common. Jenny had followed this up, and finding that the thin wooden planking had apparently been chewed through at a weak point.

The second was at a house a few doors away from the first. Here they had lost two ornamental peacocks. Vociferous birds at the best of times but they had been spirited away early one morning without so much as a squawk. The relaxed owners had never really worried about predators; the birds had appeared formidable enough. Although Jenny had never seen them, she could well imagine; and agreed the formally landscaped, half-acre setting, would be the poorer without them.

Collecting details about poor Jim Bennett's demise had not been easy either. To begin with they had had no way of finding out what had happened. The police certainly wouldn't divulge anything, he had no relatives and the medical team were unlikely to be forthcoming as well. But Jenny had hit upon the idea that, because they knew roughly where on Dudsbury Drive he had died, they could once again, in her professional capacity and on the pretext of looking for the dog, knock on doors and find out which of the residents had called it in. Or at the very least find somebody that had left their homes to find out what had happened. It was a brilliant idea and they had come up trumps almost straight away, finding David and Sarah Marsh willing to run through the events of that unfortunate evening.

Once again they had found the anomalies, such as the missing dog Cockles. Where had he gone? The traces of his blood on the pavement and road suggested an injury, but not what had happened. The fact that shock had brought on a heart attack for Jim had been distressing news. They'd known him. Not well, granted, but what they had gauged, was that he was a quiet man; lonely and a little shy. Despite this, they'd found in him a sense of humour, and a gentle friendly manner. He would be missed at their wildlife gatherings.

Jenny put down the last few pages on to the coffee table, noting that one was about Betty's housekeeper and the other blank, apart from a heading: Interview with Helicopter Cameraman. She stared at it, wondering why the person who had sent in the film had not replied to her e-mail.

Tony had gone to the toilet and she was contemplating getting dressed ready to go out, the hunger pangs growing with every passing minute. As she did so the newsreader in the background mentioned, 'some breaking news.' If that short statement hadn't got her attention, then the next one certainly did. 'A fox has attacked three children as they slept in a tent in the garden of their parent's home in Bournemouth.' She lunged for the remote and shouted to Tony to, "Get in here quick!"

The story was still young, the incident only the previous night and the overuse of 'allegedly', and the expressions, 'what we believe has happened' and "what we are led to understand is', seeming to form much of the dialogue. But through the waffle Tony and Jenny were able to discern that the three children, aged: four, six and eight, having just broken up for the summer holidays, had decided to spend the night in a tent in the garden; a trial run before the family went on holiday. The youngsters had not settled down particularly early, excitement getting the better of them, meaning they were still awake at nearly eleven pm. Their parents had had a take-away in front of the television, accompanied by a few drinks and had gone to bed shortly after admonishing the noisy campers for still being awake, and saying they would leave the sliding French door open slightly, in case of bathroom visits in the night. One of the children must have taken up this offer, choosing to leave the door wide open on their way back to the tent.

In the early hours of the morning, the children had been woken by noises, coming from just outside the tent. The oldest child seemed to have opened the tent and had immediately been attacked by the fox. The screams of all the children had scared the animal away before their father arrived on the scene. There was evidence that the fox had got into the house.

As usual, the main newsreader was soon dragging in to the hastily put together presentation, 'an expert on foxes', a representative from the RSPCA, and, an on-the-scene reporter, looking much as though, it was he that had just slept in the tent. Luckily nobody had been hurt and the experts had assured the public that this was a very unusual event, and that like as not, the animal was as shocked as the children, and, feeling trapped went to strike out.

"Yeah well I've heard enough," said Tony wearily. "Would be interesting to know where in Bournemouth. It could be miles away, nothing to do with our friends and just some incredible co-incidence."

The 'you've got to be kidding', look, he received from Jenny pretty much summed up his own thoughts.

And with yet another disturbing conundrum bubbling under and not that far away by the sound of it, Tony and Jenny switched off the television and went in search of their own prey.

Chapter 58

Tuesday 21st July

They had met straight after work, at Tony's flat, eaten a microwave-able ready meal and were on the move again by seven-thirty. Jenny had once again bluffed her way into the house with the uniform and Council Identity Card. Tony was introduced as a new member of the team joining her on a few visits. The parents were somewhat wary, not quite sure why the dog warden should be involved, especially a few days after the event', and, particularly after the incident had drawn a stream of representatives from the police, RSPCA and Bournemouth's own animal welfare officer, and not to mention of course, the press.

Jenny was prepared for that, explaining she was investigating some dog or possibly fox related incidences in Parley and, as Kinson was just literally over the boundary her supervisor had suggested she check this one out.

"No respect for council borders," she'd smiled cheekily, "these animals."

Monday had filled in the gaps. The rolling news coverage on television and front page reports and headlines in a number of newspapers had told Tony and Jenny what they thought they would hear. The incident was not in any of the other suburbs of Bournemouth, well away from Parley, it was as they knew it would be, very close. Kinson, the northernmost outpost of the town was less than a mile from the doxes assumed main stomping ground of Poor Common and the house backed on to the open fields that led down to the river.

"Easily doable in one night," Tony had said, surprised that it only seemed to involve one animal and not the three they had seen.

With the parents won over by Jenny's easy manner, particularly the young dad, and the mum distracted, trying to put pyjamas on to the four-year-old, it was easy to ask questions and elicit answers in between the normal goings on of a lively family at bedtime.

The older boy's description of the animal had been good, it was a fox that much was for sure, but whether it was one of theirs they couldn't be sure; it was tricky to obtain the finer details from the snatched view the child had got.

Wayne the eight-year-old, told them, that they had been woken by sounds outside the tent, and that it was just beginning to be light outside, but still dark enough for his brothers to be frightened. Whatever it was, moved around the small garden and they could hear it in the lounge, snaffling at the takeaway containers left on the coffee table. They'd heard the tray fall from the low table and the follow on dull thuds as the heavily stained and encrusted foils hit the floor.

They were also aware that one of the sounds was of the bin falling over and thudding to the ground, then the rustling of papers and food wrappers as the contents were carefully being searched. The two younger children were naturally scared but at this point the older decided to investigate. The noise of the zipper as he pulled it down alerted the intruder. But, instead of becoming wary or running away, the animal had in the child's words "got angry and ran at me." The boy had had the presence of mind to pull the zipper back up just as the fox hit the tent; but the fox began to scrabble at the thin material. The children had shown Tony and Jenny the rips around the base of the tent.

At that point all the children had started screaming which alerted the parents. By the time the father had got outside the fox had disappeared. However, "the mess that this one fox had left was incredible," the father had said.

The living room had been trashed; the remains of the Indian take away foils littering the floor, crisps and naan bread crumbs scattered like a giant's case of dandruff. The kitchen too had been visited; overturned cereal packets and fusilli pasta had been shot across the floor from a half-open cupboard.

"The place stank to high heaven too," the mum had said. "It had wee'd on some of the furniture and poohed in the kitchen. I can still smell it, even after spending most of Sunday trying to clean it up."

Although the boy had only seen the one fox, the way he had described the ordeal, which seemed to last for no more than a few minutes, Tony felt sure that there had been more.

"Stands to reason," Tony said to Jenny, as they belted-up, back in her car. "The boy said it happened so fast, suggesting no more than two to three minutes at most. The various noises he'd heard appearing to come from different places, but the sounds clashing, implying more than one animal - he wasn't sure about this admittedly. Besides, I doubt one animal could have made so much mess and in so many places in that time frame. The mum told me the police even found Masala paw prints on the landing upstairs. I mean, I know they're fleet of foot an all that, but it'd have to be one heck of a dose of performance drugs to achieve that sort of speed, let alone be in two places at once."

"Yeah well they seem to manage it in Harry Potter," levelled Jenny distractedly, the comeback made as she manoeuvred the car out of the tight space and away from the curb. "So you reckon this was down to our little thugs then?" she asked as the car pulled away.

Tony gave an exaggerated shrug, "Who the hell knows." His demeanour was one of pure frustration. "How in God's name are we going to pin these little buggers down? Every time, we come away with sod all, nothing concrete, just conjecture and supposition. It's getting on my tits."

Jenny was pensive for a few minutes, seeming to concentrate on her driving. Inside though, she was wrestling with how to put her next idea forward and without winding her already taught boyfriend up any further.

"You know, if this was down to our friends," her voice growing serious, "then those little people have been very lucky. That is assuming, and I take it we are… assuming, that poor Martha was killed by these animals."

"It's hard to believe it, I know." Tony shook his head. "But yes that is what we are saying. But how do we prove it?"

"Well, sooner or later…We… might not have too."

Tony's brow furrowed up, "How do you mean?"

She glanced across at him, "How long before the next one Tony, and then the next. I can't see cute rabbits and scrawny chicken cutting it for long. Can you?"

Tony noticed that her voice was harder and the driving edgy, not aggressive but determined and more assertive. He had known her long enough now to see she was working up to something.

"These… happenings Tony are becoming more frequent; they're getting closer together. We've been aware of something going on since early May, but in the last few weeks there have been too many to be coincidences. And those are just the ones that we know of."

Tony had an inkling of what she was driving at.

"So what are you saying?"

She wasn't shouting but her voice had force and the intonation was clear. "How long before the next Martha is taken… Tony?"

They drove in silence for a couple of miles, allowing Jenny to cool off and Tony to reflect on what Jenny had been implying. Deep down he knew she was right. People should be alerted, warned of the possible danger, as unbelievable and incredible as it may sound. By the time he spoke again he had come up with a course of action but he wasn't thrilled. The familiar prospects of shoving his head above the parapet again were unenviable, but at this moment in time they were still some way off so he could brush them to one side. The caveat he knew, would be regret, the moment it became reality.

"Ok," Tony said with a resigned determination. "Here's what we're going to do." He corrected himself. "Actually, what you're going to do."

"Oh yes?" the intrigue and trepidation boiled menacingly. "And what pray, might that be?"

Chapter 59

Saturday 1ˢᵗ August, Bank Holiday weekend.

The view through the part open curtains was dismal. It seemed as if the sun was ignoring the world, hiding petulantly under the covers, as the grey sheets of rain lashed at the windows.

"Sod that," Tony breathed and decided to snuggle up to Jenny for a few more minutes of warmth and comfort.

He listened to the bucketing rain being whipped into a frenzy whilst thinking, like millions of others, *it's a bank holiday weekend what did you expect?* The rain didn't actually bother him, he was quite happy working out in it. However, it did mean the country Park would be deathly quiet; there would be a few hardy souls and the weather might pick up a bit, but inevitably the day would drag. He suspected there would be some mundane duties found for him: catch up on paperwork, finish planning the later season events, Christmas perhaps, or, failing that, tidy the office. God he hoped the weather would pick up.

The forecast he remembered was actually quite positive, the morning's rain accurately predicted would sadly remain all day, changing over Saturday night as a burst of high pressure would force it out of the way; leaving Sunday and the bank holiday Monday with increasingly sunny weather. But, as one of the great weather-sceptical British public, he could do nothing but wait and see.

When Jenny awoke for the second time that morning, having dropped back off after Tony had gone, she felt guilty. *It's nine thirty!* The feeling didn't last long and she languished a while longer allowing herself to ease gently into the day and become, 'fully with it'. There were no plans to do anything, apart from some grocery shopping and her promise to try to finish off the dox folder. She was regretting having suggested a PowerPoint presentation, persuading Tony that it would look far more professional than scrappy bits of paper and flimsily printed photographs. Besides the video clip was potentially the most important and persuasive piece of evidence. The various screens being still chronologically configured would seamlessly culminate at the disturbing footage. The fact that she had never used Microsoft PowerPoint before had not deterred her, "Jill uses it at work all the time," she had told Tony, "and she's not even very good with computers, so how hard can it be?"

With the seasonal higher workload at the council stretching her day, she had not always found the time to concentrate on it. She was painfully aware that it would be nearly two weeks since Tony had laid out his action plan, the main thrust of which relied on this presentation being ready. Somehow though, the enthusiasm hadn't so much waned, but being busy all day at work, trying to get to grips with the new software, and things appearing to have quietened down on the dox activity front - no new incidences, at least none of any significance that they were aware of - the urgency to get it finished had become less pointed, and the days somehow slid by. However, it was all but ready, and, looking pretty good she felt. Tony had been impressed. Whether it would have the same effect on other more discerning and certainly cynical beings she could only guess. The other part of 'Tony's Master plan' she had already actioned, albeit that the meeting arranged would not take place now until Wednesday of the coming week. But at least that gave her time to hone the almost finished article.

The cynical being whom she had arranged to meet was someone she'd met before and had used this advantage, to help open communications. It had taken further powers of persuasion to win him over, but she had managed it. The clincher had been Betty's dogs. He had remembered the Pit-Bulls only too well, and the thought that this dog warden had information on a sensitive matter, illegal dog fights, drew him in. She had understood that this wasn't really his domain but implied that she would go down the right channels having had the opportunity to run this past him. Some of the gangs and owners involved, she explained, were local, and his working knowledge would add weight to any action to be taken.

Managing to avoid a meeting at the station by explaining she was concerned about too many people knowing at the moment, they had agreed for him to make a home visit. What he didn't know was the address given was Tony's. She presumed he wasn't aware of this in spite of Tony's not so recent telephone conversation with him. However, he would soon work out he'd been had the moment Tony was introduced. And that, she thought, was when the proverbial might hit the fan.

Chapter 60

Sunday 2nd August

They woke to a day in sharp contrast to the previous one. The early morning was still a little jittery; a lively breeze flicking round the treetops and high white cotton-wool clouds buffeting the newly washed blue backdrop and suggesting a day of real promise. And by midday no one was disappointed; the breeze had all but gone, the clouds were packed away and the sun was out in strength.

Like many residents of Dorset fearing the extra bank holiday traffic and a bonus two days off work, Tony and Jenny decided to stay local. Their Sunday would include: a late emergence from the duvet, lunch with Jenny's parents a few miles away in Lower Parkstone, and an afternoon stroll through one of the Chines down to the beach. Tony counted himself more than fortunate to have hit it off so well with Barbara and Kenneth. He had met them briefly a few weeks back and had liked them straight away.

It was only five forty-five when they made for home. The sun was still blisteringly hot, the roads were pretty clear, with anyone who was going anywhere, clearly having got there, so the run back to Ferndown was even more pleasant.

The icing on the cake, for many people, was the fact that the next day was a bank holiday, and the prospects of a fine evening, running through to another scorcher the next day, sent trails of smoke billowing into the blue yonder as evening barbecues fired and the smell of burning charcoal, pervaded the route home. The empty roads gave the impression that the whole world had slowed and making Monday, seem like an age away.

As they drove up through Longham approaching Ferndown, the White Hart on their left looked exceptionally busy, the pavement tables and chairs all taken as revellers from inside spilled out to take advantage of the rare summer evening.

"That's an idea," said Tony looking enviously at the array of cool drinks on display, the glasses frosted and slick with condensation. "I could just murder a pint. Fancy stopping at the Angel?"

"Yes, good idea, we can sit outside. That film we want to watch isn't on until ten so there's no need to hurry, we might as well enjoy it while we can. Besides it will be far more pleasant than sitting in the flat."

Within five minutes they were pulling up wooden seats and drawing in mouthfuls of chilled liquid: a Tanglefoot for Tony and Weston's Stowford Press Cider, for Jenny. The pub's western-facing garden was bathed in strong evening sunshine, and they lounged, heads resting on the high backs, eyes closed against the glare and feeling the penetrating warmth.

The beautiful weather, a relaxed day, delicious beer, chosen company, what more could one ask for? It seemed that the gods were on their side and that nothing was going to upset the tranquility. Indeed only moments before they had walked into the dim bar, Tony's erstwhile new friend, Gary, had been guided out, as luck would have it by some fateful unseen hand.

He had only been in the pub since just before five o'clock; still wary of the reception that might be meted out, he kept the stays short, and the few exploratory visits had been timed to encounter less familiar faces. But Gary too was more relaxed than he had been in recent weeks. He and his mate Dave had been to the cinema in the afternoon, and the prospect of a day off, plus a couple of pints, had set him up nicely. David had already gone home after his first pint, a barbecue at home beckoning, where he too, appreciated the finer monetary advantages of living with his parents. Gary, on the other hand stayed. There was no edible incentive; his mum was out that evening and so he planned on a takeaway, watch a film, maybe… if there was anything on. He doubted there would be, and the prospect of sitting up in his stifling room didn't appeal. He wanted to do something, something exciting! His mind wandered and the urge grew. He weighed up the options, reflected that as all the hoo-hah had died down, resumption would be possible. The beer had emboldened him and as he ambled, began to map out his evening, *pick up a takeaway, nip home and have it, perhaps start not so close to home, I'll need my bike.* With a renewed eagerness buoyed up by a sense of purpose Gary's step became determined and focused.

Poor common had seen little activity all afternoon, the dog-walkers and suburban strollers wiped-out by the heat, preferring to exercise in the time-honoured lazy day way, lifting glasses and chilling on the sun-lounger. Had they cared to venture onto the circular gravel path they would have found a cool interior, shaded and serene, the traffic's roar almost non-existent and humanity in general, quiet and subdued. However, the lack of noise and footfall signalled an opportunity for earlier activity amongst the family of doxes. As their nightly scavenging took them still further afield to find pickings of any value, the advantage would be useful; the stillness drawing them out from the hideaway amongst the rhododendrons and out onto the more open common. Sensing the air, tasting it and catching the strong odours of cooking, it caused chaos and confusion to the olfactory impulses reaching the brain. Being both inquisitive and wary the animals moved cautiously off, the former though, driving them to explore and to probe.

Some two hundred metres away across the common Mr and Mrs Anderson were clearing supper from the table in the garden, a ham salad with vegetables from his greenhouse and tomatoes from the patio. They had, as normal, had a quiet and unremarkable day, Sunday papers, the crosswords and games and were now looking forward to an evening's viewing, a Midsummer Murder or Miss Marple, they couldn't remember. It was a few minutes past seven o'clock as they moved carefully through the house, the glare of the day still imprinted on their elderly retinas, making the rooms dull and the contents near invisible.

In the house next door to them, Bridget Morley and her mother Dorothy were bushed and consequently enjoying a well-earned nap. They had entertained Bridget's brother and his wife and two children; with the heat it had been exhausting. In spite of the boiling weather, they'd had a traditional Roast Lunch, followed by a walk to the park allowing her brother's older children to let off steam, and give Declan a breath of fresh air in the heavily shaded buggy; getting back to the house in Linford Close, for tea in the garden of home-made scones and Jam. With the added effects of wine, perhaps more than either woman had realised at lunch, and Bridget settling down once their guests had left, to polish off the remaining half bottle of Rioja, meant that by six fifty-five, baby Declan was snoozing in the garden and both Dorothy and Bridget were blissfully asleep in the cool of the lounge. Not much was going to wake them as they drifted away, aided by overindulgence on all fronts, and certainly not the faint buzzing, as bees bumbled erratically through the deep border at the back of the garden.

The Anderson's television came on, not loud, but just audible through the thick Privett hedge, a car horn sounded away in the distance, a telephone chirped two doors down, the unfamiliar tone, like the other noises having little effect on the sleeping three. Even when a blackbird flustered belligerently out from beneath a low growing Ceonothus a few feet from the house, violently shaking the dark blue flowers, it had no affect either. Dorothy and Bridget were dead to the world. Only Declan woke to the sudden noise, his eyes shocked into opening, but was content to watch the sky and the gentle movement of the trees.

In the cool shade of the dense shrubs at the bottom of the garden, just a few metres from the happy gurgling child, a pair of eyes with long slit pupils gazed out across the parched grass to the sleeping people in the house. Stealthily it moved out, parting the leafy undergrowth with nothing more than a whisper of sound. There was a faint rustle as it moved through the arching sword-like leaves of a Phormium, pushing its furry body against the plant, smearing it's scent as a warning to others; and on over the French marigolds, regimented and brash, like some thin defensive line that edged the border in shocking orange. Without cover, the risk of exposure became much greater, and in response it moved more swiftly over the lawn. Stopping once as a noise emanated from next-door's garden and turning to listen, its pointed ears were alert and twitching. Satisfied that there was no threat, it covered the last few metres at an increasing pace, halting by the leg of the Moses basket to quickly scan the garden and check the house. It made to jump, but was startled by a short sharp cry, and it hesitated. The sound wasn't overly loud adding to the difficulty of locating its direction. Unsure and wary the animal's fur began to rise in an effort to increase its own bulk as it sensed potential danger. Within a matter of seconds another high pitched but soft bark came from a different aspect of the garden and the animal below the basket began to move its body in a sideways crouch, baring its teeth and hissing violently towards the end of the garden. Senses on full alert, it knew something was there and whatever it was - hiding in the shadows, watching and waiting - was beginning to stir; the odd leaf trembled as its supporting branch was nudged from below. Another movement, then another and across the garden a whole bush shook.

Above, the child softly cooed, unaware of the animal below and the mounting tension, that was filling the silent garden. Fearing for its exposed flanks and untenable position the feisty creature let out another venomous hiss and shot up the garden towards the house, its only option for retreat. As it drew close to the wide-open doors, the rhythmic sounds of heavy breathing and the occasional satisfied grunt caused it to pull up outside on the stonework of the patio, its claws scraping as it fought to gain purchase with front feet, whilst the rear swung round. Facing off down the garden the weighty creature stared out defiantly. Emboldened by the unseen threat, now suitably distant, it sauntered across the last two slabs, looking back casually with practised indifference as it slunk into the shaded room. With soft paws and retracted claws the self-satisfied bulk of the household's ginger Tom slipped quietly through the sleeping forms, into the tiny kitchen and safety at the bowl that bore his name, Napoleon.

Chapter 61

Over on the other side of town, Patrick Stimpson was retrieving the last sausage from the barbecue and placing it in the serving dish. Glancing at his watch he was triumphant, "Only a few minutes late," he advised. Marjorie gave him a withering look and reminded him that she had said seven o'clock not seven-thirty.

"I can't believe this weather," Patrick said, and on a bank holiday too… mind we'll probably pay for it later, flooding or pestilence, I shouldn't wonder."

"Starvation, more like," Sally commented over the top of her book, teasing her father and joining in on her mother's side.

Patrick made a great show of looking around the garden, before settling on his daughter. "She speaks," he said in mock amazement, adding, "About time you got off your bottom and helped your mum bring out the rest of the food."

"Can't Simon do it?"

"If I could see him I'd ask him… I can't, so you've drawn the lucky straw."

As he was giving this answer a thought flashed into his mind. "He's not still on that blooming computer, is he? I told him to come off ages ago. SIMON!" Patrick yelled through the open French doors. The intonation was clear; you're not still on the computer are you? The call elicited a lengthy silence, followed by, "SIMON?"

"Whaaat?" was the distracted reply from away in the study.

Patrick rolled his eyes at the off-hand response, "Are you still on that computer?"

"Yes, I'm just finishing my homework," was the overly quick response.

"You'd have thought by now your brother would have realised, my job has given me a nasty and suspicious mind. Homework? Who does he think he's kidding?" Before Patrick had made a move to investigate, his son bounded guiltily onto the patio, the look of relief and mild triumph well concealed. Patrick gave his son a warm stare. "Oh smelt the food have you?"

"I was Dad, honest." A mixture of innocence and amazement sat smugly on Simons face.

"Good, you can show it to me after supper," Patrick challenged.

As Marjorie placed the basket of garlic bread amongst the other goodies now adorning their patio table, she chivvied her daughter to the table. "Come on. Put that book away and sit up."

"Yes, come on," agreed Patrick. "I'm starving." He poured the wine for himself and Marjorie, taking a healthy swig as she shared out the barbecued meat items on to each person's plate.

He settled back in his chair whilst he waited for Marjorie to serve him last. The awning attached to the house shaded them adequately at head height but allowed the sun to radiate warmly around their legs prompting a further comment from Patrick.

"This is absolutely glorious," he said to no one in particular and staring out over his newly mown domain. "Looks so much better when it's done," he said, genuinely pleased and realising, once again, that too often he let it go; the lawn becoming over-long in places for even the petrol driven rotary mower.

As further thoughts of another morning to come, filled with pleasant gardening duties formed loosely in his head and a plate full of food being slipped in front of him, he relaxed and felt content.

In the hall, on the table under the stairs, the telephone began to sound, unheard by the happy group on the patio. Half a second later the telephone in the study began to copy the shrill notes adding its own volume in an effort to be heard. But it was the kitchen telephone that broke through the relaxed atmosphere of the patio, its insistent ringing looking for a response. Patrick, glass in hand, looked to his wife. As soon as he had heard the first piercing tone his insides had jumped in apprehension. There were times when he hated the phone, and this sort of time was one of them. He was hoping she would answer it. As she got to her feet, he knew he was being paranoid but the continuous ringing always seemed to imply an urgency. It could be anybody, he reasoned to himself. Besides, I'm not even on call, and he called out to his wife as she disappeared into the kitchen, "If it's the station tell them I'm out with the kids or something."

For a few uneasy moments Patrick, eyes fixed on the doorway and leaning forward expectantly in his chair, was unable to contemplate food. *It would be just typical*, he thought, *first decent weekend break he had had in ages, ruined by some bored colleague.* The certainty of the outcome already sitting acidly on his empty stomach brought a burst of irritation and he fought hard to ignore the lively debate on the opposite side of the table, that had now become annoying and overtly distracting. Straining, he could just hear Marjorie's voice, a muffled sound from behind the solid brickwork, and only certain words. Even more frustrated he lashed out.

"Quiet, will you." Glaring at them both, "I'm trying to hear."

The children looked away surprised and hurt. They hadn't seen it coming; unaware of the tension that had so quickly racked up behind the relaxed façade that was only now changing fast. For a fleeting second as Marjorie loomed into view, he thought he'd got away with it and she was coming back to the table, having dealt with whatever it had been.

"I'm sorry Pat," she said with a face that held a myriad of emotions, annoyance, angst, empathy, sympathy, resignation. "It's Thomas. He's really sorry, but there's a problem."

"Bloody great!" He pushed his chair back with force and the plastic leg caught on the floor causing it to spring wildly about at his feet. His vehemence exploded, "For God sake!" The momentary rage got the better of him and he lashed out with his foot, clearing his path and sending the light four-legged object across the patio and into the pond a few metres away.

Marjorie was shocked, although hid it well. Rarely did Pat blow a fuse, she considered. But equally she understood that the last few weeks had been exceptionally trying and particularly, as there had been no acceptable result to the little girl's abduction case.

"What is it Thomas?" he barked down the telephone, knowing that because it was his trusted oppo, it would not be trivial.

"Hi Pat, I'm sorry to be the bearer of bad news, but you need to know."

With anger subsiding at hearing his colleague's discomfort, he asked, "Okay, what's up?"

"I've just been called at home too, but, according to control, a telephone call, just come in, from a one Bridget Morley, living over on a road where her garden backs on to Poor Common."

At the mention of the all too familiar piece of land, a feeling of dread came over Patrick and a terrible premonition as to what Thomas was about to say next, swept over him.

"Don't tell me?" he breathed down the line.

"Is reporting her child as being taken." Thomas paused as if he couldn't believe it either. "The report's still a bit sketchy. The mother was not, as you might expect, very coherent, but it sounds frighteningly like the Docker case. Mum wakes from a nap to find cot overturned in the garden and baby gone. Apart from the cot there is no evidence to suggest a break-in, the house is still secure to the front, there is no direct access to the common but the bods on scene say the undergrowth and hedge is open enough for someone to get through."

"Okay Tom, Where are you?"

"Just getting into my car, I'll pick you up in ten," adding as if it might help, "Everyone's being called Pat, it looks like upstairs is taking it very seriously. I'm afraid it doesn't sound too good."

Chapter 62

Standing in the empty and darkening lounge, framed by the open French doors, Patrick and Thomas stared out at the well-tended Garden. Apart from the police officer, standing a couple of metres from the overturned Moses crib, nothing seemed much amiss. The light was fast fading and it was just after eight pm.

"Right Pat, where do you want to start?"

The diminishing light, a woman crying upstairs, the retained warmth of the room, the overturned crib with sheets and light blanket strewn casually across the lawn, all had a cloying effect on Patrick and the question went unanswered. They were really up against it this time, he was thinking, building further pressure to his role as the officer in charge. Very soon there would be no daylight, the common would be so dark and by the time any officers in number arrived, they would not be as effectual. It wasn't a large area but they could not floodlight it all. He was contemplating asking his boss to organise road blocks on the major roads out of the area, but he didn't do it. He was almost numb at the enormity of the idea. It was a bank holiday weekend, the traffic would be pouring out of the Bournemouth area; the main arteries, he guessed, already clogged, engorged by day-trippers leaving the beaches. Organised stop and search points would cause absolute chaos, the roads would be snarled up for hours, probably way into the early morning. *Surely,* he thought, *these guys would know not to risk making a get-away on such a potentially busy evening, then again, the added volume could be ideal; just another car amongst tens of thousands.*

Scenes of crime, he had been told, were on their way. The only good thing about the bank holiday from his point of view, he reflected, was there wasn't much happening elsewhere. Dorset's criminal fraternity, regarding the holiday from their work, equally as important as the rest; meant units, whether on stand-by or not, were, like he had been, readily available.

Patrick noted Sergeant Ball, the capable policeman, now familiar with this particular type of crime scene, talking to an officer outside in the garden. The uniformed constable moved off around the side of the house and the Sergeant approached the two men in the house.

"Evening Sir, Tom," he nodded to Thomas, "I've just asked the lad to go and ask next door, Mr Anderson I believe, if we can use his side passage and back gate to gain access to the common. It would be useful. We don't want our lads traipsing through that border at the back, assuming that's how the abductors have entered. The side gate was locked and the women were asleep in here."

"How long ago was this?" Thomas asked.

"Call came in at seven thirty-six. Luckily I was on duty and grabbed a couple of lads so we were here within twenty minutes. But I reckon the child was taken any time between seven, when the women say they dropped off, and seven twenty-five. The mother was alerted by their cat wanting food and, on waking, found the basket empty. I've left a couple of lads at the station. They are ringing round and trying to gather the troops. There are a couple out on the common now, trying to organise the neighbours. The place is already crawling with locals."

The Sergeant was reeling off what he'd quickly put in place since his arrival, his arms pointing swiftly to the places of note.

"And on the other side of this border and back fence area," he pointed down towards the bottom of the garden, "the lads should be taping off an area to try and preserve the ground behind for SOCO when they get here. I've also asked for some floodlights, for the garden and out the back. It'll be dark in less than an hour, particularly out under the trees."

Feeling somewhat inadequate, Patrick gratefully acknowledged the man's quick responses.

"Well done Sergeant. As you said, it's a good job you were on duty."

His own mind, though, was in turmoil. How the hell could this be happening again? *They're either stupid or it was all part of the original plan, assuming that we'd all be thinking lightning doesn't strike twice.* This second abduction now seemed like a personal affront. As yet, he hadn't issued any orders or directed his team but the feeling of helplessness was beginning to get to him already; the gall rising in his abused and hastily fed stomach.

Feeling somewhat depressed, but not wishing to pass it on, he said flatly to Thomas "I don't know about being up shit creek without a paddle. But Christ! We haven't even got a boat!"

The warm, thick air inside was overwhelming and his head was foggy and unclear, as they walked out into the cooler air of the garden. Patrick wandered around the overturned crib, studying it from a few angles. He looked down the garden to the well-stocked border. Behind the formal shrubs he could see a laurel hedge rising to nearly three metres, and beyond that, the trees of Poor Common, the tall pines looking grey and foreboding in the dimming light.

"So which one did he use this time, eh Thomas?" Patrick waved his hand towards the thick canopy. "Speaking of which, take a uniform with you and go and pay a visit to our Mr Brown. He lives even closer for this one. Find out where he's been all evening and if you're not satisfied, haul him in. Meantime, I'll talk to Mrs Morley and her Mother."

Patrick knew talking to them was going to be difficult, the rawness still painful and wrenching, but he needed answers, and this time he wasn't prepared to wait for them. He wanted to make headway with this investigation, and hopefully within twenty-four hours, so he asked Bridget difficult and embarrassing questions about her ex-husband; where was he? Was the divorce amicable? He wanted a list of her friends and enemies and of Dorothy's too. He made her go through the sequence of events right up until she made the call.

"We knew something wasn't right the moment the cat woke us up," said Dorothy, through tear stained eyes. "Nothing you could put your finger on..." she hesitated as if trying to do exactly that, but unable to find the words to explain, "You just felt it."

"And then," continued Bridget, "when I saw the overturned basket, I knew he'd gone without even having to look."

At this point the floodgates opened again, the women clutching at each other, hugging and squeezing in an effort to draw what little comfort they could find. But Patrick's resolve was undiminished, and he pressed on, despite imploring looks from the female liaison officer.

He'd been told that the little boy, Declan, was ten months old, and Patrick tried to visualise the child lying in the basket. It had been so long since his own children were that age and he found it hard to gauge the boy's size. In fact, it was difficult to imagine anything about him. *What developmental stage would he be at, crawling? Walking? Cruising around the furniture?*

"How mobile was Declan? I mean presumably he can crawl, stand up, that sort of thing?"

Bridget nodded over her mother's shoulder and through a tear-wet and stained face she sobbed an answer.

"He's crawling," clarifying it with, "but not that far."

A call to his mobile, from Thomas, told Patrick two things. The first was that it was now five to nine and the second was that Gary Brown was not at home, nor was his mother. Thomas had called into the convenience store on Glenmoor Road, where Trisha Brown worked, and had found her restacking some shelves. She hadn't seen him all day, not since their paths had crossed at a late breakfast, about ten-ish.

"All I know is," she said wearily, "he said he was going to the flicks in the afternoon with Dave, his mate from next door. They're probably in the pub as we speak," she had advised Thomas. "Try the Angel."

Leaving the uniformed officer in the car, Thomas had tried the Angel. Gary had indeed been in there but much earlier. The staff couldn't be sure but they thought he had left at about six o'clock.

"He's not at his mate's house next door," Thomas told Patrick. "In fact they parted company at the pub. Dave Fisher left Gary to have another pint. And that was the last he saw of him," Thomas concluded, but added, "So at the moment, time-wise, he could be in the frame."

"Ok Thomas, I want him found. Alert uniform and have him picked up."

The lights had been switched on in the house now, accentuating the dark outside. The garden was in the last throws of dusk and the fast retreating light, silhouetted the ragged skyline of Scots Pine.

Chapter 63

As Thomas had been questioning the staff at the Angel, he was aware of a change in the atmosphere. When he had walked in, the lively Pub had been a cacophony of sounds. Within a matter of minutes the noise level had dropped; voices more subdued and hushed. People were finishing their drinks and leaving. Soon whole tables were clearing and the regulars at the bar swallowed deeply and shuffled out. By the time Thomas was set to go, the exodus had reduced the mass of heaving humanity by well over fifty percent, dragging a concerned landlord from his office.

Outside, on the now cooler patio, Tony and Jenny were taking the final swigs before leaving to go back and watch the film in Tony's flat. They saw a woman visit the table next to them, a small group of five. She clearly knew them, perching herself on the edge of a chair and leaning into the table, and drawing the others in, as if to meter out some piece of bar room tittle-tattle. Jenny watched, fascinated by the faces as the look of interest quickly turned to shock and disbelief as the woman made to go. Clearly she was agitated, and seemed to search the remaining faces around the garden for others she might know. By accident Jenny caught her eye and gave a shy smile, knowing that she had been staring at her for some time. But far from concerned the woman lent in towards them and apologised,

"Sorry, I'm just looking to see if there's anyone I know… only," She stopped and re-evaluate the two before her. "You're local are you?"

They nodded.

"Only there's been another child taken, up on the common by the sound of it. People seem to be going up there to help search."

Sitting bolt upright and blood running cold, Tony demanded, "When?"

"No more than a couple of hours ago, by all accounts."

"Come on Jen," Tony said grabbing her hand as he got up. "We've got work to do."

Five minutes later, and after grabbing a torch from the boot of his car, they were picking their way up the poorly lit track that would take them to Poor Common. Emerging from the overgrown pathway, they watched in fascination at the points of light flashing ahead of them through the trees. The place was alive, Tony thought. They walked on up the path towards the activity, passing the ponds some way over to their left and on into the heart of the tiny woodland. They could see the torches more clearly now. A long row of about thirty, Tony estimated, was moving slowly through the trees and would eventually cross their bow, in another few minutes. The torches by the pond were not so regimented, the expanses of water forcing the lines to break and flow around or between. They saw, right on the far side, an area of intense light, which from their vantage point, Tony guessed, must be the crime scene; the tree trunks in line of sight, creating a weird barcode effect.

Tony had advised Jenny that rather than help in the search for the boy, they would do a bit of their own snooping. However, it wasn't until Tony had got on to the common that he appreciated, his hope of tracking the doxes was probably an unlikely one, with so many people milling about. But ever the optimist, and with a burgeoning feeling of guilt at not having gone to the authorities sooner, he was of a mind to stay out and try.

"If these animals have got any sense they'll stay underground for a while," Tony said to Jenny in a normal voice. There didn't seem much point in stealth.

They walked back along the southerly gravel route, heading west and away from the mayhem behind. This part of the woods, the furthest point from the crime scene, was virtually untouched save for the odd torch appearing out of nowhere, attached to a teenager who was guiding a giggling girl beside him. To their left, and all along this path the bank of rhododendrons looked, in the dark, like an impenetrable wall.

"That would be a good place to hide," he said pointing to the black mass beside them. "If, indeed, they are still using the common as their home base... Come on."

And with that, Tony moved off the path and swung his torch, illuminating the towering green monster and looked for a way in. A suitable gap found, they began to negotiate the internally twisted branches that held up the huge screening leaves of its extremity; disappearing completely to the world outside. Once in, it was like another world, and where these huge shrubs grew side-by-side the canopy extended over two, three or more bushes. The result was a vast internal space like a marquee with too many strange poles.

Twenty metres in, they came upon the remains of a chain link fence. Guessing that this must mark the extent of the properties down on Christchurch road, Tony suggested that they respect the boundary and see where it led them.

"It's pretty creepy in here," Jenny said keeping as close to Tony and the light as she could.

As they moved, the torch's beam cast shadows that constantly changed, dark shapes fluidly dynamic as the source of light itself moved and was blocked or absorbed by physical objects. They pressed on through this underworld of twisted wood and soft leaf mulch for nearly a hundred metres. Soon though, the ancient boundary was swallowed up by foliage, and the two of them had to push their way through, unsure where they would emerge.

Chapter 64

Feeling somewhat useless again, Patrick sort to broaden his view, the back garden and, now cooling, house having become restrictive. He wanted somewhere to ponder. He noted the time. It was nine forty-five. He went out of the side gate, around into the Andersons and through the back garden, to the opening in the hedge. Pulling open the well-fitting gate, it was like going through a portal to another world. The searing light was almost unbearable to his narrowed eyes. He looked around at the over-clad figures, delving through the undergrowth, shuffling or on all fours, and grubbing around like foraging animals. Sergeant Ball came over and advised him that the initial house-to-house searches along Linford Close, and much of Christchurch Road, had been completed, and a team was just on its way to Heatherlands Avenue just around the corner.

"Difficulty is, most of them are probably here." He jabbed his pencil out into the night. "Having said that, many are leaving now and we've been advising them to check their own properties, if they haven't already done so."

As they talked in the full glare, insect danced about them in confused and random flight. With nothing of significance to be shown, Patrick moved out from the insect's newly created stage and into the darkened auditorium of Poor Common. Orientating himself by the warm glow of the neighbouring conurbation, he followed the gravel path and pondered on just how it had been done this time. He would bet any money that Gary Brown had something to do with it. The fact they were having trouble locating him further damned him in Patrick's eyes. *He's got it right on his doorstep*, he reasoned, *but how the hell does he... they*, he corrected, *get the kids off the common and away to wherever they're going*. Patrick was sure Gary was working for someone; these kids had been singled out and the families watched. Immediately Patrick wondered if others had been studied, until he narrowed it down to these, the final two. *Surely they wouldn't risk taking any more?*

Disturbed by these thoughts he hadn't noticed that he had come to the far edge of the common. Debating which way to go, he heard a sharp crack like a twig being broken. The sound had come from behind him and away to his left. He turned to listen for a while, thinking that whatever it was had to be quite heavy. He tried hard to come up with a list of possibilities, but the only sensible two were a deer or a human; everything else was too lightweight. He cocked his head towards where he thought the noise had come from and strained his senses; there was definitely something! He could hear the occasional footfall; muffled and dulled by the thick leaf mulch and it was coming from the block of darkness directly to his front, a few metres away. Patrick felt the results of a little surge of adrenalin as his heart rate moved up a gear. Fear would be too strong a word for how his body was reacting;

apprehension would probably have covered it as he peered into the gloom. Standing on unfamiliar ground out in the open and with the blackness impairing his vision he felt exposed and unready for the thing that appeared to be drawing closer.

Suddenly, in his head, a thought process fired and he remembered the day that he'd all but panicked in the garden of that vacant house. The house, he now realised, he was actually standing behind at that moment, with its creepy summerhouse, pungent odour and uneasy vibes.

There was movement in the foliage ahead. He heard the subtle scrape of dry leaves brushing against an object in motion and then a flicking swish as the buckled branches let go their tension. The more he stared into the pitch the less he was able to discern. The blackness began to shift and shape, creating the illusion of movement. From somewhere in the recesses of his mind an urge to back off, to run, nudged into his consciousness, and the familiar sensations enticed his heart to pound and blood to rush. His rational side fought hard not to let emotions get the better of him and he hesitantly stood his ground.

Some three metres away from where he had imagined the disturbance had come, Patrick heard a disembodied cry that started off as a shushing and ended in a loud... it! The sight of a light flashing through the air and a couple of loud thuds, preceded by the heartfelt expletive reassured him, it was a person. One of the searchers no doubt having gone off on their own tack, he surmised.

"Good evening," Patrick said with all the aplomb of a welcoming maitre de.

There was a short high-pitched scream, accompanied by a low exhalation, forming the word, "Jesus."

Patrick saw there were two of them.

"Bit off the beaten track, aren't we?" he enquired with friendly authority as a light blinded his eyes.

"Christ! ... You nearly gave me a heart attack," spat Tony.

Patrick grappled the torch away and said casually, "Yes sorry about that." And, turning the torch on the two dishevelled youngsters as they regained their composure asked, "Fell over did we?"

"Yes something like that," was Tony's non-committal reply as he brushed himself down.

"It's Inspector Stimpson, isn't it?" Jenny piped up flashing a smile.

Beside her Tony stiffened at the name.

"I don't know if you remember me," she said hesitantly, "Jenny... Jenny Spader. We spoke on the telephone the other day... you're coming to see me, us actually, on Wednesday."

Tony winced, feeling that this probably was neither the right time nor place for introductions, but accepted the inevitable.

"This is," she paused sensing the change in atmosphere, "is... er... Tony Nash."

It took a moment to sink in.

"Oh yes, I remember." Patrick's voice was mildly threatening, "I believe we've spoken before, haven't we?"

Tony nodded and felt the man's level gaze assessing him.

"Looking for… what was it - panthers?"

"You might well mock Inspector, but I hear you've got another missing child on your hands," Tony challenged. "It wouldn't surprise me if you don't find this one either."

A nerve touched, and Patrick took a step closer. "And what would you know about that then, Mr Nash?"

Wrong footed, and not wishing to discuss his ideas whilst feeling threatened, Tony answered weakly, "Look we didn't want to talk about it like this. We wanted to explain our theory to you properly." He shrugged, "But it can wait till Wednesday, I guess."

"I'll be the judge of that," was Patrick's cold response. "Where are you headed?"

"The Angel," replied Jenny.

"Right, you can tell me all about it on the way."

Without the benefit of the PowerPoint presentation and video clip, Tony felt that, with every word he spoke, he was digging a deeper hole. The policeman listened and asked pertinent questions, but still, even Tony had to admit, it sounded fantastical. Jenny tried to back him up, adding in details that Tony had omitted.

"All we're saying Inspector is that something is not right, domestic animals are disappearing…"

"Foxes," said Patrick butting in matter-of-factly.

"No, not foxes as such," said Tony in frustration. "The deer, too big, the fawn brought down by three animals hunting aggressively, these kids… no way could an ordinary fox do that. They just don't work that way."

Tony stopped by his car in the well-lit pub car park. Patrick gave the sleek Scimitar an approving glance.

"Look, first it was big cats, panthers I believe you said." He looked at Tony expectantly.

"Yeah… but -" Tony began but Patrick cut him off.

"And now? Do you really expect me to believe that there is some creature … this dox… whatever, wandering the streets of Ferndown and devouring little children? Christ! It sounds more fairy tale than one of Han's Christian Andersons!" Patrick shook his head in disbelief. "You can e-mail me the video clip, if you like, but I doubt it's going to change my mind."

Tony took out his keys and unlocked the car, saying as he opened the substantial door, "Well don't say we didn't try to warn you Inspector."

"Duly noted, Mr Nash." He looked over to the passenger side of the car. "Nice to see you again Miss Spader."

He watched them purposefully through the glass as Tony fired up the engine, its throaty roar seeming to reflect the rage trapped within its stylish bodywork.

"Well that went well!" Anger, frustration and sarcasm, clearly coming through in Tony's Voice

"Cretin," was Jenny's vicious contribution as they moved off.

"Let's hope he can't lip read," said Tony far more calmly than he felt. "We might be in enough trouble as it is."

Patrick spent the next fifteen minutes walking back to the crime scene and pondering on what he'd just been told. What he couldn't get to grips with was that the two individuals seemed level-headed people. He reflected on the telephone conversation he had had with Mr Nash a few months back, and his first impressions about the guy's social standing and communication abilities would remain unchanged, sensible, intelligent and educated. And Jenny? Undoubtedly a bright kid, head screwed on the right way, he'd been impressed by her no nonsense attitude when handling the dangerous dogs.

But how, he asked himself, *do two bright people... allow themselves to come up with something so... completely off the wall... and believe it.* In a world of facts and evidence Patrick would have difficulty making the huge leap required. *Foxes*, he thought, *they're animals you glimpse at night, they don't hang around waiting to be seen by humans.*

A dog and a fox cross, he mused, *a hybrid they called it. How come there aren't hundred's of them.* He'd never contemplated that it was possible. *Surely if dogs and foxes could mate, there would be others?* Try as he might he could not think that he had ever come across... never mind the animal, but even the concept before. Newspapers, media, books, magazines, general conversation, his Army life, the time on the force, never had it come up. On re-entering the bubble of extreme light that had been designated a crime scene Patrick concluded his internal deliberations with, *absolute rubbish!*

Chapter 65

Monday 3ʳᵈ August

The morning briefing with his CID team and the uniformed officers on his duty was a swift affair, in by six-fifteen and back on the scene by six-fifty for most. Top priority for Thomas and a couple of other detectives was to track down Gary Brown. There had been no sign of him at his house by midnight and the team watching had not reported any change at the time of the briefing.

"I want him found," was the clear instruction. "Check with his boss, his neighbours, the pub. Somebody must have seen him."

A press conference had been hastily arranged for eight am that morning, which meant Patrick, had to stay around the station. Like the investigation before, there would not be much to tell, except, at this early hour, they could at least blame the night for slow progress.

When it had finished, escaping relatively unscathed, he drove through the milling journalists and out on to the, still holiday-quiet, roads heading for the crime scene. It was just turning nine o'clock.

Three hours later, at midday, and after a ring around to the various team leaders, Patrick was disturbingly none the wiser. This time though, the officers on house-to-house had found many people at home, some who'd been out searching the previous night, others only just informed by early morning viewing and still aghast at the news. Pretty much all though, would have been found in a sluggish state, bleary eyed and still fond of sleep, the holiday mode disturbed by the early and persistent ringing and rapping of door furniture. They had started early, the familiar questions and demands jarring residents to answer wearily and with a resigned sense of déjà vu, but in the end offering nothing of value.

Thomas had described Gary's complete disappearance as bizarre.

"He's on cctv in the town centre, on his bike, coming up from New Road towards the fire station at just before eight pm. We can see him turning right onto the Ringwood Road, heading west, and coming back towards Poole, but after that there are no cameras so we don't know where he goes. We do know he was in the Angel pub earlier, up until about six-ish. He picked up a take-away at a Chinese, on Glenmore Road, and paid for it with a debit card at twelve minutes past six. Assuming that he went home to eat, he must have been back out again, at the latest, by eight-fifteen because that's when we tried to pay him a visit. But in fairness he needn't have gone home, his neighbours have no idea, they haven't seen him; therefore he could easily have been involved."

Patrick agreed but found it difficult to assuage the idea that this was somehow totally premeditated.

"I mean, how did they know the child was going to be asleep at that time, outside and in an exposed situation? And, for that matter, the two adults, mum and grandma, fast asleep. It's like the other case. They could not have known that the toddler was going to be… available at that particular moment, or accessible and unguarded. There has to be an element of opportunity. But, at the same time, if they were able to spot this opportunity, and with sure knowledge of the surroundings and household routines, take advantage quickly, then the child could be god knows where, within a few minutes."

"True," agreed Thomas. "We know the window of opportunity must be quite limited because the mother said they'd dropped off to sleep by seven and were awoken by the cat at seven-twenty five. So that, in itself, implies that the abductors must have been watching and ready to strike as soon as they felt the coast was clear, i.e. that the women were well asleep. The watcher could easily be Gary; it's literally a few minutes from where he lives. He might even have eaten the take-away there."

"Well in my book, this Gary Brown is part of it," Patrick was adamant. "And having played his hand, twice now, he's gone to ground. He might have even have gone off with the abductors to clear the area."

"Well he's not been home. The lads watching his mum's house are sure of that."

"Right, Thomas, let's get his mug shot in the papers. Police are keen to interview this man etc, you know the drill. I doubt we can get it in the Echo's late edition but we should be able to hit the nationals for tomorrow morning."

"How about Phillip Carver?" Thomas said eagerly. "After all, he broke the terms of his parole the moment he went missing. I know we had him in the papers before, but surely he's still fair game now? For all we know he could have come back into the area just for this. Somebody might have spotted him."

There were no objections from Patrick as he tapped in a number on his mobile phone. A thought had occurred to him during the conversation and, via the dependable Sergeant Ball, he requested that two officers go to the traffic control room to watch hours of cctv covering the major routes out of the area; their brief, to spot Gary Brown in a car or light van. It was going to be mind-numbingly boring and about as hopeful as finding intelligent life in the universe. However, if there was a chance and, if they concentrated to begin with on the four or five major junctions within close proximity to Poor Common, within the narrow time period, they might just get lucky; bank holiday traffic notwithstanding Patrick remembered, shaking his head at the poor luck.

Tuesday's headlines and accompanying photographs led to a flurry of activity in the incident room, at Headquarters. The information was passed on swiftly down the line to Patrick and his team; sightings were followed up of both men, locally and much further afield. Gary's distinctive clothing, namely his camouflage jacket in the middle of summer, had caused an angry pedestrian, whom he'd nearly knocked over with his bike, to report him fairly accurately and with some certainty, as having been cycling up Evergreen Road, a few hundred metres from The Angel, at around about half past ten on Sunday night. Patrick had found this strange. Why, if he had been involved, would Gary be coming back into the area? It didn't make sense. He should have been well away by then. This phone call made him review the need to check the traffic cameras, much to the relief of the two bored and over-heated detective constables on that particular detail.

But the question Patrick kept asking was where had he gone? He still hadn't been home and hadn't been seen, apart from the man on Evergreen. The house-to-house searches that had moved into the roads leading away from the common, and through the estates, had not come across him, and the common itself had been well and truly searched on Monday. This was a very limited area in which to hide, Patrick reflected, so he must have left here, perhaps picked up late Sunday. So where's his bike? Or did he take it with him? Something else he would request the team to look out for, having obtained a description from Trisha Brown.

On visiting the said Mrs Brown, Gary's mum, later that morning, they had come away no wiser about his movements. She had no idea where he could have gone. He hadn't taken any clothes with him or wash bag, and it hadn't looked like he was planning to stay away. But it was Thomas's keen eye that had alerted Patrick to the anomaly. They had been talking with Trisha in the kitchen when a familiar garment was spotted behind the opened back door.

"What's that behind the back door, Mrs Brown?" Thomas had asked, levelly.

"That? Oh, that's just Gary's coat."

"How long has it been there? Mrs Brown?" There was a slight edge to his voice as he continued, "Think about that please, it might be very important."

Fraught already by the whole situation, and now, with the two detectives beginning to ask more pointed questions, she was naturally upset but guarded.

"Well, a couple of days, I can't be sure."

Thomas had looked at Patrick who was beginning to cotton on, and asked another question.

"How can his coat be here when the last sighting of him on Sunday was in his camouflage jacket? Either he's sneaked back without you knowing or you're not telling us the truth Mrs Brown... and you **have** seen him. Which is it?"

"Neither," she said with indignation at being accused of lying and, as a result, was reluctant to offer any clarification.

"Mrs Brown," Thomas quickly chastised in a disbelieving and menacing voice, "how can that be?"

"He's got two," she replied meekly, the implied threats working, making her see that being deliberately obtuse was not going to help anyone's cause.

"Pardon," Patrick said very clearly and slightly thrown that she hadn't appeared to be caught out and, indeed, was now offering another alternative.

"He's got two of those combat jackets. Doesn't seem to wear one more than the other. I think, it's just whichever one happens to be at hand, that he puts on. That one looks like his old one."

By now, Thomas was inspecting the hem, and working his way around the seams and on to the sleeves. Immediately he could see this coat was well worn, whereas the other one they had sent to forensics was much newer. After a few seconds he turned to Patrick, holding up one of the sleeves revealing a substantial tear in the fabric. The look on his face, said it all; this time... we really have got him.

That had been all well and good and subsequently forensics would match it to the swatch found at the previous crime scene. This would to all intents and purposes put Gary in a very difficult position when they questioned him. However, *there's the rub*, determined Patrick as they came away from the house, *we haven't got him to ask.*

Chapter 66

Wednesday, the third day of the investigation, had the Press and media second-guessing about the two 'most wanted' in connection with the children's abductions. Linked in physical print, with individual photographs side by side which, in itself, implied a connection, Gary would become, by association at least, one of society's worst nightmares; a modern monster lurking within the essence of respectability, unlike his supposed partner in crime, who was without any shadow of a doubt, a known and convicted paedophile. Phillip Carver's crimes were once again exposed to public limelight and, yet again, the questions would be raised about the right to know where in the community such evil in human form now resided. As the theories and debates raged ever more publicly, Patrick and his team kept their heads down, following up on sightings, delving further into Gary's life and talking to other forces countrywide, looking for leads.

Earlier that morning, unbeknownst to Patrick, and in fact at that juncture, of no particular relevance to his team, the already clogged Christchurch Road, with queuing commuter traffic, was suffering a further disruption. A low-loader had parked precariously and was stuck out into the road, restricting the flow and causing extra chaos. As it off-loaded its heavy cargo, a substantial mechanical digger, it brought the road to a complete standstill. The whole process, lasting just twenty minutes, was the vanguard of a small army, soon to arrive and detailed to clear the site, house and all at number three. Once demolished, the new owner's architect and builders would have free reign to begin construction of their future luxury home.

The first job of the day was to clear space at the far end of the garden, to allow a portable office to be sited, along with a twenty-foot storage container.

By lunchtime, there was more foliage compacted on the lawn than was left at the bottom of the garden. Just a ten metre square block on the western edge remained. In front of this last stand, and looking starkly exposed, was the decrepit summerhouse. The driver had only caught a few glimpses of the low building before his elevated cab broke through the thick curtain of leaves surrounding the clearing to its front. He checked over the contents of the shack on the off-chance of some useful find, but decided there was nothing of value. The dangerous building, he assessed, after removing the worst of the glass, would best be 'torched' and the ashes scattered. His intention therefore, after his lunch, was to scrape the whole pile of crap he'd just cleared into the middle of the space and set light to it. In that way he could clear the final corner whilst keeping an eye on the fire.

The huge robot-like arm extended over the broken roof and lowered to the ground on the other side of the summerhouse. The driver toggled back his joystick and the outstretched arm was drawn slowly back towards the metal body. The huge bucket on the end, with its jagged metal teeth, bit deeply into the soil as it dragged all before it. The sound of aged wood, dry and crisp, flexing only briefly before snapping and splintering, was unheard by the operator cocooned in his cab and listening to the radio on headphones. He repeated the manoeuvre four more times, the wide mouth of the bucket tearing through sizeable chunks and enveloping nearly a quarter of the structure at each clawing. On the final pass he attempted to gather the stray debris into one pile, shunting the massive machine in various directions to gain purchase. As the bucket was pulled solidly towards the controlling operator it gouged up an even deeper furrow, teasing to the surface a small collection of yellowy-white fragments.

Jumping out of his cab the driver went to the jumbled mess and set light to some dry papers stuffed inside for the purpose. The seasoned wood gave in quickly to the enveloping flame and in no time the ragged pile was engulfed. On returning to his cab the driver caught site of the strange objects scattered along the bucket-hewn entrenchment. Most of the items were just fragments, indiscernible as any particular thing; indeed, he thought they were pieces of flint or chalk. But looking back along the gully towards the, now flattened, site his eyes were drawn immediately to another piece. Even half-buried, he could see a smooth dome shape with a large round hole in its side. He recognised it immediately and pushed away the loose dirt to confirm he was right. A skull.

"Hallo, who have we got here then?" He turned the object around to view it from all angles. The elongated form with two little bone structures protruding from the top told him. "A deer, I shouldn't wonder," and continuing to talk to himself. "Not very old judging by the size of it." As he went to stand, his eyes flicked back down into the void left by the skull.

"Oh Shit," was his only response as he fumbled for his mobile and dialled 999.

Chapter 67

Ten minutes later and no more than three hundred metres from the find, Patrick's mobile chirped excitedly in his pocket. Taking it out, and glancing at the screen and noting the familiar number, he said to Thomas, "Let's hope this is some good news."

"That was control Tom." Patrick's voice was bordering on gleeful. "A body's been unearthed, and they think it might be one of ours."

"Oh yes. How did they work that one out then?"

"Because, it's just over there," Patrick pointed through the trees. "Follow me."

They took the gravel path for a short while and branched off, up beside the little field, and out onto the Christchurch Road.

"If it's the house I think it is, then a few things could fall in to place," Patrick said as they walked down past the boarded-up nursery and noting the for sale sign.

"Having said that," he continued, "it was empty. Had been for a while. No sign of recent life as far as we could tell." Patrick's brow furrowed in thought, "It struck me, at the time, it would've been ideal - secluded, an overgrown back garden and at the end of a row of houses. And I tell you what, there was an old summerhouse, really hidden away, been a good place to 'hole-up' in for a while. SOCO's going to have their work cut out. It was a big house and the summerhouse won't be easy, the state it's in."

Four minutes later they were picking their way over the devastated back garden. Patrick was suitably amazed at the clearance, but niggled that he could not visualise how it had been when he had visited previously. They walked up to the hunched JCB driver still carefully clearing earth from around other bones sticking out of the ground.

"I think you had better let us deal with that now sir, if you don't mind," said Thomas.

"Tell me," Patrick said somewhat sternly to the driver as a nasty feeling had set off alarm bells in his head. "There was a summer house somewhere here, where is it?"

The man heard the intonation and gingerly pointed to the fire.

Patrick stared, fixated by the huge pile of red-hot silvery grey embers. "Unbelievable!" was his only comment.

They confirmed that the skull was human and took a statement from the driver, then sent him on his way suggesting that he might like to inform the owners that this was going to be a crime scene for the next few days. Patrick called in the find to Chief Inspector Bryant, suggesting that the skull was almost certainly that of a child and that he was assuming, till proven otherwise, that this was probably one of the missing children. His next call was to the control room, requesting that Scene's of crime attend along with a Forensic Pathologist, and any uniforms they could spare to secure the area.

At six o'clock, after nearly four hours on site, the crime scene investigators were still finding bone fragments as they dug deeper into the soil. However, it had become clear that many of the pieces they had found were not human, belonging to any number of smaller creatures. But the larger bone sections and those fully intact would have to be taken away for further examination to determine their provenance. It was suggested to Patrick that what the digger had unearthed below the summerhouse was an animal den, probably a Fox or Badger, hence the array of differing bones.

"Fairly typical prey for such predators, I should think," said the plastic-clad female scenes-of-crime investigator. "I'm not an expert but I am surprised that there are so many pieces left. I would have thought a mature fox would have crunched its way through all of its victims. Which might suggest this was a den occupied by cubs."

As the woman expounded her theory, thoughts of Tony Nash stole into Patrick's mind. And in particular his parting words, sprung uncomfortably to mind.

"Sorry," he said, fixing the woman with an incredulous stare, "Are you telling me that foxes or badgers are responsible for killing this child?"

"No, no," she smiled, somewhat sympathetically at the evidently stressed detective jumping to wild conclusions. "No, more likely the body has been dumped here, or nearby and the animals have just taken advantage," adding in a voice bordering on admiration, "Ever the opportunists, you know."

Unfortunately, Patrick did know... he'd recently been told and he wasn't happy that somebody else was saying much the same about these interfering creatures. *Still,* he thought, *why snatch a child and dump it here, so close to where they had taken her from?* He was assuming that the remains were those of Martha Docker. *Had they bottled it or botched it? But why try again? Perhaps either one of those was the reason?*

"Do you think the body was dumped here for that very reason, you know, to remove it, or to cover up any incriminating evidence?"

"Possibly," the investigator looked sceptical. "Not exactly the most foolproof method. However, with only bones to work with it's going to mess up any autopsy, that's for sure."

As Patrick drove home, weary from the long day and mentally exhausted from all the conundrums stacking up in his head, his mind couldn't switch off. *Where was Gary... and Phillip Carver, for that matter? If these two aren't involved, then who is? There are no other leads or pieces of evidence implying others.* Once again, Tony Nash invaded his thoughts. *Could it be we are looking at this the wrong way?* He thought about the story in the Echo a couple of weeks back about the kids attacked in their tent. He hadn't paid much notice of it, *but that was Bournemouth somewhere, wasn't it? Still,* he pondered, *What if.... What if he's right?*

He pulled up in his drive and switched off the car. It was nearly eight-thirty. He sat for a few minutes looking at his home. He could see a light on in his son's bedroom and a flickering in the study; somebody was on the computer, signs of normality that jolted him out of his reverie. "Come on Pat," he said to his reflection in the rear-view mirror, "get a grip!"

Chapter 68

Thursday August 6th

The raid had been planned for a nine-thirty start and the troops, well breakfasted and hyped, were assembling at the designated rallying point. The operation, although hastily thrown together, had been sanctioned by those on high, who were glad to get their charges out into the field to expend the pent-up energy that had built over the last couple of weeks. Rations issued and weapons ready, these elite troops were awaiting the final member of the assault team, their officer, entrusted with the orders and tactics to ensure a successful mission. The nervous tension was obvious; a couple of the lads looked enviously over each other's weapons, whilst Jake picked his nose.

From a doorway three buildings down, the final member emerged, Captain Ryan. As he strode purposefully towards his men a call followed him up the street causing him to wince inwardly and to roll his eyes.

"I want you back by twelve. Your Aunty Lucy is coming for lunch."

With wary mums waving across the road to each other from their neighbourly positions, the four boys, ten and eleven year olds, set off down the little path away from Fitzworth Avenue and on into the best play park a child could have. Unleashed from parental control, they entered the wooded area and postures changed; hunched, wary, guns held at the ready and faces in earnest. Ryan led the way.

"I know! Let's pretend like, our base has been taken by the Germans, yeah, and we've got get it back. We can use our den as the base."

The plan was accepted roundly. They moved off the path and into the undergrowth, quickly immersing in their fantasy, as generations of boys have done before. Taking up their positions for the final push, having crept the final fifty metres, nothing else would cross their uninhibited consciousness.

"Chaaaaarge."

The excited, high pitched, but somewhat bloodless cry rang out from the Captain's boyish mouth. As one, the young soldiers hurled themselves forward to meet the imaginary foe; noisy imitation gunfire stuttering from the plastic barrels and animated explosions issuing from the attacker's mouths; a spirited attempt at battlefield mayhem, causing callow hearts to pound wildly at the rush toward the face of imagined death.

Ryan broke through the thick green outer defences of the hidden den. The change from dappled sunlight into deep shade and the fact his eyes had been closed as he pushed through, left him momentarily disadvantaged and he squinted to check his surroundings. Despite the impaired vision Ryan was immediately aware that something was wrong, as a huge swell of flies took to the air, irritated and buzzing loudly. Recoiling, his eyes closed again and he let out a cry.

"AAAGHH GROSS!"

******

In his boxy little office in the modern Police station, Patrick was staring out of the window in the direction of home when his desk phone rang.

"DI Stimpson."

"Calls just come in sir," the voice at the other end advised him. "It looks like we might have found Gary Brown."

"Ah good news for once."

"I'm not so sure, sir. He's dead."

Chapter 69

Half an hour later Patrick and Thomas were swishing through the belligerent undergrowth; stinging nettles, brambles and holly; all objecting in the only way they knew how.

"Uniform says - it looks like he's been there for a few days," Patrick said conversationally as they approached the site, and unhooking himself from a grappling stem.

"If he's been here that long Pat, it begs the question, how did we miss him? The common was supposed to have been thoroughly searched."

Patrick looked back the way they had come, and noted the fences either side of them were no more than a few metres away and still narrowing in the direction they were headed. "It's a bit of a backwater down here. Not that that is any excuse."

Ahead, about twenty metres away, the two detectives could see the familiar plastic tape wrapped around various supporting trees, denoting their destination. The distance between the back fences of the properties either side of them was no more than five metres. A gully filled with stagnant water ran though the narrow defile suggesting that, weather permitting, some days it was a stream. Clinging to the overgrown and slippery banks, they only just managed not to find out how deep the water was. Their shoes, though, were covered in cloying black mud.

"Surely there's a better way in?" said Patrick inspecting his shoes.

"I shouldn't be surprised," Thomas replied knowingly, and then, spotting and pointing to a patrol car parked a little way through the trees in front of them, he added, "but I think it's just uniform, playing their little games with us."

"Yeah good joke," was Patrick's scathing retort. "So…" and wiping the excess mud on a convenient mound of moss, looked questioningly at Thomas, "our boy's dead then?"

"So what do you reckon Doc?" Patrick asked of the now overworked pathologist craning right over the body as another plastic-clad investigator took pictures.

The Doctor didn't turn round, "He's dead," was the weary reply, "as I'm sure anybody could have told you, having seen the mess he's in."

"Any ideas yet how he died?" Patrick asked warily, knowing that these guys preferred to answer this with the benefit of a full autopsy under their belt.

"Difficult to tell at this stage, to be honest." Standing back up, he stretched and looked at the Inspector. "Blood loss probably. He's got a huge gash in his stomach, and it's deep, plus it looks like he's been hit over the head, possibly with that lump of concrete there." He pointed to a blood stained, jagged piece of builder's rubble a metre away from the body. "The trouble is, he's been interfered with by the usual wildlife, rats, foxes, maggots, you name it they've all had a go. Course, the fall could have killed him outright, at least, by the way the body is angled and the torso has been snagged in the guts, it would suggest he fell."

"What makes you think he was hit over the head?" asked Thomas. "It seems strange, if he's just fallen out of a tree, that someone should want to hit him."

"Well yes, I agree with you Sergeant, and in fairness, that's why I would like to get him back to the lab, but as far as I can see, that nasty bit of concrete is not close enough for him to have fallen onto it, so..," he paused thinking it through, "either, somebody clouted him over the head with it, or he fell on it here," the doctor pointed to the partly submerged head, "where the victims head hit the ground and it has somehow been moved since, perhaps by an animal digging around."

Patrick had noted that the doctor had used the 'F' word. *That animal seemed to be cropping up everywhere*, he thought, and consciously pushed the insidious theory out of his mind, once again. Besides, with crime scenes and bodies stacking up, he had more than enough to try and get his head around.

"Everything all right Inspector?" Patrick didn't turn. He barely heard the distant voice, so absorbed was he.

"And he is?" asked the Inspector.

"Ranger from the country park that oversees this area." The Detective Sergeant advised his superior and scanning his notebook for a name, added. "He brought the key for the gates. Let our boys in, a Mr Nash."

"Him again!" Patrick barely contained his displeasure. But as if a light had come on, he flashed a look across to his perplexed colleague. "Thomas, go have a quiet word in Mr. Nash's ear will you? I want to know his whereabouts for the morning of Martha's disappearance, the evening of Declan's abduction and the last few days."

"Is he a suspect?"

Patrick shrugged, the flash dimming, "Probably not," he said flatly. "But – I don't know – he seems to be getting under my skin of late." He turned back towards the Doctor adding casually. "See what you think."

"So was it an accident or was he killed?" Patrick said almost rhetorically to Thomas as they wandered back to their car.

"Well I suppose, we'll just have to wait and see, Pat. But one thing's for sure, his death can't be coincidental. Here he is, our most wanted, and the next thing he turns up dead."

Thomas's hand ran through the stubble he laughingly called a haircut, and absently scratched his scalp a couple of times.

"The way it looks to me, somebody is covering their tracks, perhaps... getting rid of the weak link?"

"Yes it's possible," agreed Patrick. "If Gary was the eyes and ears for someone else, and he's now a wanted man... and don't forget we've had Gary in Custody already. That would make that someone nervous I should think.... Presuming that is, Gary knows who that someone is. The trouble is, with all this electronic and cyber communication, they might never have actually met."

"True, but we found nothing on his computer to suggest he had any relationship with a person like that, admittedly loads with his on-line gaming friends. No, the more I think about it he knew that person and they wanted him silenced before he could implicate them."

"Well if you're right Thomas, perhaps we need to dig deeper within his circle of friends and acquaintances. Either this person is amongst them or they can point us in their direction. Why don't you make a start on that? I, meanwhile, need to go and break the bad news to his mum."

Before they went their separate ways Patrick looked questioningly at Thomas.

"You know Tom, what I can't believe is the gall of this Gary bloke. Here he is, looking as though he's fallen out of a tree, presumably whilst up to his old tricks of setting up another family to trash. And yet, he must have thought we'd be keeping an eye on him from when Martha went missing and now, with this second child. I mean, how on earth did he think he was going to get away with it? Doing it once," Patrick's palms sprung apart in open conciliation, "I can believe, but to keep doing it when you might still be a suspect... is madness." He shook his head, "It just doesn't add up Thomas. We're missing something but, for the life of me, I don't know what."

Throughout the rest of the day, the still fresh, and breaking news of a child's body being found the previous day, was later overtaken by the death of Gary. Too late for admission into the local evening papers, but the rolling news media would soon be flashing the story around the globe. By six o'clock, news of one of the country's most feared outlaws would have permeated into nearly every home. Communities would breathe a sigh of relief and paranoid, over-protective parents, encouraged by positive and repetitive reports, could thankfully downgrade their guard.

Chapter 70

After a full day at work, Tony and Jenny watched the early evening news with intense interest. Tony had calmed down now from his chat with the surly Detective Sergeant earlier that morning; a feat that had taken most of the day. So with meals perched on their laps, and mugs of coffee at their feet, they were incredulous of the storylines unfolding. The child's body being found in a foxes den! How much more evidence did the Inspector need? And yet, from the reporters and experts the impression being given was that Gary was being accused of these heinous crimes or was, at least, part of a team that had carried them out.

"I don't see it," said Tony, a forkful of spaghetti hovering above his plate and awaiting entry. "Gary's no paedophile, bit of a geek maybe and lives with his mum. At 24, you have to wonder?" He gave Jenny a knowing look. "And admittedly we don't know him that well, but, the last time I met him in the pub, I got on with him okay. Apparently, the police found his medic alert on the common, which he says, he must have dropped on his way home from the pub, and they'd hauled him in for that. Frankly, knowing what we know now, I'm more than inclined to believe him."

"Yeah but," Jenny began as Tony's fork found its mark, "by the sound of it, the police have got no other leads and now he's dead, there's no one to defend him. Fitting him up would be too strong a word for it, but he'll be blamed because they've got nothing else." She gave a snort, "And they're certainly not going to entertain our ideas."

Tony nodded in agreement, "So unless one of our doxes bites a reporter on the arse, our evidence is as good as worthless, I can see this being swept under the carpet, can't you?"

"Well… not until it happens again," Jenny said seriously.

******

Patrick had spent the early part of the afternoon with a distraught Trisha Brown. Assuming her son had just run off to avoid the storm, she was shocked at the stark reality. Gary, her only child, had been taken from her; and not just physically, but also mentally. His persona had been wrenched from her consciousness and soiled beyond measure; stolen, as the accusations and expanding rumours, became to all intents and purposes, fact and not fiction. The unconditional love that any mother has for their offspring would now be tested beyond measure. Trisha knew her son was unexceptional, was aware that he didn't run with the pack and was quirky in habit, but that didn't make him a killer… or worse, by current parental hysteria.

Vehemently and publicly she would defend her own, but a gnawing doubt would unjustly disturb her for the remainder of her days.

Patrick had been patient and understanding, his gentle questioning subtle and undemanding. Between outpourings of uncontrollable distress he enticed a fuller picture of the dead man they were now accusing. He looked for suggestions of a trigger, a moment in his personal history that could have changed this awkward adult from relative normalcy, to accepting molestation and abduction as a way forward. Gary's family life although not perfect, was unremarkable; couples break up all the time, Patrick reasoned following questions about her ex-husband. After fifteen turbulent years Jack Brown had gone off with a younger model. Trisha had seen it coming and coped. Gary at an impressionable age would be mentally scarred. Evidently Jack had never had a lot of time for Gary even whilst growing up, but when, as a young adult, he might have benefited from a males perspective, Jack had left. Gary's emotions had been confused and diverse, from further betrayal by his father towards him, to anger and hate for his mothers suffering.

At the end of it though, whilst Patrick could see potential influences that could warp any man, it was by no means conclusive. In fact, far from bolstering his case, Patrick was left even more undecided about where Gary Brown fitted in. It would not explain Gary's alleged predilections to the most vulnerable in the community. It seemed the more Patrick found out about the hapless Gary, the more questioning he became about his involvement. He was still adamant that Gary had had something to hide, something he wasn't telling them, *in all fairness,* he thought *who hadn't?*

Chapter 71

With concerns about Gary's credibility as a suspect in the two abduction cases still foremost in Patrick's mind, he found himself wandering the familiar gravel path along the back of the houses on Fitzworth Road. The eventful day was drawing to a close and the diminishing light nudged a part of his brain into suggesting that perhaps he ought to go home. But something spurred him on; he wanted to have a look at the places where Gary had been spying on the families. The first stop would be behind the Dockers', the second Bridget Morley's and the third… well, he didn't know who that was behind, and the thought intrigued him.

The Dockers' house had been in complete darkness, either an early night or they were out. Next door though, an illuminated upstairs room, windows and curtains wide open was issuing forth a thumping beat; the annoying rap music causing Patrick to look up and scowl. Movement at the noisy window drew his eye. A girl, a teenager, had stood up from out of sight, off a chair, he presumed. She went into the room next door switching on the light; frosted glass distorted her shape and movement. Patrick began to feel uncomfortable, inadvertently realising what he was doing. The girl appeared back into her room and began to unbutton her blouse.

"Definitely time to go," he said silently to himself.

Feeling somewhat abashed, he rejoined the path and went swiftly, intent on going to where Gary's body had been found earlier that day. The distance was about three hundred and fifty metres and, to begin with, he would cover the ground easily on the compacted stone surface. He chided himself for not bringing a torch as he turned off onto the uncertain ground of the forest floor; and, for the fact that he should have walked the further distance to approach the scene from the other road. Instead, he would be trying to follow the pathetic little partings in the undergrowth, in the hope of finding his way there. Although knowingw that if he could keep one of the fences in view all the time he would eventually pass through the muddy chicane and out into the slightly wider area behind where he hoped the white police tapes might still be draped.

Fortunately, there was some residual gloom and distant street lamps gave off a subtle glow, whilst lighted windows, glimpsed through the undergrowth, shone useful points of reference. He was aware of the odd person on the reverse side of the fences, moving around their gardens, putting away tools and closing shed doors. Other than those noises and the occasional passing car in the roads beyond, the tiny forest was still, and swiftly darkening.

"The dark," he quipped recounting a line from an old Goon show, "ideal conditions for night!"

Smiling, he caught sight of the thin broken white thread, running horizontally across his front some twenty metres up ahead. He had just negotiated the narrow strip between the fences and the stream, when he heard a noise in the undergrowth from where he had not long just come. Assuming it was some branch flicking back from where his body had pushed it, he moved on. But it struck him as odd because the sound had been some way off, and it was unlikely that a twig would have waited a while before deciding to return to its original position.

"Perhaps, it came from one of the gardens," he reasoned.

Unable to really see anything amongst the solid shapes of bushes and saplings, that seemed to grow darker as his eyes tried to probe further, he turned and moved off. There were street lights about seventy to eighty metres off to his left, where the cul de sac ended, and where the Police cars had parked earlier in the day. Their warm glow sent some light in his direction but not nearly enough to illuminate the crime scene, too far to be of use, but close enough for the lamp itself to affect his night vision. As he looked towards the light a memory stirred, it was a feeling he remembered that, occasionally, he used to get as a child in similar situations and which lingered through until his early teens. He was surprised, maybe even a little shocked that it had resurfaced, but try as he might to suppress it, the angst began to worm its way into his struggling mind.

He remembered the sensation as if it had happened only yesterday, faced as he was now, looking into a light source with blackness behind. In his youth, it had been the open patio doors of his parent's house and a harsh fluorescent strip light guiding him some way down the garden. But at the end of their seventy-five metre garden it was pitch black, and as now, he often hadn't taken a torch. It had always seemed light enough from up by the house. And the inky blackness whilst he was down there was not much of a problem either; although it enveloped and consumed, it hadn't seem to bother him. But the nighttime was fickle, for when he'd begun to walk back up the long garden towards the light, what lay behind began to take on a new perspective. It was all in his head he knew, but he could not quell the welling sensation of fear, a fear of something behind him in the cloying dark; it messed with his perception, growing blacker as the light source drew nearer. As a young child it would have been monsters and ghosts or the bogeyman, as a young adult it became aliens or vampires. What, it, might be was really almost immaterial, in that instance of happening, but he remembered all too succinctly getting an overwhelming belief that something was almost at his back and the night was cloaking it. And with every sound he'd heard, a rustle in dead leaves or the wind murmuring through the trees, the notion would intensify and he would break into a jog unable to look back, and then a run, as he sought to quickly close the gap, launching himself through the open door and into the light, into safety.

It was irrational and ridiculous but it was affecting him now. What he once believed was a childish hang-up, was in danger of taking hold, once again. Suddenly there was a splash, *something's in the water.* He spun round to listen. *It's coming up the stream!* His eyes, wide and straining, could see nothing; no movement of any kind, yet he could hear the water and mud being sloshed aside as if something was moving stealthily through it.

He turned and moved with urgency towards the tree that Gary had been found in, and all the while he tried to rationalise, offering any number of explanations, a frog, probably a rat maybe even a deer. But somehow his brain would not allow them to fit, the answers not meeting the audible criteria.

"What the fuck is it?" he breathed and wondering why he was so wound up.

Somehow, Tony Nash hove into his mind's eye, saying, "Don't say I didn't warn you."

"And you can piss-off," Patrick said as his hands scrabbled up the trunk searching for the footholds he'd seen earlier in the day.

Grabbing one, and placing his foot on a nearby low-slung branch, he began to climb. Hastily he pulled himself higher, and just as he began to feel safe, a short cry, low and soft, told him he was not alone. He hadn't imagined it, something really was out there. Sitting astride an outstretched branch some four metres off the ground, he looked out trying to see what it was. The street lamp's glow was now behind, and off to his right, and on his lofty perch he sucked in cool mouthfuls of damp air while his heart slowed and the night engulfed him and he felt calmer.

The woodland beneath him grew quiet and still, no more erroneous sounds, just noises of humanity a way off in the distance, but he continued to search for the animal that eluded him. A badger most probably, or a weasel or was that stoat? He always got those two mixed up, might even be… *go on say it… a fox. Bloody Tony Nash and his stupid ideas! Whatever it was seems to have gone now.*

Feeling just a tad pathetic, having been effectively, chased up a tree by some diminutive woodland creature; he chose to take in the wider view. What he could see were the lights of houses nearly all around him, in some places no more than twenty metres away, and others, at forty or sixty metres. Thoughts of who Gary had wanted to spy on from up here, pushed out the wilder elements that had up until a few minutes ago consumed him.

"So, who was it you were watching then?" He scanned the closest dwellings.

The house directly to his front was in near darkness; a light was on somewhere at the front, a porch light, he wondered, shining through the glass front door? He spotted an elderly couple watching television in the house to the left, a single table lamp allowing only a limited view of the room. To the right, the snapshot he got there was of a middle-aged couple, he, watching television and she making a hot drink; no other movement was evident in the house, *not that that meant nobody else lived there,* thought Patrick.

"Doesn't look very promising so far," he said to himself. "But I wouldn't mind knowing who's in that house?"

He mentally pointed to the house ahead of him. As if somebody had heard him, a glow appeared seemingly at the centre of the house, *the hall light,* thought Patrick, *somebody has just come in.* He watched as a door opened and, from the borrowed light coming through from the hall, he could see it was the kitchen. Within a second, the room was flooded with functional lighting and a young woman, perhaps early twenties, walked over to the sink, grabbed a cup off the drainer and drew water from the tap. From his dark vantage, all inside the room was as clear and as sharp as that of a photo shoot. He could see details of colour, of furniture, of layout and, he could see most of her.

A pretty girl, and shapely, Patrick assessed; dressed in a black tight-fitting skirt and with a white blouse. The impression he got was that of a waitress, perhaps just come off shift. His powers of deduction, had he known it, would have been spot on, for Janet Coleman had indeed just got home from waiting tables at the Angel; a regular occurrence as Monday through to Thursday she covered the afternoon and early evening stint, finishing up at about nine and then walking the ten minutes through the estate to her mum's house.

Patrick stared vacantly at the window as a thought occurred to him and he began to mull it over. This, in turn, raised the familiar concern he had been having as to where Gary actually fitted in to the abduction case; indeed did he fit in at all? He had been chewing this one over since his long interview with his mother, *had they got it wrong? Had he jumped to the wrong conclusion? What if?* He began to think to himself as the girl in the window looked down at her blouse, inspecting it closely. *What if he visited the common for some other purpose?*

The girl clutched the front of the garment, lifting it away from her chest and rubbed it with her other hand, trying to scrape off a stain. *And what if that purpose* he continued to think, *was also, not strictly legitimate either?*   As if to add weight and reality to his conclusions, the girl loosened her grip and the taut material dropped, revealing once again the swell of her breasts. In a short movement both hands were up around her neck and her head tilted backwards as she picked at the top button. The collar moved apart on its release. Automatically her hands slipped down to the button beneath. With that clasp unfettered then the next the overlapping seams drew further apart. Patrick's blank stare only just registered the movements but it was enough to distract him from consciously concluding his supposition. In reality though, he'd got there and with some certainty as to what Gary had been up to. He just hadn't said it out loud in his head. Bizarrely, he might not have to, as the female, now fully in the spotlight, was graphically about to show him.

With the final button undone, the blouse hung casually over the waistband of her skirt. The girls' head moved from side to side, evidently using the reflective qualities that the night outside gave the glass to study herself. Transfixed, Patrick watched as, slowly, the girl began to gyrate sensually as if performing some erotic dance and, all the while, her unmoving head kept her eyes rigidly on the image she created. Shimmying left she made use of the full length glass door to continue her show, uninhibited and unsuspecting. Her hands, now moving seductively across the loose material, made it ruck and pull, the seams edging further apart to reveal the soft flesh beneath. *My God!* realised Patrick, as they pulled apart, exposing a narrow strip of skin from neck to navel. *No bra.* Even from that distance, Patrick could tell, from the well-defined cleft between, this girl was 'stacked'. Furtively he looked around him, out into the darkness, uncomfortable with what was happening… and yet reluctant to move.

"Gary, Gary, Gary…" he said under his breath in unbelieving wonder. "What have you been up to?"

Chapter 72

The buzzer droned again, like some ensnared bluebottle.

Tony glanced groggily across at his digital clock, "Fur Christ's sake," he breathed, only just having dropped off, "it's not even midnight."

Equally still half asleep Jenny's words seemed to roll into one, "What's the matter?"

"There's somebody buzzing the door downstairs."

"Probably that pissed bloke from number one, lost his keys again," Jenny said turning over and eyes tightly shut.

They ignored the next reverberations hoping that whoever it was would go away, allowing them to remain under their duvet.

"Right," Tony flung back the cover as it went off again, and leapt out of bed, now resentfully awake. Out of the bedroom door, he crossed the darkened living area to the tiny hall and pressed the intercom button.

"Who is it?" he said, annoyance clear in his voice.

"Mr Nash," was the distant voice and Tony couldn't quite place it. "It's Detective Inspector Stimpson... I- I'm sorry it's so late, but... could I come in?"

"It's nearly midnight," Tony protested. "We were in bed... asleep. Can't it wait?"

There was a heavy silence on the other end of the line. Tony wondered if he'd gone.

"Hello, are you still there?"

"Yes... I'm still here."

"Well?"

"Well what?" said the Inspector

"Can't it wait?

"I," he hesitated, "I don't think it can, Mr Nash."

Tony not only registered a formality in the Inspectors voice but also a sense of entreating urgency.

"Okay, flat four." Tony pressed the release button to open the communal front door.

"**Jenny**," he called. "Better get up. We've got company."

In the moments while he waited for the knock, Tony filled the kettle ready to make coffee and slipped on a dressing gown.

He got back to the door just as the gentle tap sounded, and opened it.

"Inspector," Tony said warily, as the policeman's bulk was framed in the doorway and he moved aside to indicate Patrick should enter.

He had assessed the police officer, at their accidental meeting in the woods, as a strong willed, blunt, and probably reasonable character, but certainly not one you would wish to mess with. Naturally, rank and size bestowed him with an air of power and with that, a solid dependability, and although Tony hadn't exactly hit it off with him, he didn't feel overwhelming animosity towards him either, despite the hour. Indeed there was something about the Inspector this evening, which gave him cause for mild apprehension. And, although they had hardly exchanged many words, Tony was detecting edginess in the man, as if he was uncomfortable, perhaps about being there. Certainly the lateness of his visit was a bit out of order, and that might have been it, but somehow he didn't think so.

"So Inspector...please," Tony began, and indicated to a chair. "What's so important that you need to get me out of bed?"

At that moment Jenny wandered into the room, clearly a little dazed and somewhat taken aback at the sight of the visitor. The oversized sweatshirt she had pulled on, in an attempt to make decent, was evidently not hers but Tony's, the large white letters announcing that 'Rangers do it out-doors', attracting the Inspector's attention and an inkling of a smile.

Tony saw where the detective's eyes had been drawn, and was unsure whether the accompanying smile had been to acknowledge the humour of the shirt, or the disarming attractiveness of his girlfriend in her state of near undress. But he said, perhaps a little defensively anyway, "Don't worry. It's not an official work one."

Patrick just raised his eyebrows, tilted his head back slightly and smiled in recognition of Tony's apparent awkwardness. Moving to sit, as he had been invited to do Patrick, swept his gaze around the modern interior, noting that it was fairly compact, but well laid-out.

"This is very smart." Patrick seemed to announce in an effort to make conversation.

"Yes... it is. It's ideal really. I... live on my own." He gave Jenny an embarrassed look and felt himself colour up. "Although, not all the time, obviously." he added quickly. "Jenny stays over if we've been out late or had a bit to drink, or something."

Patrick smiled again, pleasantly. Tony was beginning to get twitchy and wondering, not unreasonably, just what exactly the Inspector was doing there? Patrick sat forward in the armchair, as if ready to speak, his backside perched on the cushion's edge and forearms resting on his thighs. Large hands came together, fingers knitting solidly and thumbs extended upwards gently tapping against each other. By now, Tony and Jenny had settled next to each other, somewhat primly, on the sofa.

"Look Mr Nash."

"Tony and Jenny, please," Tony requested openly.

"Okay," he acknowledged with a small nod in Tony's direction.

"I'm not quite sure how to begin really... how can I put this? I'm not here in any official capacity, if you understand me." It was Patrick's turn to look awkward and his thumbs tapped faster reflecting it. "Let's just say, I personally want to review what you told me the other day. Don't get me wrong. I am not accepting of it nor denying it. I just want you to convince me. Oh, and nobody knows I'm here, not my superiors, or my boss...the wife, that is," he let out a nervous laugh. "And just for a while I'd like it to stay that way, ok?"

The couple on the sofa were wide-eyed. Both nodded their agreement and glanced at each other in a look that said, 'Where's this going?'

Patrick saw the look and evidently decided to weigh straight in.

"You never sent me that video clip that you said you had. Don't suppose you've got it to hand now?"

"Actually I have," said Tony and reached over to the coffee table for his laptop.

Whilst it booted up and Tony searched for the file, Jenny was still having trouble with the detective's sudden change of heart.

"Has something happened Inspector, to make you change your mind? she asked directly.

Clearly agitated by the question he sought to fend it off.

"Miss Spader... sorry Jenny, by the way, please call me Patrick. I am merely trying to keep an open mind, but, as some of my colleagues are not so receptive of such ideas, I thought it best to do some digging in my own time, as it were."

"So it's not because you found that body in the fox's den, or that, suddenly, your only suspect Gary Brown is dead."

Patrick held her stare but noticed the flash of anger that had sparked.

"No. I can honestly say it was neither of those," he said, but again, he looked very uncomfortable and a thin sheen of sweat covered his brow. "I'm sorry. I don't suppose I could have a drink of water could I?"

"Yes of course." Jenny rose to her feet, "You wouldn't prefer something stronger would you? And looking concerned said, "Are you feeling OK."

"Yes I'm, I'm fine, thank you, just water please."

"Here we go." Tony clicked the mouse on the little arrow in the centre of the screen and immediately the video began. "This," he explained "was taken by a cameraman, a professional by all accounts, from a helicopter, and we are sure this is Parley Common. We haven't been able to track him down to verify it, but Jenny and I are certain that's where it is."

Jenny joined in, "Yes it was actually sent to my boss at work. The cameraman was concerned that these dogs should be investigated. You'll appreciate that this is literally just up the road from here."

"Right," said Tony pointing with his finger at the screen. "This is a doe with her newly born fawn here." He waited a few seconds before continuing his commentary "and here just coming on to the screen are the three doxes."

The what! Patrick wanted to say but was cut short by Jenny

"By the way," Jenny added as Patrick continued to watch, "that term 'dox' is not ours, we found it on the internet. It appears to have been used in folklore and, in more recent times, to describe the offspring of a dog-fox hybrid."

"Right," was Patrick's barely audible reply, transfixed by the events unfolding.

On the screen the three hybrids had, by now, taken up their final positions ready for the strike.

"They seem…" Patrick struggled for an appropriate word, "well," he shrugged, "organised, is the only way to describe it."

"Exactly Inspector, but whether you choose to believe our theory, as fantastic as it sounds even to us, or not, you cannot get away from the fact that these dogs… foxes… whatever, are hunting in a pack formation."

"Good God," was Patrick's only comment as the 'trap' was sprung and the kill was over within a matter of seconds. He stared at the screen as if unsure what to say.

"That was pretty slick," he finally said.

"Yes, slick and deadly," Tony acknowledged, "and I'm willing to bet that those three could easily be responsible for the missing children and possibly for the death of Jim Bennett, maybe even Gary Brown."

Patrick shook his head. "Look, I can see where you are coming from with this, but even if I were to believe that, which at the moment I reserve judgment on, I need to see the autopsies on the child's remains and, of course, Gary's. You do realise of course, that any dead body, left out in the elements, is nearly always interfered with by some animal. Doesn't normally affect the findings, but in this case, I doubt we'll be able to say with any certainty that's how the child was killed, because unfortunately, there's very little body left. Besides that, we haven't confirmed yet that this is one of ours."

With that the Inspector slumped back into the armchair, looking pale and weary.

"God I'm tired," he said, and with that involuntarily stuck his hand down to rub his ankle. "I must go… full day tomorrow."

As he drew his hand back up, the other two stared at it.

"You're bleeding," said Jenny.

Before he could wave her away with an accompanying, "it's nothing," she was pulling up his trouser leg to inspect the damage. Grabbing a tissue off the table and gently cleaning away the worst of the blood, she noted the puncture wounds grouped in a loose oval shape around the lower portion of his calf.

"Now correct me if I'm wrong Inspector," she looked at him sternly, "but being as I have seen a few of these in my official capacity, I would say, you've been bitten by a dog; something sizeable judging by the wound… and recently. Am I right?" The bite was big, bigger than she had seen before and a large chunk of skin hung loosely, the bloody flesh angry and inflamed.

Tony caught the scent. "That's why you're here," a flush of excitement animating his face. "You've seen them. They've attacked you haven't they?" He stood up and pushed his open palms through his hair and looked down at Jenny. "Well he's not a reporter and that's not exactly his arse, but it's close enough."

With just a hint of a smile Jenny shot him a warning look.

Patrick looked puzzled and Tony added waving his hand, "Don't worry about it."

"So what happened?"

Chapter 73

Patrick began. "Earlier this evening, just after nine, I was over at the site where Gary's body had been found this morning. I wanted to clear something up in my mind about the scene. I guess I hadn't really taken in how dark it had got until I was almost there, so I pressed on anyway, no torch or anything. You know where I'm talking about... you were there this morning.

"Yes," said Tony. "There's a ditch that runs right through it, carries away the overflow from the pond, always pretty muddy even if there's no water in it. Narrows at one point, I think, and then widens out again."

"That's it," Patrick acknowledged. Having established that his audience knew where he was talking about, he continued. "I'd just got through that narrow part when I heard a noise, some way off but from where I'd just come. I didn't think much of it; you don't expect total quiet in any outdoor situation and particularly so close to the houses. But something up here," the Inspector tapped the side of his head, "obviously wasn't convinced and I began to feel edgy. And then, when I heard movement through the water in the ditch no more than a few metres away, not loud or boisterous like some dog splashing about, but carefully. Maybe it was my imagination playing tricks, but the impression was deliberate and stealthy. To be honest, I began to panic." There was more than a hint of incredulity on his face and mild embarrassment. "Bloody ridiculous. It had only been a few minutes since I'd left the main path and yet I was really spooked. Before I know it I'm terrified and legging it like some frightened animal. I climbed a tree. In fact, it was the one we think Gary had fallen from, and then I heard a call, a soft bark and knew I hadn't been imagining it."

Patrick went on to explain why he had wanted to revisit the site at night time, hoping that he might see what Gary actually went there for. He wanted to confirm his hunch that Gary might have had other reasons for spying on the houses.

"I'm pretty sure Gary was up to no good, however, as it turns out, and, particularly with what happened to me this evening, I'm not so sure he had anything to do with the abductions. Our Mr Brown I believe, was satisfying some voyeuristic tendencies, or to put it another way, he was a Peeping Tom."

"Sounds about right though," Jenny said matter of factly. "You always said he was a bit weird, didn't you Tony?"

"Yeah," Tony looked thoughtful, "but I wouldn't have guessed that. So what happened next?"

He explained his need to get out of the tree and that, by then, he had completely calmed down. And although he hadn't forgotten that some woodland dweller was possibly lurking in the undergrowth he had rationalised it as a badger or a fox, and thought, 'come on, who'd ever heard of one of them hanging around waiting to be seen? Let alone wanting to have a confrontation'.

"No, feet back on the ground… in both senses," Patrick looked at them checking they understood, "and I turned away from the trunk towards the lights of Henchard Close. I thought it would be sensible to walk the longer way round than get messed up again through the woods. But just as I went to move off in that direction I saw a shape just inside the edge of the tree line. It was silhouetted by the street lamp on the pavement at the end of the cul de sac. An animal, and at thirty odd metres away, not big or particularly threatening, but it was just sitting there, poised like some expectant dog waiting for a treat. I could tell that it was looking, not out into the road, where you might have expected it to, you know, searching for any man made dangers, but back into the trees. And you know what my first thought was? It's guarding the exit." Patrick gave Tony and Jenny another quick glance, checking they didn't think he was off his trolley. Seeing their rapt and eager expressions he continued.

"I swear, no sooner had I taken one step, than the animal was up on all fours and it let out another soft bark. It was calling, do y'see?" Jenny could see Patrick was beginning to get agitated. It seemed the experience was still having an effect on him. "Anyway, at this point I was wondering what the hell to do, should I go back the way I came, or just walk on and challenge the beast head on? After all, it didn't seem that big. I mean, I was actually contemplating having a run in with this thing. God, for all I knew it might have slunk away before getting anywhere near it, but somehow I didn't think so! Something in the creature's stance, and its posture, was warning me; and the thought of that bark… it could only have been to alert another, or more worryingly, others, and that really started to make me nervous. Then I heard more noises, one, some way to my right, a soft thud like something had just dropped from a height onto the ground and another from the route I'd come in from. As you can imagine, it's dark, I can't see much and it sounds like there's movement all around, and to cap it all it seems my mind is now batting for the other side, cranking up the fear until once again, I'm absolutely terrified." Patrick shook his head in total disbelief. It was clear he was struggling to accept a side of him he wouldn't have thought possible.

"When I was in the Army, we had some scary moments; Belize on night exercises, snakes and spiders, Northern Ireland the threat of bombs and snipers. And even now in the force, stand-offs against knives and guns or the aftermath of a road traffic accident. I've dealt with all of those, but I've never felt as scared as I did at that moment."

Tony and Jenny sat in silent awe, amazed at what he was revealing, but also in admiration for this big policeman who, despite his superior age and evident experience, was admitting to being scared witless.

"Anyway, my eyes were all over the place, searching the darkness, trying to catch a glimpse of anything, and after a few moments, when I looked back over to the close, that animal had disappeared. I'd hoped, off into the road, but a quick check of the well-lit turning circle told me what I feared and knew already. It had slipped into the undergrowth and was heading my way."

"Jesus." Jenny exhaled, but it was all that ushered from the stilled sofa as the couple continued to listen, hardly daring to move, let alone breath.

"Well I turned and made ready to run, I wasn't sure where to, but the only option they were giving me was towards the back of the houses on Fitzworth. It also occurred to me, that there were high fences at the bottom of the gardens, but at that moment I didn't give a monkeys. Adrenalin was kicking in and I was either going over, or through ... all I knew was, I had to get the hell out of there." Patrick took a swig of water, his hand trembling slightly as he set the glass back on the table.

"As I started to move I could see a light shining out from an upstairs window from the nearest house, and I made a beeline for that. I tried to run but it was pitch, and I kept running into bushes and dodging round trees. It was a bloody nightmare. And of course, the moment I started to move, I was aware of these things picking up speed also. Obviously there was no need now for caution; their prey... me, was well and truly spooked and stumbling about like a helpless prat." Patrick spat out the last word in disgust, angry at the thought of his feeble impotency. "I made it to the fence and luckily the area was relatively clear enabling me to get a bit of a run up. Lunging at one of the posts and grabbing the top I jumped for all I was worth. Not elegant, I can assure you but I was over and scrabbling about on all fours in their flattened plants. And on the other side of the fence, I could hear them jumping, trying to get over, claws scraping on the thin wood. Well as you can imagine, my thoughts of now being safe, you know with a bloody great fence between us suddenly didn't feel so solid and I was up again, running across the back lawn of some body's house. As I got to the side gate between garage and house, all the time praying it would be unlocked - because there was no way I would be going over this one, it was so high - something clamped around my calf and that's when the pain hit me. I was nearly overwhelmed by the sense of panic and fear as I saw this... fox thing, hanging on to my leg and the other two just clearing the fence. I knew I had to get through the gate with or without my hanger on, because if the other two joined in, then that would be it. I wouldn't have stood a chance. The relief when the gate opened, first pull was incredible. I dragged the still clinging animal through with me, and felt its hold soften as the streetlights unnerved it. Managing to slam the heavy gate into its side it let go, slipping back behind as I yanked it home. My car was about a quarter of a mile away up the road," as he knew the story was about to end Patrick tense and agitated, visibly relaxed and by way of relief added, "Tell you what, that's got to be the fastest I've ever run, and I used to run the hundred metres for the regiment."

"Sounds like you had a lucky escape," Tony said seriously.

"Tell you what an' all, I didn't feel safe until I'd locked the doors on my car. I sat in there for ages, just shaking."

The Inspector took another large slug of water, draining the glass and setting it back down on the coffee table. Patrick had felt reluctant to tell them what had happened or even to acknowledge that he had been bitten. To do so would be to admit the existence of these animals, which despite his recent ordeal, he was still coming to terms with. After all, had he not just spent the last hour or so sitting in his car trying to do just that? The first twenty minutes notwithstanding, he'd been so overwrought; it had taken him nearly that long to stop shaking. He still couldn't believe it. As a copper he'd liked to think he'd seen it all… well… evidently not, but this, this was just too incredible. Apart from his injury he had no evidence to prove what had happened, he couldn't go with this to his superiors they would laugh him out of the station, despite the video and whatever else these two might have. And yet, although he hardly knew either of them, it seemed in this instance they were probably his only option. He'd needed to tell someone; and who better than a willing and receptive ear. He just didn't want it to go any further.

"Okay," he said adding firmly, "this goes nowhere else," looking pointedly at Tony, "No rushing off to the Echo, okay?"

"What!" Tony looked aghast, "I didn't want to be in the paper," he said indignantly. "If I remember rightly, no sooner had I spoken to you, then hey presto, my mug-shot's in the paper the very next day. I got a lot of grief thanks to you."

"Well okay, but let's keep it to ourselves. At least for the moment anyway."

"What I still can't get over, is," Patrick sounded incredulous, "this is Dorset, not…" he blustered, thinking of something appropriate to say, "Transylvania or the Great Grimpen Mire. It's Ferndown for God's sake. Those things acted like they should have been on the African plains, not piddling Poor common."

Tony handed Patrick one of the pictures he had taken of the doxes's down by the ponds. "Well that's them and whether you like it or not they're on Poor Common. I took that less than a hundred metres from where you were tonight."

"The thing is Patrick," Jenny cut in, "you, of all of us, know that they are real and what they're capable of, so my question is what are you, or should I say what are we going to do about it?"

Before he could answer Tony added further considerations.

"What we also have to remember, is that we have been focussing on the three adult hybrids, as if they are the only problem, but consider this… Jenny and I have seen what we believe are their offspring. So as likely as not there are another four more to consider."

"What like these?" Patrick pointed to the picture.

"Well I suppose it might be a bit presumptuous to assume that they would have the same inherent traits as their father, but I think we have to assume it. They are after all going to be brought up and taught by these three. Therefore, it would be a fair bet to say that they would probably grow up enjoying the same palette as their parents, don't you think?"

"Yes put like that, we might have a little bit more of a problem," Patrick agreed.

"Actually," Tony began again with even more caution in his voice. "This little bit of a problem as you put it, is going to get worse very soon if we don't stop it now."

Patrick looked quizzical, "How do you work that out?"

"Those cubs Patrick, are about twenty weeks old. They're not far from being old enough to leave and find territories of their own. Another month or so they could be off terrorising another area." Tony paused allowing it to sink in, then added, "In fairness, they've got to get lucky. Most fox cubs die before they get to ten months; killed on the roads, usually, particularly in urban areas or from disease. However I have a feeling these guys," he studied the picture as if re-appraising, "have been born lucky; lucky, because they are different. If they are, as we suspect, a hybrid, and the other side of the gene pool is from a Pit Bull Terrier, then their combined abilities might be truly awesome, don't you think?" He didn't wait for the nodded agreements that came a second later. "Let's be realistic, the adaptability and the opportunistic nature of the Fox... swift, agile, mixed with the strength, determination and possible aggression of the pit bull, makes it quite a daunting creature. We also have to remember that the fox is not usually a pack animal and these 'critters' seemed to be going against the grain, big time. As we've seen, their hunting skills, as an organised pack are as good as any pride of lions. To be honest," he said, his face looking even more concerned as the thought truly dawned, "this heightened sense of pack, might be just what sets them apart. They could clean up."

"You think they could spread, go further afield, then?" Patrick asked, somewhat naively.

"Who knows, but take the Grey squirrel as an example, it's much more adaptable than our own Red and look what happened to them. There's hardly any left! A much more aggressive hybrid Fox could push out a population of its own kind, whether by predation or just removing the sources of food." Something else occurred to him, "You also have to remember that the Red fox has a wider geographical distribution than any other Carnivora species and they are the most common. You'll find them all over the place, Tundra, deserts, highlands and cities. So our super fox has the potential to go far, don't you think?"

Jenny had been listening to all of this and was attuned to what Tony was saying, having spent hours discussing it together. But perceptively she didn't feel that the Inspector had quite cottoned on to the real crux of the matter despite Tony's efforts at explaining his concerns. So she drew the Inspector's attention,

"Of course..." she began, holding up a newspaper with a picture of Martha, the first missing child, "the other most disturbing thought, Inspector, is that as Tony said, our super fox could do pretty well, but of course for a predator to do well it has to have an abundant and easy source of prey, wouldn't you agree?" Patrick nodded. "And which of all the animals in this overcrowded little Island might fit that bill?" She flopped the newspaper in front of him, Martha side up, and gave him a wide-eyed and expectant stare, adding pointedly, "We might just have been moved down the food chain, Inspector"

"Right," said Patrick still sounding a little sceptical, "I see where you're coming from, but..."

"But nothing Inspector," Jenny sounded angry. "We're lucky... in this country, we can walk where we like, when we like, in the country, parks, playgrounds, night or day and nothing, people aside, is going to do us any harm. But just think… what if we couldn't wander down a road or walk the kids to school or go to the shops and all because, at any moment, something might attack us? And not just one thing, but a pack stalking us, in our gardens even. We wouldn't feel safe anywhere."

"Jenny's right Patrick. If these animals still look fox-like, how is anyone going to know the difference? But besides that, foxes are just as much at home in urban areas as they are in rural ones, and are as much a part of modern life as we are. But given an aggressive predatory streak we might find it very difficult to fully control them. Like it or not we have to act fast, they cannot be allowed to disperse"

Patrick didn't really need to be convinced; his throbbing calf was testament to their reality, but he was struggling with the wider implications. It hadn't crossed his mind that this might not remain just a local matter. Indeed thoughts of the heavily populated English countryside taking on a wilder side, something akin to a jungle, where the threat of savage animals was real and commonplace, was stretching his imagination too far, at this late hour.

The chair was comfortable, and he was incredibly weary, but Patrick was finding his hosts pressurising, almost hostile and he felt he wanted to go; he needed time to himself. Tiredness was affecting his frame of mind. The hostility he'd felt, was, he guessed, just concerned people feeling as useless as he did at that moment. And yet, even after what had happened to him and with everything he had just heard, and indeed, could not really refute, he left Tony's flat, still with niggling doubts and issues of credibility. *Could this really be happening?*

Chapter 74

Friday 7th August 9:05am

"Tony, meet my boss Chief Inspector Jonathon Bryant." The lean unsmiling man shook Tony's hand but looked somewhat bemused. Turning to his subordinate and with annoyance bubbling under the bewildered expression, "What is all this Pat?" Jonathon Bryant asked. "I thought they said you'd called in sick? Now I find you here with these people. You said it was urgent. What's so urgent that you see fit to divert me from my duties at the station, eh?"

Patrick had called his boss's mobile at about eight-thirty, guessing that he would be on his way to work and luring him to this meet on the pretext of having new evidence on the abduction cases. He also asked that the chief inspector not mention it to anyone at the moment. Intrigue got the better of the Chief Inspector and he called in to the station to rearrange his appointments. The plot thickened when he was told that, Inspector Stimpson had, not long ago, called in sick.

Tony was also taken aback. Last night the three of them had agreed to meet up again in the morning. Tony was on a day off but Jenny would reluctantly have to feign illness, all in the cause of thrashing out a plan. However, he hadn't bargained on a fourth person and a senior police officer to boot.

"Come in, come in," Tony garbled beginning to feel a little nervous, intimidated by the sharp blue uniform bristling with emblems of high office. Although Patrick had only just got there himself, he hadn't seen fit to mention this addition to their group. The idea of getting some sleep on the problem was to work out what they could do. But Tony was now wondering, *had the Inspector had a change of heart, was his boss here for some other reason? Were they going to be warned off, or worse?*

Jenny was not so fazed and with the help of one of her winning smiles offered, "Coffee, Chief Inspector?"

The atmosphere in the little flat was tense as they stood around awkwardly waiting for the coffee to be handed out. Tony was completely thrown and sat at the compact dining table behind the sofa, gesturing to the two police officers to take the more comfortable chairs. The ideas, which he and Jenny had been up half the night discussing, and were expecting to put across to the Inspector that morning, were, he worried, perhaps not appropriate any more. One thing was sure, no way was he going to lead the conversation. He'd leave that one to Patrick. As if reading his thoughts Patrick began.

"Can I just say thanks for dropping everything to be here sir." The formality in his voice suggested, he too was uncomfortable with situation. "I hope you will, after reviewing what we have," Patrick gestured to Tony and Jenny, "understand, why, the cloak and dagger meeting. I also hope that you will keep an open mind on what we are about to tell you and not dismiss it out of hand. To be honest, I am still coming to terms with the idea as it is indeed, somewhat hard to believe."

"Yes, yes Inspector," the chief said a little more irritably than he meant, adding, "I've known you long enough to cut you some slack. Just fire away."

******

At the same moment as their meeting stuttered into an awkward existence, a young woman was parking her progeny-laden buggy within the protective compound of Parley Play Park. The groaning pushchair creaked and squeaked in weary protest as it was relieved of its burden. The two-and-a half-year old scrabbling out from the forward facing seat, headed for the slide. Moments before that, a chunky lad of four had alighted from the back where he had been precariously hitching a ride. Mum had told him to get off as they entered the wood chipped covered park; no way could she push him as well on the difficult terrain. He'd barely held the mesh covered gate open long enough for his mother to get the buggy into the enclosure, before he was off and dangling from the wire-like climbing frame.

It was barely nine o' clock and, consequently, the tiny park was deathly quiet. A swathe of green, not much bigger than a football pitch, lay alongside the play park which, in turn, was part of a wider complex of adult playing fields. Mature trees, dotted here and there, gave it a proper park feel and they merged at its northern extremities into a large copse known as Parley wood. Beyond that, lay the open heaths of Parley Common, and with the southerly aspect sheltered behind a row of houses on the main Christchurch Road, it was still relatively peaceful.

Tracy had chosen this time knowing it would be empty and was happy to get out of the house and wanted the boys occupied, because she needed somewhere to seethe undisturbed. Her partner, the kids' dad, was once again content to sit on his arse all day instead of looking for work; the video games and films he watched were just not suitable for the children. But no sooner had she settled herself on one of the conveniently positioned wooden benches around the twenty meter square, play area, than a familiar urge alerted her… God she needed a pee.

"Boys stay in here, Mummy's just going to the toilet." She pointed to the functional brick building a little way over towards the car park. "I'll only be a minute. Josh make sure Sammy doesn't go on any of the big stuff, yeh, while I'm in there…." she gave him a meaningful stare, "Ok?"

Forty-five seconds later, and relieved of the insistent fluids, she noted the graffiti scrawled on the door whilst fumbling for cigarettes in her bag. The kids were laughing. She could hear them through the open windows and, content they were ok, decided a quick fag wouldn't hurt, despite the unkempt surroundings.

Out in the play park, and just as soon as his mother was out of view, Sammy had naturally made a beeline for the high slide. Maternally empowered, Josh headed his brother off chasing him from the steps, with a playful, "No Sammy, too high," much

271

to the toddlers delight and squealing, tottered obliquely away towards the outer reaches and the chain link fence.

"Woof, woof." The chubby little figure pointed falteringly, as he wobbled to a stop half a metre from the mesh.

"Yeh, that's right, a doggy," agreed Josh, his voice high and encouraging, full of imitated grown up praise for his brother's deduction.

"Woof woof," he said again and pointed in a different direction to where another animal was inspecting the wire, sniffing it and snuffling at where it met the retaining gravel board.

Josh swung to look at it and a movement caught his eye over by the gate. A third creature was now patrolling the enclosure.

"Look Sammy, novver one."

As the two diminutive figures stared out at the animals behind the fence, they became aware of the agitation and insistence of the dogs. Moving briskly around the perimeter, every so often stopping suddenly at a spot on the fence, the animals tested it with their pointed snouts, clawed at it, then moved on.

Unsure of what was going on but disturbed by the unfamiliar behaviour, Josh moved closer to his brother. Dogs didn't usually upset him, but he was on his own and becoming perturbed. Mummy wasn't there! Usually he only ever met one at a time, and always with mummy or daddy, but now... now there were lots. Nervously Josh scanned the open areas outside their cage sensibly looking for their owner. But there was nobody.

He grasped his little brother's hand and drew him to the centre of the enclosure, an involuntary action, to be as far away from them as possible.

Outside the high fence, frustration was mounting and piercing eyes kept throwing glances at their focus of attention. Two sets of paws scrabbled urgently at a decaying board, whilst the third jumped wildly and hopelessly in an attempt to assail the barrier, the mesh jangling as it rattled against the metal poles.

"Where's mummy...where's my mummy?" the little boy began to chant, his voice quivering with mounting agitation. The chill vibes quickly transferred through the clasped palms and the toddler too became unnerved. His face would say it all, bemused innocence, unknowing of what he should be frightened of, yet the wide eyes watered and inside a feeling of dread clouded his limited consciousness.

Angry snarling and frustrated whining upped the ante. Feeling utterly exposed and abandoned the children sobbed, jumping at every unseen noisy movement from beyond their prison. The normal safe zone, that constant protective bubble they took for granted and which exuded from the two most important beings in their short lives, was now missing. Suddenly isolated... they were alone and absolutely terrified!

******

"Right," continued Patrick, "the reason for meeting here is that Mr Nash and Miss Spader came to me with an alternative scenario to the alleged abductions, and I

272

believe it is worth giving it a hearing. However," the Inspector looked agitated, "I don't think we want this to go any further than these four walls, just at the moment. Anyway, that'll be for you to decide," he said looking pointedly at his superior.

Tony was still struggling with the fact that the Inspector's boss had been invited to the meeting purely, it seemed, to be given the low down on his and Jenny's theory, and he almost didn't realise that Patrick was now asking him to do just that and go through their evidence.

Jenny thrust the laptop into his hand and said encouragingly, "Let's use this to help us." Feeling less on the spot now that Jenny had indicated her intentions to help, he brought up the opening page of their presentation.

Tony explained that the sequence of events that they had put together were all incidences, that taken on their own would almost certainly not draw much attention, "but pulled together, and in light of the recent abductions, they offer, we think," he said looking at Jenny for support, "compelling evidence to back up the, some might say, fantastic idea that we are suggesting." He continued by telling the chief of all the insignificant incidences that had happened in and around Poor Common over the past few months. It took a little while and they backed it up with the statements obtained from those involved and the diary entries that they had made noting their encounters. From the various chicken strikes and the loss of beloved fluffy pets to the vanishing of dogs, all with strikingly similar tales to tell; here one minute and somehow gone the next and nothing apart from damaged cages and empty enclosures to show for it. And apart from the ever-excitable chickens, little evidence was left of any real struggle; suggesting in nearly every case, a clean and swift removal, almost clinical.

Proof to show degradation of wildlife was not so easy to corroborate. They could only offer their own observations and assumptions and in particular the remains found by them of the attacked deer on Poor Common

By the end of this section Jonathon Bryant was still in the dark as to where he was being led. All he had gleaned was that, in recent months, a lot of domestic animals had seemingly vanished around the common and its wildlife population had allegedly been predated upon to near extinction. Neither Jenny nor Tony had offered a definitive answer to the individual occurrences, offering only suggestions of similarity to probable fox or possibly badger attacks. It seemed though that they were implying the sum of all these unexplained events had significance and that perhaps there was a perpetrator outside the norm. But this is where the Chief Inspector became lost and confused, unable to get past the obvious.

"Surely you're not expecting me to believe that the abduction of two children is down to foxes?" He looked over to Patrick with a look of disdain.

"No, no, Tony added quickly, aware that Chief Bryant seemed to think he had finished, "well not exactly foxes."

"Wait a minute," the Chief Inspector murmured... and a look of recognition swept across his face, "Tony Nash, I remember now. You were in the paper not so long ago, advising us of... what was it, Panthers?" He gave Patrick a withering stare unable to believe that he had been suckered again. "So this is what it's all about, eh. For Gods sa…"

"Excuse me," Tony cut in firmly, "but I, haven't finished yet, so if you wouldn't mind holding fire, the best, or worst, whichever way you want to look at it, is yet to come." Incensed by the familiar jump to the wrong conclusion, his voice became hard and determined, and the room seemed to shrink as his absolute outrage manifested itself to all in the already limited space.

"We are definitely **not**," he nearly shouted, "talking panthers here, so get that out of your head right away, Mr Bryant," his contempt obvious. "What we are suggesting is the possibility of a hybrid animal, one that records and history tells us is possible, but rare." Tony knew he was skating on thin ice with the notion that there was documentation to be viewed, relating to such hybrids. The internet was a wondrous source of data, the difficulty sometimes was in the weedling out of the facts from the fiction. In fairness, to date, they hadn't found much of either. Ignoring that potential stumbling block he swiftly moved on.

Slamming a copy of the Echo on the coffee table in front of the quietly seething superior Police Officer, the headlines and family pictures declaring, 'fox attacks children in their tent'. "Remember this from a few days ago? And this?" Tony showed him a clipping of Jim Bennett's death. He had highlighted the pertinent sentences 'Mystery still surrounds the death of local nurseryman out walking his dog. The reason for the massive heart attack from which he suffered has not been ascertained, nor has the dog been found. Witnesses reported hearing animals scuffling'.

"We believe these incidences are also connected and are down to these hybrids," Tony added still furious, and feeling that his outburst might have blown it, turned towards Patrick. "The Inspector can verify this next part of the story, as it has to do with the death of an old lady living at Homewood House, just on the far side of the common. Jenny can you?"

"Yes," she said, picking up the cue. "I was called by the police in my official capacity as Animal Welfare Officer for East Dorset to deal with two dogs that belonged to the old lady, Mrs Thomas. They had been trapped in the house for some time, possibly a couple of weeks, and they had become understandably very aggressive, as one of your officers found out."

"P.C. Foster sir, if you remember?" Patrick advised still a little sheepishly. "It was a few months back."

The Chief Inspector nodded his acknowledgement; not trusting himself to speak, still angered and smarting from Tony's rebuke. He wasn't accustomed to being spoken to like that, and particularly not from one he had already decided was wasting his time. Despite that, and because he held his colleague with some regard, had decided to hear it out.

Jenny continued. "We later determined that they were Pit Bull Terriers, banned as dangerous dogs in this country but somehow living very happily and obediently with their owner in the near seclusion of the walled Homewood House. However, we also learnt that for many years the old lady had fed the local population of foxes, who seemed to also call the garden their home. The housekeeper and gardener confirmed they witnessed the dogs and foxes mating together on numerous occasions although it is unlikely that this resulted in any viable offspring. At least not… we think, in ninety nine percent of the cases. We do, however, believe that in the spring of two thousand and eight a litter of cubs were born; cubs that were part dog, part fox." Jenny had been making regular eye contact with the unmoving face of Chief Inspector Bryant for most of her delivery, but now she noted a slight raising of eyebrows, as she mentioned this proposition. Uncertain as to whether it was a good sign she carried on. Had she known, that his perspective was still hovering somewhere just above derisory, she might not have been so fervent in her delivery.

"To clarify then," she continued, "on one side we have a fox, a vixen with all the usual attributes, cunning and guile, speed and agility, an opportunist predator and hunter, ably adaptable to new situations and environments, and on the other, we have a dog and not just any dog but potentially one of the most aggressive you could have; taut with muscle and strength, vice-like jaws, and a pack mentality born of dogs the world over. Now…" She stared hard at the chief daring him to disagree, "we think that's a pretty frightening combination."

Before he had a chance to speak, Tony cut back in and clicking through some pictures on the laptop he said, "These pictures we took very recently over on the common, are, we believe the offspring, born last year… only now adult. I can see by your expression Chief Inspector that you're wondering what I'm on about. They look just like foxes, don't they? Well that's because, to all intents and purposes, they are. It's only when you gauge them against the average fox, you can see they're considerably bigger, a small Labrador size as opposed to what they should be, nearer the size of a large domestic cat. Imagine a fox with extra strength in both limb and jaws, powerful and determined. Is it any wonder the mass produced rabbit hutches and pens, only held together with flimsy staples, gave way?"

"Look Mr Nash, I can see where you're going with this and I understand your concern, but these pictures and what you have told me, doesn't really prove anything. It's all circumstantial, besides," he said looking as belligerent as when he came in, "I can't sign up to this without something more concrete, and you're right it is too fantastical." He shifted his weight as if to rise.

"Ok, let me show you this. It's a video taken less than a mile away from here showing what these three can do."

Tony clicked the mouse and the clip sprang into life. The Chief Inspector remained still for the first few seconds, his face absently scanning the diminutive screen for information. Tony once again pointed out the relevant objects, the doe and its fawn, the first slinking predator and then the other two, wide of the first but faster and stealthier, still undetected. Jonathon Bryant leant forward in his seat, eyes glued. He wriggled closer, and Tony could see that the man had been hooked.

"My word," breathed the Inspector

"You see," said Tony somewhat triumphantly, as the monitor went blank. "Imagine that was a child, a toddler like Martha, I doubt she would stand a chance."

Chapter 75

It was not comfortable on the hard toilet seat, but Tracy was enjoying the moment's peace and a sly puff. A quick ciggy on her own wasn't going to hurt anyone; two minutes to herself, no noisy cling on's or constant, "Why mum's?" ruining the moment. Some hope!

It was only her third draw. She'd hardly noticed the first two as she justified the pleasure; the usual debate and internal guilt trip plucking thoughts almost at random. Then in a trice her precious meditations were hijacked; stolen by silence... *I can't hear the kids?*" she thought, listening for a couple of seconds.

"What are they up to now?" she said pulling open the door to her retreat.

Then she heard it... a high pitch whine coming through the open slit window, like a dog in pain or distress. But something told her this wasn't a hurting sound; there was an edge to it, a thwarted urgency that conveyed pure frustration.

Quickly she left the building, turned the corner and with relief saw the boys standing in the middle of the play area. They were looking at something, something off to her left beyond the fence. Slightly frustrated as she couldn't see properly - the viewing angle through the chain links meant the wires were close together and formed an effective screen - but moving just a few steps along the perimeter towards the gate and the image became less fuzzy, like an old black and white television screen flickering and shaking, the picture stabilising as the gaps in the mesh widened. Tracy could see movement on the ground. It was fast and frantic. By the time she reached the gate her view was unrestricted, and had taken in the two animals, dogs she presumed. They were scrabbling at the board below the fence. She could see it was flaking, pieces being clawed away by the piston like action.

They're trying to get in! was her first thought, as a sizeable splinter was wrenched away. *The boys!* Was her second, *they're after my boys!* She pushed the gate and looked around for help at the same time. From out of nowhere came another animal, lunging towards her. Its jaws widening as it came, the soft flesh of its mouth peeling back, revealing its savage weaponry. Sucking in air, like it might be her last, she sidestepped into the compound and slammed the gate. The creature just managed to pull up short as the latch engaged and the accelerated wire rattled to inertia.

"F' fuck's sake," she exhaled, her speech barely audible. The shock clutched at her heart and she almost collapsed with the rush. Another lungful of air and she was once again alert, shaken, but in control. She ran to the boys, searching through the world beyond the mesh.

"Where's everybody?"

Clutching the terrified children and enveloping them in a protective embrace, she said, "It's alright mummy's here!"

More wood ripped away. Tracy whipped her head round to see a dirty brown snout probing the gap. "Shit," she spat. "It's okay, it's okay... Mummy's got you."

They're gonna be through that in a minute. As the disturbing thought went through her mind she yanked her mobile out and with panicky, shaking hands, dialled 999.

******

"Mmmm," was the only utterance from the Chief Inspector as he slid back into the armchair, pressing his fingertips together and tapping them gently against his lips, and seemingly deep in thought. When he finally spoke it was not in the vein of earlier. He had been quite shocked at the on screen savagery and was now more sympathetic to Tony's suggestion. "Yes, yes... I see what you mean... However, I am not sure that I'm wholly convinced. Killing an animal is one thing but foxes, they usually avoid any contact with man. Surely they wouldn't be so bold as to venture into a garden with people in it?"

"I'm afraid," said Patrick, "quite apart from those newspaper clippings we just showed you, we do know for definite that they would."

"You're talking about the little girl again, I assume?"

"No... I'm talking about me."

"Sorry Patrick, I don't follow."

"Last night, not long after dark, I was on the common, pursuing an idea I had about Gary Brown, and, as I made my way to where he was found, I got the distinct impression I was being followed. As it turns out, and to cut a long story short, I was." Patrick pointed to the now sleeping laptop, "These three hunted me down."

"What?"

Patrick pulled up his trouser leg to reveal the now covered bite, the padding and bandaging making it look worse than it was. He wouldn't break the illusion. "I was lucky; I managed to escape through somebody's back garden, but not before one of them sank its teeth into me. The other two were close behind and if I hadn't managed to knock this one off and close the gate... I really think I would have struggled... not just to get away you understand, but for my life. These animals," he paused, grasping for the words that would describe their intensity but failing miserably... savage, ferocious, deadly, fierce ruthless, nothing hit the mark, "are murderous," he said finally, then added, "pitiless killers... and I was their prey." Now perhaps, you see why I was reluctant to broadcast this round the station. I think also you had better hear what else Tony has to say."

"What... you mean it gets worse?"

"Potentially, yes," said Tony. "But first, and for the sake of this argument, you have to really buy into this hybrid idea. You really have to believe it's possible."

"Okay, for arguments sake, let's say I do. Where's the problem?

"We have shown you the three adult hybrids we know about."

"You think there could be more?"

"We think at the moment there are only three of these hybrid adults, but Jenny and I have seen four cubs on the common, this year's litter, and their resemblance to these three is remarkable. What we are concerned about, apart from the immediate threat to people from the adults, is the long-term effect of allowing these animals to breed and expand their range. Now," he looked across reasonably at the Chief, "I don't know for sure that if these cubs go on to breed whether the traits they have acquired will continue to be inherent or whether they will just become watered down as you might say and die out. My suspicion is Chief Inspector… and remembering our Darwin, 'survival of the fittest', I think the superior characteristics will create an advantage which nature will be all to ready to exploit. After all, many of the characteristics will be inherent but equally many will be learnt, handed down through the generations. I see therefore a beefed-up fox capable of spreading its genes over time and creating a dominant strain. As I said to the Inspector here, you only have to look at the grey and red squirrel to see the effects of a dominant strain."

"So what you are saying is that the lesser, or for want of a better word, normal foxes could be pushed out, leaving us with a version of our friends here?"

"Exactly so Chief Inspector, but the real crux is not the effect these super predators will have on our indigenous foxes and wildlife in general, no, I think that could be the least of our worries. What concerns me more is their bold and aggressive behaviour will not sit well alongside an already over-populated countryside. If you understand me?" Tony stole a glance checking for signs of emerging comprehension, "My fear is that we, the human population who have been top dog for so long as it were, might be shunted sideways sharing the podium of top of the food chain with an equally destructive animal. Imagine the fear a pack of these creatures could conjure in a neighbourhood, particularly if they weren't afraid of us anymore, and, especially if they considered our weakest and most vulnerable, as fair game!"

"Yes I see…" The chief conjured the frightening prospects in his mind's eye, packs of foxes savagely hunting children and the infirm, his officers unarmed and next to useless needing to carry a different armoury; the riot batons and tazers pointless against a swift-footed and elusive foe.

"I'm sorry. I hadn't looked much further than the now really. You've obviously had time to think about this, let's say…" he paused as if giving it some more thought, "I've gone beyond the argument stage Mr Nash… what do you propose is done about them?"

With a lifted heart Tony continued. "We have really got to stop them and quickly, the adults and particularly the cubs. I don't know exactly how old they are but in the normal way of things they should be beginning to disperse and to find new territories of their own. That might be in a week or two away, but for all I know it could be the next few days."

"How on earth do you catch a fox?" asked the Chief Inspector reasonably. "They're pretty wily"

"Traps," said Jenny. "Big ones. Cages like they use for rats and squirrels where you entice the animal in with bait and once in, they inadvertently trigger the door to close, trapping them inside."

"Well that seems straightforward enough," Jonathon Bryant seemed to concluded but added, "although, I imagine it's not that simple in practice."

"Absolutely right," Jenny agreed looking at the Chief Inspector. "I have a few contacts, pest controllers mainly, both within the council and private companies, and they say setting the trap is the easy part. Where to put it, is the most difficult challenge. Obviously, on a regular run, but somewhere where other animals won't get caught, domestic pets etc. Then disguising the fact that we have had anything to do with it, is the next; our residual scent will put them off, you see."

The chief nodded his acceptance of this fact.

"Despite all that," she continued, "and, if the animal is happy with this strange object littering its regular route, getting it to go inside is another thing."

"Yes, that's right," Tony nodded in agreement picking up on where Jenny was going. "The average fox is an incredibly wary animal, highly suspicious of its surroundings and probably with good reason. Hunted by humans on horseback, killed by cars, chased by dogs... hounds, shooed off by home owners and farmers - who wouldn't be cautious? However, it's not all doom and gloom. Put the right bait in and most will overcome their fear with the chance of something tasty. But there are guidelines for the lethal control of foxes, trapping, snaring, and shooting amongst others, as laid down by Natural England. They are accepting of the need for control but are mindful that it is done humanely and not cause any undue stress to the animal."

"Bollocks to that," was the chief's blunt input. "As far as I'm concerned, if these animals are the cause of the abductions then the gloves are off. We catch them by any means practical and safe. Besides nobody else is going to know about this...understood." He coerced acknowledgements from the other three,

"We don't want to start another panic or anything do we?"

Nobody was going to argue with him on that point, although the practicalities of keeping things quiet in a public place had not escaped them all.

"Patrick?" The chief gave him a challenging stare. "I'll leave this in your capable hands, let me know the finer details of when and how you are going to do this and I will endeavour to help in any way I can." His head inclined to take in Jenny and Tony and with a voice that was mildly threatening, said, "You'd better be right about all this."

That 'on side' feeling Tony had begun to allow himself with regard to the high-ranking officer, took a sudden dip and his stomach lurched as if he'd just crested a hill at speed.

"Officially though," the Chief continued somewhat menacingly, "and as far as those on high are concerned, we will run with Gary Brown as our main suspect. Luckily he can't answer back. The last thing I want to have to do is explain this...this, highly dubious scenarios to those upstairs."

Looks like we're on our own, thought Tony cynically, *bet I can guess which side of the fence he'll be sitting if the shit hits the fan!* And to Patrick, the stern looking chief wound it up saying,

"Stay out of the office if you can Pat. I'll cover you somehow?"

Just at that moment Patrick's mobile rang, halting the Chief Inspector on his way out. Patrick glanced at the screen.

"So much for being sick," he said and pressed the button to connect the call. "What's up Sergeant that you had to drag me from my sick bed?"

"You don't sound that sick to me sir."

"If only you knew, Sergeant," he said smiling, "if only you knew."

"It's just that you asked me to check back through the log and to collect any incidences attached to Poor Common and the immediate area around it, which I have done and you will find a shit load on your desk when you're... better. Lot of dross in there sir. I don't know what you're looking for specifically but rabbit rustling must be on the increase, loads of pets reported missing, not much real crime though." He gave a little nervous laugh before adding, "Funnily enough there's a shout on now. I've just despatched a car to a woman at Parley Park who says her kids have just been attacked. Can you believe this... by foxes." Patrick disconnected leaving the Sergeant to inform the ether. "Christ, things we have to deal with, eh sir... Inspector?"

Chapter 76

Sitting in Patrick's car, Tony and Jenny listened to him as he recounted what the two police officers had told him about the incident at the park; the play area in full view from the spot where they were keeping a low profile. Patrick had asked them to stay in the car whilst he checked it out. He could bluff away as to why 'he' was there, despite being on the sick, but might have more difficulty explaining them tagging along and sniffing around as well.

"The good news is," Patrick concluded, "that the officers didn't see anything and the woman's description fits. She thought they were just dogs at first, but used the 'f' word, when pressed, so it was obviously them."

"I reckon she was pretty lucky," added Jenny nodding towards the play area. "Let's face it, if that fence hadn't been there or it was a metre or so shorter, those kids would have been out in the open and you would have had another disappearance on your hands... probably two."

Patrick winced and shook his head. "Doesn't bear thinking about, does it?"

"Having said that," Tony began, "Just say, there was no fence here, or this was another park even. The woman said there was nobody about, which is pretty unusual. It's not a big area but there's normally somebody about, and particularly in the holidays; Mums, kids, dog walkers, etc... What it says to me is, it's not going to take much for the luck to swing their way, and the more that happens the bolder they'll get.

They took advantage of being in the car together to discuss how they should proceed in the capture and eradication of the doxes and, soberingly, all without making a fuss. Jenny quickly volunteered that she could get hold of some traps if she spoke sweetly to the right people. Coming up with a plausible excuse as to why she needed them might be trickier, but she would work on it.

They also agreed, Tony and Jenny would go back to Poor Common later on to try to find the dox's new den and look for possible sites to set the traps. Tony would organise the bait. A phone call to his father requesting whole fresh rabbits, shot that evening if possible, would he knew, give his father the excuse needed to dust off the shotgun. He might even find the time to go down and help him, reflected Tony. He enjoyed the sport of it and used to like the resulting stews and pies. Not that these particular carcasses would see the dining table, more's the pity, he thought.

"We're going to need a firearm of some sort," mused Patrick, "because as soon as we've trapped them we'll need to despatch them." He watched their reactions, wondering if there might be any objections, but neither flinched. It wasn't a pleasant thought but it had to be done. At least they were realistic about it and a gun was probably the quickest and most humane. "Besides, I'd feel a lot happier with a gun in my pocket if there's any chance of meeting up with those three again." He looked thoughtful. "I'm not sure the Chief constable is going to be overjoyed at the idea. Still, at least I've had my fair share of firearms training. I'll see what I can do."

"Using Dad's shotgun on the farm is one thing," Tony added, "but I'm almost certain he wouldn't lend it to me even if I had a bloody good reason."

"Ok, well good for him," said Patrick approvingly, "but that'll have to be our back-up plan if we can't get one through the proper channels. We'll just have to come clean with your dad, persuade him to help I guess?"

Patrick dropped Tony and Jenny back to the flat so they could make their calls. They parted, exchanging mobile numbers and resolving to try to get all the various elements up together by the following day, with the aim to start setting traps in the evening. They were going to have to work fast and they would need to get lucky with the vital traps.

Despite the short notice Tony's father jumped at the idea of an evening shoot.

"We haven't done that for a while, have we?" he said, delighted at the thought of an evening with his son. "Besides, your mum would like to see you anyway. I'll tell her you'll be over for supper." There was a pause and Tony knew what was coming. "Will you be bringing Jenny then? You know your Mum's dying to see her again."

"Probably not dad. She's got a lot on at the moment, but if anything changes I'll let you know. OK?"

After six phone calls, a lot of flannel, and white lies flying around like verbal confetti, they had five traps. Tony had been listening in. He couldn't believe the nonsense he was hearing, some of it bordering on out-an-out flirting. 'Hello gorgeous', or 'how's my favourite rat-man then?' and 'I need a big favour, and I'll do anything for it!' the intonation obvious.

"You, are something else!" said Tony incredulously. "You're lucky I'm not the jealous type," his head shaking in disbelief.

The smug look, and the accompanying wide smile, disarmed any jarring of possessive thoughts he might have entertained. Even so, "Right, <u>WE</u> need to go and pick them up then," he said playfully.

"What and cramp my style?" she countered, and grabbing the keys to her car moved to the front door. "I don't think so… Besides, I could be a while!" she said, eyes wide and suggestive, "and anyway you're going to Bridport. So I'll see you later." She blew him a kiss and threw a casual wave as she closed the door.

"Yeah, bye," he said to the empty room.

Chapter 77

It was just after midday and Tony had decided to take a walk on Poor Common for a fresh look at the area in daylight. He realised even with all that had happened over the last few months, it was probably about four to five weeks since he had last visited it in the daytime.

On entering the common, from the Heatherlands Avenue path, the first thing that hit him was the vegetation. Where, in his previous visit it had been lush and fresh from the recent spring growth, now it was like a veritable jungle in places. Tall bracken stands, some five, nearly six feet high, interspersed with the new shoots of the cut-down rhododendrons, plus substantial clumps of grasses topped with wispy tresses, brambles, honey suckle, in fact the whole gamut of vegetation, from the lowest scrub to the highest pines, radiated a mass of new growth. Within a few minutes of being there, Tony realised the difficulties they would face. In the great scheme of things a relatively small common but it might just as well have been the proverbial haystack; any animal, even the larger deer could slip unnoticed through this green explosion, let alone the sylph like fox. He could see they were going to have a lot of trouble just keeping a look-out for them, let alone trying to find any signs or track them somehow.

It was another good reason to use traps, rather than go down the route of openly hunting them. At this time of year, when the foxes were very active through most of the night it was possible; using torch and a rifle, to track them on their regular routes and blinding them momentarily with the light, shooting them. Even with stealth you had to get lucky. The range a fox could cover, often meant, you were in the wrong place at the wrong time. Tony had done this with his father on occasions at the farm. They had also buried bait on a particular site where they could, from a suitable vantage point, wait and entice the animals to come to them. This had been quite effective. The lure of an easy meal would not fail to attract them. Success on both counts would be dependent on how good you were with a shotgun. And there, Tony had assessed earlier, and Patrick had agreed, was the problem with using these methods here. The open space on a farm with no population was one thing but the total accessible area of Poor Common, in comparison, was not even a fifth of his Dad's farm. And that was surrounded by neighbouring farms with similar open fields and low population. But Poor Common was hemmed in on all sides with people in houses, travelling on roads or seeing to their horses. Whilst a shotgun was designed for relatively close work the danger of stray shot could not be overlooked, particularly if you were trying for a snapshot at a fast moving target. Besides, it was one thing to dispatch the fox in the cage with one shot. That might not draw too much attention but to have somebody blasting away half the night so close to a built-up area, would hardly be a recipe for keeping it under wraps, or indeed, avoiding panic.

With such thoughts playing on his mind, he went to search the area where they had first caught sight of the cubs, hoping to find some fresh signs of habitation. There were recent scats, which suggested they had been there. However, Tony knew that, with their tendency to roam over a wide range, they would leave their pungent territory markers in many obvious places. The only thing he could say with some certainty about this particular clearing was that they evidently came back to it; and it would seem fairly regularly judging by the droppings in their various stages of decomposition.

He moved off again wondering where to look next. The unearthed den where the skeletons had been found didn't seem much of an option and he wasn't aware of another earth anywhere else on the common. Not needing to be down on his parents' farm until about six-ish, and it was one-thirty now, he decided to make use of the three remaining hours before he needed to leave, and try and give the area a really good search; poke his nose into places he hadn't been before, under aged plants, tree roots, earth banks and old buildings. Surely he should be able to find some evidence? He took this thought further, *what if I actually see one – what if I come across all of them?* Not too concerned, as it was mid afternoon, it was unlikely they'd be above ground, wasn't it? Casting his eye around and collecting a hefty stick on the pretext of needing to probe the undergrowth, he felt a little more prepared. Although it would of course be handy, if push came to shove!

******

Patrick, meanwhile, was on the telephone to his boss and, as he expected, was having difficulty in persuading the 'by the book' senior officer to part with a gun. Luckily the serious looking bandage wrapped around his leg had afforded him an excuse to be home.

"The boss told me to take a few days off," he explained to Marjorie, "after this bloody dog had taken a chunk out of me when we were trying to make an arrest. Little thug had one of those trophy dogs tagging along. Vicious bastard... probably get put down!" Patrick had given his wife a sly grin saying, "They'll probably do the dog at the same time!"

The joke had thrown Marjorie off her guard and the usual concerned probing was greatly diminished. Ensconced with a mug of coffee, and a couple of biscuits, he had retreated to the study to ponder the request he was about to cast and how best to make the approach. Patrick was also one for following procedure. He'd found that, in the disciplined confines of both the Army and the Police Force, cutting corners or cheating the system only produced a quick fix. Longer-term gains came from doing it properly at the outset.

So his need for a gun without any real justification - well none that only he and his boss would be allowed to know about - was not sitting comfortably with him in the first place. And, he realised, was likely to prove more than just a fly in the ointment. However, if the chief constable could be won over, how 'he' swung it, would be his problem. *So…* Patrick reasoned, *all I need to do is convince him why it is absolutely necessary and that I can't do this without one.* With that goal set firmly in his mind he'd made the call and had spent some time backing up his argument.

"Well you said it yourself sir, and I quote, 'the gloves are off.'"

"Yes, yes Patrick, I know what I said but…"

"Well what **are** we going to do with them once we've caught them?" Patrick countered quickly. "If we want to keep a lid on this, I can't just pop them up the vets!"

A long breathy sigh emanated through the speaker and Patrick sensed the frustration.

"Surely there's some other way Pat, I don't know drowning, gassing… poison… for all I care you can club them to death!" Patrick let his silence do the talking.

Jonathon Bryant knew Patrick was right. Sensing the Chief Constable's acquiescence, Patrick guessed he was bordering on a climb down.

Another noisy exhalation assailed Patrick's expectant ear, before saying somewhat wearily… "Right… leave it with me Pat," and then more resignedly, "I'll see what I can do."

It was four-thirty and Tony had covered a lot of ground. The back of his hand would seem less familiar than this piece of countryside, he thought as he began his walk back to the car. He had ranged down beyond the ponds and halfway down the track that led to the Ringwood Road. He had crawled into bushes, hacked at the bracken, roamed under huge canopies of Rhododendron, found a pond he'd never realised existed, fought off brambles, been stung by nettles and to be honest had had about enough. Sadly he had found no den as such.

There was a distinct possibility, in what looked like an abandoned badger set, which he had found within the last half hour. It was beneath a large oak set off from and some way down the path he was now walking back up. The tree, probably three or four hundred years old, he'd guessed, judging by the trunks girth, appeared squashed by its vast spreading canopy. Over the years, and where the roots disappeared below the ground, a tump had formed, a hillock built from the accumulation of weather strewn detritus; composted and rich, it proved viable for the tree to flourish and for wildlife to move in. The numerous holes dotted in and around about its base, some filled in over time or covered up by new growth, suggested it was unlived in. One entrance though, looked like an attempt had been made to use it. Earth scraped and scattered around the dark void looked recent. Exposed roots could be glimpsed at some depth and it seemed there was no end to it; at least, not one that Tony's stick could discern. There had been no extensive evidence in the form of fox spoor, as one might have expected, particularly if an extended family had been using it. Although he had found a few scats here and there, some close, some further away, some very recent, some not. It was inconclusive Tony felt, but he would still keep it in mind as a possible place to set up a trap or two.

With no solid thoughts of where to place traps he mulled an idea over in his head as he walked. The advice he had read about setting traps and snares was to place them at known sites where the animals could regularly be found or on routes often travelled by them. It also mentioned that they should be set away in positions where non-target species might fall foul of them. This bit Tony ignored, remembering the no-nonsense approach dictated by the Chief Constable. 'Whatever it takes' he'd said, and if that meant a few casualties then so be it. In reality Tony reflected, it was very unlikely that any animal would get hurt in the traps and they could be released straight away. In fact the only other animal, he could think of that would be likely to get caught was probably a badger. The design of the wire mesh was of a size that pretty much everything else could get out; *they'd have to be pretty obese rabbits or squirrels to detain any of them*, he laughed to himself.

The guides also made it sound easy about how to confirm a regular fox run; 'the use of field-craft would help determine habitual use', it had said. Tony was no slouch at recognising some of these signs for various animals. He was often called upon to identify a footprint in mud or wet sand, and the inevitable dollop or pellet of faeces. "Who did that pooh Tony?" was imprinted on his brain and the kids accompanying squeals of laughter still ringing with every memory. The problem was, finding the signs, a footprint or droppings, by chance, when you are out in the forest with a small army of helpers, eyes darting everywhere, was one thing, but when you wanted to find something, when you actually wanted to try and track the little bastards down, it wasn't that easy. 'Watch out for long reddish brown hairs caught on brambles, twigs or wire,' it had said... what like every fence! Every twisted stem or shrub! It was obvious you needed to look close to the ground and where there were designated run-throughs, but... either these foxes were forensically aware or they were just plain lucky. Evidently it had to be the latter. The dry soils had offered no imprints, the scats were widely spread around, like markers in some bizarre orienteering course, and the stench of fox urine pervaded many a low bush or sapling. He hadn't really known where to start and had been limited by time.

In some ways though, the fact that he could not settle on a particular place only confirmed what he thought they should actually do. The fact that there was evidence, that Poor Common was a regular haunt of the foxes, pushed him that way too. The method that he favoured would also be easier for them to monitor and control; easier too to keep unwanted members of the public from blundering into the traps and disturbing the process.

This was all well and good, Tony acknowledged, but the real crux was, they were going to have to get very lucky to catch one or two at the same time, even with five traps set. Once one was caught and became distressed, the others would be even more wary. The more Tony thought about this the more he realised that this was not going to be sorted overnight. It dawned on him, somewhat negatively, that it was quite likely, in fact, more than likely, that although they might trap one, maybe two, and quite probably the inexperienced youngsters quite quickly, the others might not be so obliging! Yes, one or two, maybe even three was possible. Seven on the other hand, was going to need divine intervention!

Deep with these thoughts rattling around in his head, Tony was almost oblivious as he sauntered along the path.

"Well if it isn't the quiet one," said a jolly-faced woman approaching him along the path.

Tony recognised the face, but just couldn't quite place her.

"Where's that lovely girlfriend of yours? She's a cracker. You want to look after her."

Who the... thought Tony defensively, the over familiarity from one he could hardly recall, making him wonder at such blatant questioning and advice. "Sorry?"

"You don't remember me do you?" she laughed heartily and with excess volume.

Now I do, thought Tony. "Its Mrs Hoe isn't it?"

"That's right dear, Julie, we met up at Homewood House. Your girlfriend still chasing dogs then?"

Tony smiled, thinking, *in a manner of speaking.* "Yes she still works for the council."

"You live round here then?" she demanded.

It's almost like an interrogation, thought Tony. If the woman hadn't been so near to breaking into laughter at each sentence, he might have felt more threatened.

"Yes not far. You?"

"Up on Carmel Road. I'm just off to the big house now. My daughter and her family are due in day after tomorrow from the States, thought I'd take some bits in for them." She held up a couple of bulging Tesco bags. "Help them get settled in after their long haul."

"Right," said Tony "I won't hold you up then," expecting, and hoping, she'd trundle on.

"Oh don't worry about that. She's got four you know?"

Tony was non-plussed, *what eyes, legs, what?*

Registering his confusion, she added, "Children," in a way that seemed to imply she was talking to the village idiot. "Four children... Jack's seven, Lily is five and the twins are just two. I'm so excited about seeing them."

"Yes I'm sure you are," he said warming to her genuine animation. "Look, nice to see you again, but I've got to crack on. I promised my parents I would be with them by six and they live in Bridport. And traffic will be a nightmare at this time."

"Ok deerie," she said walking on and raising one bag as substitute for a parting wave.

Five seconds passed and the gap between them lengthened. At twenty-two yards she turned her head and tossed her last comment, "Look after that girlfriend of yours...mind!"

Later that evening, as Tony drove home from his parent's house, with two brace of Coney, as his father had put it, stretched out in the rear foot well, he received the final notification that all was now in place.

Patrick had texted him. It was short and to the point. 'Got gun. When do we meet next? Pat'. Tony replied, saying that he was at work the next day, and so was Jenny, so they should meet at his flat at six pm if that suited.

The replying text from him was even briefer, 'OK.'

Jenny had also called him earlier, whilst they were eating a quick supper before venturing out into the fields. He went out into the farmyard to speak with her. Her enthusiasm was evident.

"I've got them," she announced. "Talk about cloak and dagger, I couldn't get all of them in my car at once, so I had to take the first three home and try and get them into my flat without half the world seeing them. Anyway, you'll need to collect those three sometime tomorrow. I've also got some throwaway plastic gloves. I used them to handle the traps and have got spares for all of us as we set them."

"Good thinking Batgirl," said Tony jokingly, but also impressed, "I hope you've got a sack of luck in that utility belt of yours," he added.

"Of course," she said positively, "but these traps are the business. No way are those doxes getting out."

"Mmm, it's not the getting out I'm so worried about, as the getting in," he said guardedly. "Hopefully though, if Dad and I can get some fresh rabbits this evening," and, sounding a lot more confident than he felt… "might just be half the battle."

Chapter 78

Sunday 9th August 05:50am

Patrick had taken the last watch and so had been awake from four o'clock and had kept an eye, or ear to be more precise, over the selected clearing, still dark but now awaiting the imminent dawn.

In fact there were two chosen areas that Tony had suggested. This one, beside the den where they had first seen the cubs, and the second, down by the large oak tree, that Tony had inspected on Friday. He had explained the reasons for his choices, advising that although they knew the doxes appeared to range widely throughout the common, it seemed more practical to concentrate the traps in two areas. Mainly because if they set five traps in five different places around the common, they were far more likely to be found by the human population out for their constitutional, and interfered with in some way, than if they split it the way they had. The main site, with three traps, could be kept under surveillance at all times and the Oak tree was so off the beaten track that he doubted people ever went there, and placed the remaining two beneath its broad base.

So, at seven o'clock the previous evening, Saturday, they had begun to set up. Patrick had brought with him more rolls of the Police tape with the idea of taping off all the main entrances to the common in a hope to deter as many people as possible from coming on to it. He figured that, whilst it might not be possible to tape off every individual residence that had its own access, it should at least minimise traffic. Whichever way, he felt it might help to create some breathing space whilst they set things up. Tony had, for want of a better word, purloined the spare gate key from Moors Valley allowing them vehicular access off Fitzworth Road, to just inside the green swathe and away from most prying eyes. As soon as the two cars used to bring in the kit were not needed, they were removed and parked elsewhere, so as not to draw any permanent attention.

Patrick had gone off quickly, rolls of police tape encapsulated in a plastic bag, to seal the other entrances as best he could. Aware that the local residents had seen these adornments before, and that most would realise that this current masking was a fresh attempt to block people from their favoured amenity; he expected that most would obey. There would, of course, be those that would see the obvious white tape with blue writing as nothing more than the proverbial red rag and would endeavour to cross, seeing it as some perverse right, a snub at the system or direct challenge to authority, despite the possible consequences. He was not in any mood for nonsense and those foolish enough to ignore it openly would be ejected swiftly, with warrant card to the fore and hand to the scruff, if needed.

Tony and Jenny, hands gloved in sweaty plastic, had moved three of the wire traps down to the open space by the original den, leaving them there as they searched close by for suitable sites. Not wishing to have them too near to each other they had explored some of the sinewy animal pathways. Wherever the track opened onto a small clearing or a trampled area of foliage, providing it was flat enough for the cage to sit solidly, then that was a possibility. After following a number of these trails they had soon got the traps sited, all no more than 30 metres away from where they would be holed up, and at least twenty to thirty metres from each other.

Even if members of the public managed to gain access, keen eyes would be needed to see any of the traps directly from main gravel path, but as further camouflage they draped some trailing stems over the mesh. Tony also threw some debris from the forest floor inside to try to cover the mesh on its base and to help disguise any lingering human scents. The cage was just less than one and a half metres long, half a metre high and had a sliding door at one end. The idea being that, when the fox was inside and had pulled on the bait, it triggered the door to fall under its own weight, trapping the animal securely. Once Tony was happy that the structure was firmly in position, he had attached half a dead rabbit carcass to the pull wire and placed it at the far end away from the door. With the door now up and tentatively held in place by the trigger mechanism, it was ready to go.

They had set the other two traps quickly and had collected the others from the car, taking them to the Oak tree site. Patrick's hastily placed deterrents had evidently worked. They had seen no one as they'd gone about their business. By eight thirty, a little later than they had hoped, all the traps had been set and the area they would use as a hide made ready; a waterproof ground sheet over layers of collected bracken, somewhere to sleep; and a tarpaulin tied off between trees and boughs to offer rain protection, if required. Patrick had organised a Constable to patrol the common, throughout the hours of daylight when they themselves, would be absent. The area, he advised the officer, was to be regarded as a crime scene. "Stay on the path and keep the public out."

The faint aura of a new day was subtly highlighting the eastern sky as Patrick pulled his sleeping bag around him. The air was cool and dew damp, but sitting in his camping chair with the padded material drawn up to his neck and a fleece lined beanie hat borrowed from his son, he was warm and completely unconcerned by the elements, but bored witless. The other two, cocooned in their mummy style sleeping bags lay close to his feet. Hardly a feather bed he reflected, the bracts of green beneath them were soft in most places, save for a few woody stems, indenting body parts that not unexpectedly, objected. Patrick's lower back and hips had indeed drawn such a sizeable straw. Consequently he had not got comfortable and his designated six hours sleep time had seemed more like some inscrutable torture, than a period of rest, and he looked enviously at the two youngsters still apparently fast asleep. *Probably an age thing,* he mused.

They'd sat around the little hide the previous evening, after all had been made ready, making whispered conversation until about ten, the night drawing slowly in and the little forest imperceptibly growing quieter. And as the sun left the sky a chill set in creating an edge to the proceedings. At ten-thirty pm the last commercial flight out of Bournemouth International Airport had cut through the darkened forest, sounding for all the world like an Apollo rocket launch. After that assault on the eardrums the common seemed to become even quieter, not a sound, nor movement, as if everything had been set in stone and coated with pitch.

It had soon become clear to Patrick, as they'd talked, that, although they had been thrown together by circumstances beyond anyone's control, his gut feeling about the two he was now holed up with had been confirmed. Decent young people, sensible and smart and he could understand their dilemma. It must have taken some nerve, presumably, he assumed, out of a sense of moral duty, for them to come forward with this unlikely and incredible story. He also found he enjoyed their company. As a couple they were comfortable together, individually they were easy to chat with and conversations hadn't suffered from the usual stilt. Maybe it was the unconventional surroundings, the makeshift roof over their heads, as opposed to a more permanent structure, that seemed to engender a spirit of openness and a lack of concern about what he did for a living. It wasn't so much a conversation stopper at a social gathering, but he was aware the revelation often would stiffen the flow, with informal comments somehow sanitised and dialogue more cautious. Or perhaps it was the fact they had a combined sense of purpose, a coming together in a common cause; or more simply, was it just a bond forged from engaging in somewhat dubious activities that helped level any inhibitions. Who knew?

It was almost six am, Patrick noted. It had been only eight minutes since he'd last checked. "God will something happen," he whispered to the waking world. The other two had also passed on reports of 'no shows and all quiet' from their shifts. Jenny had taken the ten till one, and Tony the one to four. The lack of any excitement from the other two and now, subsequently, with his own equally disappointing stint drawing to a close, the heightened expectations of the night before were dwindling; sinking, it seemed, in direct antithesis to the drab light now gradually brightening the new day.

In fairness, the black hours had not been devoid of any activity, just none that would come to anything. Apart from the man-made noises stealing in from a distance; metallic clacking as gates closed, thumps and bumps and doors slamming, the virtually lifeless common had, itself, grown darkly animated. Much, it could be argued, would emanate from taut senses straining for input, and fertile imaginations making merry, of eardrums on full stretch and pupils like black holes. A pine cone falling unseen to the ground would sound as heavy as a brick, an insect scuffling in dry leaves as substantial as a fox and a mean glint off a glossy leaf, to shape and shift, the longer you stare.

But, for all the games the dark played, there would be genuine movement and credible sounds; an owl's silent swoop, glimpsed through the trees, the noisy snuffling of a badger, the flapping of a roosting bird high overhead. Of these, the eyes might capture a fleet or flicker, but for many it would be the auditory system that perceived the most, literally working in the dark and collecting the sounds that the brain would try to make sense of. And so, as each took their watch, perceptions would be teased and intermittently peaked, hopes unfairly excited and their anticipation eventually repressed. Disappointingly, there would be nothing of consequence and as six-fifty showed on Patrick's watch and the two prostrate bodies began to stir, a feeling of time being wasted edged into his mind. *Was this going to work?* He asked himself. They could be doing this for weeks! Perhaps they were being way too optimistic.

"Anything?" Jenny whispered to Patrick. He shook his head.

"No nothing."

She gave him a disappointed smile. "Oh well, I suppose it is only the first night." Her face brightened slightly. "And we've still got to check the other traps."

Tony sat up, his head still shrouded by the sleeping bag hood, looking like an enormous writhing grub.

"I don't know about you two," Patrick said in a low voice, "but I've been mulling this over for the past hour. If this doesn't work, or we don't catch them all, then what's plan B? And how long do we give plan A to work? This is all very well for a few nights but let's face it, we can't live like this for too long. Marjorie knows night shifts for me are few and far between, so it won't be very long before she suspects.

"I suppose," Tony said through a yawn, "it's not essential that we are here all night, and in fairness, I hadn't realised someone would be patrolling throughout the day, so we just need to check the traps regularly. The guidelines are once or maybe twice a day. The trouble is though, I doubt we will be able to keep the public out of here for long, and the longer an animal is trapped in one of these cages the more likely some stupid bugger is going to poke their finger in, or worse let the bloody thing out."

"Yes," Jenny added as she pummelled the groundsheet, "one or two nights, is a bit of fun, but I could see it palling somewhat without our normal creature comforts."

"Well, maybe give it another night and have a rethink," Tony started. "If…" There was a sudden crash away in the undergrowth! They exchanged excited glances.

As silently as they could, they scrabbled out of their warm bags and peered over the protective wall of scrub. Within seconds of the first, there was another screeching of metal as another door slid home. Then from out of the undergrowth a fox darted, followed by another, into the clearing some 10 metres away. They were clearly agitated and nervous.

"That's the vixen and a cub," Tony's voice a mixture of hushed excitement and amazement. "It's got so big! It's definitely a young one though. You can see how gangly it still is… but it's the same size, if not bigger than its mother."

The two animals turned and made to go back, but the sounds of distress coming from up the little path, halted them.

"I think we might have one… maybe two," Tony whispered again.

The cub's head was jerking left and right as it seemed to hear other sounds and it hardly moved from its spot but it didn't keep still. Its worried paws picked the ground nervously. The vixen trotted quickly a few metres up the path, but rejoined the fidgeting cub, seemingly wary of what she would find. She did it again, stopping just a metre further along, then came back, she repeated this manoeuvre three more times, each time her movement seemed more urgent than the last and it pushed her further along the path. Eventually the undergrowth hid her from view, and the cub moved to follow, tentatively he chose a line towards where the vixen had vanished, his head constantly moving, checking the ground at his feet, the plants to the sides and back over its shoulder to where the watching three held their breath.

"What do we do?" Patrick said, and his hand involuntarily clasped a bulky object at his side as if checking it was still there.

Jenny saw the movement and realised it must be the holstered gun hidden under the fleece jacket he was wearing. Patrick had not shown it to them and they hadn't actually asked to see it. In fact, thoughts of the gun had not entered their heads as they'd talked happily the night before. But now that the moment was fast approaching when it would be used, it stirred feelings of anguish and dread. She knew it would have to be done, but that didn't mean she had to be happy about it, or indeed wouldn't get upset. She picked up her own defensive weapon, her dog grasper, and checked the slipknot, wondering whether they would get that close.

"I can't see any of the others... the three adult's," Tony whispered straining to look out beyond the vast protective shrub. "Perhaps they are off hunting elsewhere, still moving as two separate groups. That could be to our advantage."

"Yes," agreed Patrick, realising what Tony meant. "I suppose it would be a little too much to ask, that the others are somewhere near the other site, or perhaps have already been ensnared?"

"In answer to your earlier question, what do we do now?" Tony said in a still hushed voice, "I suggest we sort these out," he nodded out towards the recent activity, "and then move to take a look at the other site. Ok?"

The Inspector nodded his agreement. Then Tony added soberly,

"It might be best if you lead and have your gun ready," he looked at Patrick meaningfully. "If you can get a shot off at one outside of the traps, then you might want to take it; cubs a priority over the vixen, yeah?"

"Right... Ok... Good idea," he acknowledged with a hint of respect for Tony, and realising he should, perhaps, recall some of his military training. After all, he now had a firearm, a lethal weapon, and he was about to venture out into a public area, albeit hopefully devoid of people, but, he reminded himself, that even on the police ranges, they followed strict procedures. Just because he was, 'off the leash', didn't mean he could forget some of those valid lessons. He too, like his current adversaries, would need to be cautious.

Chapter 79

The sudden chirping of her bedside telephone nearly made Julie Hoe spill tea down her nightdress.

"God preserve us," she said looking at the clock "Who can that be… and at this hour? It's only just seven."

"Only one way to find out then," were the sage words offered by her husband in a way that suggested he'd offered this advice many times before.

Julie reached for the slim cordless receiver, pressing the connect button as she gripped it. Immediately she picked up excited speech, muffled and distant which clarified as the device nestled against her ear.

"Nanny… Nan," two high-pitched voices proclaimed, boisterous and over-excited. "We're calling from the plane…. Nan… Nan, can you hear us?"

"Lord save us Neil, it's the kids," she said, and sounding about as high. "Oh take my tea will you, 'fore I spill it."

"Haloo," she bellowed back to further shouts and greetings and could hear that someone was shooing them away from the mouth piece at the other end.

"Sorry Mum, hope we didn't wake you," Justine began, "only they've been pestering me for the last couple of hours to call you. But I reckoned you and dad would be awake by now."

"Oh yes, just having our morning cuppa, in bed"

"And that's where these two are supposed to be. It's effectively two in the morning for us, but they just won't settle."

"How about the little ones?"

"Yes they're fine," she said advising her mother with a degree of certainty, "and let me tell you, those two are zonked out. Anyway mum, just wanted to call and let you know we're on time, arriving Heathrow about mid day… your time, and should be into Ferndown late afternoon-early evening. So we might see you later or, failing that, tomorrow morning. We'll see how it goes."

"Ok Love. Can't wait to see you. I've just about got the house sorted, but we're going up later to open the place up a bit, get some fresh air into it."

"Thanks mum, you're a star and we can't wait to see you either."

******

Back on Poor Common and ground level, three pairs of feet were carefully and stealthily following in the doxes' wake. Patrick crouched and leading, was feeling a little self-conscious, arms raised in front of him and a Glock pistol gripped in one hand and the other steadying from beneath. The rather dramatic pose, he felt, might be seen as a little over the top, akin to something off the telly, CSI or some other American cop show, but he knew that, if he wanted to get a quick shot off and have any chance of a hit, he needed to be moving with one eye to his front and the other sighting along the stubby barrel. Even if he had had a shotgun or rifle, his reactions were going to have to be like lightning, to shoot a relatively small fast moving target, hell bent on getting away.

As they drew near to the cage that was sited further up the path, Patrick caught sight of the wire mesh roof. He motioned for the other two to wait. He wanted to see how close he could get without disturbing the vixen or the cub, assuming that they were still there, distracted perhaps by the caged youngster. Still crouching and using the luxuriant foliage for cover he inched forwards, trying desperately to keep his not insubstantial frame from noisily brushing and swishing the vegetation. Momentarily he saw them. A glimpse through the fern-like bracken leaves and they were no more than four metres away. Easing the Glock forward and parting the fronds that limited his view, he lined up the barrel on one of the unsuspecting creatures. As he gently squeezed the trigger, the subtle shift in his body weight as he tensed for the shot, crushed a hollow stem, making a soft popping sound and all hell broke loose. Already on a heightened sense of alert, nervous and jittery, the doxes' ears twitched towards the sound. At the same time their bodies lurched away, in full flight mode. The report was deafening. The sound reverberated and echoed in the quiet sanctity of the hallowed morning. Tony and Jenny, a few metres back down the path, hidden and unable to see Patrick, were expectant of the weapons wrath, but still they jumped, shocked at the severity of the sharp explosion. The time for silence had gone; whispered words and hushed speech unnecessary as high overhead crows took to noisy flight and roosting pigeons exploded into slapping wing beats.

"Pat?" called Tony; his voice questioning as if somehow it hadn't been Pat who'd fired. "You Ok?"

"I think I winged it," Patrick called back breathlessly. Tony gathered from that one short sentence that the policeman was giving chase and was moving at speed.

"Come on Jenny, let's go see what we caught." They covered the few metres quickly, pushing away the undergrowth with enthusiasm. And then they saw it, the cub. It was cowering away from them, its gangly legs pushing it hard up against the far end of the cage trying desperately to ooze its way through the mesh. Wide innocent eyes filled with raw fear bored into them.

No matter that this was a potentially dangerous animal, and that its temperament was questionable, or that its size belied its age, and that it had possibly engorged itself on human flesh… it was still, just a baby, a pup and Jenny melted. Its immature face, compacted, cute, like a child's teddy bear, bore two dark orbs and, although hardly moving, held such expression.

"Oh my God, Tony," she whispered as if seeing it for the very first time, "it's just a baby." The dark eyes implored as if sensing an ally and, despite extreme alarm and behind the anxiety, it sought to play its best cards - natural, innate, alluring and beguiling, a bewitching charm of pure innocence. "Surely we can't …"Jenny started to say.

"I'm afraid we must, Jen," Tony said despite feeling much the same. "Come on," he rallied, "let's check the other one and then find Patrick… we'll leave it to him."

There was no more gunfire and Patrick returned, red in the face and an excited sparkle in his eye.

"I'm pretty sure I hit it," he said with a modicum of triumph and breathing heavily. "There's blood spatters where it was standing. But it still managed to run off, the little bugger. No idea though, what it was… cub or vixen."

"Well amazingly, we've caught two here," advised Tony matter-of-factly. "They must have both been sniffing around the two traps at exactly the same time. Luckily for us, being young, their naturally inquisitive nature got the better of caution. However, they look pretty sorry for themselves now, so I think we need to put them out of their misery straight away." He gave Patrick a pointed look, "Don't you?"

Patrick's next job would quickly remove any latent exhilaration, it was one thing to kill an animal where elements of skill, of the chase, of giving it a chance; in short… to hunt, were involved, but to stand there, to level the gun, to point at the animal, a cub, defenceless, helpless… hopeless. It was almost too much for even Patrick to cope with. He shot it quickly; knowing that to delay would stretch out the anguish unnecessarily. This time the noisy report seemed louder to Patrick, perhaps, because the shot was more deliberate, premeditated, not diverted with the thrill of the chase, as was the first. He cringed and wondered about what effect the violent explosions might have on the dormant population's day of rest. Should they hurry lest the common fill with inquisitive souls or uniformed others, summoned at their behest? He continued however, but with one ear cocked, seemingly in anticipation of the familiar two-tone sounds of the blues and twos.

They wrapped the young body in a black bag and tied it off. The dead weight was of hardly any consequence, but its lifeless form was difficult to control as it slid against the shiny interior. Placed in one corner of the temporary hide, rather poignantly Jenny felt, as she went to reset the trap, amongst the accumulated rubbish they had swept to one side before laying the groundsheet. Patrick went to dispatch the second cub, leaving Tony, to dig. Burying the carcasses properly, and ensuring they lay undisturbed, would need a hole just over a metre in depth. It would take Tony some time, so Patrick and Jenny, their deeds done, decided to take a stroll to the oak tree and inspect the other traps.

Being a sleepy Sunday at the beginning of the summer holidays, much of the Ferndown community would be contemplating a lie-in or at best a quiet start to the day. Some, with bulging newspapers and extra coffee rations, and others, allowing children free reign with the television remote, whilst sneaking a few more zeds. The hushed streets around the common bore little traffic and despite windows thrown wide to counter the heat of the night, few took notice of the sudden noises that sharply emanated from the familiar fragment of countryside. Even close to, those that heard the three shots would not recognise them for what they were. The distance, no matter how short, would tone the sound, trees and fences creating baffles and absorbing the harshness. Whereas more solid objects would deflect noise, causing echoes and reverberations, and deceiving even the most expectant ear. Was it a car door slamming, someone hammering, a child's balloon bursting? There were a hundred things more likely and more readily grasped than something so unexpected.

There was, however, far more consternation as dog walkers guided their pooches throughout the day to the taped up entrances surrounding the site for the mornings constitutional. Impromptu gatherings as disgruntled owners discussed their options and frustrated dogs, straining on the leash, sniffed at the surrounding gardens and assessed theirs. As luck would have it, only the law-abiding appeared to surface that day, for the usually busy common did not feel the trudge of any footfall outside of those already within. Outwardly everything was normal, or at least acceptable, as the Lord's day progressed less urgently, than those of the rest of the week. But even still, a modern Sunday, less holy and respected than in bygone times, would swell in busy commerce; the locals noisily taking to the adjacent roads, editing the common into a sound bite of calm.

As they neared the other site, Jenny's mind was in turmoil. Half of her was wishing for empty cages, and the other half for full. Rationally she knew that if the cubs in their little pack had found the other traps, then at least if anything had been caught here, they would be adults. They she reflected, trying to kid herself, were the monsters, the killers... and needed to be removed. The cubs on the other hand, had had no choice. It didn't seem fair. *Although I suppose...* as she thought about it a bit more, it wasn't exactly any of their faults, *they're only doing what comes naturally.*

Despite the inner struggle, she noticed, from a distance away, that both the doors had dropped, and was immediately excited, "Wow! Looks like we've got two." In the closest one she detected a churning mass of dirty brown fur; a fox, big, one of the doxes for sure. It was seething, hurling itself at the sides and door making the cage rattle and jump. Unsure about getting too close, they stood a couple of metres from the cage. Memories of a few nights ago pervaded Patrick's thoughts. The animal inside, filled with rage, charged as best it could in the confining space and for a moment it looked as if the sturdy frame might collapse, making Patrick and Jenny start in a spasm of angst.

Designed to fold, flat pack if required, the simple retaining clips that held the mesh rigid in its rectangular shape were being tested to the full. Patrick became concerned, and looking more closely at the construction of the cage began to think actually how fragile it looked. The animal had thrown its weight three or four times making the opposing side physically lift from the ground and shunting it ten or twenty centimetres towards them. The ferocity of the animal was unbelievable. It seemed, to Jenny, totally unconcerned or frightened about them being there. It just wanted out. She also got the distinct feeling that, if that were to happen; it wasn't just simply going to run away, as any normal wild animal would do at the first chance of freedom. No, despite being outnumbered and out-sized, it was going to attack. It unnerved her, and although the animal was restrained, its teeth and claws rendered ineffective, why was it that she felt vulnerable, so exposed, and in danger?

Evidently Patrick felt much the same way, strode two paces forward and took aim.

In response Jenny jerked her hands up to her ears, wincing at the impending detonation.

Eight hundred metres away and digging, the muffled crack was still quite loud and Tony hoped that it signalled further success. The soil was soft and pliable with much organic matter, but the roots of the aged pines were causing trouble and Tony was every so often, having to hack and sever them. He had moved further into the vastness of the Rhododendron world, in the hope that any disturbed soil would not be seen at a later date. It had taken him a few minutes to find a suitable spot, one clear of ground-hugging twisted branches and sunken stems but roomy enough to work unhindered from above.

By seven-forty as the others approached he was not far off his target depth and a large pile of soil banked beside it, marked his presence.

"Happy hunting?" he asked a little out of breath and devoid of any pleasure that the question might have implied.

"Yes and no," Jenny said, causing Tony to furrow his brow.

"How do you mean?"

"Well two traps sprung, and we got this one here," she pointed to the black bag, hanging down Patrick's back like some macabre swag. "A real vicious piece of work, angry as hell, frightened the life out of us even though it wasn't going anywhere."

Patrick, clearly struggling with the weight, allowed it to drop heavily on to the forest floor. Intrigued, Tony climbed out of his hole and studied the lifeless mass. It was difficult to gauge how big the animal inside was, although, clearly, the heavy duty plastic had pulled tight in places and had stretched and thinned. He hefted the bag needing a second arm to actually lift it clear. "Blimey," he said and decided to untie the bag to get a closer look at the creature. Pulling the bag away from around the familiar shaped torso, the sheer bulk of it, immediately struck Tony. He had seen dead foxes before, handled them, strung them up on fences at the farm in a vain hope to deter others; they were lightweights compared to this. Ordinarily, he could pick up a dead fox by its brush in one hand, the strain no more than an easy bag of shopping, six or seven kilo's at most, but he guessed this was probably fifteen, maybe even more? Once again Tony struggled to find anything, apart from its size that made it look different to a normal fox. Yes, its fur was an unusual colouration, but he had seen some pretty mangy looking foxes in the past, and not dissimilar to this.

What was it, he wondered, that made these so different? For all he knew it was just a big fox. Clearly it had not taken on any obvious physical characteristics of the Pit bull. A slightly barrel chest maybe? But any larger, more substantial fox would be likely to display a heavier set than a lighter one. The websites he had visited to expand his knowledge of the red fox gave the average male weight as around six and a half kilos and female five and a half, although globally a maximum was felt to be about fourteen kilos. The legs were, it seemed, a bit more solid compared to the usual rather frail and lanky limbs normally attached to the equally lightweight frame. Maybe the distinctive pointed snout was a little shorter, more rounded, blunter and its jowls heavier set, but Tony wasn't about to swear to it.

"Dam' it," he said out loud, his thoughts culminating in frustration. "I can't see anything different. For all we know, this could be just a normal big fox?"

Patrick stopped pouring the now tepid coffee, and fixing Tony with an 'are you mad?' stare. "Let's get this straight," he said. "There is absolutely nothing normal about this animal. Apart from having half my leg ripped off by it or one of its mates, if you could've seen the absolute venom in its eyes you would know this wasn't any ordinary fox."

"Yeah," said Jenny nodding in full agreement. "I appreciate I've never really come eye to eye with a normal fox before, but pictures I've seen, television programmes, and the like, all say to me it's more cutesey and playful, than cruel and aggressive... I don't see a hint of anything sinister about them, despite it being a top predator. But that thing, as Patrick said, was just... pure evil. Blazing eyes with thin dark slits for pupils, looking nothing short of demonic; daft I know, but if we'd let that thing out it would have gone for us."

"Okay, point taken," said Tony. "It's just what your boss said," looking at Patrick, "about hoping we're right, just unnerved me a bit particularly as they really don't look that much different."

"Trust me," Patrick assured, "They're not normal, end of." And looking at his watch said, "It's nearly eight. We need to get these animals buried and get out of here."

"By the way," Tony suddenly remembered, "What was in the other trap?"

"Nothing," said Jenny amused, "and when I say nothing, I mean absolutely nothing, no animal and no bait; no rabbit bones, no blood - clean as whistle. So we'll need to re-bait it."

"I wonder what clever little sod had that away," Tony mused. "A stoat or weasel I shouldn't wonder. Small enough anyway, to get through the mesh."

"So what should we do about tonight?" asked Patrick casually and secretly hoping they wouldn't have to sleep out again, but not wishing to be the one that pulled the plug, "I'm game for another night if you think it's necessary."

Tony studied the ground mulling it over for a few seconds. "To be honest, we've just been incredibly lucky. Some people have traps out for days, or weeks, before they catch anything. But what concerns me a little, is, that having caught three, one adult and the two young ones, they are likely to be really spooked and go to ground. I wouldn't be surprised if we don't see them for a few days so I don't think there's much point." He looked around at the others and nobody seemed about to argue.

"That's settled then," adding a little wistfully, "It's a nuisance that we don't know where the current earth is, I mean, I've no doubt they've got a few but I'm sure that, as they've still got the cubs in tow, they'll have a safe one somewhere deep, and secluded. As far as we know they aren't in this one and the one under the summerhouse was destroyed, so that's got to narrow it down for them. I just wish we knew where they went."

As they packed up the camp, they talked about meeting up at six thirty, later that evening, to search again and see if they could spot any fresh signs whilst it was still light. And then, when it had got darker they could check the traps, and perhaps maybe get lucky, spot them on the move. Being a Sunday evening, Tony reasoned, it would be quieter than most days and hopefully the adults would still come out to hunt.

Sounding more optimistic than he felt, and realising that they, or more specifically… he, hadn't really thought the whole process through properly; he should have expected them to go to ground for a while, or worse just move away. The latter option, though, he felt was unlikely. If the range they were covering was still providing them with food and shelter, why go elsewhere? And finding a new range would certainly mean stepping on some other foxes toes. But, Tony argued inwardly, so what? These doxes are more than a match for a normal fox and the thought of them dominating and ousting local populations suddenly took on significance and a real possibility.

The other problem he was toying with, was, the size of their range. The adults had evidently pushed out from their natal range, stretching it as the food within it dried up. So, as far as he was aware, he knew they had travelled east, presumably through the leafy streets of Parley and as far as Parley Common, some two miles from Poor common. He was also sure that it had been them attacking the children in the tent and that was due south a couple of miles. So, assuming that they might travel North and West a couple of miles… that he assessed, would take them across the Ringwood Road and on to Ferndown Common, plus taking in the main estates of Ferndown itself, although he had no confirmation of this, and all the incidences they had documented were so far, to the east and south. Depressingly he thought, and not counting the latter area, that's nearly eight square miles on its own; not huge in the great scheme of things but difficult for three of them to cover, particularly as thirty to forty percent of it was private households.

A positive thought did occur to him and it bucked him up a little. The cubs, up until now, were evidently still being kept within the close natal range for some reason, and that was why the adults were returning; bringing back food. How long that would go on for was anyone's guess. What they had to hope for now was that the vixen and the cubs continued to remain on Poor Common for as long as possible, and that they would continue to be the draw for the others. This final thought, once again spurred Tony, *if they're still on Poor Common then we've got to find them… and quickly.*

Chapter 80

Tony just managed to scrape into work for his nine o'clock shift to start. He had come straight from the Common, hadn't changed, washed or anything, neither had he had any breakfast; apart from a luke-warm coffee, which according to his groaning stomach, obviously didn't count. Thoughts of getting a bacon sandwich from the café at his first break, a couple of hours away, did nothing to quieten the internal reminders.

The fact, also, that on arriving at work he had been requested (which was to say required) to stay on for an extra couple of hours, to cover one of the other rangers who had to leave early, was not exactly meeting with rampant cheers from the rest of his weary body. *Great,* he thought, *just when I could do with getting away early.* He would text Jenny later to let her know that he would not be back until seven-thirty that evening. In the meantime though, there were the joys of a noisy morning with a group of families destined for the wide outdoors and bush craft; building shelters, traditional fire lighting, having a go at natural cordage and, Tony flinched at the thought, remembering somewhat shamefacedly his own shortcomings… animal tracking, not exactly on top form!

Very soon though, he was into the swing, with excited children sword fighting with sticks destined for the temporary lean-to, demanding mothers wondering, just how they would keep designer clothes from becoming ruined, and dads, from raising the entire forest to the ground in their efforts to light a fire. Brilliant!

At the same time Tony was dousing the conflagration that was the campfire, Julie Hoe and her husband Neil were attempting to walk back home through Poor Common. It was three o'clock. Confounded earlier in the morning by the tapes across the path on the Fitzworth entrance, not just hanging loosely and barring their way, but criss-crossing it like a giant spiders web and forcing them to go the long way round; the serious usage of police tape seeming to suggest that somebody meant business and did not want them, or anyone else for that matter, to enter. But now, as they approached from the paths' opposite end in the hope that there had been a mistake, they had found that the giant arachnid had been there too.

"Oh really Neil, this is too much!" exclaimed Julie her voice sounding to anyone overhearing as if it were his fault. "Why can't we go through? What is going on?" Unmoved by her outburst and ignoring her questions he carefully fed a leg through a convenient opening in the flimsy web.

"Neil what are you doing?" Julie demanded. When his foot touched earth on the other side, he cautiously shifted his weight and dragged the other leg through. With the 'Police, Do Not Cross' now facing away from him, he stared back at Julie. "What?" he said, as if ignoring the message was the most natural thing to do.

"It's there for a reason Neil."

"I know, just thought a quick look wouldn't hurt?"

They had walked up about a couple of hundred metres from Homewood House and were beside the high fences of Evergreen Road, when the temporary barrier had obstructed them. To Julie it meant they would have to walk back down to where they could divert through the estates, but to Neil it was a temptation waiting to happen.

"For goodness sake Neil. Come back, before somebody comes."

"Stop fussing, woman," he answered her not unkindly; "I'll have a quick look up the path. See if I can see anything, I won't be a tick."

"That's right sir," said a stern voice from behind him. "You won't be!" And from the path, emerging from behind a dense bush a couple of metres away, Neil saw what looked like a twelve year old in shirtsleeves addressing him.

"I think," added the young man, that Neil had now assessed was a Police officer, "you might want to do as the lady says, don't you?"

Looking a little abashed as if he'd just been caught scrumping, Neil slid back through the plastic strands to stand next to his wife, a sheepish grin spreading slowly across his weathered face.

Julie broke into one of her big smiles. "Sorry about that officer," she said laughing. "I think he's on the turn." The young copper smiled, and waved a hand as if no harm done. Neil was still assimilating the 'on the turn' comment, with surprised eyes and lips now displaying a wry hint.

A classic Julie manoeuvre, disarming through humour, but was ready for the attack. "So what's all this about, officer," a chubby finger pointing and tracing along one of the tapes? The young man didn't really have a clue. He didn't buy the line he'd been spun at the station, but gave it anyway.

"It's just routine. The whole common has been designated a crime scene, what with all that's been going on. CID wants another opportunity to sweep the area.

"Well I'm good with a broom if they want a hand," Julie shot back and gave the youngster a taste of one of her riotous laughs. He barely acknowledged the intended humour.

"I can't see anything special," he said offhandedly. "God knows what I'm doing here… it's just a piece of waste land."

"It's quite a nice bit of wasteland," Neil countered.

"That's as maybe," the policeman continued, "but I'm bored stiff. Obviously there's nobody about to talk to, nothing to look at, nothing going on at all, I've been up and down this path and around that gravel one, don't know how many times, I could do it blindfolded."

Feeling a little sorry for him Neil asked, "Been here all day I suppose?"

"No, I only took over at one, but I've got another three hours to do yet and you're only the second lot of people I've talked too." He looked somewhat grateful for that fact.

"Well there's usually somebody walking over here at any time of the day," Julie acknowledged. "Best time though is early morning. You'd be surprised at what you see. The number of times when I went into work early, you know up at the house there," she turned and pointed back up the path, expecting the lad to know where she was talking about. She ignored his blank look, and continued with her thoughts, "You get deer, badgers, foxes, and loads of rabbits in the fields over there. Fixing him with a look, "you ever see a stoat, or a grass snake?" she challenged. He shook his head dutifully. "I have," she said, "and all on that little bit o' common back there... so you want to keep your eyes open." He glanced around as if expecting to be assaulted by something at any moment.

"I shouldn't worry too much though," added Neil. "There doesn't seem to be much about these days, I haven't seen a rabbit in the fields for weeks. And I'm over here quite a lot."

"That's probably what the traps are for," the officer said nonchalantly. "An our lot are not going to find anything, that's for sure," he said half joking, "They couldn't catch a cold."

"Traps? Where? What sort of traps?" asked Neil. He'd never seen any on the common before.

"I suppose like, a rat or squirrel trap... only bigger." He held out his hands, almost at full stretch.

"That's a fox or badger trap," Neil said knowingly and looking a little perturbed. "Why are they there, I wonder?"

"If they want to catch a fox they'd best put them over in Homewood," Julie said to her husband with a laugh, and turned to the Policeman.

"Yeah, little buggers," Neil smiled. Digging up the lawn, pissing on the patio pots, and crapping all over the place."

Julie remonstrated at the language with just the one word, "Neil!"

Eyebrows shot up beneath the helmet's brim, "It's all right love," said the now amused copper winking at Neil. "If I'm honest, sounds like your average Friday night in Ferndown."

Chapter 81

An hour and a half later, a boxy Mercedes people carrier, drove up to a set of large wooden gates and stopped. The short unmade road had given the weary travellers a bumpy wake-up call. All had succumbed to the comfy seats, the unusually warm air conditioning and the smooth ride. Being intermittently on the go for the previous twelve hours and, for these travellers, effectively seventeen hours, if you included the time difference, they had readily nodded off at various points along the two hour journey from Heathrow.

Justine woke first and looked around the spacious cab at her sleeping brood. *They've only had... what? four or five hours of broken sleep in the last twenty-four.* She tried to work out. *They're going to be a nightmare,* she thought. As if somehow reading her mind, the impending bad dream began, the lack of movement and the car stopping with a certain finality, woke the children. Disparate voices called out still doused with sleep, "Are we there yet?" – "Are we done here. Mom?" - One of the twins began to grizzle.

"Yep we're here," she called out.

The taxi driver had got out and was fumbling with the gates. Only Justine knew what to expect when they opened. She had been here many times in the past, with her mum. The secret garden was how it had always been referred to, from when she had been a child herself, to even now. She would always call it that, hidden away as it was. All at once she saw the opening of the gates in her mind's eye and reminisced, a multitude of moments and memories suddenly unlocked. Warm scenes of happy days swept through her, the scented rose garden, helping her dad in the vegetable plot, chasing the dogs, climbing trees, summers on the patio doing homework, homemade lemonade... Betty. Ah yes Betty... a little frightening at times, intimidating even when she shouted at the dogs... but like an extra grandma, warm, big hearted and kindly. It seemed fitting they were to live here for a while. It was like coming home. Not home as in family, but home as in a place, a special feeling like stepping back on to home soil after being away too long.

And now, as the first heavy gate swung away, its foreshortened travel, initially revealing only a narrow perspective, that familiar anticipation grew... she had been away, too long. Although moving at the same speed the slim aperture soon widened and broadened more quickly as the gate drew back further. All necks, still restrained by seat belts, were craning for a view. The angle of the halted car was such that the house was completely hidden behind the second gate. Somewhat disappointingly, all that could be seen through the half open portal, was a high yew hedge bordering the gravel driveway, that disappeared behind the wooden structure at a point in the near distance.

Justine turned to watch her children, as all parents do at significant moments in early lives, hoping that the sight of their new home would spark similar reactions to those of her childhood; wanting to see the expectation grow on their open faces, turning to genuine amazement and then bursting excitement. Time and time again, it was a thrill you couldn't bottle.

As the driver walked over to unbolt the opposite gate, Justine's anticipation mounted. She noted heads incline, eyes widen and brows to gently wrinkle, ready for the next reveal. Obviously the kids had seen big houses before, she reminded herself. In America there were loads; grand and imposing, old and new. Indeed, the home they had just left was modern and spacious, a little larger than average and it, too, had a good size plot. But this one would be different. It was typically English for a start, and although it was big, it wasn't vast or brash like some she'd seen in the states. Set in its own modest corner, but in reality probably twenty times bigger than the average UK garden, she thought, but it didn't feel grand. It was an intimate space; in reality spaces, gardens with-in a garden. And, it had a history. In parts, the building was older than her husband's country, and although internally rejuvenated by Betty and her husband, it still had that air of another time, another era. Its high boundary walls kept it isolated and secure. That was it, she mused, the refining notion; it was like stepping into a different world, a bit like walking through the arch into Disney land… from reality to a kingdom of magic. Not that she was expecting quite such an explosive reaction on this occasion, from the eldest two, who had actually done that.

No, these individual significances would probably be lost on the kids, she thought, but the whole package couldn't fail to impress, and, to top it all, this was where they were going to live. Their English, home, in a land of castles and palaces, kings and queens and fish and chip. She had sold it to them heavily and was looking forward to now showing it off. And so as the view expanded laying out the reality beyond, a growing amazement filled the Taxi's interior, "Wow!" was the first words said in almost silent awe by Lilly, the five-year old. There followed a more boisterous, "WOWIE," from the seven-year old Jack, "Are we really going to live there Dad?"

"You betcha," managed Brett. At thirty-five, a high flier with JP Morgan Bank, and not easily flummoxed he too was just a little taken aback. Transferred to the extensive Bournemouth Office for the next two years, he knew his wife had managed to swing some nice accommodation and, at a reasonable rent, one that the Bank was happy to sanction. But he'd had no idea what she had actually rented. "It's a goddam stately home," he said in delighted amazement to his beaming wife.

The Taxi driver took them up the drive, the low profile tyres, compacting the gravel stones, making them crack and pop. He deposited them, with bulging bags outside the front door. Before he drove away leaving them to their own little world, he advised them that the Angel just around the corner would be a good place to grab a quick bite at this time. "Open all day," he said.

With the key found under the allotted pot, they unlocked the front door and went in to further calls of admiration and disbelief. A swift tour round the front part of the house gave them their bearings; the hall, the kitchen, the lounge and, most impressively to Brett, the Library.

"Willya look at that," he said in wonderment and, running his free hand across the acres of green baize that was the Snooker table, "I ain't never played on one this size before." As they climbed the sweeping staircase winding around the front hall, Brett couldn't help but notice the paintings and the beautiful décor, from the rich wooden floorings to the ornate cornice around the ceiling. It was a lot to take in and a long way from the clean lines of their previous home.

"That reminds me," said Justine with one of the babes in her arm and pointing out some dusty footprints on the polished floor. "We need to close the windows. Looks like we've had a visitor already," she joked. "You can tell there's been no dogs here for a while. The local cats seemed to have checked things out for us already." *Big cat!* She thought absently as cresting the stairs on to the landing, and then went into the first room. "Who wants this one?" she called to the older children already disappearing through into the next room.

With bedrooms allocated, windows all closed and confused stomachs getting the better of them, they wandered around to the pub. "Our local," she informed Brett.

Chapter 82

About the same sort of time, Patrick was sitting in his car, in the lay-by, on Ringwood Road. He was about to get out and walk up to the Common. Jenny had just texted to tell him that they would be meeting at Tony's flat at about seven thirty, so he was going to have a wander to kill some time and maybe check the traps; when his mobile rung.

"Stimpson...?"

Patrick recognised who it was by the way his name had been forced down the wires; his boss, Chief Inspector Jonathon Bryant.

"Yes sir."

"What's been happening? Any news?"

"Actually, yes." He was surprised that his boss had phoned. It was, after all, a Sunday night. "I was going to call you in the morning."

"Well I'm saving you the bother," he said abruptly, alerting Patrick to the fact that his boss sounded a little... off. "So what's the news?"

"Three down four to go," Patrick said rather triumphantly.

"Is that all?"

"You're joking aren't you?" Patrick now sounded irritated. "Tony thought that was bloody miraculous for just one night of trying, and I'm inclined to agree with him."

"Well I wouldn't put too much store in what Mr Nash says," said the chief ominously. "And I would strongly suggest you distance yourself a little from him."

Patrick was now more than a little irked. It sounded like the chief was backtracking from his positive position the other night. "Why?" he asked rather belligerently. "Has something happened? Something I should know about?"

Jonathon Bryant changed his tone, realising that he wasn't going to win over his colleague by brow-beating him. "Look Patrick, I don't want to fall out with you over this, and I don't know how much digging you did before you swallowed Tony's explanation of hybrid foxes?"

Patrick stayed silent, hoping it was a rhetorical question and that the chief would continue. The fact he hadn't done any checking because the hole in his leg had seemed convincing enough, probably wasn't going to cut it. Now though, he felt like he should have.

"Some," he lied hoping not to be interrogated about it any further.

"The thing is Patrick," he continued, "I have it on very good authority that there is no such thing."

Patrick knew exactly what he was alluding to but felt like being less than cooperative,

"As what?"

The even-tempered approach was short lived, "A bloody hybrid fox, Patrick. Don't be obtuse."

"Says who?" Patrick demanded. "Somebody up the golf club was it? Perhaps he'd liked to have a look at my leg?"

"Now look here Pat," the chief countered, irritated and ignoring the bit about the leg. "This guy I know works for Defra and when I put the question to him... casually you understand... we were having a drink... well yes all right it was at the Golf club, as it happens, not that it makes any difference, the information he found from other colleagues in the know, said it just cannot happen. Something to do with different Chromosome counts making it virtually impossible."

"Virtually, is not the same as totally or completely impossible," argued Patrick, not really sure why he was having this conversation.

"For God's sake Patrick, you're splitting hairs. You know what I mean... It's not possible, and that's it."

"I see, so the fact that my leg nearly got ripped off... its bloody painful by the way... and that I shot the most vicious looking killer I have ever come across, this morning, not forgetting that you saw what those creatures did to that fawn, and all the evidence pointing to the missing children going the same way and you just want to leave it; walk away. I honestly can't believe it."

"I haven't said leave it." The exasperation, clear in the chief's voice, "I just said don't get too chummy with this Tony Nash. What we should be doing is handing this over to... animal welfare, or whichever department handles dangerous dogs. This isn't Police business Pat."

Patrick was incredulous, "I hear what you're saying sir, but irrespective of whether a fox and a dog can or cannot hybridise, these animals are real. And by the way," his voice lowered a tone and became a little threatening, "those missing children... of course now I know what we should be looking for, I bet you forensics will be able to find some pretty damning evidence to prove it was them. What are you going to do then?"

It was evident that the chief had had enough of the argument and cut in menacingly, "Patrick, what you do in your own time is up to you, but tomorrow I want you back in the office. Is that clear?" And, as an afterthought, "Oh and I want that gun back."

"And what about these animals, we're just going to let them pick off a few more kids are we?

"Leave it up to Mr Nash and Miss Spader," he said abruptly. "She is a dog warden after all. And as I say... what you do in your time..."

Patrick jabbed at the red telephone symbol on his handset. "Arsehole," he annunciated angrily, accentuating the sounded vowels. It didn't make him feel any better.

Chapter 83

Ten minutes later, and with some fresh air circulating in his lungs, he was beginning to calm down. He'd walked up the lane to where Julie and her husband had been turned back and climbed deliberately through the still taught plastic tape. Remembering that there would be a beat officer around somewhere he decided to leave inspecting the traps until a little later. He kept up a brisk pace as he headed along the gravel path that would take him past the second set of traps set back in the undergrowth, and up onto the common.

Taking the left hand path at the first junction he made towards the Ponds. A few paces along and he became aware of a large tree trunk that appeared to be sprouting a pair of black boots. As he drew closer and then almost level with the trunk, the boots, he now saw were attached to legs clothed in dark blue trousers and stretched out on the ground. The rest of the body was still hidden from view.

"Good evening constable," Patrick said calmly.

Legs and boots scrabbled to heft the emerging torso into a vertical position. The wrong-footed copper took in the senior detective and straightened visibly.

"Tired are we?" Patrick asked, an amused smile sitting devilishly on his lips.

"Yes… eh, no I mean, I literally only just sat down sir. Honestly."

"Relax, I'm sure you're allowed a break at some time. Who's to say it wasn't just then…eh?"

Looking a little relieved, the officer was hoping he might get some straight answers from this detective, rather than his own senior officers.

"I was wondering sir, why I was here? I can't really believe forensics is going to do another sweep. Besides… the place is dead."

"Well you're right. They won't be going over the whole area, but there are one or two places of interest and the further away we can keep the public and press the better. So you might not realise it but you are doing an important job."

"Fair enough."

"Found many people wandering on the common, or trying to get on it?"

"You must be joking. As I said, it's absolutely dead. Four people, that's all since one o' clock, two kids on their bikes trying to sneak in; I got rid of them quick enough, and an elderly couple pissed off at having to walk the long way around. Actually, we had a bit of a laugh. The old boy was moaning about the foxes… what did he say?" The young officer screwed his face up and dredged the words out. "That's right – 'little buggers, digging up the lawn, pissing on the patio pots, and crapping all over the place', and I said, 'if I'm honest, sounds like your average Friday night in Ferndown!'"

Patrick wasn't laughing.

"Yeah, well it was funny at the time... you understand,"

"Did they say where these foxes were?" Patrick asked trying to hide his interest.

"She said something about a big house down the path a ways." He pointed back the way Patrick had just come.

Patrick's mind was turning quickly. *My god! Is that where they've gone...? Obvious when you think about it. Tony had said that was where it had all begun.* Without saying anymore to the bemused policeman, Patrick swung round and marched off the way he came. Checking his watch and noting it was five-forty, he assessed there was plenty of time; his intention - to try and get in and have a look around. As far as he could remember the housekeeper had told Tony that Homewood House was still unoccupied.

******

In the brick pigsty of Homewood House, wedged between the long shed and a dry store for produce, the doxes had been resting. One of them was licking a wound in its tail that continued to weep. They were all still deeply disturbed; the shock of the morning's ambush and entrapment had left them jittery and nervous. The vixen, particularly, was still pining for the cubs that were missing.

She had soon realised that the cubs were in danger, the instant the traps had fallen. Ill-equipped to understand what had happened, she had lingered for a few minutes in a forlorn hope. The sudden violent sound and the emergence of people had mobilised her to flight, leading the remaining pups back through the common and straight for the protection of Homewood House. The other loud noises that she had heard whilst in flight would have frightened and spurred her even more, although she could not have understood their significance. But innate senses, engendered over thousands of years, would lead her basic instincts to suspect that the pups were no longer of their world. The loss almost palpable, even at a distance, but it had not stopped her from searching.

Housing the near adult pups in the sty, a place she had been shown by the big male and where they had often found food, she knew they would be out of harm's way. Joined by the other two adults, similarly stunned, they had all slept for a good part of the day, but were now fitful and, when the unfamiliar sounds of heavy gates being dragged back and the gravel relenting under the press of tyres, penetrated their silent refuge, they became agitated once again. They heard the thump of car doors and voices of differing levels and then muffled sounds coming through the brickwork. This was followed a short while later with more loud voices and gates again. The inquisitive alpha male hunkered out of the sty and stole a sly look, unseen in his scrape under the yew hedge, bordering the drive, as the family left through the gates.

Chapter 84

Sunday 9th August 19:05pm

The scented terrace, ablaze with summer flowers took full advantage of the south westerly sky; its attuned and elevated aspect ensuring it caught the very last rays of any setting sun. Staring up from the accurately positioned loungers nestling in the crook of the warm brick building, Justine and Brett, travel weary but relaxed, marvelled at the sheer beauty of a spectacular Dorset sunset.

Overhead a near perfect mackerel pattern stretched from the solid walls restricting the view behind them, to somewhere just above the level eye on the horizon; the thin wispy streaks of cloud, regular and uniform a dappled grey against the light hue of the firmament. Across this vault and towards the dipping sun each striation reflected a glimpse of its dying radiance; subtle changes from flat tone to ones tinged with gentle pink, eventually descending to a fiery orange glow streaked with red and gold. At this distant point, the compacted clouds, now dense and damp, collected in futile effort to block the radiant lustre, their huge billowing forms only adding depth and majesty to the vast natural canvas.

With the leftover chardonnay they had re-corked and brought back from the pub, now sparkling in tall crystal glasses they luxuriated in the warm glow; a perfect end to what had been a very stressful day… *two days,* Brett reminded himself, *actually more like two months* he thought, reflecting on the time frame from when they had first really begun to wind things up in their previous life.

They had departed the United States from JFK the day before, at just before midnight, American time. Brett, giving a long lasting stare out of the airplane window, as he had left his vibrant homeland, for a new and uncertain future, in the gentler folds of the United Kingdom. They had arrived in London, just before midday. The overnight flight had afforded them some sleep on the plane, albeit fitful and disturbed, but the five-hour time difference would upset body clocks for maybe a few days yet.

Travelling for a holiday was stressful at the best of times, particularly if it involved air travel. Moving house was another source of extreme angst, but now Brett and Justine had found themselves doing both, and to cap it all, they were upping sticks and changing continents. As if that wasn't tortuous enough, their four excited children aged: seven, five, plus twin toddlers of twenty-three months had tested their patience to the absolute limit. But finally the taxi driver of the pre-booked nine seater vehicle had deposited the bulging suitcases in the front hall of Homewood House at just before four-thirty pm. They were full of clothes and useful items to see them through the first few weeks, or at least until they could be fully repatriated with the rest of their clobber. Jet lagged and out of sorts they had given the house a quick tour of inspection before wandering around to the Angel Inn, to grab some much needed sustenance before a planned early bed.

But parent's plans are oft broken by the determinations of their young and, on this occasion, they had not been objected too. On returning from the Pub, Jack and lily were intent on exploring the garden, and frankly, neither adult could blame them on such a gorgeous evening. Although, where they could find the energy from, was still something of a mystery. Mum and Dad though, were more than happy to lie back and just drink in the peaceful atmosphere of their new surroundings. The twins had dropped off in their buggy on the short walk back and were now laid out on top of a king-size bed with pillows placed under the duvet and encircling the pair like a nest, ensuring they stayed put and fast asleep. Justine would get them ready for bed later. She hoped it could be done without really awakening them, and maybe... they would sleep through till morning. And of course, Pigs might fly!

"Whatever," she had said, draping a single sheet over them. "Best just go with the flow!"

Whilst Justine had been taking care of the two babies Brett had taken a stroll down into the lower garden stretching out from below the wide Patio. Justine had told him that there used to be a large pond in the far corner and, although she could remember it being enclosed behind a picket fence, and so, in theory safe from the kid's point of view, they ought to just check its integrity. "I'm talking ten or fifteen years ago," she'd added, "so for all we know they might have taken it away by now."

From the southwest corner of the patio Brett had gazed out over a large lawn that swept away and around the property to the east, looking for the pond. Below him, at the bottom of the steps, was a path running around the base of the patio and which, in fact, encircled the whole house. Stretching directly ahead of him and all the way to the long borders of the southern wall, this pea gravel path denoted the westerly border of the lawn. On the other side of this walkway was a substantial bed of mixed and mature shrubs nearly twenty metres long. Despite their age and propensity to sprout in random profusion, they had been well tendered, trimmed and shaped, so that from his overview, they looked like a landscape in miniature; a diorama of rolling hills, undulating and folding. Behind this pleasing green strip the plants seemed to take on a wilder side, much taller and unkempt. From his high vantage, it looked like a jungle. He recognised the giant leaves of a plant he knew was a water lover. At nearly two metres a leaf span, there had to be a serious amount of water to support something that size, he'd guessed. So with that helpful clue, he had descended the stone steps to the scrunchy surface of the path and strolled beside the lawn, the ground sloping imperceptibly down as he went. Almost at the end of the garden he had been offered a choice, by way of a staggered crossroads. Immediately to his right was a route denoted by a boardwalk through the wild garden he'd glimpsed a few moments ago. Carry on a few paces and he would hit a 'T' junction, one way running along the bottom edge of the lawn, all the way back around the house following the outer wall to the east. The opposite direction also followed the eight-foot high brick fortification, but wound, like a woodland walk, through the screening shrubs and trees.

He'd turned off the path onto what, he assumed, was a trail through an area that was likely to be marshy, hence the slightly elevated slatted wooden causeway. Within a few paces he caught sight of a picket fence to his left and the open water behind. Another ten metres and he was at a further crossroads, left to the pond through a latched gate, right he had assumed went back to the house and straight on... to meet the western wall at some point. He had stood for a few moments amazed at the foliage above him. Suddenly he remembered the name of the plants, Gunnera. He hadn't seen them this size before, their fleshy stems thicker than his leg and supporting vast platforms of green, half a meter above his head. Interspersed with these were aged tree ferns, woody stems of over two metres high that exploded lengthy fronds high into the air. On the ground, between the dry mounds supporting the massive ferns, there was no standing water as such, but the soil was boggy and moist, other low ferns and mosses thriving there; cleverly making this whole area feel like some primordial swamp.

Taking the boardwalk directly ahead, and following the picket fence around to where it joined the pea gravel path, he realised that the route had cut the corner off the garden. He had satisfied himself that the pond was indeed secure and took another path; this one had curved back towards the house through high spires of colourful bamboos, palms and other exotics. Brett was not a gardener but inspired by what he'd seen so far, he figured... *that could change.*

"This garden is incredible," said Brett still semi reclined and surveying his temporary domain with a refreshed chardonnay. "We ought to take a stroll a bit later before it gets dark. I only went down to the pond, but there's more to see, I guess at the front of the house."

"It was her life's work really, and his too, after he retired from the army," Justine advised with eyes closed and enjoying the residual heat. "They both loved it. Everything planned out by them, from the various formal areas, veg patch, orchard, pond etc to where they kept ducks chickens, and pigs at one time. My Dad came to work for them after Mum had become housekeeper. He helped tend the gardens and grew veggies for Betty and her husband, and for us as well." Justine sat up and adjusted the backrest giving a little laugh, "We had some high old times here, me and my brother, playing with the dogs, climbing trees and making dens whilst Mum and Dad cleaned or gardened."

"Certainly loads of space," Brett agreed, acknowledging her good fortune. "And the old couple allowed you to play here? That was sure swell of them."

"Yes we were really lucky, although of course it was only in the school holidays, but Betty and Owen would always make us feel welcome. They only had a few simple ground rules, like not going near the pond, only climb certain trees and be

314

careful of the plants. Other than that we had free reign pretty much. Like our kids will have now; plenty of space, totally enclosed, secure and safe."

Chapter 85

Tony arrived home to his less palatial abode, at seven thirty-five and was greeted by Jenny in the kitchenette, offering him a steaming plastic pot with a fork lodged inside.

"I know I said, let's have something quick for tea," he said with devilment in his eyes, "but you really shouldn't have gone to so much trouble."

Jenny pulled a face and flicked a playful 'V' sign. "Nothing wrong with Pot Noodles," she informed him as the door buzzer cut in. Patrick had arrived.

He was hot and had made himself bothered again in the car, by going over the argument he had had with the Chief Inspector. Politely refusing the offer of a 'noodle refreshment' from a smiling Jenny, he launched into the dilemma that he was now faced with. After he had finished disparaging his boss, and wishing that he had never decided to keep all this quiet, the other two looked at him dismayed.

"So where does that leave us?" asked Jenny. "You know yourself, how dangerous these creatures are. We can't just leave it."

"Jenny's right, Patrick. We can't just ignore it. I know we've been operating somewhat below the radar up to now, but without your bosses blessing, we are truly on our own. Mind you, I had that nasty feeling when he left here the other day."

"Well I'm not proposing that we just drop it, but I've had time to think it over and, if the three of us can't sort it, and I do have my doubts. Then we are going to have to make this public soon, force some hands as it were. That is, if our friend Brian at the Echo doesn't do it for us," Patrick said acknowledging Saturday's Echo lying on the coffee table with 'Feral Foxes attack Play Park', splashed across the front page, "which will piss his lordship off, but I'm not sure what choice we have. The fact that a fox and dog can or can't hybridise is not the issue. There are dangerous animals out there and they have got to be removed. I can understand… up to a point," his voice lost some of its aggression, "my boss's concerns. He's worried about his career. Without hard evidence, and not having had a chunk of flesh taken out of him, like I have." Patrick smiled wearily, "he isn't even going to whisper his thoughts to those on high. And even if they did give him a hearing, they'd all be too worried about their own prospects if all went tits up. Nobody's going to want to come clean, let alone moot this idea in the public domain, unless there was proof positive. And even then," he added sounding defeated, "with the panic it would cause, they'd want to manage what information was given to the public." He shook his head, "No… The idea, as we've said is just too fantastical."

"I know what we've got is pretty damning, but it's not exactly conclusive…" began Tony hesitantly "and I'll be honest with you, I'd be a little reluctant about going public with it. As you know, I've not had very good experiences with the press." As if a sudden thought just popped into his head he said, "Surely though, with three dead animals, someone should be able to prove evidence of hybridization. Plus, using whatever techniques your forensics boys have, couldn't they tie the animal to the child's remains?"

Patrick gave Tony an appreciative look, evidently he had come up with the same thoughts as himself, but more importantly he felt, Tony was not about to let it go either.

"Look," Patrick said a little cautiously, unsure as to how they would react. "If you guys can continue for a few days on your own, I intend to do exactly that. If I can direct the forensic boys to look for evidence that would positively show that the animals were responsible for the children going missing then that would force the Chief Inspector's hand. However," Patrick advised sounding more like a doctor bearing medical complications, "as I said before, crime scenes like these are often interfered with by animals of all kinds. Therefore the fact that the area might be covered in fox hair or that the child's bones look like they have been gnawed upon, it still doesn't actually prove they took them. The argument will be that it was somebody else who abducted them, dumped them on the common, allowing the foxes to take advantage, along with half of creature kind."

"So what you're saying…" Jenny said thinking it through, "is that we might never prove it."

"Fraid so. But if we manage to get rid of these animals, at least there should be no more children going missing. And whether the brass upstairs accept what we find, and join in the credit, or they just sweep it under the carpet, then so be it. The alternative of us doing nothing," he said with an inevitable look, "is that another child goes missing and eventually the truth will out, with all and sundry asking why we didn't stop it at the time. My career would be toast, that's for sure and no doubt my boss would be distancing himself from me, like he suggests I do with you."

"Well it looks like we don't have a choice," added Tony sucking up the final slippery noodle. "I suppose," and looking like he was wondering what to do next, "we'd better go and check the traps."

"Oh yes the traps," said Patrick looking annoyed with himself. "That was the other thing I had to tell you. Sorry the chief making me see red put me off my stroke." His face brightened a little. "I reckon I know where the doxes are hiding out."

Chapter 86

As the troubled three despondently made noises to pursue their quarry, a similar hunt was just beginning in the lush gardens of Homewood house.

"Thirty one, thirty two," Jack said quietly, then mumbling for a couple of seconds began again, "forty nine, fifty!" before shouting, "Coming, ready or not!" His head spun round, taking in as many aspects of the views available, hoping desperately to catch a glimpse of his sister in flight and giving him a useful clue as to whereabouts in this big garden she was likely to hide up. Annoyingly, his foreshortening of the countdown was not enough and she had obviously scuttled away pretty quickly. So with further shouts of, "I'm coming to get you," and a warning shot from his mum, "Do not go near the pond Jack." He bounded down the stone steps and out onto the lawn.

Even with the pond area out of bounds this was still an awesome place for hide and seek, Jack had assessed excitedly. He doubted they would run out of places to hide even by the time they went back to America. It was a pity he couldn't show this to his friends at school. *Now that would be truly awesome*, he thought as he scrunched onto the path that ran past the old duck and chicken coop to the south-east of the house. Wondering whether to look in the sheds further up beside the house, or to head off down the path, he decided to go down to the bottom of the garden. The sheds and buildings were way too obvious he thought, but the huge trees and shrubs that ran along the bottom wall looked much more promising, and particularly the one standing on its own at the front, the one with its leaves dangling on the grass beneath. This was a beautiful Weeping Willow, its bright green tresses gently moving, sweeping the floor beneath and tantalisingly offering a suitable refuge for those wishing to avoid capture. Jack continued to intone his threats "I'm coming to get you, I'm gonna find you!"

From the count of one, Lilly had run away giggling with intent. She knew exactly where she was going to hide, had caught a glimpse of it as they had driven through the gates in the taxi. And later, she'd had a better view from the front window on the half landing; the little wooden building looked so pretty. Roses trailed over the front veranda and Wisteria writhed behind it on the back wall; cascading flowers over the roof like a tumbling stream. So the moment it had been suggested by Jack that they play hide and seek, the five year old had made her decision. By the time the count had reached ten, Lilly was halfway up the path at the side of the house, determination written across her chubby face and blonde curls bouncing with the pace. Every so often she would let out a high-pitched squeal of excitement; she just couldn't help herself.

But away on the other side of Homewood House the excited shouting had not gone unnoticed. A nose nudged its way out of a low door and sniffed the air. A noise emanating from the front of the house, suggested there was movement on the gravel drive. It enticed the snout to advance a little, slowly and warily until erect ears were unhindered by solid objects and allowing the collection of full-on stereo sound. Curiosity dragged the rest of its body out from the low building and into the open pen. Long shadows, cast from the nearby house threw a dull light and the sinking hues tinged with the merest hint of gold, were strange and ethereal. The calm evening had been relatively quiet up to this point and the conditions had not felt right to foray from their new home. But now as the day began to slip away and fading light cooled the air, it signalled a change in their natural rhythm. Within a few moments the first attentive animal was joined by another, marginally smaller, this female caught the mood, she stretched her sleep-tight limbs and made ready.

Chapter 87

"Homewood House," said Patrick sounding as if they should have known all along. "
I was talking with the beat officer who'd been charged with keeping the common
clear, and he told me about a conversation he'd had with a couple of the locals. When
he'd mentioned in passing, the traps he'd found, the old girl alluded to the fact that
they would be better off at Homewood because of all the foxes there. As soon as he'd
said it, I saw the possibility." He glanced at Tony, who by the look on his face was
also making the connections. "You'd said this was where you thought it had all
kicked off from."

"Christ yes… it's so obvious," was Tony's reply. "They're going home!"

Lilly left the gravel driveway down a long straight path. Half-metre high box
hedges lined the route. She was entering Betty's more formal garden. Caring not for
the neat design and regimented rows of plants, the little girl was just so excited.
Allowed to run free and unhindered by a protective hand or cautionary word, she had
got away from her brother, who was now shouting far away at the other end of the
garden. The little thing had never known so much liberty. Every time she rounded a
bush or found a bend in a path a new horizon opened and she soaked it up like a
sponge; borders full of summer flowers, heady fragrances, a statue, a sundial and a
tinkling fountain; all magical to unblemished eyes.

This part of the garden was laid out with precision and symmetry. The whole area
was bisected by two paths running from each corner forming a St Andrews cross.
Halfway distant from the saltire's centre, paths connected each arm to form a
continuous oblong route. Clipped box hedges bordered the walkways and the spaces
between had been planted with roses. A different variety blossomed in each ordered
section.

Lilly had run to the stone sundial in the middle expecting to reach the
summerhouse directly from that point. It was no more than fifteen metres away but
there was no obvious path to take her straight there. Using the plinth of the sundial to
gain just a few extra centimetres of height and a different perspective over the neat
box, she saw the layout and decided on her route.

It had been literally a few seconds from the first noisy shouts that had awakened
their interest to them crossing the expanse of stones leading away from the front door
of Homewood House. Soft footwork, quick and light made no sound as they padded
beside the high yew hedge bordering the gravel drive. Their ears pricked, to the sound
of high squeals and soft excited shrieks sifting through the close cropped barrier.
Tails low and lithe torso's slightly hunched, the pair clung beneath the bushes

overhang. Suddenly they disappeared, one second there and the next gone; slipping swiftly through a familiar and well worn tunnel in the dense greenery,

The fact that the foxes were going home was good news, but Tony was worried and it now showed on his face. "When did she say?" he said to himself, albeit out loud.

"Who… What?" asked Jenny quizzically, wondering what might have concerned him. She had already reasoned, if they could relocate the traps to the walled garden, it meant they could unseal the common and hopefully keep this under wraps. Surely that had to be good news? Tony was now beginning to get tense. He had an unpleasant feeling, and it hinged upon remembering what the woman had said.

Patrick cut across his thoughts and, mirroring Jenny's conclusions said, "If we can put the traps in the gardens of Homewood, that would be ideal. It's secluded so no worries that somebody is going to interfere with them or indeed disturb the foxes. But the big plus might be that we don't have to work in the public domain anymore. We can reopen the common and nobody needs be any the wiser… Thank God it's unoccupied."

"That's just it," Tony countered exasperation surging to the fore. "It is, or… or it's just about to be."

Patrick looked confused, "About to be what?"

"Occupied, it's about to be occupied, for God's sake." Tony's face was full of concern. "If I could just remember when the house-keeper said they were coming."

"The house-keeper?" Jenny queried in a way that under any other circumstance might have been taken as a jealous streak. "When did you see Julie Hoe? You didn't mention it."

"Oh the other day," said Tony, too distracted to register the tone. His face lit up as the words suddenly jogged out of the grey matter. "Day after tomorrow, that's what she'd said…" his expression became focussed as he interrogated himself. "so when **did** I see her?"

"So…" Jenny asked expectantly "somebody's moving in…?" The slight pause held for just a few seconds before she too suddenly registered. "Oh my God… yes," she said excitedly.

"Anybody like to tell me?" implored Patrick.

"Her daughter and husband," Jenny continued quickly. "She told us that day when we went to see her. They're going to rent it, aren't they?"

"That's right, but I just need to figure out when. Now I saw her… Friday." Tony determined, adding urgently, "That's right, so … day after tomorrow is…" trepidation gripped limpet like, to the eureka moment, "Oh Christ, that's today."

"Well there was nobody there just now, when I was up there," concluded Patrick with an air of authority. "The house was all shut up, tight as a Tick. Didn't look like any-body was in it and I had a good wander around the garden."

"If what she said was right… then it's definitely today."

"That could be any time in the next four hours," added Jenny. "They could even have arrived since you left," she nodded at Patrick. "It's been what… half an hour or more?"

Patrick's head tipped to one side in acknowledgement.

"And," Jenny continued, "didn't Julie say they had children!"

"Right," Tony began in a determined voice. "We need to get round there, pronto."

Chapter 88

Jack had expected to find his little sister much quicker than this… she was so annoying! He had assumed she would run to the nearest hiding point, which in this case was the high shrubs and trees just on the other side of the path, that's what she would normally do when they played hide and seek back home. It was easy, he always found her really quickly and she never seemed to mind, always laughing and giggling. But whenever he went off to hide, usually somewhere really good, she would soon lose interest and never find him, unless Mum or Dad helped. Even though he hadn't found her quickly, the fact that this was a whole new play area, meant, he was actually still up for the chase. His warning protestations, exuberant and shrill rang out through the lower garden disturbing only a late foraging blackbird.

Lilly heard the muffled shouts reverberating off the solid brick building in the middle of the plot; it made her shriek with excitement as if her brother were just behind her. Standing on the short path, made of brick, leading to the veranda of the wooden house, Lily studied the little house that seemed so perfect; she would bring her dollies here for tea she thought. Made of interlocked logs hewn to a standard size and with decoratively carved weather-boards hanging down from the pitched roof, it had the appearance of an alpine chalet. It had charmed the tiny tot from the moment she'd set eyes on it, and now as she looked into the full-length pains of the doorway, saw herself reflected, as if standing inside it. She waved and giggled, but something caught her eye, a movement in the glass. The mirror image had caught a ghostly shape clearing one of the box hedges behind her. Unsure of what the image meant or where the movement had actually happened, the diminutive figure, peered harder into the glass. Confused but inquisitive, she stepped on to the wooden deck.

Clasping the door handle at head height, she dragged the door ajar. As it swung she caught yet another glimpse in the glass, a momentary vision captured on screen… "Doggy," she said with apparent delight. Still high on freedom and exploration, with chocolate box images filling her little mind and fanciful creatures flashing before her-she was lost in a world of her own. Another step and she was inside, the smell of stale air, of dust and of wood, wrinkling her button nose. Alerted by a scrabbling sound outside and the door closing noisily on the latch, she swung round.

"Doggies," she said immediately and went to reopen the door. As she raised her arm, one of the creatures jumped and slammed violently into the thick safety glass. Shocked, Lily's tiny body spasmed and within an instant her face visibly shaken, became stricken with fear. The creature backed off, bemused and frustrated. Through bared teeth, and issuing low growls, the two animals nosed around the base of the door tasted the air and collected the child's scent.

Once again, foiled by something they could not possibly understand, they swept the ground around the base of the cabin, desperate for a hint of the prey within and searching for another access point. Their probing was urgent, back and forth they moved, a few paces in one direction, then lurching back in response to an interesting smell that had enlivened the senses.

Inside Lily backed jerkily away from the door, almost apoplectic with fear; silent tears moistening her white cheeks as she managed to squirm behind the wicker sofa. Thick cushioning and bamboo struts offered false protection. Imprisoned and frightened, with animals beyond her reasoning she curled up into a ball, distraught sobs pleading for maternal rescue.

Outside her brother's noisy shouts continued to permeate the air from the other side of the garden. The happy shouting, designed to spook his baby sister from her concealment, drew only unwanted attention.

Totally unaware of the mounting danger their daughter was in, Justine and Brett were as chilled and relaxed as they could be, the heat of the day captured by the patio was reluctant to leave and encouraging them to stay.

"I noticed Mum put some beer and wine in the fridge. Do you want a top up or beer?" asked Justine. "Not that I really want to get up."

"Force yourself," encouraged Brett laughing. "I'll have a beer if you're going."

With her third glass of wine and a Budweiser for Brett placed between them on the low table, she sat back down. "I can't believe I'm actually back here," she said wistfully. "Don't get me wrong, I haven't missed home particularly, since living in the States. Not having Mum and Dad around was a wrench at first, but, as you know... you soon get swallowed up with everyday life and its relentless pace; it helps distract you."

"Sure does. Hell, seems like only yesterday when we got hitched, and look at us now... four kids, a world away and a stately home. Some distraction!" Laughing, they watched their son in his efforts to find Lily

"When do you think we should tell him...? She went that aways" Justine said, mimicking her husband's gentle twang and pointing towards the front of the house.

"Oh give it an hour," chuckled Brett.

"At least!" agreed Justine.

"Come on Lilibeth," was the shout from the end of the garden. As Jack emerged from the pendulous branches of the willow, he looked somewhat despondent. Spying the tunnelled boardwalk of the bog garden from across the lawn, he perked up and seeing new possibilities charged off in that direction.

Justine followed her son's movements across the near perfect lawn, "Whichever way he goes he's getting warmer," she said, "assuming Lily's in the front somewhere." As the huge plants of the bog enveloped her son, she caught sight in her peripheral vision of a darting movement amongst the sweeping leaves of the graceful willow. Her immediate thought, *Lily!* Assuming her daughter was not exactly playing fair. "You little devil," she said out loud.

More quick movement and a longer glimpse -"hang on," she said, realising her mistake. "What was that?" Her attention now switched to the beautiful tree. Even without a breeze the weeping variety seems to move and sway at the best of times but now with a soft huff gently agitating the slender leaves, it swayed and gaps appeared in its hem of foliage. "There's an animal in the willow down there," she said. "Looks like a cat."

"Probably the one that paid us a visit earlier," added Brett not bothering to open his eyes.

"Oh…" Justine squinted, "there's two."

In response to the boy's shouts the two foxes had given up on the trapped prey of the front garden and moved swiftly back around the house past the sty and down through the undergrowth that masked the high wall. It was indeed hide and seek, but the dimensions had changed; from innocent fun to deadly intent. The concealed to prey, the hunter to hunted, and unsurprisingly the foxes would have the upper hand, for this was familiar territory. The erstwhile gardeners had brought together all their skills to design and create a most glorious setting, lush, tranquil and varied. But inadvertently it was also a garden for cover and deception, offering tracts of furtive connectivity, between nooks and crannies, hidey-holes and tunnels. And the high walls that had, in the past, offered privacy to human kind and their livestock, plus anonymity to its incumbent foxes would still serve to enclose, albeit in a perverse twist, not to keep the world at bay… but to contain and confine… and this new prey would not find it so easy to escape.

Together they broke cover from the sweeping leaves, tails low and heads focussed. Keeping just on the lawn, they hugged the lower path, a slightly longer route but it kept them within darting distance of cover in the nearby shrubs. High on the patio Justine watched them amused at their cheek. "Look," she said. "It's foxes."

One animal left the path just before it reached the boardwalk and melted into the jungle like foliage and the other carried on up the path. "I don't know who's going to get the bigger shock," added Justine still amused, "Jack or the fox."

"How do you mean?" asked Brett still reclined, but with eyes now open and trying to search from behind his subtle paunch.

"Well either the fox hasn't seen Jack, or he's following him, because he's just disappeared in the same direction."

Brett manoeuvred himself up on to one arm to get a better view. "Well providing your Brit foxes are as nervous of us as their Yankee cousins, then I'd put my money on him high tailing outer there in just a few seconds."

By now the second fox coming up the garden had been lost in the dead ground below the patio. "Wonder where that second one is going?" Justine said, beginning to look a little quizzical. "Mind you they probably know the run of this place better than we do. Betty used to feed them you know." Justine had seen the foxes many times in the past, had watched them being fed and any cubs, often playing on the lawn. However, there had been an irregularity about these two, nothing obvious or disquieting and so unable to pin it down, she let the thought go.

Down amongst the giant foliage, Jack's eyes were everywhere, *there were just so many places to hide*, he thought. Ten metres in, he swung round in response to a low sound, a sort of scraping, as if something was being dragged over a rough surface. He noticed through the dull and dappled light one of the leathery gunnera leaves, three or four metres away and low to the ground, shiver to a standstill.

"Lily?" he called out in a low enquiring voice. "Lily... I know it's you."

Nothing. He shrugged and continued along the creaking planks until he reached the gate in the picket fence into the pond. *Which way now?* He asked himself.

By the time he had turned sideways to look up the path towards the house and then back to his original direction of travel he was surprised to see an animal, a fox he guessed, coming up as if to meet him. He remembered somebody telling him 'foxes are harmless, more frightened of you, than you are of them.' It didn't take Jack very long to assess this creature was bucking the wisdom. It came at him with unblinking eyes and, although its legs seemed to grow shorter, lowering the body to a slouch in readiness for action, he knew exactly where its gaze was locked. Feeling suddenly alone, in a rather strange place, in a new country he didn't know, Jack's concern grew quickly to alarm. From somewhere over his right shoulder, caught at the limit of his periphery, he saw the second fox and his heart sank as a wave of panic swept over him. With adrenalin fuelling his reasoning, he turned to the gate, flicked the latch as he pushed it to. With only moments to spare he slammed the gate and ran up the boardwalk. Without looking back, he knew they had jumped the fence, their claws retching at the wood, gaining purchase and then a solid thud as they landed on the walk-way.

The boardwalk turned to jetty as the marsh below turned to shallows and then deeper water. A few metres up ahead, he saw a bridge humped over the expanse of dark liquid below. It seemed to be his only option. But it was no option. Even in his panic he knew the animals would outrun him. Casting glances as he ran, stepping stones in the water just ahead gave him an alternative. As he leapt to the first one, he could see they led to a small island. Caring less about how slippery the flat stones covered in a green film were, he didn't falter and bounded unsteadily, almost losing his balance, onto each one. Fear and body impetus, like being on skis and unable to stop, got him across the ten stones that led him to more stable ground. He whipped round and saw the foxes hesitate on the jetty, unafraid of water but unsure of the irregular pathway, they seemed to be assessing whether to jump or to swim.

Taking advantage of the momentary respite, shaking and absolutely terrified, Jack screamed at the top of his voice, "HEEELP - MUM – DAD – HELP ME – DAD!"

Chapter 89

"If he's in that water," Justine threatened half-heartedly to Brett, "I'll smack his bottom!"

She could have guessed when they'd warned him off. The word no, evidently saying so much more to her son. No! Means whatever is in there must be interesting. No! Was for Lily not me, I'm seven and I can swim. No! He reasoned - Dad would probably say yes.

"I'll skin him alive," she said as they both scuttled down the steps, concerned but not overly worried. He was still shouting, after all, and he could swim. Following the sporadic yells, half absorbed by the dense vegetation, they eventually found him. Tears streaming down his face but with a defiant look and a large stone in his hand; he crossed carefully from his island realm.

The water had foiled them. Reluctant in the first place to reach him, the foxes had begun to test the first two stones and were about to attempt the third when Jack had hurled rocks at them. The great churning of water as they plunged sent plumes of spray which startled the foxes. They retreated back to the jetty only to be stung by smaller stones accurately flung from the valiant defender. When Jack's parents had drawn close, the foxes slunk off unseen, fearing further pain.

Realising their son had not fallen in but was obviously distraught, Justine had enveloped him in her arms and quizzed him on why he was so upset. When he explained about what happened, they believed him up to a point. They assumed he had been surprised to see the animals and, perhaps frightened, he had run off without realising that they too had probably gone in the opposite direction. Somewhat prone to exaggeration and like many kids of his age not always given to telling the truth, Justine and Brett were a little wary about how he had to throw stones at them and fight them off. They suspected he was trying not to lose face. Sneaking in to the pond area, which he knew was off limits, getting stuck on the island somehow and becoming uncertain, frightened even, and so just wanted help. Mind you, she thought, he didn't have to make up the foxes, they were real enough; elements of his story true but others difficult to swallow.

"What do you think?" Brett asked Justine when they were back on the patio and not within earshot of Jack. "You think those foxes attacked him?"

"I doubt it," she said looking over at her husband. "Our wildlife doesn't do dangerous. No, I should think they just spooked him." Turning to look out into the garden, and, a decision made, "anyway it'll be dark in another half an hour or so, we ought to be thinking about getting this lot off to bed."

"First of all we've got to find Lily. Come on sport," Brett called to his son kindly. "Let's go and find your sis."

They all went round to the front garden where they believed the little girl had gone. Both parents stood on the wide turning circle in front of the house, calling her name and telling her that it was 'game over' and time for bed. After a few minutes of no reply and them moving onto the formal paths lined with box, they were beginning to get a little anxious.

"Where on earth is she?"

"Do y' think…" Said a tearful voice, "the foxes might've got her?"

"No. Now stop it," Justine said tetchily. The fox thing was getting out of hand. "Foxes do not attack people. Understand?" The boy began to cry again.

"Come on Tine," Brett placated, "he's tired, we all are. Let's find Lily and get an early night."

A few more minutes passed as they searched for Lily and the onset of night was more than just a hint. The sun had now disappeared from view and was in danger of setting. The garden had become gloomy, a dull flat twilight, where the edges of buildings softened, hedges and shrubs blurred into one and vision became poor as it recalibrated for night. And how quickly perceptions changed, this incredible garden, inspirational and beautiful was fast becoming disorientating and forbidding. Almost under his breath, he added, "Come on Lily. Where are you?"

Justine was over by the summerhouse when she heard a low sob and an intake of breath, quick and short. It was so quiet she wasn't sure if she had imagined it. She spun around to the wooden building and peered in through the glass, shadows and darkness was all she could see. Pulling open the door it came again, from somewhere at the back of the room and she knew- it was Lily. "She's here!" Through the cell-like bars of the cane furniture she could just make out the foetal shape of her child.

"Lily?" she called softly. "Lilikins it's Mummy." The child sobbed again but made no other response. Concerned, Justine picked her up and snuggled her in close, saying, "Let's get you inside."

The front door to Homewood had just closed as Tony's Green Scimitar drew up outside the gates.

"Right, this is how I think we should play it," said Tony. If there's nobody in we try and search the gardens, but we stick together OK?" Nobody argued. "If it is occupied… then Jenny you flash your council ID and tell them we have a dangerous dog on the loose and we would like to search the grounds. If we find the foxes then I think we should ask them if we can set some traps up in the garden tonight. After that, we'll have to wing it, especially if we catch one. Disposing of them might not be so easy with an audience."

"I could use the van from work, take them somewhere quiet and then…" she looked at Patrick, "you can deal with it."

"That's a thought," said Tony, "although I'll be amazed if they fall for it again so soon. Anyway let's go… see what we can find."

Lights in the house told them they were going to have to bluff it out, as they walked up the drive; the compacting shingle loud against the peacefulness of the evening.

Behind the smart front door the Adams were having a family hug. Lily was snuffling back tears, but still not communicating very well. Through speech thick with spittle and punctuated by sobs and quick breaths, the shocked little girl spoke falteringly, "oggy... iss-was an oggy."

"What's she saying?" Brett asked.

"Oggy, she's saying oggy." Justine said, looking equally as perplexed.

"It's doggy," said Jack looking fearful again. "She's saying doggy."

There was a moment's silence as Brett and Justine exchanged a glance, surely not... foxes?

The loud rap on the front door, just behind them, made the huddled group jump. "What the f...," began Brett, stopping himself before the expletive made a full appearance. Irked at the sudden interruption of their efforts to calm things down, Brett opened the front door. Not expecting a minor delegation, he was surprised to find three people standing on the other side and appearing somewhat menacing.

"Can I help you?" he asked not unreasonably.

He noted the girl spoke up while the others looked mildly uncomfortable.

"Sorry to bother you so late," she said, holding up her council ID card, "but I'm from animal welfare at Dorset County Council." She took in the distressed children and assumed tiredness and bedtime tears. "We have a problem with a pet gone missing, a dog..." A look of more than just interest flashed across Brett's face, and she caught it. "Oh it's nothing to be concerned about," she hastily added with a hesitant smile thrown in as back up. "Only we need to..."

Justine cut her off acidly, "And it needs three of you? Just how unconcerned should we be?"

Jenny was angered by the woman's unnecessary vitriol, but she could not find it within herself to tell her, 'it was all ok and they had it under control,' because they didn't! Knowing she had been put on the spot, she felt pressurised. *I can't tell her now, when she clearly suspects something*, Jenny struggled... *that it's nothing to worry about.* Jenny looked back at the young children and made her mind up. "Look I won't lie to you but we do have a dangerous animal out there..."

"Just the one?" Brett said accusingly.

Tony had been watching the exchange and read something more in the children's distress and the parent's apparent awareness of the situation. As he assessed the scene his eye was drawn to the floor, and he knew the game, was clearly up. They had to come clean.

"May I ask?" His voice a mixture of genuine concern and empathy, "Have you had a problem here?"

"I don't know," Justine glared. "Until you turned up... we thought we had a couple of overtired children and a game of hide and seek gone wrong." Justine was furious. God knows who these people were, but they were hedging around something and she had a nasty suspicion it involved the foxes. However, she was not about to offer it to them on a plate, nor indeed would she let them get away without telling them the truth.

"What problem do you think we've had?" she challenged.

Tony had been noticing Patrick's furtive glances out into the garden behind, and too felt the unease of being out in the half light, the bright hall bulb disrupting his vision out beyond its immediate influence and making the world behind, darker and more ominous.

"Would you mind if we came in?" Tony asked justifying it with "keep the heat in!" As soon as he said it he realised how pathetic it sounded.

"Okay," said Brett standing back, "but you better tell us exactly what's going on? And why you don't want to be out there... Although I guess it might have something to do with foxes scaring the crap out of my kids."

At that same moment, a distant grizzle from one of the bedrooms reached Justine's attuned ear. "The twins," she said and looking alarmed. "They've been up there all this time!"

"Is the house secure?" demanded Patrick, speaking for the first time, the authority obvious as was the intimation.

"No, the French doors in the day room have been open all evening," Brett's voice was showing signs of concern.

"Oh God! The house has been open all day," Justine said in horror and beginning to move towards the stairs, looked down at the paw prints, "I knew they were too big for a cat!"

"You mean!" Brett too looked horrified, "they've been in the house!"

"That's definitely fox," confirmed Tony, following Justine. "Jenny you stay here with the children, Patrick?" Tony pointed to the stairs.

They took the wide risers two at a time. Tony grabbed Justine allowing Patrick to take the lead. As the Glock appeared from beneath his fleece, she let out a short gasp, "Oh my God. Who are you people?"

"It's okay," Patrick acknowledged. "I'm a police officer. Which room?" With no time to weigh up whether he was, or why he was involved with dangerous animals, or even why he had a gun, Justine pointed to a door along the landing. "In there."

Both the babies were crying now. And even to Justine's practiced ear, and unable to match it with visual clues, the crying sounded urgent, more pained, and it frightened her. She couldn't begin to imagine what she might find. Patrick ran just inside the high ceilinged room and flicked on the light. He remembered the airy feel that all the rooms had had, from his earlier visit in the year, and the death of the old lady. The head of the double bed was tight against the wall nearest the landing and opposite was a large sash window; closed.

Patrick could only see one child and held his hand up to stop Justine from entering. "You said twins?" The inference in his voice was not lost on Justine and she pushed past him panicked. "They must be there, I heard them!" she screamed.

She ran to the bed confused, Patrick and Tony following. Tony saw the streak of dirty brown in the adjacent room, a bathroom, with a second door on to the landing. Before he had time to alert Patrick, shouts were coming up the stairs.

"On the Landing!...Tony!... They're on the Landing!"

The two men charged out back the way they'd come and on to the wide space that led back to the stairs and looking down through the balustrades could see Jenny and Brett pointing. "They saw us and shot off, towards the back," called Jenny.

"Come on, the back stairs," yelled Patrick.

Although internal doors were wide open throughout the house, from the morning's airing, Patrick guessed that the animals were heading for the way out and he ignored the other rooms, and made for the back stairs. Within seconds they seemed to have moved into another property, all finesse and luxury gone replaced with a utilitarian and functional decoration. Heavy feet on bare wooden floorboards echoed around the lesser stairwell. "They're heading for the day room, I reckon," breathed Patrick heavily, his body trying to catch up with the unexpected exertion.

As they rounded the stout newel post Tony's eye swept the gun cupboard. Patrick read his mind and internally saying, 'What the hell,' smashed the glass with the Glock, grabbed a torch fortuitously placed beside the rear door and said, "Take your pick."

Yanking out a shotgun and appropriate cartridges, Tony fell in behind Patrick who had gone through into the darkened and now inaptly named, day room. Pulling the French doors closed behind them, they went out on to the patio.

There was still a substantial amount of bronze tinted sky to the west. The sun had set but seemed reluctant to leave. Grateful for what residual light they could get, Tony and Patrick moved to the edge of the patio scanning out across the lawn and into the shrubs and shadows beyond. The evening was warm and the air still, sounds of traffic a distant murmur, the screening effect of trees planted with foresight, cocooning and protecting.

"There." Tony quickly pointed with his left hand as his right hefted the shotgun sharply, snapping the loaded barrels closed. In one smooth action the weapon was up to the shoulder, right hand gripping the stock and fore finger curling around the triggers. In half a second and with left hand now fully supporting, he was taking aim. He tracked the movement for two seconds and fired. The discharge burst through the night as he let fly with one barrel. One second later, with his body still smoothly turning, he fired again. In the poor light it had been difficult to accurately pinpoint the moving body, amongst the low shrubs, in the border off to his left. But with the spread of buckshot widening with every metre it flew, Tony knew that a closely aimed shot could get lucky and do some real damage.

Straining to see movement, Tony and Patrick watched for ten to fifteen seconds. With no positive activity, save for the darkness's trickery, they left the patio and headed for where Tony confidently expected to find a wounded or dead animal. Patrick's torch swept the lawn and into the plants ahead whilst Tony hastily reloaded.

Chapter 90

After alerting, and pointing the way for the two pursuers, Jenny and the family group, standing helpless in the hall, began to edge up the stairs. Having heard his wife shriek in trepidation and the two men give chase, all had gone eerily quiet. Brett was naturally disconcerted, even with the passing of just a few seconds his apprehension was deceiving him into accepting the worst. He called up nervously hoping to elicit news, but wondering what on earth to expect,

"Tine... you okay?" He thought he could hear her crying. "Tine... honey, please is everything all right?" With fear ramped to almost desperation he wanted to charge up the stairs. However he knew he couldn't, anchored as he was by the responsibilities held in both hands.

"Dad... is Mum ok?" the elder one questioned, his voice trembling.

At that moment Justine appeared out of the doorway. In her arms she was clutching two wriggling forms.

"Harry must have fallen off the bed." Tears rolled down her cheeks but the smile conveyed the truth. They were fine. Brett and the other two children ran over for another group hug.

Seeing all was well, but feeling awkward, intruding on their shared moment of relief, Jenny descended the stairs into the hall. She wondered what was going on. She'd heard the two men go down the back stairs, the glass break and had caught a glimpse of them down at the far end of the back hallway as they nipped into the day room. She remembered being here only just a few months ago, and pondering on the pit bulls in that very room. According to Patrick's boss they didn't feature in the creation of these – whatever they were...foxes, hybrids! She puzzled over it in the hushed hallway. If they didn't feature, then why aren't those foxes, just foxes like every other? Even if they had been fortunate enough to be born bigger, or grown that way through plentiful food, where did the aggression come from and the other changes in behaviour: unafraid, hunting in packs, and since when, did foxes start attacking people?

The powerful blasts shattered her thoughts as they made the windows rattle and destroyed the silence. Once again Jenny had been caught off guard, but the huddled group upstairs just beginning to break and recover, collided back together, all shocked and the kids tearful.

"I didn't think you had dangerous animals over here?" Brett said clutching his elder two and shouting crossly down the stairs.

"We don't," said Jenny shortly.

"Sure as hell don't sound like it, sweetheart!"

Out in the garden the powerful torch beam picked up a moving animal. It was travelling in the cover of the shrubbery up towards the sheds and barns. The stop-start, almost faltering motion, suggested a wariness or a deliberate attempt to avoid detection, instead of outright flight. Understandable, perhaps under the circumstances, but Tony wondered whether it could also be the gait of an animal that had been injured. Besides he thought, normally a fox would just belt for the nearest hole in the hedge, rather than hang around working out a means of deceptive escape. *Mind you*, he corrected himself, *we're not talking normal!* He made a mental note to be careful. These creatures had shown a remarkable grasp of aggressive tactics.

Patrick was tracking the animal with his torch and Tony had it clearly sighted at the end of his twin barrels. The animal, Tony could see, was about to run out of cover. Needing either, to double back through the underbrush, but risking a closer encounter with them, or run the gauntlet of the open lawn up to the vegetable patch, a distance of some twenty five metres. If you put your money on it, the safe bet was back the way you'd come, but Tony couldn't call it; so hedged his bets. Swinging behind Patrick and lessening the distance to the cover, but forcing him momentarily to lower his aim. At that very moment the beast took off, skidding on the gravel as it turned sharply on the path. It shot past the old chicken run, up beside the long shed and disappeared over the low gate of the pigsty.

"Come on," yelled Tony. "We might have it cornered." In the dark they had no idea as to which animal they were chasing. It could have been a cub or an adult. Tony guessed an adult, it had seemed way too sure of its self; he doubted that a cub could have been so... cool and calculating! Good grief! He was actually giving these things qualities that were hardly credible.

As they drew level with the sty it was obvious that the small courtyard was empty. Along the high back wall was a low hut, barely a metre tall, and it had just one entrance. The square black hole that led to a sleeping chamber off to the right was devoid of all light, and it begged the question to Patrick's pointed beam, what lurked in those inky depths? In the entrance to the tiny stall there was nothing, no loose straw or aged bedding. It had been swept and cleaned out long ago, when the last Gloucestershire Old Spot had given up its bacon. But the torch's rigid beam sent shadows dancing, from the bucket by the door, the leaning shovel and off the heavy protruding hinges of the door. But no amount of arm and body twisting could illuminate the inner sanctum, the dark place behind the brick screening. To do that would have required crouching down, creeping on all fours whilst precariously clutching a torch and gun. Tony sized up the void, as did Patrick.

"Sod it," decided Tony, and swung the heavy wooden door against its aged architrave, "buggered if I'm going in there."

After the two explosions, the house soon returned to quiet. Justine and Brett had taken the children into the large front bedroom in an effort to take them as far from any more likely disturbances as possible. The beleaguered family, tired, tetchy and bewildered, tried to come to terms with the end of a day that they had always known was going to be stressful and exciting. Unsurprisingly, they just hadn't factored in terrifying as well. Their mobile phones, frustratingly, had no network and the landlines had not yet been connected. They were effectively cut off from the world, virtually imprisoned by God knows what, and being protected by... well who knew?

Jenny, meanwhile, went through into the back hall and into the kitchen switching the light on, heading for the day room. As she circumnavigated the long pine table she heard a soft clacking sound, coming from the dining room, behind her. It sounded like somebody was rhythmically finger tapping on a hard wood table. It was alarmingly familiar and in the microseconds of hearing it she knew the noise was not elevated, it was lower down, like off a wooden floor... A dog walking on a wooden floor!

"Shit," she breathed her heart suddenly percussive in her ears. *They're still in here*! Subtly, the tapping changed, and she detected, *there's only one,* it had reached the kitchen flags.

Without turning round to look, Jenny lunged through the day room door, and immediately decided to leave it open. She heard the persistent sound change as the animal revved up, its claws scrabbling for purchase; she didn't have long. Cutting right she ran through the day room and into the back hall but this time pulling the door to. With adrenalin and blood surging throughout, a hasty idea was already being actioned. However, unaware that there was only one animal left in the house, Jenny was hoping to trap this one, before running into the other. She sprinted up the hall and had just re-entered the kitchen as the animal lunged at the door back up the corridor. This was going to be a close call she thought. The interconnecting door through into the day room, across the kitchen, was a marginally longer distance because of skirting the table, than the fox had to cover to get back to the door. The trouble was the carpet in day room, gave no clues as to the animal's whereabouts and it had already gone ominously quiet. Jenny hesitated and it was fortunate that she had, as through the open door, halfway along the kitchen wall, appeared the relentless dox.

Without hesitation, it came at her and she turned and fled the kitchen, slamming that door closed as well. She couldn't believe this thing. Never, in her three years as an animal welfare officer had any dog behaved in such an aggressive way. It was like a heat-seeking missile, locked on and unstoppable. 'I'd hate to think what it might do if it were cornered,' Tony's words flitted through her frightened mind.

"Fuck you," she responded angrily. "Just who's cornering who?"

Running straight ahead, into the expansive lounge lit only by borrowed light from the main and lesser halls, she slammed the door behind her. In an attempt to put as much distance between her and the pitiless animal, she carried on around into the library. Yanking the library doors closed, the noise seemed to reverberate around the house as she searched for the light switch.

Only a poor light fell through the open doors at the far end, from the main hall and, pooling just inside the long, book lined, room, it gave her no help. Frantically feeling her way around the door, she heard the distant ticking of a clock; but as her hands swept the smooth surface she realised with dread, it was getting louder! She found a bank of switches and swiped them all, lights flickered to brilliance as the fearful clack, clack, clack, continued, alerting her to the creatures quickening pace across the spacious hall.

As if tracking her with X-ray eyes, the animal had been forced back through the dining room, and entered the library just a few seconds after Jenny. Heart still pounding, and seeing a row of potential weapon, she struck out to the opposite end of the room. Grabbing two she turned to face the beast that was now passing the snooker table and coming inexorably on. Immediately to her left was a ladder set on tracks and movable to attain books at height anywhere along that wall. As the creature moved steadily forward its grim eyes locked on her with menacing intent and, despite her threatening motions with the snooker cues, it continued on unperturbed.

It would have to be high enough she thought, hurling a cue like a javelin and making the brute jolt back, cringing. In that brief respite, Jenny flung herself on the ladder and scaled it as high as she could go, her head touched the ceiling. She brought her legs up another couple of rungs and squatted uncomfortably hanging on with the left hand, whilst her other swung the heavy end of the cue in readiness. She didn't have to wait long; the fox leapt at her from a standing jump, testing the height, the angle, her defences.

"HEEEEELP!" she shouted as loudly as she could, "TO - NYYYY!"

With her feet, effectively two and a half metres from the floor, its vile teeth came far too close for comfort and this, on its first attempt. Her swing had been hampered by the awkward position and the solid cue missed by a few centimetres. Fortunately the angle of the steps was severe, making it pretty much impossible for the animal to climb, but it didn't stop it from trying. As Jenny continued to shout, half jumping, half climbing, it sought to bring down its prey by biting on any available part, aiming to lock its jaws and then clinging on until the pain or weight dislodged it. If allowed to happen, it would stand a good chance of achieving its single-minded aim, but Jenny was having none of it. Despite her left arm aching, with the effort of holding her body close to the ladder, she swung out at the monster that was threatening to tear at her lowest leg.

Unbelievable, she thought as another blow struck the animal on its next flight. Twice now she had really connected, both on the torso, *surely that must have hurt?* But it seemed almost unaware in its frenzy to engage. And this seemingly unswerving determination, coupled with her arm now beginning to tremble at the physical strain brought a feeling of real panic to Jenny. It was getting to the point when she would be forced to either, change supporting hands, losing the cue in the process or jump down and fight it out. She hit out one more time, a glancing blow to the head and ditched the cue. Clenching the top most rung with both hands, relief flooded through her left arm and she tried to bring her feet up another level. Not a permanent solution she knew, but there had been no choice, and once again she shouted, but this time her voice was filled with desperation. She wouldn't be able to hold on much longer!

Chapter 91

Out in the partially illuminated sty and even through its solid wooden door, Tony and Patrick could discern a stirring. Whatever was in there was not happy. With the only entrance tight shut and the means of escape denied, the movement became more frantic and sounds of distress, high whines and squeals grew louder.

"We'll work out what to do with them later," Tony advised Patrick. "The trouble is we don't know how many are in there. We only saw one come in, but by the sound of it, there's more than one. But for the moment though, I think we must assume we haven't got them all."

"Yeah I'm with you on that," agreed Patrick. "Let's continue a sweep around the garden as best we can, see if we can't flush something out."

With one or maybe more in 'custody' it left a nagging uncertainty and both men were silently weighing up the odds. How many more were out here? Were they lurking in wait or had they run away? Where would they go? How could they get out of this garden? How did they get in? Whatever each one had been thinking, they had both begun to feel vulnerable, standing as they now were out in the open, in near pitch conditions, and with a failing torch, to boot. The weaponry gave them cold comfort. If you couldn't see it, how could you shoot it? And what's more it didn't help also, that both men were now painfully aware that their adversary was completely in its element.

"Let's see if we can't find some more light, first," said Patrick, heading for the back door.

No sooner had the door unlatched and it began to swing open, than the shouts of distress piled out.

"Shit, that's Jenny," cried Tony pushing past Patrick and shoving the hinged obstruction out of the way. With the loaded shotgun at high port he charged through the kitchen heading for the hysterical screaming.

As he entered the library he took in the bizarre scene. His girl friend was virtually clinging to the high ceiling like a huge fly and below, hidden sporadically as it leapt repeatedly into the air, by the sweep of the snooker table, was a mass of writhing fur, legs and teeth. Without much thought Tony sidestepped to get a better view around the massive bulk in the middle of the room, and at the same time swung the twin barrels down towards the ferocious creature. Only now did it become aware of the threat and on landing immediately kicked off with powerful hind legs, thrusting it forwards straight at Tony.

The explosion of two barrels, fired almost simultaneously, was deafening in the extreme; a sound the fox may have registered briefly, before a hail of shot blasted it backwards and shredded flesh. For seconds after, the violent sound seemed to bounce off the hard surfaces in the large room, ears rang and eyes slowly opened. Looking truly shocked Jenny climbed down almost dropping to the floor as her arms gave way.

"Christ Tony," she wept as he held her tight. "Thank God you came. I couldn't have held on any longer."

They allayed Jenny's concerns of another fox somewhere in the house by searching each and every room. As they moved through the last rooms, it struck Tony that if he had just killed one downstairs, and Patrick and he had chased one into the sty and were certain of at least another one in there, possibly more, then the total count was at least six that they had captured or killed in the last two days. That left potentially just one on the loose, out of the seven probable hybrids. He didn't include the vixen, which they believed to be a normal fox. Tony also knew that the one he'd got in the library was an adult; a female. He also presumed quite reasonably, that as the adults had travelled as a pack, then he reckoned the one they had chased in the dark and now trapped in the sty, was the remaining adult and that surely had to be the big male. He also reasoned that if the two that had been in the house were the adults then those originally in the sty, either had to be the cubs, or cubs and vixen.

With Justine and Brett out of the way, trying to get the children to calm down and off to sleep, Tony was able to talk openly. He was cautiously optimistic when he expounded this theory to Jenny and Patrick over a cup of tea around the solid pine table in the kitchen.

"So I think," he said hesitating as if still trying to think of a detrimental reason, "we may have removed the threat, at best, completely, and at worst, almost completely."

"How do you mean almost completely," asked Patrick looking quizzical.

"Well," began Tony, "if we have eliminated the big male and its siblings, then that is the immediate threat dealt with. If, by chance, the cubs were not in the sty, it was just the vixen and the male, then, although the cubs might be free and probably ready to move off and find a territory of their own, they are still not yet equipped physically, nor indeed experienced enough, to cause the same sort of havoc. And, even when they do grow up, they might not go down the same path as their older relatives; for example, they might not have the same level of aggression, or drive or skills. And I suspect, so far, their hunting achievements have been limited to frogs, worms and the odd rodent, and that's a far cry from attacking humans, or killing deer in a pincer movement. Plus, we can't be sure that the cubs have not been involved with any of the more serious hunting trips, although somehow, I doubt it. Whenever we have seen them they have been under the control of the vixen, and, as I have said many times, the urban fox that grows to live beyond eighteen months to two years is quite a rare beast. So amazingly…" he stretched out with a satisfied look, "I think we may have just cracked it."

Jenny had now calmed down and had got over her humiliation at being brought to near physical harm and tears; by an animal not dissimilar to those she worked with every day of her life. Tony had comforted her and laid her concerns to rest saying that these animals bore no relation and were totally unlike the domestic pets she was used to. She had been grateful for those words, but badly tainted by the experience, she wondered how she would view her charges in the future. Would she still trust them in the same way? Somehow she didn't think so.

Grateful for the timely demise of her vicious assailant, she was still mindful that there was a sty full of trouble, and sadly they would need sorting out. "So how are we going to kill the ones in the sty?" she asked, "as I'm assuming you won't want to open the door."

"Ah, well I've thought about that," Tony said looking even more pleased with himself. "You're right. We don't want to open the door to shoot them. There's a good chance, with a few in there, one could get away. But, if we nip to the chemist and buy some sleeping pills we can stuff them in the baits from the traps, slip them through the top of the door and within a few hours we should have either dead or sleeping foxes."

"Not exactly humane or legal," Jenny countered.

Patrick gave her a withering stare, saying off-handedly, "Like I could give a monkey's," and rubbed his bandaged leg.

Chapter 92

Monday 10th August

It was business as usual for Patrick and Jenny. Despite a late night, they both had to be in work that morning. In fairness though, both would have preferred to have seen the task right through to the end. Without knowing the final count of dead foxes, they seemed reluctant to accept success. Neither had any desire to see dead foxes per se, but to be able to physically and personally do a head count would bring each a sense of finality, a real conclusion to the events. However, it was not to be. Only Tony had got the day off and, perhaps justifiably, as the instigator and mastermind, he had gained the right.

Chief Inspector Jonathon Bryant's comment about wanting 'you back in the office' had not been followed up with, 'and that's an order' but Patrick knew him too well to defy him. He was, on the whole, a good senior officer and they jogged along pretty well together and, as luck would have it, there had been no need to cross him. His short absence from the team had fortunately not raised any major suspicions. His close colleague Thomas had wondered about his day off sick, and the report that Patrick had been seen on Poor Common when he should have been at home, worried him. He suspected that perhaps things had just got on top of him and Patrick just wanted some breathing space. The major investigations that they had been involved in, and which had stalled badly, would have obviously affected him. Even with Patrick's robust constitution and level outlook, renowned amongst his colleagues, the constant pressure from the forces hierarchy was bound to be getting to him, Thomas concluded; the stress had got to be taking its toll.

As it happened, the stress for Patrick now was not how to solve the abduction case - that effectively had been achieved. No, the real problem was how to convey this to his superiors. The proof was not there to positively condemn the foxes, and it might never be, and without it, he doubted very much, whether the establishment would wish to support such a wild theory. However, knowing what he did, the current official explanation to the children's abduction would never be proven. The children might remain missing, no perpetrators would be caught and punished, the case would effectively remain open, unsolved, a black mark in his own book, let alone the local constabulary's.

Patrick also felt that Tony and Jenny deserved a bit of recognition for their part in sorting this out. If it hadn't been for them this might not have surfaced for a lot longer, and who knows what the consequences of that might've been. *Another missing child?... Quite probably! Not to mention the wider implications if these animals hadn't been stopped*, thought Patrick. It was hard to imagine what a British countryside might be like with real, dangerous animals in it. That would add a certain frisson on the walk to school every morning, never mind dirty old men in macks.

Jenny had had to be in work by eight that morning, she'd got up at six forty-five and left Tony's still prone body lying in bed and waving from under the covers.

"Lazy git," she'd admonished sleepily. "Go and see if they're dead and how many we got."

"All in good time," Tony advised stifling a yawn. "I wouldn't want to wake the residents of Homewood too early, now would I? Anyway, no point in both of us being knackered after being up half the night clearing up."

"Yeah thanks for reminding me," she said sarcastically.

It had taken an hour and a half to get the lethal overdose ready. Patrick had been detailed to find a late night chemist and get the drugs whilst Tony and Jenny ventured over to the Common, collected the bait and moved the traps over to the vehicular entrance, ready for a swift extraction later on. They then had the grisly task of cleaning up the library, fortunately the solid wood floor made life easier but no less gruesome. By ten-thirty, they were bracing against the door of the pigsty in case the foxes tried to use their weight to break free, and trying to open it just a sliver, wide enough to slip the doctored food through, but not too big that anyone felt threatened.

The three of them had then sat down once again in the kitchen with Justine and Brett and tried to explain what had happened that evening. Tony had gone back right to where they felt it had all begun; from the foxes being fed over the years, the ever present Pit Bulls, the questionable mating between species, the loss of pets, the over-predation of wildlife and the culmination of the fawn being killed. Diplomatically, and because he'd twigged the family had only been in the country less than twenty four hours, and therefore had probably no idea about the missing children, or at least, if they had, might not make the connection, Tony decided not to mention them. Instead, he cited the recent incident with the children in the tent, saying that the animals in question, the ones they now had trapped in the sty, were nothing out of the ordinary. They were just foxes who had become a little bolder due to over-familiarity with humans i.e. Betty. They hadn't actually attacked the children but were just inquisitive and seeing an opportunity - food scraps - had popped in to join the party. The council had obviously become concerned because wild animals should remain wild and that, whilst there was unlikely to be any danger, it was better to be safe than sorry.

Brett had mumbled something about 'the biggest load of bullshit' he'd heard in a while, but frankly was too tired to argue and Justine was much the same. They'd parted at just after eleven pm, leaving the family to much-needed sleep and saying they would be back in the morning to deal with the animals in the sty.

Now, as Jenny sallied forth in her white van into the yellowing Dorset Countryside, the fields and hedgerows colouring nicely in the sunny weather, she reflected on the close shave she had had the previous evening. *Not one to tell the kids!* she thought. This made her think of Tony. She hadn't known him that long but something about him felt right. Maybe it was his timely rescue, the 'Maiden in distress' bit, and smiling at the thought, acknowledged, he was dependable, cool under pressure, and he'd handled the family well. One of the good guys, she thought … and pushing the wheel to make a turn, said distractedly, "Play my cards right..."

When Tony arrived at Homewood, he soon gathered that, despite a worse previous day than his, the family's day had begun at six thirty; one of the twins alerting the subdued household to the presence of morning. He had hoped that they would be out; that would be favourite, he'd thought, but unlikely. Wondering if he could slip in unnoticed had also been scuppered; the gravel drive giving the game away and bringing Brett to the front door. They exchanged a few pleasantries, although Tony wanted to get on and avoid any awkward questions if he could and luckily Brett was still not really with it, so he managed to keep it short.

He'd wandered around to the pigsty, thinking how different the house and garden looked in the daylight. When they'd turned up the previous evening and he had seen the light on in the hall, signalling further complications, he'd been quite despondent.

But now, optimism restored, all seemed quiet as he approached the door of the sty. He crouched for a minute with his ear cocked almost touching the wood; no sound of movement or of distress came though the rigid planks. That didn't necessarily mean anything, he assessed. They could all be just sleeping, and the thickness of the door and solid construction of the sty would absorb any subtle shifting of soft bodies. And, he was definitely not about to open the door without giving them a chance to declare themselves, because if they were tucked right around the internal screening wall, it meant he was going to have to crawl in there. Being certain they were incapacitated was essential, so he banged sharply on the door, rattling the hinges, hoping to startle docile forms into frightened life. Nothing.

After giving the door a good kicking and still not detecting even the slightest signs of activity, he carefully drew back the sliding bolt. He held his breath and readied himself, placing a foot against the base of the door to control its travel. Pulling it open just a sliver, he peered in to check and delved into his pocket for the torch he'd brought. It was one that he could strap on his head allowing free hands. The narrowed beam showed all was clear immediately behind the door, so he pulled it further back, and continued until he had revealed the entire shaft to the back wall. Bugger he said to himself, hoping to have seen at least one corpse this side of the wall, indicating that his plan had worked. He did though, know something had been inside, the bait had gone. All four pieces of bloody rabbit had disappeared. They had obviously enjoyed it; the floor was clean, no tell-tale stains of long standing carcases, which also meant, they had eaten it pretty quickly from when they had been dropped in.

So at least one was in here, he could assume, but he wondered how many more. Unfortunately, there was only one way to find out! He was going to have to crawl down this tunnel-like structure, about three metres, to reach the opening of the sleeping quarters, knowing that just on the other side of the wall, were the creatures he sought. He grabbed the old spade that was still leaning against the wall of the sty; it would be useful to collect the bodies without having to touch them, he reasoned, but actually thinking… *and a weapon*! They were dead he was sure… weren't they?

Try as he might, doubts kept teasing his rationale. *What if they are just heavily sedated and suddenly wake up when I get close. Or worse… when I touch one! In such a confined space too!* He spent a few moments getting the torch to stay on his head and pulling on his gloves and making sure the thick plastic bags were open ready to receive their grim contents.

"Right", he said to the hushed garden. "I'm going in!"

Chapter 93

At one o'clock, later that day, Tony was sitting in the White Hart and sipping a real ale. He was waiting for Jenny and Patrick to appear. They had prearranged the meet so that they could hear the expected good news direct from Tony, and... celebrate. Why not they'd agreed? Jenny would use it as her lunch break and Patrick knew he could find some good reason for being out of his office at the appointed time.

At a few minutes past the hour Jenny breezed in, turning the few male heads resolutely studying the bottle-lined back bar. As she sat down next to Tony, planting a big kiss on his cheek, the doorway darkened as the tall detective followed close behind her.

"Patrick," Tony called and getting up to go to the bar. "What will you have?"

Patrick hesitated. He wanted a pint, but he'd have to be back to the station in under an hour - not ideal. "Oh sod it!" I'll have the same as you."

When Tony joined them with the drinks, he sat down and his face was difficult to read. He looked relaxed, albeit tired and a little drawn.

"Well?" said Jenny expectantly.

"Yes thanks," he teased.

"Tony," she said forcefully.

"Okay, okay, what do you want first?" he said flatly, "the good news, the bad or the worst?"

Both looked at him, and again found it difficult to gauge any probable outcome.

"Let's have the good, I could do with a bit of good, considering the morning I've had," said Patrick, the negativity of the previous few hours resonating in his voice.

"Okay," said Tony looking as if that was the right choice. "The good news... When I finally managed to drag the last one out, there were three foxes killed in the sty."

"Well that's brilliant," said Patrick beaming. "That's all seven then?" He looked over to Jenny whose face had also lit up at the news.

"Sadly not," Tony said rather deliberately, "and this is the bad news. One of them was the vixen."

"Oh, I see," said Jenny nodding her head and grasping what news the worst would be.

"Sorry, I've had a hard morning, so I'm being a little slow" Patrick said, smiling sheepishly, knowing that whatever it was, he was obviously missing it.

"Do I presume," Jenny began guardedly, "The one that is missing... is the big male?"

"You guessed it."

The smile left Patrick's face, but he was wondering why Tony didn't seem overly bothered. After all, this was the animal, the leader, the one presumably that had started it all in the first place. If he was still on the loose then the problem wasn't sorted.

"I don't understand Tony. Why aren't you more concerned," he asked. Surely this creature is just going to mate again, and before long we'll have the same problem."

"Potentially… yes. But do you remember when I shot at it and we gave chase following it to the sty. Well I was confident that I had winged it, and although we didn't see any evidence of that at the time, I noticed this morning before I left the sty, that there was a fairly hefty smear of blood on the roof. It looked to me like he used the sty to jump the wall and obviously got away."

"So you think he's wounded. Can't be much if he managed to get over that wall," Jenny added.

"Well, in fairness, we don't know. But I wouldn't be surprised; an animal in flight, even an injured one, could probably attain things that might look impossible to us. You know what I mean; the adrenalin pumping can make us all do extraordinary things when forced. I'm sure it's no different for a fox. But, I should think it's more than likely now severely disadvantaged. It could be that it is unable to hunt, it might not even be able to scavenge and lack of food will lead to poor health and poor health to wounds not healing, becoming infected, and fairly quickly leading to death. Even if it can feed, I suspect the wounds will still be its downfall; they are hotspots for contamination and bugs. I give it very slim odds for survival."

"You're probably right," Patrick said cheering up a bit, and then changing tack. "But what of the chief's revelation that you can't have a dog-fox cross. He was banging on about it again this morning. It rather buggers up your theory and makes it more difficult to try and prove our case."

"I did think about that this morning," Tony said. "So I tried a bit of googling around the dog-fox hybrid notion. I probably came up with much the same stuff that you did Jen, but I did find an interesting site, in that it suggested that foxes could be domesticated. I followed a number of links and ended up at none other than the National Geographic site. The article I found was reporting on a long running research programme in Siberia with Silver Foxes. They were basically, over generations, breeding foxes that were not just wild foxes that had become domesticated, as in captured and tamed, but they had actually been bred, as I say over generations, to be domesticated in the true sense of the word. They seemed to be suggesting that the animal's genes could be altered through the selective breeding and that they hold the key to it being truly domesticated. Now," Tony paused allowing a moment for them to catch-up. "What I was thinking was, and this is only me talking off the top of my head, you understand. If a fox in Siberia can be changed with selective breeding, then why couldn't a family of foxes over here?"

"Go on," said Patrick warily wondering if he was about to be blinded with science.

344

"Well, we know that there have been foxes at Homewood for possibly thirty years. And, as far as we know, Betty has fed and watered them all that time in a secluded and secure place; so it begs the question - why leave when your basic needs are taken care of? With their close relationship to Betty's potentially aggressive dogs over that time, is it not possible that some way down the generations, their behaviour has modified. The traits and skills passed from the dogs' way back, could well have been fine tuned, as you might say, by a form of selective breeding. It would apply to being unafraid of humans as well. That boldness around people, growing stronger as each year passes. So our big male, and probably his siblings, not a hybrid, but dare I say… sort of selectively modified."

Patrick looked at him with false scorn, "Sounds like the realms of fantasy to me," and nodding at Tony's pint added playfully, "You been here long?"

Amused by the inference Tony clarified what he was suggesting. "Look I don't know what happened to those foxes but we cannot deny they were different. Perhaps not by a huge amount," Tony looked across the table. "Patrick, you surely must have seen sensible, normal people forced when they are up against it, into taking desperate measures and doing things totally out of character?"

"You're not joking," Patrick acknowledged.

"I don't see it was any different for these foxes, except their instincts are baser; no sense of right or wrong or guilt, just survival. The old lady died, they became hungry, having not been fed, and so quite literally bit the hand that fed them. Once Betty's body was removed they would have been forced to venture out and look for food in pastures new, i.e. Poor Common and beyond. And what they had learned from the mock fights and pack behaviour in play, might very well have reshaped natural hunting and foraging skills to a more co-ordinated and deadly level."

"You come up with that all by yourself did you?" Patrick grinned, but recognised the logic behind it.

Tony Laughed, "One thing's for sure, we'll probably never know. Let's face it, the likelihood of conditions being right for anything like this to happen again, is highly improbable."

"That's as maybe." Looking more serious, Patrick added, "What gets me, though, is that this is all going to be hushed up and I'm not particularly happy about that. People out there should know. And I'm not just talking about the general public. I'm talking about the likes of the Docker family, Bridget Morley, Gary Brown's mother, my lads at the station. These are all people who are not going to know the truth but they deserve to. The families have a right to know that their children didn't suffer at the hands of some paedophile. Mrs Brown should know that her son was not involved in any abduction. The lads at the station should know they did everything possible and right, but they were beaten because they weren't allowed to look in the right direction."

"Trouble is," said Tony, "the damage is done. The papers have seen to that. Gary's face has been plastered in every tabloid in Britain and probably elsewhere. They've condemned him as sure as anything just by implication alone."

"I know," agreed Patrick. "Of course, he was obviously up to no good. Albeit, in the great scheme of things, pretty innocently really. Just unlucky, leaving a few clues near the scenes of crime to put him right in our crosshairs." Patricks brow furrowed. "And that's what bugs me. My boss is quite content to use that circumstantial evidence to advocate that Gary was guilty and part of a paedophile ring, particularly now he's conveniently deceased, and can't say otherwise." Patrick tilted his glass inspecting the contents, "So unfortunately," he began again wearily, "it seems the hapless Gary fell out of a tree, smashed his head open and died. Wrong place, wrong time; no involvement whatsoever!"

Tony nodded his agreement. "And you know what? In light of what we know about our doxes," he added cynically, "you might be tempted to acknowledge - deaths were all of natural causes."

Patrick and Tony, acknowledging that proof positive was unlikely ever to be found, endeavoured to do their bit to set the record straight, sending anonymous information to Brian Maidment at the Echo and helping him on his way to seeing connections. Brian's 'investigative journalism' culminated in various articles offering an alternative, but plausible, explanation to the abductions, and supporting Gary's innocence and, they went some way to setting the record straight. Some of the national papers even gave it print space, but mainly it was eclipsed by the breaking news stories of the day and before long the wider world would forget.

But, in Ferndown the newspaper articles would touch a chord, particularly to close friends and relatives of the two stricken families. They would find Brian's evidence compelling and, although knowing it could not be substantiated, would accept it as the truth.

Patrick ignored Chief Inspector Bryant's remonstrations about leaks to the press, and suggesting that his superior should not jump to him as the immediate conclusion, there were, he intimated, others freely available to do with the information as they wish.

Tony and Jenny were somewhat peeved about Brian claiming the glory but accepted this as inevitable; Tony had had his fifteen minutes of infamy, and was not keen for another slice. However, in their local pub, the Angel, a number of regulars would continue to tease Tony, implying that the articles smacked of the 'experts' doing. Luckily the one drinker that might have blown the deception was permanently unavailable for comment, because of course…

Our boy…Gary, was dead.

Epilogue

October 2010

It was mid October and the spiders, it seemed to Tony and Jenny, as they wandered onto Parley Common early that morning, must have been up all night. Perhaps making ready for the winter months; having cast their fine nets in such profusion, as to sieve the very insect dregs, from the rapidly cooling skies. For all around, the unforgiving gorse was covered in delicate strands of silk. Sheer threads, water coated and sparkling like tinsel, cascaded from the top of each spire and down over its lower protrusions. An enchanted scene, a 'gossamer morning' where each spiky plant took on a magical structure,

"Like fairy castles," Jenny whispered.

As they wandered through the glistening structures, the true heath opened up to them. From the drier raised ground they looked out over the low carpet of muted purple, jaded by the early days of winter, to a new world, where the flat and, in some places, sodden landscape was dotted by similar fortifications; vaporous shards jutting mysteriously out from the wet heathers and moor grass, and each one it seemed, a realm of their own, suggesting a patchwork of tiny kingdoms.

"It's so beautiful," murmured Jenny not wishing to disturb the air. It was so still and peaceful that she felt a raised voice might send ripples, like a shock wave, loosening the droplets and destroy the moment.

"It certainly is," agreed Tony, "and you know what amazes me?" his tone reverential and awed. "Tomorrow they'll all be gone. One day this," he gestured to a shrouded spire of gorse, "and the next, nothing, hardly a cobweb to be seen. There must be literally thousands of spiders here to be able to create this spectacle and yet it seems, you only ever see this just a few days in each year." And then smiling, "God knows what they're doing for the rest of it?"

"Taking baths I shouldn't wonder," said Jenny her volume back to normal. "Did you see the one in yours this morning? Bloody Tarantula it was."

"Notice you left it for me to deal with!"

"Your bath – Your spider," she laughed.

Whispered communication cast aside, and the morning's soggy silence broken, but still… the enchantment remained.

And although it had been over a year since they had put paid to the foxes of Homewood, they had not forgotten them. For a few days immediately after, they had scrutinised the local papers and listened out for snippets of conversations in the pub, whilst Patrick flicked casually through the incident logs, hoping desperately not to find news that might suggest a come-back. But as the weeks slipped by, and no news was good news, Jenny and of course Patrick breathed their respective sighs and accepted... they had gone for good. However, Tony, although confident of his predictions, still wondered about the injured escapee. There had been a tiny part of him that hoped, maybe it had survived. He found himself at times regretting the animals' demise. But they had all found that often a memory would be nudged by some day to day incident and an aspect of the previous summer's events would slip back into conscious thought.

For Jenny, handling dogs day in and day out served as constant reminder of the 'family's' darker side. Any future crime scene reported to Patrick as, 'interfered with', would send him regressing straight back to Poor Common and to the likes of Betty Thomas, Gary Brown, Jim Bennett and of course the two little children. Tony on the other hand, found any prompted moments of reflection were often severed by noisy members of the public high jacking his attention. He didn't mind there were plenty of other opportunities for recollection and particularly when he was with Jenny. Often out walking together, all manner of objects, words and creatures would set them off, pondering once again on what had occurred and what might have been. The most obvious of course, foxes... and they had seen plenty since their ordeal. It hadn't put them off liking them, but it did make them wonder. So they scrutinised each one where possible, looking for signs, a familiarity or a nuance to suggest it was their old adversary; and, if not him? Well who knows, could he have survived to sire again? It seemed though they had been thorough and they were all... just foxes.

As they moved off down the path that cut eastwards across the long narrow stretch of common Tony pointed to a small dark flash of movement, a bird diving into the scrub next to the path up ahead.

"Dartford warbler," he said, his finger tracing the low flight. "Hope this winters' not too hard on them. A really cold snap could decimate the few that are left." They stopped walking; a crossroads, the sandy trails offering three possibilities and looked out to where they thought the bird had gone.

"There," Tony said pointing once again, "on that bush." The little bird perched jauntily with its long tail cocked, was emitting a harsh rattle, angry no doubt at being disturbed. "It's really only these few patches of Dorset Heath where they're found in any number." he said poignantly.

"It's sad," Jenny said, "that we seem to be pushing forward the boundaries of science enabling our species to live longer and use up more space, but you have to wonder at what cost. Extinction of creatures like this little bird seems inevitable and, the thing is, I can't really see an end to it."

"Yes it is does seem rather depressing when you put it like that. But you know," he said, a wry smile gently widening his lips, "I have a hunch nature will get its own back; perhaps not tomorrow, but sometime in the future. And I also reckon," he smoothed his day-old stubble with an open palm, as if still thinking it through, "there'll be quite a few more incidences like the one we've been involved in. As humans infringe more and more on this planet, we should expect to cross swords with the natural world at some point."

"Well hopefully not tomorrow. We're going down to your mum's," she reminded him, adding glibly, "Only I wouldn't want to miss out on one of her cakes!"

"Good point," he said exaggeratedly, glancing down. "Look at that." An irregular saucer-sized slimy brown parasol caught his eye. "Wish I knew more about mushrooms and fungi," he said staring at it, "might be edible? What do you reckon?"

A few seconds went by and he turned to look at Jenny who hadn't answered him. She was staring intently off into the distance, up the path. Tony followed her gaze. Thirty metres away was a fox. It was sitting slap in the middle of the path.

"Is it me?" She asked cautiously. "Only… it looks a little bigger than the ave…"

Tony cut her off, "Leave it!" he said in mock admonishment and holding up an open palm, as if training a dog. She looked at him indignantly, although a smile played cautiously on her lips.

"Just don't go there," he teased. "Every time we see a fox you say something like that!"

"So do you!" she countered.

"Not as often as you though."

"Rubbish," she said.

They looked away from each other back up the path to get another look. But it had gone.

"Oh well," said Jenny, "that settles that, then."

But as they began walking again, Tony toyed with the scene in his head. He wasn't sure, but there had been a look about the animal, the way it had just stared at them, and the faintest inkling of unease broke loose, niggling at him. Something about the animal had not been right, and despite the growing pangs of suspicion, a subtle thrill shot through him and he swung round in a delayed double take,

"I wouldn't swear to it," he began "but that fox…."

Authors note

In reality, attacks by foxes on humans are not common place; but they do happen and it's probable that they happen more often than we realise. Recently, the ever hungry press and media machines have reported a number of incidences deemed more noteworthy than most.

In June 2010, nine-month old twins were savaged by a fox in their cots. (The Independent)

Later the same month, a toddler was reported to have been attacked by a fox at a school party. (The Independent)

February 2013, Five week old baby seriously injured when dragged from its cot. (London Evening Standard)

July 2013, fox attacks man, woman and cat in their home in South London. (London Evening Standard)

Just a few examples of articles with the usual sensational rhetoric, stirring up fears that one of our most endearing wild animals, is on the turn; from opportunist scavenger to blood thirsty predator. These are not, they seem to be implying, just some cornered animal lashing out in an act of self preservation. Rather that these creatures are deliberately and actively seeking out human activity in order to cross swords with us.

I don't really believe this is the case; foxes are wary animals at the best of times and particularly when it comes to humans. So, not actively checking us out, but it is inevitable that our paths will cross. There are simply too many of us. Besides which our urban environment offers such rich pickings, overloaded bins and excessive food wastage; hard to resist.

The key is in the word opportunist. These intelligent creatures are bound to take advantage of any prospect that might further their well being. Whether fed by animal lovers or routing around in our bins they are inadvertently drawing themselves nearer to us. The consequences are bound to involve minor confrontations similar to the ones above and they are likely to increase.

Therefore, in this book the truth is hardly stretched. No blood lusting foxes bestowed with supernatural abilities, merely a possible and plausible scenarios to the consequences of those confrontations.

The National Geographic article, referred to in the book, is real; '**Designing the Perfect Pet'** was the headline and 'Can a fox become man's best friend?' the by-line. It was published in the March 2011 edition.

Made in the USA
Charleston, SC
02 April 2014